DEATH COMES BUT ONCE

Decker's War — Book 1

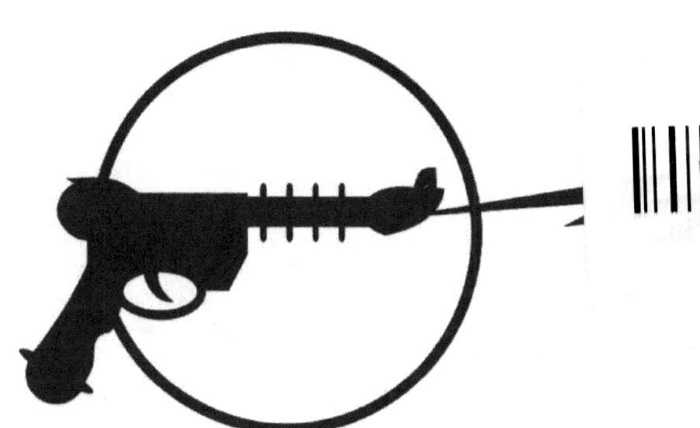

ERIC THOMSON

Death Comes But Once
Copyright 2014 Eric Thomson
This paperback edition February 2019

All rights reserved.
This book, or parts thereof, may not be reproduced in any
form without permission.

This is a work of fiction. Names, characters, places and
incidents either are the product of the author's imagination
or are used fictitiously, and any resemblance to actual
persons, living or dead, business establishments, events or
locales is entirely coincidental.

Published in Canada
ISBN: 978-1-989314-02-9

— PROLOGUE —

Plasma rounds cracked over Command Sergeant Zack Decker's head in a steady stream. Pinned down by the enemy behind a jumble of granite rocks, he still waited for Captain Sarratt to do something that might relieve the pressure, such as calling back the assault shuttles to provide air support.

Little remained of Decker's patience, a virtue in short supply at the best of times. None of his Marines had become casualties so far, but the operation was turning into the expected clusterfuck.

Decker's first public argument with the captain occurred in the middle of the mission briefing aboard ship, and things had gone downhill from that point. Sarratt wasn't the 902nd Pathfinder Squadron's regular commanding officer, and his inexperience was all too clear in the way he planned the mission.

There was nothing easy about taking a marauder group's hideout, and Sarratt's plan made it even more complicated than it had to be. If it hadn't been for their orders to collect intelligence, they could just as well have destroyed the outlaws from orbit with a kinetic strike. There weren't any civilians around who could become collateral damage. The closest town on this shithole planet was a few thousand kilometers away.

The squadron's executive officer tried to dissuade Sarratt from carrying out his plan, suggesting a workable, if less spectacular alternative, but to no avail.

They should have jumped in guns blazing, covered by the Gatlings and rockets of their assault shuttles. Instead, their acting CO wanted to sneak up on the enemy, gain the element of surprise, and then run through them like plasma through plastic. Decker would have gone straight to the last part and replaced surprise by massive firepower.

After one look at his designated drop zone on the scans taken by the frigate from high orbit, Decker had decided to disobey his orders. Of all the possible DZs around the hideout, this one was not only the closest but also the most obvious. The marauders were neither blind nor stupid. They'd have figured out it was a great place to drop Marines hunting for them.

Sarratt's complicated plan hinged on having Zack's troop land there before advancing on the target. His troop's job was to pin them down, while the captain brought the rest of the squadron around for the killing blow. He had resisted all attempts to change Third Troop's DZ.

Instead, Zack had a quiet chat with the assault shuttle pilot and landed his Marines in a less visible but far safer spot a few kilometers away. By the time Sarratt found out, Decker was already halfway to the original DZ, but on foot.

The captain had threatened Decker with disciplinary measures for his disobedience, but he had ignored him. Provided their communications were over a private channel, no one else would be privy to the exchange and Sarratt would calm down once they concluded the operation with success.

Zack had wanted to send a small patrol to scout the marauder base from the ground and warn of any ambush along the way. Sarratt would hear nothing of it, ordering him to press along at speed, to make up for the time wasted by landing further away.

The original DZ had turned out to be a well-prepared ambush site. If Decker and his troopers had landed there, the enemy would have wiped them out almost at once.

*

"Three this is Niner," the radio crackled to life. "Why the hell aren't you moving?"

"Because we're fucking pinned down," Decker replied, furious. "How fucking often must I repeat myself? We're not moving until someone can take the pressure off one of my flanks. They have us covered from all sides."

"Three, this is Niner," Sarratt replied, voice trembling with rage, "mind yourself when you speak with me. As I've told you more than once, I can't spare anyone to help you correct your mistakes. Thanks to you, I now have to take the target with one less troop than the plan called for."

"Niner this is Three," Decker's tone dripped with sarcasm, "perhaps my holding down a fair chunk of the enemy's firepower might make it easier for you to carry through your abortion of a plan. In the meantime, we'll try not to die. Three, out."

Decker knew he would pay for his intemperate words later. However, risking the lives of his Marines because an idiot of a captain wanted some combat time before the next majors' promotion board wasn't on the menu.

A stupid training accident had sent the squadron's real CO to the hospital, and Sarratt had used his connections to get the temporary command. Though Pathfinder qualified, he had spent most of his career in a rifle battalion. Commanding a 'leg' company wasn't anywhere enough experience, and he was too arrogant to listen to his troop leaders, all of them experienced Pathfinder noncoms.

Decker cursed his regimental commander for dumping Sarratt on them, but the colonel had no reason to expect orders sending them into battle on the fringes of the Shield Cluster. No matter what favors someone owed Sarratt, people needed to be slapped upside the head for this.

A rocket-propelled grenade smashed into the ground in front of him showering the Pathfinders with shrapnel and debris. So far the enemy hadn't brought up enough firepower to turn this into Decker's last stand. But now that they were shooting RPGs, it could only mean they were breaking out the heavier stuff. If they had mortars, they could make it very uncomfortable for the Pathfinders.

Just as that thought crossed Decker's mind, he heard the dull thud of a mortar round leaving its tube.

"Shit," Decker swore, then shouted, "Incoming!"

The mortar round landed a few dozen meters to Decker's right, throwing up a shower of earth and wood splinters. It was a small caliber shell, but a direct hit on one of his Marines would be fatal in a very messy way.

Decker debated informing Sarratt that the enemy was using artillery, but discarded the idea. If the captain wasn't smart enough to notice the heavier ordnance, there was no point.

Without the assault boats flying cover, there was no one to relay news of progress by the main body. For all Zack knew, the enemy could have pinned them down as well. With the squadron's executive officer aboard one of the shuttles, there was no tactical command post on the ground to coordinate the attack.

Another mortar round exploded, this one nearer.

"Niner, this is Three," Decker gritted his teeth as he called Sarratt, this time on the squadron push. "We're coming under effective mortar fire. If we don't get relief soon, you'll be able to scrape us off the ground with a shovel. Even one pass by an assault shuttle would help."

When Sarratt replied, Decker knew things weren't going well on his end either. He sounded out of breath, anxious and there was heavy gunfire in the background.

"I've called the shuttles back, Decker. Just hold on. Once they've made a pass at the enemy positions in front of me, I'll have them support you."

"Suggest you have them take down the enemy mortar team first." He ducked as a shell came down in the center of his troop's position, throwing a geyser of earth and stones into the air. "They have our range."

Before Sarratt could reply, the voice of the lead shuttle pilot came on the push.

"I have eyes on the mortar position and will engage as a priority target."

"You will engage the objectives as I laid out," the captain shouted.

Neither the pilot nor Decker replied. Mere seconds later, he heard the sound of tearing cloth as the lead gunboat's Gatling cut loose, followed by the next and the one after that. A larger explosion, followed by a mushroom cloud of dust, erupted from the jungle as the plasma cooked off the mortar's ready rounds.

"Any chance you can do a pass in front of my position?" Decker asked. "If I can escape from this trap, I can relieve the pressure on the others."

"Affirmative. Paint your perimeter and we'll fry anything beyond it."

Decker quickly passed the order to his troopers.

"I have you," the lead pilot said moments later. "Hug the ground. We're coming in."

Ignoring Sarratt, the four assault shuttles turned the forest beyond Decker's position into a nightmare of fire and death. This was how they should have come down on the marauders in the first place, instead of pissing about trying to surprise them.

The moment the shuttles broke away to engage the targets to Sarratt's front, Decker stood up and motioned his squad leaders to move out towards the target. There was no point in dawdling. The only play left was to hit hard and hit fast.

They rushed through the smoking ruins of the jungle, their way cleared by the air strikes and when they neared the base, all sounds of fighting had stopped. The only noise came from the burning vegetation, and stray ammunition cooking off at random in the fires.

Urged on by Sarratt, Decker didn't pause to figure out why the marauders had given up the fight. It was as if they had dematerialized, leaving nothing but ruins.

As the perimeter of the installation came into view, he realized that the enemy had played them for suckers. Before he could warn the others, the fake base erupted in one giant blast. Decker's last thought before his world went dark was how he'd strangle his CO the moment they were back on the ship.

— ONE —

"What should I do with him?"

The *Dragon's Tooth*'s plump, gray-haired waitress nodded towards the far corner, grimacing at the proprietor, a paunchy ex-Marine with tattoos on his arms.

They, and the customer snoring with gusto, his head on his folded arms, were the last living beings left in the bar. It was a little after three in the morning. Late. Only the whorehouses in the spaceport precinct stayed open later. Most never closed.

Tren, the innkeeper, shrugged. "Leave him be for now, Mara. By the time we finish down here, he'll wake and wander out on his own. Poor fucker has enough problems without getting tossed out of a joint like this."

"Your place Tren. But don't take on no pity cases now," Mara replied, shaking her head. "I know you too well." She pointed a red-tipped fingernail at him. "Can't resist an old Marine in trouble, can you? Give him a free beer and a free meal, sure, but don't take him home with you as if he's a stray cub. Hell, the sad sack's large enough to frighten the living shit out of the cub's mother."

"You know, Mara, you sound just like we're married." Tren snorted in mock disgust as he wiped a stain off the scarred counter.

"Near enough, Tren. Near enough." Mara hoisted another battered chair on an equally battered table, grunting at the effort.

"You wanna fuck Mara before going to sleep every night, you have to listen to her speak." She leered at him. "Anyway, on some planets, the law would say we are married."

"Which is why I retired here, you foul-mouthed old hen. I don't aim to repeat my mistakes, and I've been through that sort of hell once already. What a mistake to make." Tren spat into the imitation brass spittoon, making it ring like a bell at the impact.

"Who the hell is that drunk, anyway?"

"Old Marine, Mara."

"I know, you old fool. He even looks like you — ugly puss, drools when he tries to speak like a human, and drunk from sunrise to sunset."

"Fuck you, Mara."

"Later." She wiggled her fat bottom at Tren, chortling. "Hey, your old buddy seems better looking than you. Maybe I should trade. Maybe he's better than you in the equipment department too."

"You wouldn't want Zack, trust me." Tren suddenly turned dead serious, and that brought Mara to a halt. She looked at him and frowned as if trying to read the answer on the ex-Marine's broad, prize fighter's face.

"Apart from being drunk, which seems to be normal for everything that wears a uniform, what's the boy done?"

"Dunno. Zack doesn't want to talk about it. But that's not what I meant."

"You want to tell me, or is this one of those off-limits things?" Mara knew by now not to press Tren when he didn't want to speak. Though he never laid a hand on her like her first husband had, he was scary as hell when he was pissed off.

Tren shrugged. "Zack's a mean fighter. Lived for the Corps, didn't have time for nothing else. He has a kid somewhere he's never seen. Wife fucked off when Zack refused to leave the Fleet for a civvie job. Hurt him bad too. Never wanted to get close to another woman since then. Became a super trooper: Pathfinders, special ops, every fucking war the Corps fought in the last twenty years. There are people think the man isn't quite human anymore."

He shook his head, eyes far away, in that place where Mara never went.

"Now Zack's on early retirement, which can only mean they've kicked him out. And that'll kill him for sure. Zack Decker was one hell of a Marine, but he'll never make a civilian. Either drink himself to death, pull out a gun, and blow a hole in his head. Or else, bust up someone or some place and get gunned down by the Militia in a blaze of glory.”

“That’s why you’re kinda soft on him?” Mara asked in a gentle tone.

“Yeah. I figure old Zack don’t have too much time left in this universe unless a miracle happens and he finds a job that’ll keep him alive.”

“Like what kind of job?”

Tren tossed his soaked, grimy rag into the stainless steel sink beneath the counter and rubbed his chin with a calloused hand.

“Well, Colonial Army’s out. Don’t hire no noncoms forced to retire. Too many of ‘em are bad news a court-martial couldn’t convict. Merc outfits aren’t so choosy, but there’s none in the area. It’s too quiet on Aramis.” Mara nodded. Tren had already given it thought. “Rent-a-cop? But that’ll drive Zack nuts so fast he won’t have time to collect his first pay. Hire on a fast trader? Some of ‘em need good gunners where they go for business. But none are hiring these days either. Anyway, a lot of ‘em are half-pirate, and that’s no place to send a man who spent twenty years fighting the scum.”

Mara patted Tren’s still muscular forearm.

“You really seem to care about this guy.”

“Yeah, I do. Zack Decker saved my life a long time ago. We were both buck sergeants in the same platoon, on Hispaniola before the war became a war. Old Zack pulled me out of a crowd of angry *pesans* who were looking for someone to rip apart. Zack Decker, all alone with a fucking carbine and no damn ammo. The guy has more balls than brains sometimes. But if he hadn’t stared the fuckers down, I’d be dead, so I owe Zack.”

“Listen, Angel, if he means that much to you, we can put him up for a while. No trouble.”

“Thanks, Mara.” He kissed her with a tenderness surprising in such a hard man. “Appreciate the offer. But Zack, he doesn’t live on no charity. Take free beer and food from a pal, sure. We’ve been paying each other a treat since he was a PFC with no more sense than a puppy. But Zack’s getting his pension, little as it is, and he won't take anything. Proud bugger." There was admiration in Tren's voice as he looked at his sleeping friend. "Command Sergeant Zachary T. Decker was one hell of a Marine."

Tren pulled a chipped shot glass out from under the counter and poured himself a measure of whiskey.

"I'll stay a while, 'till he wakes. You go on up, Mara, and get some sleep."

For what seemed like a long time, Tren Kinnear stared at his friend's resting shape, sipping contraband hooch and thinking hard. Pathfinders take care of their own, even when they weren't Pathfinders anymore.

*

Zack Decker shuffled through the deserted streets of Heaven's Gate, kicking at empty booze bottles, cig packs and flyers advertising cathouses with his scuffed work boots. Hands in his pockets, shoulders hunched, and head pulled down into his jacket's raised collar, the big man only superficially seemed like any other drifter in any other spaceport on any of the Commonwealth's planets.

At one-ninety centimeters height, one hundred and ten kilos weight, all of it muscle, and with a face chiseled in granite, Decker looked like a mean drunk, a mean ex-Fleet drunk. An even meaner hangdog now that his head started pounding with the inevitable hangover, his efficient metabolism already recovering from the ethanol binge at the *Dragon's Tooth*. Who knew what he'd been tossing back near the end. Could have been hyperdrive coolant for all he cared.

He had a twice-broken nose, sharp as a hawk's beak now, sandy hair still cut in a short brush, a jagged white scar running from his left ear down into his collar and dark blue eyes, almost purple, bright and old beyond his years.

To the rats lurking in the slum's dark alleys, his appearance, and athletic stride, honed by years of wearing heavy armor battle suits, marked him as a veteran, someone to avoid. Vets knew one hundred and one ways to kill a body with their bare hands, and few of them ever went anywhere unarmed. The cutthroats and footpads had good survival instincts. They left him alone, even though there wasn't another soul in sight, at three-thirty in the morning, in the seediest part of Heaven's Gate.

They wouldn't have found much for their troubles. Zack Decker was just about broke, his meager pension barely holding out from one month to the next, especially since he'd crawled into a bottle and stayed there, day and night. With nothing else to do and no money for the better places in the city, he visited seedy bar after seedy bar in the spaceport precinct, each worse than the next, his itinerary without rhyme or reason, searching for something without knowing what.

The Heaven's Gate slums had plenty of flyblown bars. Zack had been at it for three weeks straight, ever since a tramp freighter had dumped him here when his money ran out. Not that Decker minded. He didn't know where he was headed, anyway. One planet was just as good, or bad, as the other. He'd lost the only home he knew when they handed him his pension papers.

Tonight, he'd stumbled on an old pal, Tren Kinnear, once sergeant first class in the 9th. Gone to fat in his old age, but they'd been through plenty of tough times together and become tight buddies. Tren had always wanted to own a tavern somewhere, near enough to a spaceport so he could hear the transports land and bring more thirsty spacers to his place, and he made that dream come true, for what it was worth. Had himself a woman too.

The night air in Heaven's Gate was chilly, and a thin mist was spreading from the open sewer the Heavenites called their river. Zack shivered and tried to burrow deeper into his jacket, in vain. A uniform had been good enough for twenty years, and Decker never had much of a civilian wardrobe. Now, when he needed the rags, he didn't have the money. Couldn't even remember where the dough had all gone. Cheap booze, it had to be. Couldn't have been cheap hookers. Even dead drunk he had more sense than that.

Muffled thunder broke through the still night air and resonated in Zack's skull. He glanced back at the port and saw a sleek trader ship heading off for parts unknown. At least her captain had a purpose in life.

Laughter and music poured out of an open doorway across the street, and a splash of multicolor light fell on the cracked, grimy pavement. Two men in spacer coveralls, much worse for wear, stumbled out of the whorehouse and stood on the sidewalk, swaying as they fought to get their bearings. The music and illumination vanished, leaving them stranded in the night.

Zack gave them a glance and decided the footpads would take whatever the whores had left in their pockets before they had walked one block. They should have stayed with the hookers until daybreak. It was safer that way. But some guys were too dumb to survive. Decker shrugged and kept walking. Not his business. Survival of the fittest in his universe and that meant not only the healthiest body but also the sharpest wits.

A few minutes later, he heard a strangled yell behind him, but he didn't even break his pace. Survival of the smartest.

*

When Decker reached his rooming house, he was cold stone sober, with a headache to beat all headaches, and no hangover pill to be had for love or money. The ship's sawbones used to hand them out like candy whenever the crew of *Musashi* took shore leave. But there were no naval surgeons in the seedy areas around the spaceport. They all had enough money to sleep in fancy hotels, drinking good hooch, instead of Tren Kinnear's rotgut.

The rooming house was an old tenement a few blocks from the spaceport and had been built so long ago that its original owners were long forgotten. It had seen no maintenance since before Zack's birth, but it was cheap enough, and it came furnished if you could call the crap he had furnishing.

The plascrete stairs squeaked under Zack's weight when he walked up to the third-floor landing. The building's lift had broken down so long ago that they didn't make spare parts anymore.

It was a big place with a clientele that included every variety of loser imaginable: hookers, thieves, welfare bums, goons and more, everyone jammed together on five floors of warehouse-grade concrete. At four in the morning, most of them were coming home from work or play, and Zack did his level best to ignore the young prostitute next door as she struggled to open her lock. It wasn't easy, the way she was dressed.

She wore indigo leather tonight, a bustier that left her midriff and nipples free to the admiring eyes of potential customers. The nipples, painted a screaming shade of green for the occasion, to match her hair and eyelids, were of admirable proportions, especially under the assault of the cold night air. A matching mini-skirt attempted to cover her nether regions, but as designed by its makers, it failed.

Zack was sober enough to notice Rosette's obvious intoxication on whatever drug she had bought with her nightly earnings. He didn't know her age but would have sworn she wasn't a day over twenty, even though her eyes could easily have given her ten, fifteen years more. Part of it was thanks to her choice of career. But most of it was thanks to the hard drugs she used.

Decker might have crawled into a bottle, but he hated hard drugs with all his being. He had spent enough years chasing the scum who smuggled the crap into the Commonwealth so it didn't end up in the bloodstream of mixed-up kids like Rosette. Zack felt sorry for her, but he refused to get involved. Or in her bed.

The girl suddenly realized she wasn't alone and looked up.

"Hi, Zack." Her white grin seemed unnatural in a dusky face darkened even further by the uneven lighting. "Wanna come in and spend time with me?"

"No thanks," Zack shook his head, immediately regretting the motion and unlocked his door before she could grab his arm and try to pull him into her room. Decker didn't believe in taking advantage of a zoned-out girl who should be in school and falling in love instead of turning tricks and snorting junk. Then, there was Zack's fear that the whore had scary bugs lurking in her privates, diseases just waiting for a stupid prick.

With a loud snick, the door closed behind him, cutting off the sound of Rosette's voice. Decker looked around the room, feeling a deeper depression than the one usually brought on by too much alcohol. To call the place dingy didn't do it justice. Though it was larger than his cabin aboard *Musashi*, it wasn't as comfortable or as clean. It didn't even come close to being as clean. Nor did his old cabin have resident scavenger insects, a few of them larger than his thumb, which seemed to thrive in the rooming house.

No hangover pills meant only one solution since Zack didn't want to try sleeping with an artillery barrage rolling through his skull. He pulled a half-empty bottle of cheap whiskey from under his bed and pulled the cork. Not even bothering with a glass, he took a swig and swirled it in his mouth, trying to kill the sour taste of Tren's rotgut. The whiskey burned a trail of fire down his gullet and added to the lethal stew in his stomach. Perhaps the booze hadn't such a good idea. Still, the headache faded, replaced by heartburn. But that was something Zack could live with.

Unfortunately, this time, it didn't take many king-sized swigs to put Decker back into the swim again. And the more he drank, staring out of the grimy window at the first pearly gray of dawn, the worse he felt.

His eyes wandered over to the closet door. Like everything else in this building, it was broken, jammed wide open. There, hanging as if in his shipboard locker, was his black Marine uniform with the stripes and crossed-swords of a command sergeant on the sleeves, Pathfinder jump wings on the breast and all the other ribbons and devices that came with twenty years of memories, good and bad.

Staring at the uniform gave Decker painful pangs of homesickness

He took another swig of whiskey and leaned back in his chair to open the drawer of a scarred white dresser, from which pulled a battered but serviceable blaster. Meeting Tren tonight had reminded Decker of too many things.

The blaster came from a Shrehari marauder he and Tren had fought years ago. Like most Pathfinders, Decker had kept his trophy and carried it with him in battle, after getting it chambered for Fleet-issue ammunition. When he retired, he had held on to the gun. It was his private, if unlicensed, property.

With practiced movements, he stripped the weapon, checked each piece, and reassembled it, satisfied that it was in perfect working order. He rammed in a full magazine of Fleet-issue ammo, unaccounted for when he left *Musashi* and armed it.

On some worlds, suicidal gamblers still played Russian roulette with old six-shot revolvers. Zack had seen them at it once. But you couldn't play Russian roulette with an automatic blaster: each pull of the trigger was a sure winner.

He looked at the pistol in his hand and took another swig of whiskey. Then he raised the gun, eyes staring at the pink line of clouds on the horizon, and stuck the barrel into his open mouth, muzzle pointing up at his brain.

— TWO —

The universe, in its infinite wisdom, wasn't finished with Zack Decker yet. Not by a long shot. Just as he was about to pull the trigger and blow his brains across the room, he heard a scream that tore through the haze of self-pity and booze. Admittedly, it was a muffled scream, but the sounds of a body thrown against the wall separating Zack's room from Rosette's was convincing enough.

Fights weren't unusual in the decrepit rooming house, and sure as hell not in the slums. But this sounded like a young, screwed-up kid getting the living crap beaten out of her, and that was different. At least in Zack's eyes. Though he wouldn't admit to it, he felt just a bit protective about her. She was young enough to be his daughter although he hoped his real daughter wasn't out turning tricks and getting high.

With a speed surprising in a man his size, and with the level of alcohol in his blood, Zack was across the landing, kicking in girl's door. The plas shattered around the simple lock just as whoever was giving Rosette a licking did something that made her scream again.

Without thinking, Decker closed the few feet between himself and the sharp-faced, greasy goon who was holding her by the wrists with one hand and doing something painful between her legs with the other.

He smashed the butt of his blaster against the man's skull, feeling the bone crack under the impact. The goon gave a last grunt and slid to the floor, blood seeping from his scalp. Rosette merely stood there, almost naked, the glittering costume jeweler and green dye making her look pathetic in the dingy, smelly room.

She stared at Zack wordlessly, scared by the violence in the former Marine's eyes. Decker breathed in and out a few times, working to regain control of himself. After a few moments during which none of the losers on the floor had come to see what the ruckus was, Zack slammed the door shut with one hand and knelt beside the man.

He reached for his neck and tried to find a pulse, without success. Zack had cracked his skull and smashed his brains. Once again, the great Zachary Decker had waded in without thinking and struck without moderation. He sobered up for the second time that night. Many people out there would call this manslaughter.

"Who was he, Rosette?" His voice was a lot harsher than he wanted it to be. The girl flinched at Zack's tone and looked out the window while she rubbed her wrists. "Please tell me this was a slime ball who won't be missed, least of all by the militia."

"Is he dead?" Her voice quavered with a mix of fear and coming down from her drug-induced high.

"Yeah. If it makes you feel any better, this shithead won't be smashing you around no more."

"Oh no!" She wailed and crumpled to the floor beside the rapidly cooling corpse.

"It's okay, kid." Zack tried to smile as he reached out and put a light hand on her shoulder. "Tell me who he is, and why he was using you for torture practice."

"He was a fucking militia cop." Her voice rose in pitch as she hid her face in her hands, crying openly now.

Shock silenced Zack, and all the blood drained from his face.

"His name," Rosette sobbed, "was Leath." She raised her head to look at Zack. "He was as bent as an old pipe cleaner. Worked the vice squad in the spaceport precinct." She sat back and leaned her head against the wall, tears streaming down her face. "Bastard runs hookers, pushes shit, and does protection. You name it, Leath did it. He isn't alone in the precinct either."

Figures, Zack thought. Corrupt bastards always ran in packs and covered for each other, which meant no awards from the local militia for cleaning up their in-house filth.

More like a quick bullet in the head to warn any other strong-arm who wants to put bent coppers out of business.

"He came here tonight," she continued, "to collect his cut from my night's take, and what I owe him for some stuff he gave me, stuff he says they seized off a trader and can afford to sell at a discount. He also wanted a quick fuck, on the house, but I told him I was too tired. So he became mad at me and started beating me around. Then he grabbed me down there, and it hurt. Oh God did it hurt."

And then I promptly stepped into it. Would have been better to blow my head off instead of playing cavalry to the rescue. I just killed a fucking cop!

But Zack Decker didn't become a command sergeant in the Pathfinders without growing some smarts. As the last whiskey fumes vanished from his system, the combat soldier in him, trained to survive, took over.

"First things first, Rosette. Put on your regular clothes, pack everything you own and prepare to move. You have fifteen minutes."

"W-what?"

"You can't stay here. I might have killed him but how do you expect this shithead's buddies to react when they find his body in your room? You have to leave. Now move it, girl."

She nodded and stood, still shaking. Gingerly stepping over the body, she went to the closet and pulled out a simple street outfit, nothing flashy. She didn't even bother with underwear. Then she wiped off her makeup and took off the fake jewelry.

With her green hair tied back into a ponytail, Rosette almost looked like the schoolgirl she should be, not like the streetwalker she was. Almost. When she'd cleared the closet of her belongings, Zack picked up the copper's corpse by the armpits and dragged him into it. With any luck, it would take a day or two before they found him. Like when he started to smell ripe. A day or two to get away. Of course, if the local fuzz had military grade scanners, it might not matter how much of a lead he and Rosette had. For further insurance, Zack jammed the closet door shut with a well-placed kick.

"C'mon, kiddo. I have to pack too, and I'm not letting you out of my sight." He grabbed her by the wrist and dragged her from of the now-empty room into his, next door. Rosette looked around with curiosity as Zack packed his duffel bag.

"Hey, you been in the Marines, lover-boy?" She asked, pointing at the uniform.

Decker grunted. "Yeah. And you can cut the whore talk, Rosette. You're too fucking young for this kind of shit anyway."

"Hah," she snorted, "what the hell do you know, Marine-man? You haven't been where I'm coming from."

"No, you're right," he replied as he carefully folded the undress tunic and tucked it into the drab green carrier with his name stenciled on it. "I've been to worse places. Didn't push me into drugs and hooking."

"No?" She held up the bottle of whiskey. "Booze is a fucking drug just like any shit you snort, inject, or plug into your brain."

That hit a raw nerve with Zack, but instead of lashing out, he snorted.

"Smart girl, aren't you? Too fucking smart to waste your life on the streets. How old are you anyway?"

"Twenty-five." There was enough defiance in her voice to make Zack doubt her word. He took her chin in his hand and forced her to meet his eyes.

"You're not a day over sixteen, Rosette. Not even legal age to sell sex on Aramis."

"Am too!"

"Suit yourself, but you'll have to find a new line of business. Heaven's Gate cops will be looking for a green-haired, green-skinned whore called Rosette who's probably underage and hooked on any kind of drug she can get. Doesn't exactly narrow it down, but it won't take smart coppers too long to end up with you in an interrogation chair. If Leath had you on a string, his buddies will know who you are."

And Decker ends up next in line for the rubber hose treatment.

He closed his duffel bag with finality and took one last look around. Nothing that could be easily traced to him, except the DNA he left everywhere in his fallen hair and dead skin cells. But perhaps he'd be lucky, and Aramis was a place where the fancy gear came out only when a wealthy or influential person was killed, not a bent militiaman. Good thing he had taken the room under a fake name.

Decker nodded, satisfied. The booze hadn't entirely rotted his brain yet. He could still think like a Pathfinder. And that might be the only thing to keep him out of an Aramis prison. If he made it that far. The dead creep might have good friends who'd swear one Zachary Decker died while trying to escape. It wouldn't be the first time a coroner's inquest overlooked the fact that the escapee died from something other than the plasma round fired at close range.

At least Zack had enough money to cover his trail until he could find a ship. Getting the funds for a passage might be a bitch, but he'd seen worse. Ironically, he hadn't even realized that all thoughts of suicide had vanished with the rising sun and that he felt more alive now than he had in months. Decker lived for action and adrenaline. This was probably as close as he'd get.

Then he saw the girl waiting for him. What the hell was he going to do with her?

"Rosette," he frowned, a sudden thought crossing his mind. "You rent the room under your real name?"

She remained silent for a moment, debating whether to answer.

"No," she finally replied. "Rosette's my street name, not my real one. The room and my hooker's papers are under the name Rosette."

"Did they check your ID for the hooker's papers?"

"You gotta be kidding, Zack," she replied laughing bitterly, confirming his suspicion she was underage and therefore not legally eligible for a prostitution license. "My papers came from a pimp who was more interested in fast money than laws. That was before Leath came along, put the pimp away permanently, and took over."

Nice cops around here: pimping, drug dealing, extortion, murder. Like putting the monkeys in charge of the zoo and giving 'em the keys to the bananas.

"So what's your name, kid?" Zack's expression brooked no more lies or evasions.

"Ellena Veillon," she replied looking down at her feet.

"You from Heaven's Gate?"

"No. My family lives in Merat Lake. It's about two thousand kilometers to the west. In farm country. A hick town of pious folks where parents beating their kids, and worse, was a regular part of growing up." Her voice was savage.

"You wanted to know why I'm a hooker, well that's why. I had to get away, so I ran. The only way I could eat once I was here was to sell myself. But I was used to that stuff. Satisfied now, Mister Big War Hero?" She cried again, silent tears running down her cheeks and shoulders trembling.

Zack just stared at her, wondering about a universe where this kind of crap could still happen on civilized planets. After a few moments, he shook it off and took Ellena by the hand.

"C'mon kid. I don't know what will happen, but we're going to visit a good friend of mine near the port. He'll put us up for a few days, and we'll see what we can do."

*

"Damn, Zack," Tren shook his head. "You never know when to stop yourself. That's your problem. Always was. You stupid son of a bitch." But there was no anger in his voice. Only resignation.

Tren, Mara, Zack, and Ellena were sitting in Tren's living room above the *Dragon's Tooth*. Both the innkeeper and his common-law wife were wearing gaudy robes over what looked suspiciously like birthday-suit pajamas.

When Tren had opened the door to Zack's insistent ringing, he'd known at once that something was wrong. Very wrong. Especially with what looked like an underage tart in Zack's wake. Refusing a drink, to Tren's surprise, Decker had told him what happened at the rooming house.

"You know," the ex-Marine chuckled after staring into his glass for a few moments, "you're lucky in your stupidity. No one in the slums, except slags, will help the cops finger

Leath's killer. Most business people will figure you've done your civic duty by topping the shithead. He was the worst scum that ever wore a militia badge. Put the squeeze on everyone he could. Never tried it on me, though, especially after I showed him my Shrehari blaster." Tren grinned at Zack and nodded towards the duffel bag by the door. "You still have yours, I hope. Good guns those Imp fifteens."

Tren took a sip of whiskey and shook his head.

"Come to think of it, not too many of his cop buddies will be awfully zealous. Either they'll be too happy to move in on his profits, or they'll be glad the biggest stain on the precinct is gone." Tren belched.

"But that don't mean you're in the clear, Zack. They have to make an effort for form's sake. After all, can't let the idea get around you can top a copper without consequences. If you left no clues behind and didn't rent the rooms under your own names, they won't find you guys. City cops don't have high-performance scanners. Even if they did, last I heard they didn't take samples of every breathing body on the planet just in case, so they won't have you on file."

"Rooms aren't under our real names, Tren."

"The contrary would have surprised and saddened me, Zack old buddy." Tren rose to his feet and clapped his hands.

"We can discuss the future later. Right now we all need our beauty sleep. Some more than others." He grinned at Decker. "You guys are welcome in my house for as long as you need."

Decker noticed that Mara's eyes said otherwise, but the woman held her peace.

"Zack, you can have the sofa here. Miss Veillon," he bowed with exaggerated gallantry towards Ellena, earning an annoyed grunt from his wife, "you'll be most comfortable in the guest room."

*

Tren took a sip of his scalding hot coffee and looked out the window at the bustle of spaceport precinct. It was close to noon, and the *Dragon's Tooth* wasn't due to open for a few more hours. He glanced at Decker, who seemed absorbed by his coffee.

"So far, all seems quiet in town. But nobody's had time to miss the scuzzbag. Still, it'd be best to stay inside right now."

"Just until I find myself a berth on an outbound ship," Zack scowled, feeling tired and angry at life in general. He couldn't even crawl into a bottle without fucking up. And his aborted suicide attempt still bothered him.

"Yeah, well that could take a while."

"No mooching, Tren," Decker warned. "I pay for my place and the girl's fair and square." *And somehow also scrape together enough money to buy a ticket off Aramis. But what to do about Ellena?*

The innkeeper nodded thoughtfully. He had expected Zack to decline what he considered charity.

"Can't have you working out in town right now. Someone might remember you living in that rattrap. And I know your pension won't cover a starship ticket plus your livelihood, plus your booze..."

"No more booze," Decker interrupted. "I need to keep my wits if the local plod's on my tail."

"Good to hear, Zack. But what I was about to say was that you can earn your keep by working around the *Dragon's Tooth*."

"I don't sling drinks, Kinnear."

"Will you stop fucking interrupting me?" Tren made an exasperated face. "You serving drinks is just as bad as letting you out on the streets, shit-for-brains. What I was about to suggest was that you pay for your keep by helping out in the stockroom and kitchen. You can also play bouncer starting around midnight when the spacers turn rowdy. You're big enough to make dickheads think twice. That work will give you rations and quarters at the *Dragon's Tooth* 'till you move on. Deal?"

Decker shrugged.

"Best offer on the table. Okay, Tren. But no charity. I work for my grub."

"You will," Tren chuckled, his jowls quivering, "you will. Wait 'til you see a deep space trader crew come in for a party. About the girl…" He turned to look at Ellena and a frown of concern creased his forehead.

"Now what's the matter, honey, you're shaking all over. Zack, is she coming down with something?"

Decker, who'd been expecting it for a while now, nodded.

"Yep. She's coming down with withdrawal symptoms. Time for her next fix."

"Aw shit, honey. Why d'ya take junk? What is it you're on? Meth? Shimmer? Blackjuice? Heroin?"

"Shimmer." Her voice shook with an uncontrollable craving for the narcotic.

"Shee-it," Tren swore. "I wish we could put the fuckers who smuggle the stuff in from the Shield out of business. Too bad the Government won't let the Fleet clean up the technobarbs."

"Government might not have a say for long," Zack smiled bitterly, "if more officers show guts like a few of our old friends. Heard on the grapevine that people we know made a raid on a Kardati colony last year. Not drug related but they put a whole clan out of business. All unsanctioned. Maybe we'll see more of that."

There was a tinge of envy in Decker's voice, envy at missing the action.

"Enough skipping down memory lane." He shook his head. "Ellena here is getting a bad case of cold turkey, and we'd better do something."

"Right." Kinnear rubbed his chin and glanced over at Mara, who'd remained silent. She was throwing anxious glances at Ellena's growing agitation. "Only thing we can do, since I won't have any shit in the house is find some nerve juice."

"What the hell's that?" Zack asked, frowning.

"Don't know what its scientific name is, but it's stuff they use in detox. Keeps off the shakes but without the high. It's legal but only under prescription, which means registering."

"Not a good idea, Tren."

"I know. Keep your fucking shorts on. Mara's has a few contacts who can get us some. At least enough until we figure what to do with the girl. Ain't that right, darling."

"Yeah," the fat woman grudgingly replied. "And I'll buy something to wash that awful dye out of her hair too. Green-haired girl's obviously a tart, and that's what the militia will look for. One of you stays with her 'till I'm back. She might need holding down so she doesn't hurt herself or go running to the streets to find a pusher."

"I'll do it," Zack replied with a weary shrug. "My responsibility. Same as payment for the nerve juice will be." *At this rate I'll never leave Aramis,* he thought. *We'll to have to find her a detox program soon, one that'll take ex-hookers who don't own a bloody dime. If she can give up the whoring too that is.*

"Yeah, sure," Tren replied, turning towards the window again, damning Zack for being so proud. They were doing good business with the tavern and could afford to help out for a long time.

"Listen, Ellena can pay off her grub and bed, and the nerve juice by chipping in around the *Dragon's Tooth* too. Not behind the bar," he added before Decker could object. "Can you cook, honey?"

"A bit. Mum made me learn stuff before I ran off," Ellena replied, hugging herself and shivering. "You want, I can do simple stuff. As long as I don't have to go back on the streets." She choked down a sob, looking more than ever like a young girl instead of a hardened tart.

"I think we can arrange that, honey." Tren patted her on the shoulder. "Why don't you go to your room and have a lie-down 'till Mara gets back."

"S-sure." Still hugging herself, the frightened girl disappeared around the corner and down the hallway. When Tren heard the door close he followed her, faster and quieter than a civilian would have expected from such a stout man. He came back smiling.

"She can't leave the room now. Door and window are locked, and there's nothing to hurt herself."

"Seems like you've done this before, Tren," Zack eyed him with suspicion.

"Rough neighborhood, buddy. You know how it is." He shrugged. "C'mon. It's time I showed you the bar operation downstairs. Last night you weren't exactly in a shape to figure your way around."

"You'd be surprised, Tren." And Decker described the public parts of the *Dragon's Tooth* in excruciating detail. Some things a guy never forgets. Like how to observe and report.

*

"Strange, isn't it, Tren?" Zack Decker glanced at his friend as he reached for another piece of bread. The two ex-Marines and Mara were eating their midday meal together in the apartment above the bar. Ellena was having a rough time of it, even with the nerve juice, and was sleeping off another restless night in her room.

"What's strange?" Tren asked, chewing on a chunk of tuber.

"It's been five days since I topped the copper and we haven't heard a thing yet. Not a fucking word in this morning's news either." Decker tapped the reader on a small side table. "Bugger must have started to smell days ago. Even in a shithouse like that, someone's bound to notice, especially with the door broken down."

Tren Kinnear shrugged irritably.

"Don't worry about it, Zack. Maybe the cops don't want to make public that one of their own was killed in a flophouse, off duty. Could be a dozen explanations, such as one of the other inmates found his body and made it vanish. So the cops don't crack down on everybody else in the place."

Decker grunted and returned his attention to the job ads in the daily.

You know more than you're letting on, Tren old pal, but I suppose this comes under the 'you don't want to know' shit we noncoms always tried to make young officers understand. Suit yourself.

Zack's work at the *Dragon's Tooth* had been tame, and he'd stayed away from the bottle, except for a small nightcap with Tren after closing. The only time he saw customers was when things got loud. Then, he'd take his place near the door and stand in the shadows, bare, muscular arms crossed, to watch the crowd. No one tried to see if he was as tough as he looked, which was just as well.   Zack didn't want to attract more attention than necessary.

The rest of the time, the ex-Marine helped Mara and Ellena in the kitchen, cooking up straightforward meals for hungry customers. Decker was surprised to find that simple as the food was, it tasted fantastic. Home cooking like grandma used to make.

After a few days, he realized that under the seedy appearance, the *Dragon's Tooth* was a cut above average. And it attracted a better clientele.

Merchant spacer captains were among the regulars, come to relax with excellent ale or whiskey and a plate of Mara's home cooking, in a place that kept out pimps, whores, beggars, drunks and other losers.   Tren Kinnear was making creds hand over fist, and he seemed to be on friendly terms with more than a dozen captains and officers.   There wasn't a night the place wasn't full of merchant types and the occasional Fleet noncoms on liberty from a passing ship.

Neither did Tren seem to have any problems with the law or the mob. Cops never visited the *Dragon's Tooth* except off duty to have a beer and a friendly talk with him. The local hoods, who ran rackets left, right, and center, squeezing businesspeople in one way or another, kept a healthy distance from the *Tooth*. Zack couldn't figure why, but Tren was above-board. He wouldn't do anything illegal unless it was for a good cause, and Pathfinders had a strict definition of 'good cause.' In a way, Decker felt happy to see his old friend doing well for himself.

As the days went by, Zack felt more and more at home in the tavern. He had a small space to himself behind the storeroom, which allowed him to keep an eye on the main floor after closing. Ellena was getting better, with Mara's mothering and the detox treatments, and she was working long hours in the kitchen under the older woman's eyes. Mara had taken a shine to the former hooker and watching them together, Zack figured she had adopted Ellena as her own. It was probably the first time the girl had something like an ordinary family around her. Nobody was beating her up; nobody was abusing her.

The only thing bothering Zack was the lack of reports on the dead cop. Nothing in the news, nothing on the grapevine, which had a regular branch in the *Tooth*, and no militia cops from CID flashing badges and asking about an ex-Marine and his floozy. But Tren had told him not to worry about it, so he held his peace, and money was accumulating in his account.

*

Almost six weeks after the incident at the rooming house, Tren walked into the kitchen, a big grin on his face. It was close to eight in the evening, and the place was in full swing.

Another of the regular spacer crews was in port, after a long haul across the Commonwealth, and Decker had been kept busy whipping up plenty of Mara's hearty, stick-to-your-ribs cooking.

"Zack, old buddy!" Tren clapped him on the shoulder, looking every inch the happy, prosperous innkeeper. Decker grunted as he finished chopping up yet another spice-onion. "Why don't you let the girls finish whatever you're doing? I want you to meet someone."

He shrugged and took off his apron, wiping his hands on the silky-smooth fabric. Kinnear led him across the crowded room to a darker alcove by the back door, stopping at the bar just long enough to pick up two beer mugs from the barmaid, a thin, sallow-faced girl who worked for Tren a few evenings a week. Decker had never warmed to her, and apart from polite nods whenever they met, he much ignored her.

"Zack, I want you to meet an old regular, Captain Diego Strachan of the merchant spacer *Shokoten*. Captain Strachan, this is my old Marine buddy, Command Sergeant Zack Decker, retired. One of the best gunners in the Corps."

Decker shook hands with Strachan, a stocky, middle-aged man with squint lines around his eyes and a silver-shot beard around his mouth. His black hair, also liberally frosted, had been pulled back into a short queue at the nape of his neck.

He wore a plain black leather tunic, adorned with silver buttons and trim. The four stripes of a merchant captain hung on a short strap attached to his right shoulder. It wasn't the look Zack had expected from a civilian ship's master. But then, the crews of the fast traders that plied the outer star lanes hardly stuck to convention. Common wisdom said they differed from marauders only in that the former were the latter's prey. The captain's handshake was firm, testing and Zack responded, pressure for pressure, all the time looking Strachan straight in the eyes.

Decker had a good idea what this was about since him being one of the best gunners in the Corps was so much bullshit. Like many senior noncoms, Zack was qualified as Marine Master Gunner and knew how to handle most types of ship's guns, and his command rank also meant he had the basic gunnery officer's ticket. But he was a Pathfinder first and best, not a gunner.

"Pleasure to meet you, Decker," Strachan said as he released his vise-like grip. Zack could read a small measure of approval in the man's expression. He seemed to place faith in the way a man shook hands.

"Pleasure's all mine, Captain," he replied.

Strachan sat down, motioning Zack to do the same, and Kinnear placed a mug in front of either before vanishing in the crowd. The merchant captain examined Decker as he took an appreciative sip of Tren's imported Shrehari ale.

"So," he finally asked, "what made you leave the Corps? You don't look like you're at retirement age yet."

Zack briefly debated whether to tell him a bullshit story, then decided the truth was best, especially if he was right and Tren had set this meeting up to get him a job on a freighter. Who knew what the other ex-Marine had already told Strachan about him. This could be another test, just like the handshake.

"Wasn't exactly voluntary retirement, Captain," Zack shrugged, staring into his beer. Telling a perfect stranger about it wasn't easy. "I was brought up in front of the colonel for disobeying stupid orders from a shit-brained officer who almost got us all killed in a badly planned combat op. Unfortunately, I also took exception to that officer once we were back on board ship, and I was out of sickbay. If I'd kept my temper, the colonel could have convinced Captain Sarratt that hauling me in front of disciplinary hearing would be bad for everyone involved, but me giving Sarratt the what-for in front of the squadron made it impossible for the colonel to smooth over. He formally considered my case and found I wasn't sufficiently right and the officer sufficiently wrong to throw out the complaint against me. He gave me a choice: retire voluntarily or face a court martial. My chances in court didn't look good, and if found guilty, it would have stripped me of my rank and sent me to a penal battalion, so I put in my twenty-year papers. They gave me my pension and an honorable discharge instead of hard labor."

Strachan nodded as if satisfied with the explanation. For a moment, Zack feared that he'd ask for more details on his story, but the merchantman took another sip and changed tack.

"How much of a ship's gunner are you anyway, Decker? I know Tren enough to figure he sells bullshit along with the best beer on Aramis." Once again, Strachan's tone and expression brooked no evasions or tall tales.

"I'm checked out on all gun and missile systems as an operator, I used to have command rank, so I also have my basic gunnery officer's ticket, along with the Marine Master Gunner qualification. So you could say I know the ins and outs of firing and fixing most of the stuff in the Fleet inventory, but one of the best gunners in the Fleet, I'm not. I'm a Pathfinder first and last, which means my specialty is recon, not gunnery."

Strachan nodded thoughtfully.

"Thought Kinnear was laying it on a little thick. He tells me you're looking for a job."

"Yeah."

"Why? You have a decent one here working with your old buddy, don't you?"

Zack shrugged.

"Too young to settle down. I still have the urge to move. Tren's right. I'm looking for a berth."

Strachan nodded again. "Kinnear recommends you highly, and I'm short a gunnery and security officer in *Shokoten*. Where we trade is where the high-profit margin cargoes are, and pirates know it. My ship has good legs, but it also needs someone to handle our weapons properly in a fight. You interested?"

"What's the job include, Captain?"

"Train the crew to man the guns and shoot straight in a fight, maintain the buggers, keep our small arms locker in order, train the crew in small arms handling, and ship's security. We pick up passengers along with cargo, and they sometimes need watching, and we have to make sure we're secure on the ground when we're sitting in a foreign port. Think you can handle that?"

"Yeah," Zack slowly nodded. "I can handle it, and I'm interested. What about pay and benefits?"

"Standard rates."

"Which are? I'm not familiar with the merchant service."

"A thousand creds a month for the first year, renegotiable every year after that, free meals, a hundredth-share of the annual profits, increased every year. You become entitled to Merchant Guild medical and disability insurance and use of Guild facilities when you're in port."

"Sounds good," Zack replied, face expressionless. A thousand creds a month was a quarter of the pay he used to make as a command sergeant, but with his pension, it would make a tidy little sum for someone who'd be living on board ship.

"When do I sign on?"

"Show up at the Guild offices tomorrow morning around nine. My first officer will see you squared away and bring you on board. We lift the day after tomorrow. I have a quick cargo turnover. You need to bring your own coveralls and leathers, and you can only bring one duffel bag of personal gear. Space is at a premium on commercial ships."

Zack allowed himself a small grin. "Same thing on frigates, Captain. And I already have leathers, good Fleet-issue battledress."

"Right then, Decker. I'll see you when my first officer brings you aboard. Her name's Raisa Darhad. You won't have any problems recognizing her."

Strachan drained the rest of his beer, stood up and shook hands with Zack again. Then he left the *Dragon's Tooth* with a parting nod at Tren.

*

"Did Diego offer you a berth?" The former Marine asked when the two friends were alone in the stockroom.

"Yeah. As the ship's gunnery and security officer."

"Good." Tren seemed genuinely pleased, more than Zack figured he would be.

"So what's the story on Strachan?"

"Runs a clean operation, as far as I know," Tren answered, looking at the stacked crates of Shrehari ale against the far wall. "Fast freighter, decent crew. Does just about every run in this part of the galaxy, including the Imperium. No shady stuff, at least not what an old Pathfinder might object to, the kinda crap we fought against for years. Does some smuggling on the side, like this Shrehari ale here, and that don't hurt no one except the taxman. You ought to get along fine and have a good time at it too."

Zack grunted and stared hard at his friend, who he noticed had kept his eyes riveted on his ample stocks.

Why do I have the feeling Tren here really wants me to sign on with Strachan? I mean more than just seeing an old pal right. Strachan's job interview wasn't very thorough, which means Tren sung him my praises and piled on the crap 'till it reached the sky. In a hurry to rid yourself of me? That's a sudden change of wind.

"What'll happen to Ellena?" He asked instead.

This time, Tren looked at him before answering. "She'll stay with us of course. Mara kind of adopted her. She could never have kids. Spent too much time working on an old tramp with shitty radiation shielding. Don't worry about the girl. *Shokoten* calls into Aramis twice a year, so you can visit."

"Yeah."

"C'mon. Let's see you paid-up and packed. No more work tonight." He put his arm around Zack's shoulder and squeezed. "We'll give you a real good sailing party!"

— THREE —

Zack Decker stepped off the grungy street and into the chilly silence of the Merchant Spacer's Guild, feeling as if he had crossed a portal between parallel universes. This close to the port itself, it was mainly warehouses, cheap, flea-infested hotels and the lowest grade of bars. But the Guildhall, now that was something else.

Decker had made his tearful farewells the night before, liberally dousing them with Tren's best hooch, the stuff he kept for his classiest customers. Ellena had hung around his neck, crying that she'd miss her 'Uncle Zack' something terrible.

By leaving the *Dragon's Tooth*, he felt as if he were leaving his family. But Zack was clear-headed enough to know the familial atmosphere couldn't last, that his wanderlust would sour it. Not to mention the inescapable fact that he'd murdered a militia officer, something that could see him arrested as soon as the other plods pinned the job on him. And that would kill Tren's thriving business.

On the other hand, Decker hadn't seen nor heard a thing about Detective Leath since he'd stuffed his body into Ellena's closet. That bothered him. After the first brush-off, he stopped asking Tren about it, but Zack couldn't shake the suspicion that his old friend had more pull than anyone knew, and had arranged for the death to become a non-event. After a month and a half living with Kinnear, Decker knew there was more to his old comrade in arms than just a retired Marine sergeant who became a gin-slinger. Tren seemed to have contacts everywhere, from the cleanest cops to the dirtiest crime gangs. It ensured his inn, and its inn-mates were left alone.

Zack had left the tavern early that morning before anyone else woke. He didn't want to go through the goodbyes again, preferring a clean break. Because *Shokoten* visited Aramis regularly, it wasn't as if the farewell was forever, like the one his ex-wife gave him when she bugged out with his daughter. Or the one he received when they walked him down *Musashi*'s gangway and into the hands of the military police.

After the automatic doors of the Guildhall's entrance had swished closed behind him, Decker stopped to get his bearings. The central area was two stories high and as big as a gravball playing field, and that meant big. Most likely, it had started life as a warehouse.

Skylights let in the morning sun, turning the austere hall into something warmer. Cream-colored panels covered poured plascrete walls while massive support pillars marked off separate work areas. The panels glowed softly under the bright, natural light, looking like brushed silk.

At first glance, the Guildhall was clean, uncluttered, and functional. It matched Zack's idea of the people who took to the star lanes for profit.

To his left, a dozen simple but comfortable looking chairs were set out in small groups around tables laden with printouts of various publications. An industrial coffee urn presided over the waiting area, chugging along as it percolated the richly scented brew in a method centuries old. Three spacers in clean coveralls were sprawled out in the chairs, coffee mugs at hand, looking as if they were recovering from a night of overindulgence.

A long table, labeled 'Employment,' with several computer terminals on it sat across from the waiting area while glass-enclosed offices lined the wall. Two business-suited Guild employees behind a high counter shuffled paper, ignoring the waiting spacers.

Further down, Decker could see signs advertising cargo and freight, passenger transport, administration, spacers' welfare and insurance, standards and at the end of the large atrium, a door that sported a sign proclaiming the Merchant's Guild Club–Aramis.

Zack walked over to the waiting area. The three spacers looked at him, bleary-eyed, and then sank back into their hangdog misery, satisfied that the new arrival wasn't some exotic apparition. Decker had dressed simply, like any spacer, military or civilian did when on shore leave: dark, military cut slacks, scuffed boots, white collarless shirt, and black leather jacket.

He dropped his duffel bag by a chair and helped himself to a cup of coffee. Taking a sip, he grinned with appreciation at the flavor. Instead of sitting, Zack wandered around the waiting area, admiring holo pics displayed on the smooth walls. They showed gleaming merchant vessels of many eras, including pre-spaceflight Earth sailing ships. The former noncom spent a long time studying the most beautiful one, an ancient ship by the name of Cutty Sark.

When he finally turned around, his eyes stopped dead in their tracks as he saw a female merchant officer walk through the doors. She wore a high-collared, black tunic of an exotic cut that emphasized her feminine curves and flared over her hips. It was cinched at the waist by a broad gray belt through which she had thrust a curved dagger half the length of Zack's big forearm. The dagger's hilt was an extraordinary work of filigree art that did not come from any human artisan.

Her trousers were of the same matte black as the tunic and hugged her form like a second skin. They were tucked into knee-high military-style boots with flat heels. She wore rank insignia, three stripes, on a leather strap dangling from her right shoulder.

Zack at once knew this was Raisa Darhad, *Shokoten*'s first officer. Captain Strachan had told him he would have no difficulty recognizing her, and he was right.

Where the captain had looked like a marauder gone legit, she appeared more dangerous than any pirate Decker had ever met, for First Officer Darhad was not a human female. She was from a predatory species called the Arkanna.

As she walked towards Decker, a flush of heat ran through his body, a strange mixture of attraction, admiration, and instinctive fear. Darhad moved like a killer, an exotic, beautiful, and deadly assassin. The trained warrior in Zack screamed in warning.

Arkanna, a humanoid species resembling homo sapiens, came from an early spaceflight planet of the same name in the neutral Protectorate Zone. Uncommon in human space, they preferred the more violent, unpredictable Shrehari and their harsh Empire. This one's presence in the Commonwealth hinted at a past life shrouded in mystery, and most likely, death.

Humanoid though she was the differences between the Arkanna and humans were more striking than the resemblances. Characteristic of her race, First Officer Darhad's skin was albino white, almost translucent, with a fine tracery of veins barely visible just below the surface. In shocking contrast, her thick, shoulder-length hair, gathered into a ponytail at the back, was crimson.

Her eyes were her most striking feature. Where human eyes were white, hers were almond shaped and of a deep cerulean blue around bright red irises. They seemed to exude an archetypal power that sent a shiver down Zack's spine. For a moment, he knew how his distant, ape-like ancestors felt when they met Earth's equivalent of her distant, predatory ancestors.

When she came nearer, Zack realized she was as tall as he was, taller than most human women were, yet her body was slender. But she seemed no less of a formidable opponent.

"Mister Decker, I presume," she said, stopping a meter in front of him. Her voice had a deep, rich modulation, sensuous, but with an alien undertone that disturbed Zack until he realized that it stirred his deeper animal feelings.

She examined Zack from head to toe after he'd nodded, speechless before this apparition. She didn't seem overly disappointed by what she saw.

"I am First Officer Darhad of the *Shokoten*." She held out her hand. Decker, struggling to recover his poise, looked her straight in the eyes and took her slender fingers in his, squeezing hard as he shook like Captain Strachan had done yesterday.

Suddenly, pinpricks of pain studded his hand below Darhad's fingertips and he released the pressure. He glanced down as they let go and caught sight of shiny talons retracting into her pale digits. Her scent, musky and exciting, filled his nostrils.

"Pleased to meet you, First Officer," he finally answered.

She considered him for a moment and then smiled, her bloodless, full lips drawing back to show sharp, pointy teeth, like those of a predatory carnivore. A she-wolf with the shape of a dancer.

"Come, Mister Decker. We have much paperwork to complete so we can turn you into a Guild-certified merchant spacer."

She turned around and walked towards the counter. Zack picked up his duffel bag and followed her, unable to resist admiring her shape from behind. Though after seeing those talons and teeth, he wouldn't even dream of making a move on her. He was sure the crew didn't give First Officer Darhad any trouble.

The Guild bureaucrats behind the counter wisely chose not to ignore her, and the elder of the two, a woman in her mid-forties, smiled at them.

"What can I do for you, First Officer?"

She pointed over her shoulder with a long thumb. "This is Mister Decker. Mister Decker is a former Marine Corps command sergeant, who is signing on to *Shokoten* as gunnery and security officer. I would have you process him so he may obtain his Guild certification and work papers."

"Certainly, First Officer. Mister Decker, do you have your discharge papers?"

Zack nodded and dug deep into his jacket's inner pocket, producing a flat, gray data chip which he handed to the clerk. She pushed the chip into a slot on her computer terminal and read the lines appearing on the screen, raising her eyebrows at several notations. Finally, the clerk typed a few commands and smiled at Darhad and Decker.

"Won't take but a minute." And it didn't.

"There," she said handing back Zack's discharge papers and a new data chip, blue in color. "These are your Guild papers, Mister Decker. Based on your military record, the Guild recognizes you as a qualified ship's gunnery and security officer, as well as a level four weapons system tech and a level six general engineer. With a hundred practical hours on the bridge, *Shokoten*'s captain can also certify you as watch keeping officer."

Darhad raised her upswept eyebrows in a good mimic of human surprise.

"You have watchkeeper training, Mister Decker?"

"Yes, sir. It's been standard for Pathfinder officers and command noncoms on patrol frigates for the last two years to take the training in case of emergencies."

"Fascinating," she purred, a small, feral smile playing on her lips. She looked at the clerk. "Anything else?"

"A few more formalities to put Warrant Officer Decker on the official Guild rolls."

"Warrant officer?" Zack looked at the clerk in surprise.

"That's what your qualifications give you." Then, seeing the lack of understanding in Decker's face, the clerk explained, all the while watched by an amused First Officer Darhad.

"In the merchant service, just like the Commonwealth Fleet, there are three levels of rank: officers, warrant officers, and ratings. Officers are concerned with sailing the ship and handling the cargo. Warrant officers are specialists whose work doesn't involve sailing the ship but who have defined jobs, like pursers, doctors, or gunners like you. And the ratings, of course, have the same jobs as enlisted personnel on board a warship. Now if you'd actually qualified as watchkeeper, the Guild could have recognized you as a ship's officer, provided a master was willing to hire you as such. But your naval gunnery ticket is enough for warrant rank."

Decker grunted and nodded his thanks.

So now I'm a fucking warrant officer. Warrant Officer Zachary T. Decker of the MV Shokoten. *Nice ring to it.*

When the retinal scan, DNA sampling, and the multiple thumbprint signatures were over, the clerk shook Zack's hand.

"Welcome to the Merchant Spacer's Guild. May you have a long and profitable career."

"Thank you."

"Well then, Warrant Officer Decker," the first officer purred, "let me guide you to our ship."

First Officer Darhad had a long stride and a fast pace, and Zack had to hurry. People in the streets looked at her with frank curiosity, and Decker saw more than one stare at her receding derriere, which he had to admit was charming. But those talons, and those teeth...

*

The Merchant Vessel *Shokoten* had none of the sleek, deadly lines of a Fleet patrol frigate, but she had a certain sinister elegance, nonetheless. She appeared built for speed, the sort of speed traders wanted in the badlands, or smugglers anywhere.

Her dull gray hull was liberally streaked with black re-entry marks and pitted from too many high-speed runs through space hazards, but it was in good repair, as were her hyperdrive nacelles and gun turrets. She was big for a lander, almost as big as a Navy corvette, the smallest class of warship in the Commonwealth.

Thick lines snaked from ports along her lower hull towards a metallic servicing block at the edge of the pad, like the tentacles of a giant squid. The broad belly ramp was lowered, and gravlifts were ferrying a steady stream of containers from the customs hangar to the ship, under the watchful eye of an officer with two and a half stripes on his black tunic. If Zack had figured out the merchant rank system right, that was the second officer, a tall, dour looking black man with gray hair, a gray beard, and a gold earring hanging from his right lobe. Darhad gestured towards him.

"Second Officer Bowdoin, responsible for ship's systems. He is your direct superior. He is also the chief cargo officer. You will meet him later when loading is completed."

"Yes, sir."

At that moment, a gust of wind pushed up the crimson hair on the side of her head, and Zack glimpsed a white, upswept, pointy ear that twitched at the colder air. It seemed appropriate for First Officer Darhad's general appearance. Zack was now convinced her ancestors hadn't been swinging from trees like his. They had hunted ancestors like his, no doubt with extraordinary skill and excessive cruelty.

*

The familiar smell of a space vessel filled Zack's nostrils as they walked up the gangway and through the personnel port. Ozone, lubricants, coolants, metal and polymers, the aromas of home.

The ship's passageways were as utilitarian as her exterior. Black, anti-skid rubber covered the decks; the bulkheads were bare metal, unrelieved by any hint of paint or the decorations he expected after twenty years aboard warships.

Each section was isolated from the next by heavy, armored hatches. No elegant sliding doors here. Right now, they were all open, their strong locking mechanisms withdrawn.

Sheathed conduits and wiring ran along the ceiling, color-coded for easy maintenance. Glowpanels hung at regular intervals, projecting a bright, uncompromising light into the smallest nooks and crannies. And there were many of those.

Decker unconsciously mapped the passageways in his mind as she led him deeper into the ship. They met crewmembers who greeted the Arkanna woman with obvious respect and gave Zack frankly curious looks, but who didn't otherwise stop their busy work.

The crew was a mixed bunch, of all human races. Most of the men wore beards of some sort and long hair gathered in queues or braids. By contrast, many of the women had hair as short as Zack's Marine cut.

They looked as hard and tough as any smuggler crew Decker had ever seen, with tattoos galore, earrings, nose studs, and other body ornaments. All carried knives tucked into belts or boot tops.

Darhad stopped in front of a cabin door, and it took all of Zack's control not to bump into her. Somehow, he had the impression she had done it on purpose. She knocked on the hatch, and when it opened, she motioned Decker to precede her.

Just as Zack crossed the threshold, she announced in a loud voice, "Warrant Officer Decker reporting to sign on, Captain."

Not knowing what else to do, Decker reported in proper Marine fashion. He stopped three paces in front of the imitation wood desk and came to attention, restraining a military salute just in time. Strachan had watched his actions with amusement, the former Marine in Decker showing through at every gesture.

He stood and held out his hand. "Welcome aboard *Shokoten*, Warrant Officer Decker. I hope you'll have a pleasant and profitable career with us. At ease, man, at ease."

When Zack relaxed, he saw Strachan pulling a bottle of Akvavit and two glasses from a drawer. Then, he picked up a datapad and handed it to Decker.

"Read the terms of your contract, if you're satisfied, press your thumb on the reader. A hard copy of the contract will be given to you when I file it with the Guild. The terms are as I laid out last night."

"You knew the Guild would rate me as a warrant officer, sir?"

"Of course. Our former gunner was a warrant officer."

Decker nodded his understanding and kept on reading. The contract was comprehensive and set out his duties, responsibilities, privileges, and pay. He thumbed the reader and saw a tag appear at the end of the document, proof of his 'signature.' Strachan took back the pad and thumbed it as well. Then, he gave Zack one of the glasses and took the other.

"A toast to our new gunner." Strachan swallowed his shot in one gulp.

Zack imitated him, sending a liquid fiercer than antimatter engine coolant down his throat. He repressed the urge to cough with great difficulty.

"Well then, Mister Decker, I'll leave the first officer to see you settled in. I trust you've completed all your business ashore? Good. We're lifting at first light, and there is much to do before then." He nodded his dismissal.

Zack snapped to attention, executed a perfect about-face, and followed the Darhad out of the cabin.

"You will bunk here," she waved her white hand across the threshold of a small cabin several doors down from the captain's quarters.

Zack stepped in and looked around. It was small all right. A two level bunk almost covered one wall while two lockers covered the opposite wall. In a corner, a narrow open door led to a tiny washroom, complete with shower, toilet, and sink. Two desks, with computer terminals, sat face to face in the center of the cabin and completed the meager amenities.

One desk and the lower bunk, showed signs of use, but there were no decorations or other personal effects to soften the starkness of the spotlessly clean quarters.

"The only other warrant officer of the ship, Nihao Kiani, is your cabin mate. She is *Shokoten*'s purser." Darhad stepped over to a locker and opened the door. It was empty save for a leather band with a single red and gold stripe on it. "This is yours. The rank strap belonged to our former gunner. Since it is ship issue, it now belongs to you. Please wear it when you report to the bridge at the start of the afternoon watch."

"Yes, sir. What happened to the former gunner?"

"He died on a planet in the Shield Cluster, torn to shreds by the natives, apparently for a violation of a local taboo. I shall leave you now, Mister Decker, settle in."

She disappeared down the passageway, leaving a very pensive Zack to stare through the open cabin door.

*

"Permission to enter the bridge," Decker stood at attention on the threshold. He had replaced his scuffed work boots with his calf-high synth leather shipboard boots and wore his black Marine battledress, the closest he could come to the clothes officers wore aboard this ship. From what he'd seen, the ratings preferred coveralls or jumpsuits, though high, military style boots were the rule for all ranks.

It was five minutes before eight bells in the forenoon watch — Five minutes to twelve.

"Permission granted. You are?" the lanky young man with the one and a half stripes of a fourth officer asked, smiling as he rose to greet the new arrival.

"Zack Decker, sir. The new ship's gunner and security officer."

"I'm Fourth Officer Gareth. Welcome aboard."

Gareth had a vigorous handshake. His brown eyes examined Decker with interest. Though younger than any of the other officers, he showed none of the innocence Zack expected from young and inexperienced Navy officers.

"The first officer said to report to the bridge for the start of the afternoon watch, sir."

"Oh, aye," Gareth nodded, "she told me to expect you. You're acquaint yourself with ship's systems and the gunnery station. Have you had lunch yet?"

"Yes, sir. Wardroom served up cold sandwiches."

"Excellent. Though you shouldn't rate the ship based on your first meal aboard. Food is always measly when we're loading. It gets better once the ship is underway."

To Zack Decker's military mind, the arrangement made perfect sense: put the greatest effort towards the primary mission, loading the cargo. After twenty years in the Marines, he'd had a lot worse anyway.

He had eaten alone in the small wardroom, as the officer's mess on a ship was called, and had enjoyed the cold meal. The next one probably wouldn't be as enjoyable, when he ate with the others. After two decades as an enlisted trooper, it would take a long time getting used to being an officer.

"I thought the food was good, sir."

Gareth raised his thin eyebrows.

"Why Mister Decker, either you have a dead palate, or you haven't been fed in a while."

Zack smiled, eyes twinkling.

"How about I get to work, sir, before I say something I might regret?"

"Yes, why don't you, gunner." He waved at the gunnery console. "It's all yours."

"Thank you, sir." Zack slipped into the seat and ran a loving hand over the smooth console. It was good to be back aboard a starship wearing a uniform, even if it was with a merchant sailor's rank and on a freighter. Warrant Officer Decker. Wouldn't Captain Sarratt have a fucking bird if he found out Decker had gone up in the world instead of down to a penal battalion, as he wanted him to?

The hours flew by as he eagerly learned his new duties.

*

When the door opened, Zack jumped off his bunk and held out his hand, smiling.

"Hi, I'm Zack Decker, the new ship's gunner. I guess I'm your new roomie, too."

In deference to modesty, and because he didn't know what sort of culture his shipmates came from, Decker had kept on his shorts and t-shirt, instead of stripping down to sleep, as he usually did.

He'd had a long day going through the ship with the second officer during most of the two dogwatches and the evening watch, inspecting each gun turret, the defensive arrays, the arms locker, and the surveillance gear.

Shokoten was surprisingly well equipped for a freighter. But, as he had reminded himself, Tren had said she often sailed through the badlands, where anything less meant suicide.

Mister Bowdoin had grilled him long and hard about his technical and tactical knowledge, often demanding hands-on demonstrations of his weapons' use and repair skills. They had stopped in the wardroom only long enough to wolf down a bowl of stew, long after the other officers had eaten. Zack hadn't had a rough day like that in a long time, but it felt good to be useful again.

When they parted, Bowdoin had muttered something about Zack 'doing okay' and told him to be on the bridge for lift-off, at six bells in the morning watch.

*

The woman who walked into the cabin didn't seem surprised at his presence though Zack knew she hadn't been on board all day. She eyed him warily, and her handshake was perfunctory.

"Nihao Kiani, the ship's purser. Welcome aboard."

Now why, Zack wondered, did that welcome not sound like one? Then a thought struck him. Maybe she and his predecessor had been more than just bunkies. Living close like this, a man and a woman were bound to think of getting even closer.

Decker climbed back into his bunk and watched her putter around the cabin in silence. Warrant Officer Kiani was a surprisingly tall and strongly built woman for a Han native, unlike most Zack had met. Her thick black hair fell straight to her shoulders, framing a broad, high-cheek boned face dominated by intense brown eyes.

When she undressed for bed, Zack got an even greater appreciation for her strong, muscular thighs and arms. As she turned the lights out, unconcerned about her nudity in front of a stranger, Zack glimpsed a tantalizingly flat stomach and small breasts.

It had been a long time for Decker, and that night, trying to ignore the very attractive woman in the bunk below, he promised himself a visit to a reputable house the moment he had a chance. It would be a hard haul, what with more than one highly attractive women on board. But he would no more make an advance on Nihao Kiani than on First Officer Darhad. Both of them looked like they could make him very much regret any unwanted attentions.

When he woke the next morning, Kiani had already left the cabin.

He didn't see his roommate again until late that night when *Shokoten* was in hyperspace. And then he saw only her sleeping face above the covers. Not that she seemed to be deliberately avoiding contact with Decker, but that's how it seemed. If she kept this up, eating at different times and ignoring him in the cabin, it would be a tough way to live.

Yet Nihao Kiani, like much aboard *Shokoten*, would stay a mystery for Decker as the ship sped towards its next destination.

*

He was busy, of course. The lengthy absence of a qualified gunner showed in the general state of her ordnance and small arms lockers. The crew treated him with the deference due to his rank and, Zack had to admit, due to his size and strength, but always with a strong undercurrent of suspicion. They didn't accept him at face value, and that was normal. But their distant looks and frequent outright distrust made him uncomfortable. Only Strachan and Darhad were anywhere close to making Zack feel at home, and then only in the line of duty. Zack Decker was an outsider, and the crew made sure he knew it.

— FOUR —

Decker was out of his bunk and halfway to his locker before he woke and realized the loud noise that had turned his dream into reality was the battle stations siren.

Without thinking, he pulled on his battledress and buckled his gun belt around his waist. When he stepped out of the door, moments later, Nihao Kiani was just starting to push her covers back. Zack grimaced as he hurried towards the bridge.

Judging by her lack of urgency, standards were lax on this ship. And she was in charge of the aft damage control party. In Zack's world, from the moment you spot a bandit until he's within shooting range you rarely have enough to time to wipe your ass. *Civilians!*

In an emergency, there was no protocol on a Navy ship, and Decker assumed it would be the same here. He stepped through the door to the bridge and headed for his station without even acknowledging the officer of the watch.

Fourth Officer Gareth, seated in the command chair, opened his mouth to reprimand the new warrant officer, and then thought better of it when he saw his intent face. A few moments later, the first of the battle stations bridge crew arrived, and Gareth handed the ship back to its captain.

Decker powered-up all the ship's guns and shields while sending the fire control sensors to probe the night. A red light blipped on his status board. Gun turret number three was refusing his commands. He stabbed the call button on his intercom terminal.

"Engineering, this is Guns."

"Engineering," a bored voice answered.

"Gun turret number three is not powering up. Please find out why and get it online ASAP."

"Hold on a moment, there, Gunner," another voice came back. "This is the third officer. First of all, you don't give my people orders. You're a warrant. Second, turret number three isn't working because I had the power interlink pulled. Since this is a drill, I'm not about to fuck around in the dark and put it back. You hear that, Gunner?"

Zack raised his eyebrows at the rebuke. He felt the captain's eyes on his back. Strachan had heard the short interchange and waited to see what the new man would do.

The third officer was a hard woman and had a particular hatred for the Commonwealth Navy. That made Zack Decker her number one object of loathing aboard *Shokoten*.

"Engineering, this is Guns." Decker deliberately used a harsh tone. "Primo, we're at battle stations, which means any order from the bridge is like it came from the captain himself. Second, I don't give a rat's ass about power interlinks. Without turret three, the aft underside of the ship is wide open, and that, sir, is your own area. We can't have that, now can we?"

Sarcasm dripped from Zack's voice.

"So please put the fucking interlink back." He paused before concluding. "And third, you don't know it's a damn drill until the captain says it's a drill. Start thinking there's a difference between training and the real thing, and the next time the pirates come and kick your ass, you won't be ready to return the favor because your head will still think drill. Pirates won't let you live long enough to figure out the difference."

"Hey," Third Officer Arlean Sonoda's outraged voice erupted from the intercom, "you can't talk to me that way."

Before Decker could reply, and Strachan was sure his next answer would be even more stinging that the previous one, the captain stopped the bickering. Decker was right, and he was doing his job. That's why he hired him. The last few days had proven his competence and his willingness to work.

"Engineering, this is the captain. We are at battle stations. You will carry out guns' request now. After we've secured ship, report to my quarters. Bridge out."

Strachan nodded at Decker, who turned back to face his screens with a small grin playing on his lips.

Yes, smile my ex-Marine sergeant, the captain thought as he stroked his beard, only half listening to his first officer's status report. But beware of our Arlean Sonoda. You have a dangerous enemy there.

Then Strachan noticed the worn Imperial Armaments blaster in the open holster on Decker's right hip. Interesting. That's a Shrehari weapon if I'm not mistaken. Did you take it off an Imperial soldier in battle, perchance? Maybe it's Arlean who should be wary of you...

As drills went, this one was a shambles compared to a well-trained patrol frigate. But for a merchantman, Decker had to concede that *Shokoten* had surpassed his low expectations. They weren't new at this.

"People," Captain Strachan looked around the mess table at his officers and warrant officers. He was using the wardroom for the debriefing because *Shokoten* didn't have a dedicated conference room. Space was at a premium on traders, and every spare nook and cranny had to bring back profit with cargo.

"I will not say I'm satisfied at the battle stations drill, because I'm not. It may be good enough for some ships, but not *Shokoten*. As our new gunner has pointed out, reivers will give us less than five minutes warning. And he should know. He has served aboard ships who did the same to those reivers, or who picked up the debris of imprudent traders."

Strachan nodded in Decker's direction. The third officer sneered silently at the reference to the Fleet, an expression Zack saw, though he pretended not to notice. The other officers remained still, staring at their captain, faces neutral.

"When the siren goes off, don't think, 'Oh shit, not another drill.' Remember that you're about to fight for your lives. Make the crew remember this. There is only one reaction, and that is the right one. Not one reaction for a drill and one for a real attack. We seem to have grown remarkably lax of late." Strachan glanced at Decker again.

"You all know we're headed for Pradyn, out in the Shield. In three days, we cross out of Commonwealth space and into the badlands. I will run drills often and at unexpected moments, just to make sure we survive the trip." The third officer seemed about to speak, but Strachan held up his hand. "There will be no discussion on this point. I know we've been without a gunner for a few runs, but we have one now. And he has more combat experience than anyone on this ship will ever have. When he speaks from the bridge during battle stations, take it as coming from me, and execute."

Zack and the captain had spoken in private before the meeting, and the gunner had made several very blunt and very accurate comments about the combat readiness of the ship. Diego Strachan prided himself on running a steady operation, better than most, but Zack Decker's merciless report on his vessel's readiness had caused him to think again.

"It can't be that bad, Gunner," he had said. "I've been running ships across this arm of the galaxy for thirty years and yes, I've had a few close scrapes with pirates, but we've always come through without a scratch."

"With all due respect, Captain," Decker had replied, "it takes only once to see you dead. Your friendly neighborhood pirates are getting better ships and people all the time, and they're getting a lot bolder. Where you might have been safe five years ago is now a hell's gauntlet, especially in the Shield. No Fleet to cover you there. *Shokoten*'s a good ship, and the pirates would give their left and right nuts to get their slimy little hands on it. I mean, how often have you been in the Shield with her?"

Strachan shrugged but didn't reply.

"Stop me if you know this one, Captain, but the first couple of times, reivers take a close look to figure out how much of a target you are: weapons, crew, cargo; stuff like that. When they have you pegged, they'll find out when your next run is and jump. They have spies in just about every port in the Commonwealth. It doesn't take much magic to pull an ambush across the border. Statistically, every new trip into the Badlands gets you one step closer to trouble."

Strachan had stroked his beard as he stared out at space through his cabin's porthole.

"You seem well informed, Gunner, and willing to part with intelligence I'm sure the military would rather keep quiet." His tone was light, but the meaning in his eyes as he turned them back towards Decker, wasn't.

Zack looked down uncomfortably.

"You pick up a lot when you serve in border patrols, and you hired me to do a job which I'm doing, Captain."

A cruel smile tugged at Strachan's lips. "Plus you have an interest in keeping this ship and your own skin out of pirate hands."

Decker gave him a defiant stare.

"Normal enough, isn't it, sir? But if you're asking whether I fear the scum, I don't. I could have been killed many times in the last twenty years. How often did you risk your life, Captain?"

Diego Strachan glared at the ex-Marine for a moment, and then burst out laughing as he sat back in his chair.

"Fair enough question, Gunner. I like your spirit." Then, as he became serious again, "what do you suggest we do?"

Decker had grinned, looking more than ever like a tough Marine Corps noncom, and had lectured his captain on turning his ship into a survivor, as he would do now, in front of the ship's officers and bosun.

"Mister Decker will explain how we will become more efficient. Zack?"

The captain's use of Warrant Officer Decker's first name was not lost on anyone. First Officer Darhad looked at the others' expressions with her predator's eyes, amusement playing on her lips. They did not like the captain's friendliness with a man who'd been on board for only a short time. In particular Third Officer Sonoda.

A good thing she didn't have talons, Darhad mused as she extended and retracted her own. Otherwise, our gallant gunner would be torn to shreds.

Now why, she frowned, glancing at Warrant Officer Kiani, while Zack explained his plan, does Nihao give the impression she'd rather listen to a lecture on agricultural subsidies than give Decker the slightest bit of attention? Lokis is dead and won't ever come back. Time to move on, girl. Darhad sighed. Though she'd been working with humans ever since she fled Arkanna many years ago, she would never fully understand many of their behavior patterns.

However, a man like Decker, she could understand. He was a born warrior, with primal instincts, a predator who could command an Arkanna's respect. Which also meant he was very dangerous. A man to watch. But she'd known it the moment she'd seen him in the Aramis Guildhall.

"Thank you, Gunner. Any questions or comments?" Captain Strachan's tone sufficed to discourage anyone but his first officer, and she agreed with his use of Decker's warrior abilities. To do otherwise would have been wasteful.

"That's it then. Meeting adjourned."

Raisa Darhad watched her crewmates file out of the wardroom, whispering among themselves. If Zack Decker had impressed a few of them with his no-nonsense professionalism, he had also made several new enemies.

The men and women aboard *Shokoten* were no choir singers and made for dangerous adversaries. They lacked the discipline Decker would expect from any crew after a lifetime in the Marine Corps, and that made the lower decks dangerous for someone like him during the night watches.

*

The door to the cabin whisked open with a sighing sound and Nihao Kiani entered. Zack Decker looked up from his desk where he'd been tending to his disassembled blaster.

"Hiya, Mister Kiani. Done for the day?"

She grunted in reply and busied herself at her locker. Decker's formal courtesy hadn't impressed her. The old noncom was out of ideas on how to draw a human reaction from her, short of stripping naked and committing an indecent act. And even then, he suspected the dour purser would merely turn away and find some busywork.

Nihao stripped out of her duty uniform in silence while Zack reassembled his blaster, satisfied that it was still in perfect working condition. The Imps might be swine, but they knew how to build solid small arms.

Naked, a towel over her shoulder and a bottle of shampoo in her hand, Nihao stopped by the door to the washroom and looked at Zack, who was trying very hard not to admire her.

"You realize you made enemies today, Gunner."

Decker glanced up in surprise, eyebrows raised. It was the first complete sentence Purser Kiani had spoken to him since he'd signed on.

"What?"

"Third Officer Sonoda is a vindictive woman, and it is clear she hates you. She also has friends on this ship, friends who will hate you too. Like the bosun. Take care of your back, Gunner. Being the captain's friend won't help you."

Zack's mouth ran away from him before he knew what he said.

"Is that what happened to my predecessor?"

Kiani gave him such a dark stare before vanishing into the cubicle that Decker felt like he'd just stepped into a minefield.

Engage brain before opening mouth, you ugly, stupid sonofabitch, he thought. Now see if she'll talk to you again on this trip. Dammit, Decker, for a former top sergeant, you're one hell of a dumb jackass.

He thought of stowing his blaster in his locker and then changed his mind. Discarding the holster in an empty drawer, he placed the gun on the small shelf above his bunk, where it would be instantly accessible. The shelf wasn't a standard feature, Zack was sure of that. Now he had an idea why it might have been there. He lay back on his bunk, still dressed in a faded shirt and loose slacks.

When Nihao reappeared, she declined to even glance at Zack and remained silent as she toweled off and prepared ready for bed. Decker spoke in a soft tone, eyes fixed on the bulkhead above him.

"Tell me, Mister Kiani, why did you warn me now, after ignoring me since I came aboard?"

She shrugged, still averting her gaze.

"I don't know."

Zack decided to let it go for now. After a few moments of silence, during which she climbed into her bunk and switched off the lights, he figured he might as well ask one question that had been bugging him.

"*Shokoten* isn't exactly your run-of-the-mill merchant freighter, is she, Mister Kiani? Morale doesn't seem too hot."

Silence.

"I couldn't just let you become a sitting duck," she finally said, "not after what happened to Lokis."

It took Zack a few seconds to realize she'd just answered his earlier question, and a few seconds more to remember that Lokis had been the former gunner, Nihao's bunkmate.

"Why would I be a sitting duck?"

More silence.

"Just watch your back, Gunner. *Shokoten* is an efficient ship. Diego Strachan would tolerate nothing less. And he punishes transgressions without hesitation. But you are right. This is not an ordinary, boring freighter."

Zack heard her turn and knew she wouldn't say anything more.

He closed his eyes and tried to sleep, but for the first time in a long time, rest wouldn't come as ordered because his mind's eye insisted on replaying the incident with the bosun earlier that day.

*

Like all Marine noncoms, Decker was used to a bit of carefully applied force to force the worst delinquents in line, or to convince them to leave the Corps. But he had his limits, and like most of his colleagues, could not stand gratuitous bullying. It smacked too much of cowardice and lack of leadership. That was why the bosun's behavior angered him so much.

Zack was coming out of a gun turret, after a routine inspection, when angry voices and grunts of pain reached his ears. He stuck his head into the maintenance niche to satisfy his curiosity and found Gavin Alers, *Shokoten*'s bosun, inflicting a carefully measured beating on a crewmember held up by two bosun's mates.

Decker stepped in, grabbed the bosun's massive forearm before he could strike again, and tossed him aside.

"What the fuck do you think you're doing, Alers?" Zack's voice exuded menace.

"Mind your own business, Gunner," the big man replied, narrowed black eyes gleaming with hate. "I'm bosun of this ship and will discipline the crew as I see fit." He wiped a fleck of saliva from the corner of his mouth.

Alers had Decker's height and weighed more than the retired Marine, but much of it was fat, not muscle. He wore gray coveralls from which he'd removed the sleeves, displaying bulging biceps and fantastic tattoos. His head was shaved except for a ponytail at the base of his skull, and a thin beard around his massive jaw. The bosun's nose had been broken many times and lay flattened against his piggish face

"Not by beating the living crap out of them you won't."

"Oh?" Alers' lips twisted into an evil grin. "You have no stomach for roughness, Marine? Then maybe you should get off this ship and take a berth on a luxury liner. As a pimp."

Zack ignored the gibe. "What has this man done, Alers?"

"He disobeyed my orders, is what. And that's none of your business. I report to the captain. Not the likes of you."

"Somehow I doubt the captain has given you leave to beat up the crew." *But this shit explains why they aren't exactly a happy bunch, what with a fucking bully like that running their lives. Does Strachan know what's going on below decks and does he care?*

"Ain't none of your business either. Now get the fuck out of here, Mister Gunner, sir, and let the real workers go about their duties. We don't need Fleet pansies on this ship."

Without warning, Zack's fist shot out and rammed into Alers' large stomach. The bosun bent over, retching and fought to keep his balance. A light tap from Zack's foot sent him sprawling across the deck. The gunner turned on the two stunned mates.

"Let him go, and tell that fat pig of a bosun if I ever catch him, or any of you beating up on the crew again, I will pop your fucking kneecaps."

The two mates complied, and the frightened crewman vanished into the bowels of the ship, fearing with reason, that Alers would take it out on him later, to make up for the humiliation. He gave Decker a terrified glance before passing through the open airlock. The accusation implied by that glance shook Zack. He had let his temper lead him into a dangerous situation without thinking, again.

*

The incident had left a bad taste in his mouth, but not as bad as when he found out Alers' victim had landed in sickbay two hours later, with several fractures, insisting he'd fallen down an emergency ladder.

Decker had sought out the bosun, but Alers had sneered and declared his innocence, challenging the gunner to call him a liar in front of his supporters. The lower decks had suddenly acquired a distinct taste of danger and Zack had prudently retreated.

He had kept quiet about the bosun's disciplinary practices for the moment, at least until he could figure out whether he had the captain's blessing or not. One thing was for sure. Alers would do his utmost to make Zack's life a misery, and worse.

*

However, enemies or not, the next battle stations drill went much better. As Nihao had said, the captain wouldn't tolerate anything less, and Zack had the feeling that the crew had a healthy amount of fear for Strachan.

Kiani hadn't spoken to him anymore on the subject of the ship's morale, or his predecessor, but she started to thaw, and now at least she acknowledged his existence. Which made the cabin a more comfortable place to live, and that suited Zack.

So far, the purser was the closest thing to a friend he had. Although the captain was making like he and Decker were old bunkies, the ex-Marine knew it was an act either to win Zack's greater loyalty or piss-off some of the ship's other officers, or both. Or maybe something else altogether. But he didn't let his suspicions show.

The only person aboard in which he had any faith, apart from Nihao, was the first officer. Arkanna were supposed to be honorable people, in their own way, and that was something Decker could rely on, even if Raisa Darhad remained professionally distant.   Still, he sometimes caught the alien woman looking at him, and for the descendant of a predatory species, she could only be measuring him up for food or for mating. Either thought made Zack shudder. But he felt a growing respect for her, because as an officer, she was good.

*

By the time *Shokoten* left the Commonwealth for alien space, Decker was confident they could beat off an attack by a single marauder, provided they detected the bastard far enough out, and the crooks had no traitor on board. It was a typical ploy to buy off a crewmember or plant an agent whose job was to disable the ship and open her up for them.

Two bells in the evening watch rang through the ship, and Zack Decker crawled out of turret five's lower housing, his coveralls smeared with grease. The second officer hadn't assigned him any techs to help, and he doubted the engineer would volunteer any, should he ask, so the gunner had to do the repairs and maintenance checks on the ordnance himself. Zack didn't mind. It kept him away from the others and let him use his skills. Like all pros, Decker took pride in a job well done. The captain had hired him to make sure the weapons fired and hit the bad guys when the time came, and they would.

He wiped his hands on an old rag and pulled his tool case out of the narrow shaft. The intensive practices of the past week had put a strain on several moving components that hadn't been maintained since the former gunner died. Weaponry needed as much care and feeding as a small child and it could be just as balky. This time, a small gimbal had cracked during a simulation. If something larger broke, he'd have no choice but to ask for help, and that could present issues.

A hatch clanked open, and Gavin Alers walked down the lower passageway with two of his mates. Decker tried to ignore him as much as he could and behave like any ordinary warrant officer.

As the bosun and his mates came closer, Zack bent over to pick up his tool case and sling it over his shoulder. He leaned into the access tube again to retrieve the cracked gimbal, to show the captain. A bad tactical move, as he realized a moment later, but it was too late to recover without showing fear.

"Evening, Gunner." A vicious grin twisted the bosun's face as he came level with Zack. Then, without warning, he gave the warrant officer a powerful jab in the sternum with his elbow. Zack, who hadn't expected this sort of treachery, collapsed into the access tube, fighting for air and looked in surprise at the man's ugly smirk.

Before Decker could recover, the bosun gave him a shove that sent him further down the narrow shaft. Then, Alers slammed the hatch closed, and Zack heard the lock slide home. As he sat there, boiling with rage and struggling to get his breath back, Zack thought he could make out the bosun and his mates laughing, though he knew that was impossible. The hatch was designed to withstand vacuum and was therefore sound proof.

Once Decker got his anger under control, he remembered that the turret module could be depressurized from the passageway. Since he was still alive, it meant Alers wasn't trying to kill him. Yet. To escape, he would have to call the bridge and ask for someone to release the latch.

It would seemed as if Decker had forgotten to secure the mechanism before going inside, like a wet behind the ears tech on his first cruise. And if Zack tried to pin it on Alers, his mates would back any story the bosun cared to tell.

Not, this time, you fucking bastard. I've forgotten more about gun turrets than you'll ever learn, Alers.

It took Decker over an hour, during which he imagined the bosun waiting anxiously for his call for help.

But in the end, the access hatch surrendered to the ex-Marine's superior knowledge. Zack dismantled the locking mechanism from his side, by removing part of the bulkhead and the security overrides. It was an old trick he'd learned from a ship's engineer who told him about the surprising number of times he locked himself into a tube or another. Handy when boarding ships by stealth too.

Once out of the tube, Zack returned everything to its normal state and headed to the wardroom for a nightcap. As he walked in, he saw the third officer glance at him with surprise written all over her florid face.

"Evening, sir." Zack nodded in her direction as he walked over to the small wet bar and poured himself a drink. He could feel Sonoda's piggish little eyes burn holes in his back.

Decker was glad he had no cuts or bruises that would arouse questions. Better he keeps this incident quiet and take care of Alers on his own terms. The bastard needed correcting before he got out of hand. Zack could ignore the seemingly accidental bumps, the malicious insolence in his manner, or even the minor pranks. He'd done shit like that to officers he disliked too when he was young and stupid. But this?

He turned around and swept the wardroom with a neutral gaze, sipping his whiskey. Sonoda was scowling into her herbal tea, looking like she'd just found a nest of rats in her engine room. The blazing dragon tattoo on the side of her head seemed to pulsate with a kind of inner pressure. In the opposite corner, the lupine first officer glanced up at him from her reader and let a small smile show on her lips as their eyes met. Zack felt an electric current run down his spine. Then she returned her attention to her technical manual.

Zack finished his glass and left the wardroom. He needed a shower and sleep, in that order. The day had started very early, and it was now almost six bells in the evening watch, close to twenty-three hundred hours.

Decker moved silently over the bare deck, as befitted a former Pathfinder, eyes and ears always alert. When he reached one of the gangways that led down to the crew quarters, he caught Alers' raspy voice coming from an equipment alcove behind the stairs. Zack stopped, glanced down the passageway in either direction, to make sure no one else was near, and crept closer.

"Fucking bastard, that Decker," Alers growled. "Come here and dump on us with his arrogant Marine bullshit. He's only been on board a few weeks and already he lords it over us. Sucking up to the captain too. Why the hell do they let people like that on this ship?" He hiccupped. "Only thing I can say is the fucker better watch himself before he gets a real accident. Wouldn't be the first."

Zack made out something that sounded like a man taking a sip of something boozy.

"Ah, that's good stuff, Alf," the bosun continued. "I showed that asshole what was what tonight. Rammed him well and good into turret five's access tube." Alers chuckled, as did his drinking companion.

Decker frowned for a moment then nodded. Alf Hartjen, the senior engineer's mate, Sonoda's right-hand man. Small guy, wiry but no threat. Hartjen hung on to Alers like a little dog will hang around a big dog. Zack shrugged and made a grimace of disgust. The engineer's mate would hide behind Alers while the latter fought until he saw an opening for a stiletto in the back.

"Next time you ram me well and good," Zack said, words lashing out like a whip as he filled the doorway to the alcove, "better make sure I'm down for the count, Alers."

The bosun stared at him in amazement and fear.

"How the hell did you escape on your own?" He asked.

"Wouldn't you like to know, asshole?" He looked at Hartjen and pointed his thumb at the gangway. "Go play in the engine room, rat-face. Now."

The engineer glanced nervously at Alers, then back at Zack and decided not to take any chances. The promise of violence in the gunner's eyes was enough to scare him. He scurried out of the alcove like the rodent he resembled.

When he was out of sight, Decker grabbed Alers by the front of his coveralls and hauled him to his feet, lifting the man until the two were face to face. Then, without warning, Zack slammed his rock-hard fist into Alers' midriff several times in rapid succession. When bosun retched, Decker threw him against the bulkhead so hard that the thick alloy rang with a dull clang. Alers collapsed into a heap, panting and coughing. A thin trickle of blood ran out of the corner of his mouth.

Zack squatted down beside him, grabbed his chin, and forced the bosun to look at him. A rictus of violence distorted the ex-Marine's face.

"Listen up and listen good, you little turd. The fucking around stops now. I don't give a shit what you like or don't about me. You're a petty officer, and I'm a warrant officer. Two different worlds, see. You have a grievance against me, you bring it up with the second officer. Next time you so much as bump into me by accident, I will make sure they find your stinking body floating outside the airlock without a suit. You hear me?"

When Alers didn't answer, Zack raised the tone of his voice and brought his face within centimeters of the bosun's.

"You fucking hear me, shithead?"

"Yes," he replied in a hoarse voice.

"Yes what, asshole?"

"Yes sir, Mister Gunner, sir." Alers coughed several times.

"What I said goes for your mates and buddies too, Alers. The captain hired me to do a job on this ship, and I'm doing it. It isn't my fault if you're not doing yours worth shit and Strachan has to ride you hard. But that's not my problem. Just remember: the next time you piss me off is the last time you'll ever do anything again. You wouldn't be the first idiot I kill, either."

To make his point as clear as possible, Zack drew his dagger from its hidden sheath and brushed the blade across Alers' face, leaving behind a thin line of blood. The bosun's eyes widened in fear and a sudden stench of urine permeated the alcove. Decker made a grimace of disgust, stood, and left the bosun alone in his piss.

Not good, the gunner thought, shaking his head in annoyance at his actions as he walked down the passageway. Alers just humiliated himself in front of Decker, and would look for revenge, no matter what. Few men would let it pass and still believe they could think of themselves as men.

*

Already in her bunk, Nihao looked at him with curiosity but didn't comment as he stripped off his soiled coveralls with knuckles skinned by his work on the access hatch. Zack took a quick shower and then jumped into bed without bothering to put on a t-shirt or shorts. His mind was on things far removed from his bunkie.

"Need the lights, Zack?"

"No. Go ahead and turn 'em off."

After a few moments in the dark, he heard her turn onto her back and put her hands under her head.

"What happened tonight, Zack?"

"What do you mean?"

"You're almost two hours late, for one thing."

Decker glanced at his watch. Shit, she was right: almost eight bells, he thought, and me so regular in my habits.

"Your hands seem to have been through a meat grinder."

"You know, Nihao," he replied sourly, "you sound just like my ex-wife." When she didn't answer, he said, "I'm sorry for that crack. You're the only one on this ship who cares enough to notice, and I'm thankful."

She grunted in reply. Not quite absolution, but close enough.

"I had a few problems with turret five. Cracked gimbal and defective hatch mechanism. Took me longer than expected to fix. Was a bastard too, hence the torn-up hands."

When her snort sounded close to disbelief, Zack wondered for the first time how fast news traveled on board this ship, and how many people knew about his confrontation with the bosun. More to the point, Zack wondered how long he would last aboard *Shokoten* at this rate.

If he was right in his suspicions, the captain wouldn't tolerate a disruptive officer for long, no matter where the fault lay. And his removal might be more than a layoff notice and a shove down the gangplank. This was no regimented company ship but a free trader that almost certainly dabbled in illegal business. They had their own ways of solving problems.

Zack frowned at another thought. "Say, Nihao?"

"Yes?"

"To who does this ship belong, anyway? I can't see Strachan having enough dough to own it himself."

"You're correct, the captain does not. The ship is owned by a holding company."

"Holding company?"

"What? Is there an echo in here?" Nihao asked with an edge of sarcasm in her tone. "That is what I said."

"Eh, Nihao?"

"Yeah?"

"What's a holding company?"

She snorted with amusement. "You don't get out much in the Marine Corps, do you? Nowadays, a holding company is mostly used as a blind, or a means to confuse people. It permits the real owners or investors to hide behind an anonymous corporate name."

"Listen, Zack, I'm not sure I should tell you this, but I found out about *Shokoten*'s ownership by accident. As purser, I have to deal with accounts and the like, and one day the captain gave me accounts he should have handled himself. I don't know whether he realized his mistake."

"Don't worry. I'm not about to confide in anyone aboard, present company excepted."

"Okay. Well, the holding company is called Intertrans and registered on Mykonos. I did a little digging during my last leave, just out of curiosity. Its board of directors comprises ordinary Mykonos businesspeople who are paid a small honorarium for the use of their names. The actual shares in the company are held by another holding company, and those, in turn, are owned by several trusts. I could not trace it any further. Suffice to say, the ultimate owner does not want his or her name associated with *Shokoten*."

"Why? It sounds like a strange way to do business. Has *Shokoten* been doing illegitimate crap?"

He could feel her hesitate.

"Not to my knowledge," she finally replied, sounding as if she didn't quite believe herself. "We've been hauling perfectly legal cargo since I was hired."

Yeah, and I have a prime piece of swamp to sell you on New-Tasman, complete with a colony of vytyrek.

Zack grimaced in the darkness, unconvinced by Nihao. The more he discovered about the ship and her crew, the more he wondered about the wisdom of signing on. All he needed now was for someone to question whether he was really a Fleet or Constabulary plant, out to spy on whatever smuggling activities _Shokoten_ did, if any.

Nihao Kiani soon fell asleep, but Decker remained wide-awake, wondering whether Lokis' death had something to do with the unanswered questions about the ship. He wanted to ask her but didn't want to do anything that would jeopardize their budding relationship. She would come around and tell him one day. Zack just hoped it would be soon enough. _Shokoten_ was landing on Pradyn in less than twenty-four hours, and that's where the former gunner met his end.

— FIVE —

"Any questions about your job once we're on the ground, Zack?"

"No, Captain. First thing, I make sure the security system's online and working. Then, I make an outside visual of the ship. When the stevedores come to unload the cargo, I post guards at all airlocks so nobody tries to sneak in, and then watch the unloading with the second officer. Once that's done, I make sure all access points of the ship except the main personnel hatch are secure and can't be opened, except by authorization from the officer of the watch, and post a guard at the airlock round the clock. Then I can take liberty." Decker grinned.

Strachan nodded with satisfaction. "Aye, but you're back on board for loading, which means less liberty than you may think."

Decker dropped his grin and shrugged, unconcerned.

"That's why you pay me."

"Pradyn is one of the most civilized places in the Shield, which means you don't have to be on full alert to make sure the natives don't steal the hyperdrive nacelles from under your nose. But it also means they're more efficient. Turnover can be quick."

"Job's a job, Captain. If I don't have time to play tourist, so what?" Decker didn't much care about getting liberty. Not on this planet at any rate.

"Okay, Zack." Strachan glanced at the chronometer. "We're about to enter Pradyn's defensive sphere, and you'd better stand by at your station. It's quite an experience to see their version of tech, funny really, but the natives take it seriously. They have enough problems with marauders, mainly human pirates, that they take no one at face value."

"Captain." Decker nodded and left Strachan's cabin for the bridge.

He met the bosun at the juncture of the central passageway. The man seemed to have recovered from his encounter with Zack's knife and sneered at the warrant officer. But he kept his distance, like a beaten dog. A vicious dog who carried a mean grudge.

Decker smiled back and brushed his hand over his dagger. He had the satisfaction of watching Alers scurry away. When the petty officer was out of sight, Zack dropped his fixed grin and sighed. Something would eventually break. Alers wasn't the kind to keep a grip on reality forever if he let hate gnaw at him.

Unfortunately, Zack couldn't help pushing him further towards the edge. He had a hidden mean streak that was sometimes hard to control, which was why he was working on a freighter instead of a frigate.

The small Pradyn guard cutter grew on the viewscreen, and Zack had to smile at its appearance. It was ornate, heavily decorated and looked ludicrous in space. It reminded him of the pre-spaceflight ceremonial barges he'd seen in the Fleet Museum.

Gold fittings seemed to glint all over the voluptuous, gondola-like hull and painted, multicolor creatures capered on either side of the cockpit window.

"Come, Mister Decker, time to greet our visitors."

The first officer's voice was a silky purr, and Zack had to suppress an involuntary shiver.

"Why isn't the captain meeting them?" He asked her once they had left the bridge for the shuttle bay. He had learned that Darhad wasn't averse to his questions if they concerned business or if her answers could help advance some personal agenda.

"Face, Mister Decker, face. The Pradyni are a status-conscious species, and it would be demeaning for the captain of a great human ship to waste his valuable time on a minor customs official. By sending an underling, Captain Strachan gains status and face with the local authorities, and that will make things smoother once we land."

"Mere underling?" Decker chuckled as he glanced at Darhad's elegant profile.

She smiled back, showing her sharp teeth.

"Do not let my choice of words influence you, Gunner, but you may be right. Perhaps a first officer is too high for those puffed-up bureaucrats. Still, they're expecting to meet a human male and it always shakes them to meet an Arkanna female. Psychological advantage."

Decker nodded his approval. He could appreciate her reasoning.

"I guess the Pradyni don't let their females in high positions."

"No, they don't, Gunner." Zack couldn't tell whether she was amused or annoyed. "Female Pradyni are mere chattel with few rights and limited education. I gather polygamy of some sort is the norm. Barbaric, especially for a space faring race. You humans are responsible for giving them too much technology too fast at a vulnerable stage in their social development. It would have been better if they evolved towards space flight themselves. That way their social structures could have evolved too and freed the females from their condition. But I suppose one should not judge an alien culture by one's own social norms, so long as it has no bearing on one's own."

They reached the shuttle bay just as the customs boat crossed the force field that kept the ship's atmosphere from escaping through the open space doors. Its hull crackled blue with energy as it passed through. Grappling arms seized it the moment it was in the bay, bled away the static build-up from the field, and deposited the cutter in the center of the pad.

Zack touched the loaded blaster at his hip. No humanoid species could mistake the large, deadly looking weapon for something other than an instrument of death. The former noncom and his gun were the only security for this encounter. When he saw the customs official step out of his boat, he smiled grimly and nodded. He would be more than able to control any problem.

"Welcome aboard *Shokoten,*" Darhad said in slow, precise Anglic. She placed her right hand over the hollow beneath her throat and nodded. Zack saw a flash of talons at her fingertips and wondered whether it had been intentional or a reflex. "I am Ship's Second Raisa Darhad. This is Warrior Leader Zack Decker."

Zack raised his eyebrows at the unusual titles she used, and then realized that these probably translated better into whatever language the alien spoke. Darhad must have dealt with Pradyni before this. Since she hadn't taught him the proper greeting, Decker decided against imitating her gestures. He remained in the parade rest position and stared at the official.

Pradyni were human shaped, but where Darhad could pass for a human mutation that hadn't seen the sun since birth, the official would never be mistaken for anything but a member of another species. His hairless skin was mottled in various hues of blue, brown, and green. It appeared dry, leathery, and wrinkled. He had no visible ears.

Unblinking, large, black eyes stared at Decker. Small nostrils pierced the tip of an elongated snout, just above a full mouth. A thin blue tongue flicked out every so often as if testing the air.

He held a four-digit hand against his throat, just as Darhad had done and bowed back. His thick fingers had black claws on their tips, and these were decorated with small dots of gold, silver, and red.

When the official opened his mouth to speak, Decker saw a row of sharp, spike-like teeth. The Pradyni had a bad case of rotting meat breath.

"Thank you, Darhad. Welcome to Pradyn. I am Frykil Bvanis, customs officer of his Imperial Majesty, the Glorious Ruler, and Guardian of the First Egg, Wesshti the Sublime."

His Anglic was labored but understandable—barely. If the female Arkanna's presence had rattled him because he expected a human male, they could tell. But Zack figured he'd never be able to read anything off that reptilian face and in those cold, dead eyes.

"Your First of Ship?"

"He is unavoidably detained, Excellency and has honored me by ordering me to perform this most important task. I am at your complete disposal and will strive to fullfil my duties to the utmost of my limited and inadequate abilities."

Bvanis cocked his head to one side.

"It is unfortunate. Please convey my deepest respects to your First of Ship."

"Certainly Excellency. How may I help you?"

"Please describe your cargo."

"Household appliances, mostly, and a few luxury trinkets."

"Please show me."

"If you will follow me, Excellency." She bowed her head then glanced at Decker. They quickly walked down to the main cargo bay, leaving the official's pilot with his cutter, under the watchful eye of a pair of brawny bosun's mates.

Darhad tapped the proper sequence to unlock the cargo bay door, her long fingers dancing over the pad. When the double doors whisked open with a sigh, she entered, stopping by the rampart of standard containers.

The official came to stand beside her and inspected the cargo with unblinking eyes. Then, he pulled out a hand-held scanner. Darhad's eyes momentarily widened in alarm, and she glanced at Decker, who'd seen her reaction.

"Your Excellency seems to have an interesting piece of equipment," she said, recovering her poise.

"Ah yes. Our government bought a significant number of these marvelous machines from a human trading firm recently. He called them state-of-the-art, which, I understand means the best."

Zack examined the small rectangular package in Bvanis' hand and recognized a civilian version of the military battlefield sensor. It was advanced tech but built for war, not precise scanning like police sensors. The Constabulary would never use them.

Darhad looked at him again, one upswept eyebrow raised in question.

"His Excellency has a good example of recent human tech," Zack said. "Our armed services have used this machine in war.

Raisa gave Zack a small, knowing smile and turned her attention back to the Pradyni official.

"What please is in that container?" He pointed at one in the middle of the right-hand stack.

Darhad glanced at the label on the side. "Cooking implements: knives, kitchen appliances and the like."

Bvanis cocked his head to the side again and played his scanner over the container. Decker, now fully alert thanks to Darhad's reaction, glanced over the shorter alien's shoulder and stared at the readout.

After twenty years of soldiering, Zack could interpret a sensor scan in a way the average civvie couldn't even begin to do. And this scan, while it ostensibly showed power tools, as the first officer had described, also showed background readings that shouldn't come from a box of utensils.

Were he ordered to discuss his thoughts about what he saw, Decker would have said there were high-tech weapons hidden between the vibrablades, autospits and other powered implements, which would explain why Darhad seemed alarmed at seeing the sensor.

Zack cursed himself for not having studied the planet further, but he'd be willing to bet the political situation wasn't too stable on Pradyn. Perhaps someone opposed to the government was buying contraband human weapons under the cover of harmless kitchen appliances.

His eyes met Darhad's over the alien's bowed head, and he saw that the Arkanna woman knew he knew. Since he wasn't supposed to find out about the contraband, his loyalty was about to be questioned. Would an ex-Marine aid and abet illegal commercial activities? Or would he run to the nearest Fleet outpost and do his duty?

The Fleet had kicked him out so he didn't have any reason to feel generous towards his former employers. And this was small time stuff. No skin off his nose if aliens wanted to kill each other. It kept them from killing humans.

"Hmmm, and this box?" Bvanis pointed at another randomly chosen container.

*

Half an hour later, Darhad and Decker escorted a satisfied customs official back to his cutter. He had placed his seal on all containers. Now *Shokoten* could land and off-load the cargo. Whoever took receipt of if would have to deal with the paperwork on the ground to remove the seals and clear the stuff, but that wasn't the ship's problem.

Darhad and Bvanis carried out the short Pradyni greeting ritual again, and the reptilian climbed aboard his cutter. Moments later, he was gone.

As Zack and the first officer walked the length of the ship to the captain's cabin, Decker wondered how he should handle his discovery. Apart from the weapons, he'd seen traces of restricted electronics hidden in the containers. Nothing that gave him heartache. Since the first officer knew he'd found out, a lot would depend on how he acted next.

The first officer knocked on the door to the captain's cabin and was ordered to enter. Zack followed.

"All went well?" Strachan asked, outwardly calm, but betrayed by his fidgeting fingers.

"Yes, sir," Darhad replied. "But there is one disturbing development. The Pradyni now have high-grade sensors."

"What?" Strachan leaned forward over his desk and looked at Raisa Darhad with incredulity.

"Tell him, Mister Decker," Darhad ordered.

"Aye, sir. Captain, the Pradyni have a civvie version of the Navy's Mark Nine hand-held battlefield sensor. The Mark Nines are still in use by the Corps."

Pathfinders had the Mark Ten, which would have made those guns show up like priests in a whorehouse, but there was no need for Strachan to know.

"Those little babies are built to be tough, work anywhere, and be used by even the dumbest trooper. That means they're not as accurate as police sensors. An experienced tech who knows what he's looking for can read a lot more into the scan than the obvious. I doubt these guys will ever be good enough. It usually takes the fear of death to become that skilled. Properly camouflaged stuff can fool most people."

Strachan and Darhad exchanged a significant glance that wasn't lost on Decker. A tiny part of him felt nervous.

"And are you good enough to read between a Mark Nine's scan lines, Mister Decker," the captain asked, locking eyes with Zack.

"Yes, sir. I know those sensors better than my mother does. Used 'em for years." Decker held the stare with unabashed defiance.

"And you saw what the customs official scanned?"

"Yes, sir. Saw his readout clear as day."

"Tell me, Mister Decker. Do you have any problems with what you saw?"

That was the question Zack had been expecting. He hoped that his face was as neutral as he could make it.

"Not my place to have problems, sir. My job's ship security, not cargo."

Strachan examined him with narrowed eyes. He stroked his beard several times as if deep in thought.

"Very well, Mister Decker. Thank you for bringing this development to my attention."

The captain didn't look very thankful. Worried like hell was a better description and he glanced at his first officer, a natural-born killer, then at his gunner, a former Marine from a Corps whose reputation for integrity was legendary. It took little for Zack's paranoid mind to spin scenarios he'd rather not contemplate.

He took a deep breath. In for a penny, in for a cred.

"Sir, if you want to make sure the sensor readouts show only what you want to show, there's ways of making that happen. Won't fool everybody all the time, but it's better than what you have now."

"Really, Mister Decker? And why would I want to hide anything from anybody?"

Zack was thrown off by the captain's reply. But interest glinted in Strachan's eyes. He recovered and shrugged.

"Just trying to do my job, sir."

"Yes, thank you, Mister Decker. Dismissed."

Zack merely nodded and left, unable to decide whether he was dog meat or not. He returned to his cabin and threw himself on his bunk. Weapons were shut down for the entry into Pradyn orbit and the landing, and he had nothing to do until they were on the ground, except fret.

Since he had decided to stick with Captain Strachan until he found himself doing something he found morally repugnant, he pushed the thought aside. The way things worked, if the Constabulary or the Fleet caught them, the crew wouldn't suffer for minor contraband, only the officers, and the owners. Provided, of course, that the crew didn't resist boarding or inspection. However, the discovery that Strachan was running illegal guns gave him second thoughts about the mysterious death of the former gunner.

*

"What do you think, Raisa?" Captain Diego Strachan raised an eyebrow as he looked at his first officer. "Can we trust him to keep quiet or will his old Fleet instincts send him to the nearest military outpost?"

Darhad ran slender fingers through her crimson hair, lost in thought.

"If truth be told, Captain, I don't know. Decker is a difficult man to judge on anything other than his efficiency, which is commendable. There is, of course, the fact that the military threw him out, and that should affect the way he sees his loyalties. Then too, smuggling weapons to alien planets is not so big a crime in a Marine's eyes. Most military minds I have come across believe in a non-human race's fundamental right to destroy itself or any other non-human race of its choice." She shrugged. "I must admit I like and admire him. He has a hunter's soul and instincts. We could do much worse than trust him. Let us wait and see what happens. If he wants to betray us, I will find out before he does so, and I will kill him."

Strachan gazed at his second in command through half closed eyes. Sometimes Raisa Darhad's bloodthirsty predisposition troubled him. But for all that, she was a good first officer, ready to command her own ship. He trusted her judgement. He had to. Otherwise, he would be alone on a ship crewed by rogues who wouldn't be out of place on a marauder, but who preferred to keep their heads on their necks in return for smaller profits.

"What happens when Alers tries to get his revenge?" Nothing remained secret on a ship like *Shokoten* and Strachan knew of the bad blood between his bosun and gunner. "He may be an idiot at times, but he's able, and he's served with me for several years. Do I sacrifice him for Decker? Is Decker valuable enough, and harmless enough to our affairs?"

"That is your decision, Captain. But consider that your bosun is spiteful and brutal. The crew hates him, and he can impose discipline only by force. Eventually, someone will kill him. Any intelligent, experienced rating can take over the bosun job, but you have only one gunner, and a good one at that. Not like Lokis. Decker did nothing stupid upon discovering contraband in the cargo, nor did he deny seeing the contraband, and he showed himself willing to discuss the subject of sensors and ways to foil them."

Strachan nodded. "I will take your words under advisement, Raisa. Meanwhile, keep an eye on friend Decker, especially if he goes on liberty. I rather like his ways and don't want to discover that he is dangerous to us after all. When do we land?"

"We will be in orbit in twenty minutes. From there, spacecon will assign us a landing pattern. It could be anywhere from an hour to two days."

"Thanks, Raisa."

She smiled to herself as she left the cabin. Strachan's orders gave her a perfect reason to get to know Decker in a less formal setting. She felt attracted to his fierce, proud professionalism. Of all the humans aboard *Shokoten*, he was the closest to a male of her species.

*

It didn't take four years at the Academy to set-up the security on a freighter like *Shokoten*, even on a technobarbarian planet. Alers' spacers and mates were detailed as guards under Decker's orders, and they gave him no trouble. The bosun, bullying and brutal when he held the upper hand, was despised by most of the crew, and he'd come down a peg or two since Zack gave him a beating.

Several ratings had given the gunner knowing grins when they reported for security duty, and he placed those in the airlocks he couldn't directly see from the hold or outside. The ones who looked like they might be Alers' pals, Zack kept with him in the hold, to watch the stevedores.

All the guards carried loaded pistols. Decker had made sure they knew how to use them, and more importantly when to use them. He didn't need an idiot blowing his toes off, or, since the possibility was always there, accidentally shooting him while 'cleaning his weapon.'

The Pradyni worked with speed and efficiency under the direction of a foreman with a disturbing tendency to snarl at his workers.

"They must not have a union, with the boss abusing his gang like that," Zack commented in an aside to the second officer.

Bowdoin cackled. "Never left the Commonwealth, have you, Gunner?"

"No sir."

"The reason these workers aren't unionized is that they're slaves."

"What?" Zack Decker, who'd fought slavery time and time again, had never seen the wretches at work in a slave-owning society. His hand reflexively reached for his blaster, and he had it half-drawn before he regained control of his instincts.

"Calm down, Mister Decker. This isn't a human world. The Pradyni can do whatever they want. Slavery is bred into this society. They had them long before we made contact, and I imagine they'll have them for a long time yet. It's not our concern either way." Bowdoin paused and studied the working Pradyni.

"Their government has forbidden the trade with off-planet slavers, so most of the people wearing the collar are natives who have broken the law, or who were born to their state. They're efficient enough and well controlled."

"I guess they are at that, sir," Decker replied, doubt and loathing evident in his tone.

"There are worse places out here, Gunner, a lot worse," Bowdoin murmured.

The unloading was quick, thanks to the strange looking container-lift machines the natives drove. Powered by some sort of primitive internal combustion engine, they spewed disgusting gray exhaust fumes that rapidly filled the cavernous hold. Even the ship's air scrubbers had a difficult time keeping up with the pollution.

Zack could have found refuge in the controller's room which would have given him the same view as from the catwalk, but he was damned if he would leave his guards to breathe the crap while he hid in an air-conditioned office. The next time, though, he would rustle up filters or masks so they could breathe without destroying their lungs. It would mean going to engineering, but such things could be arranged without facing the irascible third officer.

*

"That's it, sir."

The hold was empty. All the containers, including the ones with contraband, had been offloaded and stacked in a nearby storehouse to await pick up by the recipients. Zack was glad the guns were off the ship. No matter how much he tried to ignore the fact, breaking the law, even beyond Commonwealth borders, made him uneasy. Twenty years of training wouldn't wash away in a few weeks.

"Thank you, Gunner. Secure the locks and stand down." Bowdoin nodded.

Decker snapped to attention. "Aye, aye, sir."

*

"The shippers have advised me we have a three-day wait before they can load their cargo."

Captain Strachan scowled as he swept the assembled officers with an annoyed gaze. He was unhappy, and the reason was easy to divine. For three days, *Shokoten* would be idle, eating up expensive landing fees.

"Obviously, they want a bribe to speed things up, but the delay isn't bad enough for that. Yet."

"What happens when they postpone loading again?" Raisa Darhad looked just as somber as her captain did.

"I will deal with that in due course. As it happens, I've made sure any further delay would cost them in increased shipping fees. They can weasel out of it, of course, by getting an arbitrary decree from their king, but by now, even he knows it would be bad for business. The Pradyni obtain most of their high tech from the Commonwealth, and tech must flow."

"Meanwhile," Strachan continued, "we will have liberty. No more than twenty-four hours per crewmember. I want a full watch on board at all times, including security." He glanced at Zack. "I'd prefer that the crew go out in pairs and not alone and make damn sure they know the native taboos. If someone gets into trouble with the local law, there is little I can do to rescue them. I'd rather people get drunk aboard the ship than in a tavern. Failing that, tell them to stay in Spacetown. The natives are more tolerant there than in their own cities."

Raisa Darhad nodded.

"The liberty sheets will be posted by the end of the watch."

"That's all. Have a good time ashore. And be careful." Strachan rose and left the wardroom.

*

"You going, Nihao?" Decker asked as he changed out of his worn battledress and pulled on his single change of civilian clothes.

"No. I have much work to do. Merchant ships don't carry large amounts of perishable foods. It takes up too much space, and stasis containers are expensive. I have to negotiate the local purchase of fresh things."

"On an alien planet?"

"Some of their food can be eaten by humans, and there is a ship's chandlers business here that grows human foodstuff, mainly soy-based. Unfortunately, it will take up all of my time."

Zack nodded. Nihao Kiani didn't want to take time off on the planet where her former roommate had died, and her work gave her a good excuse.

"Be careful, Zack."

"Don't worry about me, Nihao. I checked the roster. Alers isn't allowed off the ship until tomorrow."

She looked at him with worried eyes. "The bosun will not take his revenge personally, Zack. He is too frightened of you and will have someone else do it while he is aboard and has a good alibi."

Decker paused, his shirt half done up.

"Doesn't matter. Bad guys haven't managed to kill me in twenty years and they won't now, especially not some half-assed friend of Alers. We can't carry blasters in town, but I can sure as shit take this." He flashed his black-hilted, silver-bladed Pathfinder dagger. "The bugger's already tasted its edge, and will again if anyone gets too frisky."

Nihao shook her head and muttered something in Mandarin before vanishing into the washroom.

*

Zack wrinkled his nose at the stench of exhaust fumes that permeated the spaceport. The whole city of Vortaz seemed to be smothered by a gray blanket turned a ghastly shade of red by the sun. Beneath the ship, the concrete tarmac was grimy, cracked and pitted, with sharp-bladed plants growing wherever they could.

Decker was alone, contrary to the captain's orders, but there was no one on board with whom he was friendly enough, except Nihao. He had read the condensed infopak on Pradyni culture and memorized the main taboos that could spell trouble. His dagger was strapped to his left forearm, hidden by the sleeve of his old leather jacket.

Zack spotted the terminal building the left and headed for it. Under port rules, all visitors had to pass through the control station. Though utilitarian, the building was the first example of native architecture he saw and he felt mildly disappointed. After meeting the customs official, Zack expected something ornate and alien. But it was a simple concrete block, with few embellishments.

The inside of the building seemed cleaner than the outside, but that wasn't saying much. By all appearances, the locals didn't care about off-worlders' impressions of them. The fact there was a second spaceport, on the other side of Vortaz, exclusively for Pradyni spacecraft spoke volumes.

A bored native, his colors faded by the monotony of his job, sat alone behind a scratched plastic window, and looked at him with expressionless black eyes. His office was no better than the empty waiting area: faded and dented plastic furniture, grimy, beige floor tiles, and walls that had once been white. No posters, plants or other decorations relieved the depressing grittiness of the place. Watery light streamed through cobwebbed windows that hadn't been washed since the first contact with humanity.

"Your identification." The Pradyni asked in his tongue, the request translated by a primitive AI that sounded robotic.

Zack slid his blue ID card through the slot under the window and watched as the alien shoved it into a reader. The official pushed it back to Decker.

"Have a pleasant stay."

Tired doors whisked aside with a nerve-grating screech, and Zack stepped out into an alien city, on a planet where the natives had no love for strangers, but tolerated them to obtain modern technology. The ex-Marine suspected that the day they became self-sufficient, trade would be conducted on their terms, which meant not on their planet.

Stretching out from the terminal towards Vortaz proper, Pradyn's version of Spacetown stood as an obstacle and a temptation for off-worlders, a means to keep them away from the city. Other exotic but no less unpleasant smells mingled with the exhaust fumes and Zack wondered whether he wouldn't be better off spending his free time on the ship. But for a Marine, checking out bars on a new world was tradition.

He walked further into Spacetown, keeping strictly to the main drag and saw many alien visitors but only a few natives. There were strange shapes in the dark alleys between the loud and garishly lit taverns, but Zack knew better than to investigate. Shadowy corners meant druggies, whores and their pimps, bums and other assorted scum who'd cheerfully slit a spacer's throat for the contents of his pockets.

As with most planets, the Pradyni made only nominal attempts to preserve law and order in Spacetown, preferring to let off-worlders prey on each other rather than on the local citizenry.

Non-natives could visit the planet outside Spacetown, but only with grudging permission. Anyone who broke a law there was guaranteed to suffer the full penalties of native justice. According to the guide, slavery was used for small crimes. Bigger ones started with forced labor in the mines and ended with death in various fashions, depending on the offense. Dismemberment was mentioned, as was becoming supper for a particularly loathsome, tank-sized desert creature kept just for that purpose.

When he judged he had reached the center of Spacetown, Zack looked around for the joint that seemed like the best prospect for a decent beer. A purple, two-story building with large signs in many languages and scripts attracted his attention. It looked clean from the outside, or at least more decent than the rest. It had no broken windows or lights and had a steady stream of customers going in and out beneath the flashing pink lights.

He crossed the wide asphalt street, dodging unrecognizable garbage in the gutters and panhandling off world bums sitting on the edge of the sidewalk. A gust of loud, discordant music assaulted his ears as the swinging door flapped open to let out a pair of drunk, gray-skinned Kardati sailors. They looked like the barbarians they were in their stained, rough leather and mail uniforms, now decorated with flecks of dried food and what might be vomit, though for all Zack knew, it could have been a Kardati delicacy.

The sailors looked at him unsteadily and then, arm in arm, staggered down the street, bellowing something tuneless. Decker shook his head in amusement. They must have started drinking at noon to be in such a state.

He pushed his way into the bar, wincing at the noise and smell. The air was smoky enough to cut with a knife; lights flashed left and right, hurting his eyes; loud music, played by instruments he couldn't identify, competed with a crowd intent on holding conversations at the top of their lungs.

It seemed that every spacefaring race in this arm of the galaxy was represented, most of them unwashed, if the odors were anything to go by, and each was drinking something weirder than the other.

One glass, held high by an incredibly ugly Marzukki female who must have been over two meters tall, contained something with tentacles that writhed at the bottom of the blood-red liquid. She downed her glass, hors d'oeuvre included and Zack turned away when he saw a small tentacle hanging out of the side of her lipless mouth, flapping feebly while she chewed.

He made his way through the press of beings to the bar and waited patiently for the heavily scarred, one-eyed Pradyni bartender to notice him. Attracting his attention verbally over the deafening noise seemed beyond Zack's abilities.

He was jostled a few times by drunk patrons who were either slapping each other on the shoulder, roaring with laughter, or striking each other to make a point. They and the bartender ignored him. While he waited Zack looked around, trying to find another human face, but in vain. Alien words bellowed into his ear, made him turn around.

"Sorry," Zack yelled back, "I can't speak your language."

"What you drink, human?" The bartender replied, this time in heavily accented and barely understandable Anglic.

"Shrehari ale."

The bartender vanished for a few moments then plunked a twisted bottle filled with a purplish, carbonated liquid in front of Zack.

"Thirty khlavass."

Decker mentally converted khlavass into creds and handed the bartender a twenty-cred chip, which was about three times what that inferior brand was worth.

"Keep the change," he yelled. But his sarcasm was lost on the Pradyni, who pocketed the chip expressionlessly and turned to the next customer.

Zack opened the bottle and took a sip, then grimaced. The stuff was even worse than expected based on the brand name. Inspecting the label, he became convinced that the stuff was locally made and passed off as real Shrehari ale. He hoped he wouldn't go blind from the bootleg hooch.

Decker loved his beer, and a good, well-aged vintage was fantastic. It beat the living pants off most human brews and had a good kick to boot. Too bad a lot of human worlds didn't allow the brew on-planet. Shrehari ale smugglers were the only outlaws Decker was willing to help as much as he could.

If this joint was one of the better places, he grimaced again, looking at the other patrons, and it probably was, then he didn't think he'd be having much fun on this liberty. It would be a long haul back to civilization, living in close quarters with the delectable Ms. Kiani.

But thinking of Nihao reminded him that Gunner Lokis had died on Pradyn. As he sipped his insipid ersatz ale, he felt the hairs on the back of his neck stand up, as if he were being watched. It was a sixth sense he'd developed over the years, something that had kept him from being killed more than once. Zack had learned to trust the feeling, even if he couldn't explain it.

Slowly, without seeming alarmed or even interested, he scanned the crowd. Sometimes, just by doing that, his instinct could tell him who was doing the watching. Sometimes. It was easier with humans. Body language was often hard to conceal. But trying to read the body language of a dozen species of sentient aliens was a different story.

The big Marzukki female had a fresh glass with another of those tentacle snacks writhing at the bottom. She roared at something her companion, a scaly Flaxitatt hermaphrodite was saying, and thumping him/her on the back so hard that it would have sent Zack Decker sprawling on the floor. The Flaxitatt barely moved, though he/she laughed, jaws open wide, showing dagger-like fangs, yellowed and worn.

At another table, a group of Hradin spacers, identical in black coveralls and hoods, took nervous sips of a frothy liquid, heads bowed together, bluish lips moving at speeds impossible for humans to follow.

Near the door, the five members of a pod of shaggy, broad-shouldered Gardal were uproariously pouring thin Pradyni ale over the head of an Anrytzoli crewmate, singing a drinking song in their rumbling, deep-throated voices.

Here and there, pairs or trios of Pradyni hustlers moved between the tables or sat at strategic spots to snare unsuspecting spacers, though why anyone would want a lizard hooker was beyond Zack's imagination.

His eyes almost bugged out when he saw one of them, her hide carefully made-up, sit on a Darsivian's lap and immediately become the object of his most slobbering attention. Moments later, the ursine alien spacer and the Pradyni headed up to the second floor. Zack chuckled as he tried to imagine the offspring such a coupling would produce were it genetically feasible, which it wasn't. An ugly but funny thought.

The canned music suddenly stopped and everyone's attention, at least those still awake and sober enough not to drool, turned to the small stage at the far end of the bar.

A faint shimmering caught Zack's eye, and he nodded with approval: a force field to protect the players. A group of six aliens, from six different species, each carrying an intricately designed instrument, walked on stage to the yells, hoots, and drunken heckling of the patrons.

An ale bottle flew against the force field and bounced back, catching one of the nearby customers on the head. Zack barely had time to notice the brief scuffle as huge bouncers swiftly threw the culprit out onto the street.

Then, the band played a raucous song that pleased the roaring crowd. If coherent thought had been difficult before, it became impossible now under the fresh assault of noise. Zack still felt watched and it made him edgy.

New movement near the door caught his attention, and he was surprised to see Raisa Darhad's pale face and shockingly red hair above the furry skulls of the Gardals. She caught sight of him and smiled, sending shivers down Zack's spine.   He briefly wondered what effect her predator's looks and manners had on humans who didn't have his experience with danger and death. Perhaps they died of fright. As she approached, Decker began to suspect that Darhad was doing it to him deliberately. That thought made him smile in return.

"Are you having a good time, Gunner?" She asked above the din, her mouth almost touching his ear. He felt the warmth of her breath on his cheek while a hint of pheromones sent his heart racing.

"Yes sir, though the beer's fucking lousy. And the music worse."

She nodded, amused.

"Incidentally, Gunner," she purred, lips brushing his earlobe again, "on liberty, you may call me Raisa."

"Yes sir, Raisa, sir," Zack replied grinning, feeling inordinately pleased and not knowing why.

Darhad turned towards the bar and ordered something unintelligible in a tongue Zack had never heard. Meanwhile, he resumed his slow scan of the bar, trying to figure out who, or what was watching him. Having her at his side made him feel better. If it came to a fight, the Arkanna was the one crewmate he'd most want at his back.

Zack finished his scrutiny with a close-up view of First Officer Darhad in civvies, and it made him appreciate her more visible qualities. Definitely mammalian: all the right curves in the right places.

Raisa Darhad wore a skin-tight black outfit, and while it accentuated her remarkable female shape, the former Marine quickly realized that the one-piece garment wasn't to attract males. Her pheromones did quite well, thank you. No, the outfit would give her maximum freedom of movement and a good deal of protection in a fight. Of course, it would also distract any humanoid male while she went in for the kill. An interesting choice.

Zack averted his eyes from her shapely behind when she turned around with a glass of something thick, opaque, and pungent in her hand. Darhad leaned against the scarred metal bar beside Decker and sipped her drink, eyes resting on Zack's craggy profile.

He's looking for someone, she decided after watching his eyes flick back and forth beneath a slight but unmistakable frown of concentration.

Decker wasn't only letting his gaze rove across the bar in what Raisa Darhad thought of as the 'protective scan mode,' that unconscious and automatic state that all good warriors fell into the moment they left their familiar, safe surroundings. The warrant officer was in 'active mode,' looking for someone or something specific. Someone he knew? He had admitted he had never been outside the

Commonwealth before so it was unlikely it would be a native. But why would he meet with a human on Pradyn?

She watched him for a while and then leaned over, brushing her lips against his ear again, her breath warm on his cheek.

"Are you waiting for someone, Gunner?"

If he was startled by her sudden closeness, he showed an admirable control over his reflexes. Darhad had no choice but to approve. With deliberation, he turned his head to look at her. Raisa raised her right eyebrow in question, letting a faint air of amusement relax her features.

"No, Raisa. How the hell could I? Don't know a living soul out in the Shield. And all the Shield citizens I've ever met didn't survive the introduction." He paused and glanced at the crowd again, visibly uncomfortable. "Okay, First Officer. I've had the feeling, since before you walked in, that I'm being watched. It's a feeling I've learned to listen to and trust. Saved my life a couple of times."

She nodded. He was telling the truth as he believed it to be. Why should he not be able to sense a hidden watcher? It was the attribute of a natural warrior and Mister Decker was as close to an Arkanna male as she had seen among humans.

They drank in companionable silence for several minutes, tuning out the awful band, the loud conversations and concentrating on small anomalies, such as anyone paying Zack Decker too much attention, especially when he stood beside a superbly sculpted she-wolf.

Darhad drained her glass and laid her surprisingly warm hand on Zack's, talons fully sheathed. Her fingers were dry but smooth, and Decker felt another shiver run down his spine.

"I know a place that serves better drinks and where hidden watchers are much easier to spot."

"Didn't know Pradyn had a Guildhall."

She laughed. "No, it does not. But the place of which I speak is known to few and keeps its customer list short. For that, it offers a quiet surrounding without the assorted riff-raff of the galaxy drinking unmentionable things, and it has a fine beverage list."

Zack briefly wondered about the reasons behind her invitation, especially in light of his discovery of the contraband. He had no illusions that he could take on the first officer in hand to hand combat and win. Had Captain Strachan decided to make sure he would never talk?

More to the point, did Lokis receive an invitation that led into an ambush after finding something he wasn't supposed to find?

Decker shrugged and placed his half-empty bottle on the bar. The day he stopped living dangerously was the day they could bury him, and that wasn't happening anytime soon. Plus, he really wanted to know what this lady had on her mind. Was it only getting wasted with a shipmate, or was she looking for something else? He could see only one way to find out.

"I'm right behind you, Raisa."

"Come, then." She flashed him a smile, baring her pointy teeth and turned to head for the door, pushing through the dense, unwashed crowd. Zack had no choice but to follow in her wake.

— SIX —

The streets of Vortaz's Spacetown were remarkably silent after the deafening noise in the bar. The air was cleaner too though it still attacked human throats with harmful intent.

Decker stopped at the edge of the cracked sidewalk, ignoring the drunk Kardati in the gutter, and breathed in deeply, relishing the simple exhaust and solvent fumes after the dense, choking atmosphere inside.

Pradyn's sky was dark, yet only a few stars twinkled. The haze of pollution and the riotous sea of lights washed out most of them. An unpleasant, sharp odor suddenly stabbed Decker's nose, along with a sound of rushing water. He turned towards the sound, and then looked away in disgust. A Darsivian was urinating in the shadows of a narrow alley beside the bar, humming a tuneless song.

Zack and Raisa Darhad looked at each other and grimaced. After a moment, the Arkanna walked off toward Vortaz proper, leaving Decker to follow her. She led him through a warren of ill-lit narrow streets, past bawdy houses and run-down taverns, into garbage-strewn alleys infested with all sorts of scurrying creatures, sentient or otherwise.

An average human being would have lost his sense of direction fast and grown worried at the characters lurking in the shadows. But Zack could find his way back from Hell necessary. He instinctively memorized every turn and was always calculating the shortest route back to the main strip and the safety of the spaceport.

His mind instead worried about his companion's motives and whether she was leading him into an ambush and a quick death. Smugglers couldn't afford informants, and

Decker, the former Marine noncom, had already learned enough to make even the most sanguine captain nervous. Making an embarrassing crewmember disappear was no feat of trans light physics. It could be days, weeks even, before anyone found a dead body around here, if ever. Not all aliens in this part of the galaxy shied at eating another sentient species, and humans were considered one of the tenderest races.

Decker walked with a caution born of years spent patrolling hostile jungles, hamlets, and towns, with terrorists and guerrillas lurking behind every window or beneath every bush. He had loosed his knife in its arm sheath the moment they left the main drag, but part of him wished for his Imperial Armaments blaster.

Darhad stopped, and Zack fell into a fighting stance, expecting a treacherous assault. The Arkanna first officer gave him an expressionless glance and then walked to a recessed and unmarked door on the right side of the alley. She knocked on the door while Zack, feeling foolish at his paranoia, took up a covering position behind her, as if that was what he had always intended.

After a few heartbeats, a small rectangle at face level opened, spilling light over Darhad's face. A hoarse voice asked a question in guttural Pradyni, which the Arkanna answered in the same language. The window vanished, leaving them in darkness again.

The door swung open, and a thickset native with a livid scar over his skull waved them through. He slammed the door shut behind them. Darhad led the way down a short corridor and pushed aside a plush red curtain.

"Welcome to the Unhatched Egg, or Trazujki Yar in their language, Gunner."

Zack stepped past her into a room he'd never thought would exist in the seediness of Spacetown. Dark wood panels with a swirling grain lined the four walls of the windowless club. Plush, leather-covered furniture surrounded tables of every height and size, to better accommodate the variety of sentient beings in the room.

A thin layer of smoke hung near the beamed ceiling, blurring the low light from the wrought-iron chandeliers. Soft, non-human music played from hidden speakers, and the patrons talked among themselves in subdued tones, as if awed by the opulence of their surroundings.

Zack saw Pradyni, Darsivians, Kardati, Flaxitatt and other races, but these specimens were well groomed and wore better quality clothing, a few of which he recognized as officers' uniforms. A few glanced up at the Arkanna and her human companion then returned their attention to whatever they were doing. It seemed clear that if one didn't belong here, one wasn't admitted.

Darhad led the way to a private booth opposite the bar and sat down facing Zack.

"Nice joint, Raisa," Decker commented, a wry smile on his face, as he sat back on the surprisingly soft, padded bench that ran along the booths walls. "Who'd you have to kill to be allowed in here? This isn't a typical Spacetown dive."

She smiled back at him, slanted eyes twinkling.

"This is a private club, reserved for ship's officers and merchants. Many, ah, transactions are conducted here, and admission is only through someone who is already a member."

"Sort of like a smuggler's Guildhall?" Zack asked in jest. But he preferred not to speculate about whatever business was transacted behind the club's bland facade. He strongly suspected he didn't want to know. Successful marauders could match honest traders cred for cred, and liked luxury just as much.

Darhad gave him a languid smile.

"Perhaps, Zack.   Untaxed transactions," she used the euphemism for smuggling, "outweigh the other variety in the Shield Cluster. The name Unhatched Egg refers to business deals yet to be consummated. Quite apt, I believe."

A Pradyni waiter in a simple, dark suit materialized at Darhad's elbow and silently placed a bowl of nuts on the table, then looked at the Arkanna.

"What would you like?   I believe you are partial to Shrehari ale."

"Not if it's like the swill they served at the last place I'm not."

A soft laugh escaped her lips. "Would the Zahkar vintage be acceptable to your delicate palate?"

Zack stared at her for a few moments grinning with delight.

"It certainly would."

She turned to the waiter and spat out a short sentence in Pradyni. The alien bowed and vanished again. Darhad took a handful of nuts from the bowl and popped several in her mouth, chewing daintily.

"Have some. They're perfectly safe for human consumption and so good that even a meat-eating Arkanna enjoys them." She placed a few more between her sharp teeth and crunched.

Decker shrugged and took a handful for himself. She was right. The nuts tasted fantastic, like a cross between a cashew and an apple, with Holkan gengji thrown in for good measure.

Before he had a chance to eat more than a few, the waiter returned with two platinum mugs foaming at the brim. He carefully placed them on the table and said something in his language that sounded much like 'Cheers.'

"You're partial to this stuff as well?" Zack asked, raising his beer and smacking his lips.

"At times, Gunner, at times, though I find it affects my metabolism less than it does humans, and I often prefer something from my home world."

Decker's eyebrows shot up. Shrehari ale, especially premium vintages, carried quite a punch and Zack couldn't drink more than three ordinary bottles before feeling dizzy. Considering the ex-Marine's size, a single bottle would do for the average human.

The ale tasted as good as advertised and washed away the last dregs of the horse piss he'd had earlier. It also went well with the nuts. Zack grinned at Darhad

"You sure know how to take liberty, Raisa. Now tell me there's a cathouse that looks like this, with human girls, just around the corner, and I'll be in heaven."

"Sorry. There is no such thing on Pradyn." She took a sip. "How do you like the merchant service so far?"

"Okay, I guess." He shrugged, still looking at the bar. "Can't say I care for all the people I've met, but then the Fleet's not a haven for saints either. As for the other business, so long as it's just keeping the taxman from taking his slice, I don't give a damn. That's Constabulary business, not Fleet."

"Did you like the Fleet?"

Getting personal, are we, Zack thought, focusing on Raisa Darhad again.

"It was my home for twenty years. Can't say much better than that." Pause. "Yeah, I guess I loved the Fleet."

When in doubt, tell the truth.

"Why did you leave?"

"I didn't leave, if you mean leave voluntarily. The colonel handed me my retirement papers, with no real choice in the matter." Zack's reply was spoken with a disinterest calculated to suggest he didn't appreciate the line of questioning, but he was finding it difficult to brush her off.

"Why?"

Either you don't take a hint, or you're one persistent alien dame, he thought. Then, realization dawned on him. She was testing.

"Had one disagreement too many with my superior officers. But that last argument got out of hand, and my acting squadron commander wanted to see me court-martialed. The colonel had the matter dropped if I put in my papers." He shrugged, as if the past wasn't important, though he fooled no one, least of all himself.

"Otherwise, I'd likely have ended up in a penal battalion as a private second class."

"What happened?" Her voice was hypnotically soft.

He debated how much he would tell her, but if he didn't spill the whole story, the questions would continue, and they were affecting his enjoyment of this excellent ale.

"We were ordered to raid a marauder base in the Telara Sector. Captain Sarratt, who'd been given temporary command of the squadron over our executive officer's head..." In a resigned voice, Decker recounted the story of the botched assault right up to the destruction of the base.

"When the demolition charges blew, my troop was caught in the blast radius. Had we been wearing anything lighter than full battle armor, we would have died. I flew several meters into the air and landed hard against a slab of rock. Put me completely out. They had to carry half of my

Marines back on stretchers. A couple had internal injuries. Thankfully none died."

"When I came to, I found the squadron sergeant-major informing me that Sarratt had put me under arrest and was laying charges for insubordination, behavior unbecoming, anything he could think of. At that point, something snapped in me. I left sickbay and headed to the barracks to confront Sarratt. I found him and the other troop leaders completing the after-action review. I added my own comments, mainly about Sarratt's incompetence and general uselessness as an officer and a Marine. Next thing I knew, I was in the ship's brig. A real officer would have known how to handle an asshole like me, who was still concussed from the blast, but Sarratt decided he had to make a public example of me, in an attempt to recover from his disastrous leadership."

"When we returned home, the colonel interviewed Sarratt, the other troop leaders, the pilots and me. Then he reamed me a new one for not being able to shut my mouth. I already had a reputation in the Regiment, and a track record for ignoring orders I found stupid or dangerous. Sarratt tried to save what was left of his chances for promotion by shifting all the blame on me through formal charges. If I had just waited to be home before contesting the charges instead of barging into the after-action review, I might still be there. Instead, the colonel made a compromise, which like all good compromises, pleased no one. Sarratt would drop the charges and let me retire voluntarily, and my contribution to the after-action review would be cut, meaning no official record of his ineptitude beyond whatever was in the logs."

"How could your colonel side with an incompetent officer?"

"He didn't side with Sarratt. The dickhead's career was done for, no matter what. Gossip would make sure no one would use him again. He did it to save my bacon from a court martial and protect Sarratt from public humiliation. The colonel figured that even though I had only myself to blame for my problems, my disobedience saved lives, and so he owed me the least bad outcome he could manage."

"The biggest irony of it all, as intelligence later found out, the whole thing had been a trap, designed to lure in a Pathfinder squadron. We needn't even have gone, which would have saved us a dozen casualties, as well as Sarratt's and my careers."

He took a sip of ale, staring into the distance, avoiding Raisa's gaze. He still keenly felt a loss he didn't want to share with anyone.

"Is there any chance of the balance being put right?" She finally asked.

Zack snorted. "You have to be kidding. Plenty of beached noncoms and officers like me, who were fucked by a career-seeking bastard. I put in my papers fair and square so it technically isn't as if they tossed me. No, there's no chance in hell I'm reenlisting in the Corps."

Raisa nodded. He believed that. No one could fake the emotion and the bitterness she felt. Zack Decker was who he said he was – a beached noncom who was retired for having done his duty too well, not an infiltrator.

"Do you have any family?"

Zack shrugged. "Yes and no. My parents disowned me when I joined the Corps. They belonged to a pacifist sect and wanted me to take over the farm after I finished school. But I couldn't stand the life and the hypocrisy, and I wanted to see the galaxy. Haven't seen them in twenty years. If I ever returned, the old man would probably throw me off his land. All I know is my name's been struck from the family book."

"So without the Fleet, you have no family at all?"

"Nope." Zack took another swig of beer, trying to look unconcerned. He wiped the foam from his lips with the back of his hand.

"I know how it feels, Zack." Raisa threw her crimson hair back with a toss of the head. "I left Arkanna fifteen years ago and have never been back. My chjok, I guess the closest Anglic word is 'pack,' threw me out after I foolishly challenged the matriarch for supremacy. I had fallen in love with the pack leader, the alpha, and in my society, only the matriarch and pack leader may mate. It makes us strong, for only the strong reproduce, but it's hard. I was much too young to even be considered by the alpha, and of course did not have the strength to best the matriarch."

"No other pack would take you in?" Zack was fascinated by the glimpse of Arkanna she offered him.

"Other packs might have taken me, but I would have been the most junior female, no matter how old I was and that is not a pleasant status. I preferred to find a new life elsewhere. A human freighter agreed to take me on as a deckhand and took me into the Commonwealth."

"Why not the Empire? I thought Arkanna and Shrehari had more in common."

She shook her head. "The few Imperials I had met by then did not impress me. They were brutal, uncouth and appeared to have an uncontrollable attraction to Arkanna females. It would not have been a pleasant life for an outcast."

"So how do we humans measure up?"

She smiled, looking more like a predator than ever.

"Most human males do not measure up to Arkanna warriors and leave me in peace." Her talons briefly flashed in the club's low light. "And I have discovered that even outcasts can make an honorable living in your Commonwealth. Your humanity is something a Shrehari or a traditionalist Arkanna warrior would spit on, but it has given me a life, and for that I am grateful. However, a few human males can measure up to the expectations of an Arkanna female."

"Do I?" Zack asked with a cocky grin.

"Perhaps, Gunner, perhaps. You are a warrior and have strength and honor. Perhaps more than anyone else aboard *Shokoten*."

Her smile revealed sharp teeth and gave Zack a frisson of danger. With great difficulty, he broke eye contact and withdrew his hand. He felt close to losing control, and it was not a sensation he enjoyed. Especially not with an Arkanna who could easily kill him, and who had reason enough to do so, now that he had discovered *Shokoten* was smuggling arms and restricted items to alien worlds.

The fate of his predecessor came back to haunt him, and he wondered again whether Lokis had died because he'd stumbled onto Strachan's illegal business.

Darhad did not try to re-establish eye contact. She sipped her ale and took the conversation to safer grounds. They spoke about the worlds they'd seen, the cultures they'd experienced and discovered shared interests. The earlier tension eased and Zack relaxed. Time seemed to melt away.

*

"Well, Gunner," Darhad drained her ale and gave him a wry smile, "it is long past the midnight hour. I suggest we return to the ship. It is late, and we may find the shippers will bring the cargo for loading tomorrow. Captain Strachan can be very persuasive."

"You're the boss, Raisa." He swallowed the last of his drink and rose. "Let's find the waiter and press a few creds in his scaly palms."

She laid a restraining hand on his arm and shook her head.

"At the Unhatched Egg, they don't do things as vulgar as make valued customers pay in full view of others. I have my own arrangements."

"Then let me pay my part."

"No. This was my treat. I find you fascinating. The drinks are a small price to pay for the chance to learn more about you."

"Then I could argue the same, Raisa."

"Next time, Zack."

*

They had turned the corner into an adjacent alley when Raisa suddenly froze, nostrils flaring and ears twitching. Decker instinctively turned to place his back against hers. He didn't know what had made her stop and probe the night, but he was unwilling to take the chance it was simply nerves.

The two drinks hadn't blunted his thinking, and he stifled his questions, letting Darhad figure out what had alerted her. He shook his dagger loose and waited, watching the shadows for movements.

A pair of soft thuds came from Darhad's side of the alley as if two beings had jump from the roof. A third thud attracted Decker's eyes, and he saw a dark shadow fill the narrow passage in front of him.

The three new arrivals advanced on the two spacers in silence, blades drawn. Decker took a moment to thank the gods that their attackers weren't more heavily armed. A Pathfinder and an Arkanna in a knife fight had a chance; in a one-sided gunfight, they'd be dead already.

A soft growl rose from Darhad's throat, and he felt her tense against his back, getting ready to pounce.

"I guess there's no point in asking these gentlemen what they want from us," Decker muttered at his companion. He felt her shake her head. "Then I hope they've put their affairs in order."

A chilling howl ripped through the air as Darhad jumped at the nearest of the two footpads on her side, talons flashing in the dim light. Her war cry was quickly followed by a scream that turned into a wet gargle.

Decker had no time to think about his companion. The third assailant ran towards him, long knife held low, as a professional would, preparing to rip Zack's guts out.

He tried to side step the assassin, to avoid the oncoming knife while pivoting to take his opponent from behind, but his foot landed on some unrecognizable, but slippery substance and he lost his balance. That accident saved his life.

The assassin had seen Decker telegraph his move and had shifted his knife to his left hand to counter it. As the gunner went sprawling, the blade flashed over his head and swung through empty space.

Without thinking, Decker thrust his dagger upwards, burying it in his attacker's midriff. The cloaked figure, forward momentum fatally checked, let out a shriek of agony, and collapsed. Decker twisted out from under the falling body and pulled his dagger free.

He sat up just in time to see Darhad dispatch the third assailant with a cruel swipe of her claws across his face and neck, sending a gush of dark blood across the alley. She ripped out his windpipe so quickly that he didn't even have time to cry out.

Decker hauled himself to his feet, breathing hard with the rush adrenaline in his blood. The whole attack, from start to finish, had lasted less than a minute.

He bent over and pushed the footpad's hood back, revealing a Pradyni face, eyes now fixed in death. Glancing at Darhad, he saw her wipe her hands on the other footpad's cloak, shoulders heaving as she fought to regain her composure.

"You okay?" Decker asked.

"I will be in a moment," she replied, her voice deep and hoarse. "Arkanna fight-or-flight instincts tend to be somewhat primal compared to yours."

"I can see that." He shook his head in admiration at the mess she'd made of her two assailants. "I'd hate to have you mad at me."

Both were Pradyni, just like the one Decker had dispatched, but where the gunner's dagger had left a small hole, Darhad's claws had torn her opponents to shreds. He pulled the cloak off the Pradyni he'd killed and handed it to Raisa.

"Better use this to get the blood off. These lizards bleed just as bad as humans, and we can't have you cross Spacetown looking like you came from a slaughterhouse."

"Thank you." Chest still heaving with deep breaths, she took the rough cloth and wiped herself. "We must return to the ship. On Pradyn, what we just did is called murder until you can prove you were acting in self-defense. I would rather not try to explain myself to a court composed entirely of staring lizards."

"Me neither." He leaned over wiped the blood off his blade on the dead alien and re-sheathed it, all the while staring at the savaged assassins.

The Arkanna woman was much more dangerous than he might have imagined. She could probably kill Command Sergeant Zack Decker, retired, late of the Pathfinders, in less time than it took him to belch.

"Come."

Without waiting for an answer, she walked off.

*

"Who and why?" Zack asked, staring at the star map on Strachan's cabin wall. He and Darhad had reported to the captain the moment they came aboard, and Strachan had poured them both a much-needed drink.

"Who knows," Strachan replied, a thoughtful expression creasing his forehead. "Robbers most likely. They thought that people who come out of posh clubs are loaded with creds." Something in his voice rang false.

"Rather lightly equipped for that sort of trade," Zack replied. "Only three guys with knives? If one of 'em had a blaster, they'd be richer, and we'd be dead."

"No private gun ownership on Pradyn, Mister Decker," the first officer reminded him. "Guns have been banned ever since the present dynasty took power. It seems to contribute to political stability. Anyone caught with an illegal weapon is automatically sentenced to public dismemberment."

From the corner of his eye, he caught Darhad and Strachan exchanging a glance, but whether it had to do with his comment or something else, he couldn't tell. One thing was for sure, he doubted those were ordinary footpads. He didn't know why, but his instincts told him so.

"Whatever they were," the captain finally said, "we will have to keep you and the first officer on board until we lift. Though I doubt the dead natives will be traced back to you, there is no point in taking unnecessary chances."

Raisa Darhad nodded.

"Aye, aye, sir," Zack acknowledged the order. Sensing he was about to be dismissed, he stood, drained his glass and snapped to attention before pivoting on his heels and leaving the cabin.

"Good night, Gunner."

When Decker was gone, Strachan refilled Darhad's drink. "Talk to me, Raisa."

"Not much to tell. I'm convinced Decker is genuine. He loves the Fleet but is bitter at the same time. More importantly, he's absolutely certain he'll never wear a Marine uniform again, which removes any incentive to interfere. I don't think he is a danger. And he is a formidable fighter, a very dangerous fighter. His emotions shut down when he is in jeopardy, and he becomes an efficient machine."

"If I didn't know better, you blood-thirsty she-wolf, I would say you engineered the ambush just to test Decker. Arkanna have strange ways."

A dangerous smile distorted her lips.

"And if I had?" Before Strachan could reply, her smile vanished. "I say trust Decker. When and if your business comes to include things he will object to, we can re-evaluate his employment. But, as long as it is just avoiding the taxman, he has no problems serving you."

"Good. What about the ambush, then?"

She shrugged. "Footpads? An assassination attempt? Take your pick, Diego. Whatever it was, the attack failed, as it was destined to do. A mature Arkanna and a Pathfinder Marine make for very dangerous prey."

"Just make sure it wasn't Alers. If you're right, and Decker can be trusted, we need him more than the bosun, especially a stupid brute who is fast outliving his usefulness."

"If you want Alers out of the way, just give the word," Darhad replied, "but be sure he will try to kill Decker one day."

"Wait for now. Our gunner can take care of himself. With any luck, he'll take care of Alers in a manner no one will find objectionable."

The Arkanna nodded. She tried to read her captain's feelings, to discover what he was thinking. Diego Strachan never did or said anything without good reason, and that narrowed it down to either his personal interest or the interest of their ultimate owner.

Unlike Decker, Captain Diego Strachan knew his first officer's species had developed a survival trait for a very harsh world: all mature Arkanna females were empaths, able to read and project emotions. And he had learned to mask his feelings as he was doing now.

She rose. "Good night, Diego."

*

Zack tossed and turned in his bunk, unable to sleep. He relived every moment of his brief bout of shore leave: the easy way he had told his story to Raisa Darhad, the attack in the dark alley, the secret club for select merchants and, most distressingly, his strong attraction to the Arkanna.

"Are you all right, Zack?" A soft voice enquired from the lower bunk.

"Yeah, sort of. Sorry to have woken you, Nihao."

"It is of no matter. How did your leave go?"

"Strange as hell, kiddo. Our exotic first officer rescued me from a spacer's dive and took me to a fancy, private smuggler's club. Damn posh, let me tell you. They serve the finest vintage Shrehari ale. Our Lady of the Talons pumped me for my life's story and gave me a bit of her own. Then, just as we left the club, three Pradyni footpads ambushed us. Darhad took out two with her built-in slicers and I took out the third with my knife. What the fuck that was all about, I don't know."

She made no comment and Zack fell silent as he debated whether to ask or not. Then, he rolled over on his stomach and glanced down at Kiani.

"I wonder. Did something like this happen to Lokis? It seems strange that I'm attacked and almost killed in the same port."

"Lokis vanished while on liberty here in Vortaz, last time we visited," Nihao finally said, her voice flat. "Two days later, the police found his body in an alley in Spacetown. He had been badly cut-up, possibly tortured. Pradyni go for clean kills and no torture. It goes against their code of honor."

"So why was he killed?"

"I have no idea. Maybe he fell into the hands of thugs looking for blood sport."

"Or he found out something he shouldn't have," Zack countered, rubbing his chin.

"I don't know, Zack. Perhaps Lokis was involved in something criminal and paid for it. Some otherwise honest merchant sailors are often tempted by quick, but illegal profits. Lokis and I were close, but we kept much from each other. Anyway, it's all history now, so please leave it be. The important thing is that you are safe."

"Thanks for the sentiment, Nihao. But that doesn't explain why no one wanted to tell me what happened."

"It's bad luck to speak of those who died violently, Zack."

"Really? Never heard of that superstition in the Fleet."

"Maybe because violent death is normal there. But in the merchant service, we don't want to tempt fate." She paused for a long minute as if framing her next words. "Zack, beware of Darhad. She has her own agenda and, like all Arkanna females, she can be treacherous. Goodnight."

Zack was too stunned by her warning to reply, but he let the matter go because he had just realized something else that was strange about his evening ashore. Darhad had known they were in danger before the assassins appeared, as if she had heard or sensed them, even though he had heard nothing.

*

The next day, tired but relaxed, Decker stood beside Bowdoin and supervised the loading of the outbound cargo. Darhad had been right: the captain had convinced the shippers to play straight. *Shokoten* would lift by sunset, bound for Wyvern with a hold full of refined exotic alloys. And the gods knew what else hidden among the visible cargo. It took most of the morning.

"Secure the hold, Gunner and stand down the guards. I'll have the bridge seal the ship. Unless something comes up, we're ready to lift."

"Aye, aye, sir." He raised his communicator to his lips. "Security detail, this is Decker. Check all locks and report. It's over."

A few hours later, the freighter left Pradyn's surface far below as her thrusters labored to break her out of the planet's gravity well. By the end of the evening watch, she had left Pradyn's security sphere, and Zack could unlock his weapons again. The chances of a pirate attack on the way back were less than on the way out. There was more money to be made in the Shield Cluster from human tech than from commodities, no matter how exotic, but it paid to be cautious.

He spent most of the night watch inspecting every gun and every launcher with painstaking precision, earning an invitation for a drink with the captain, though it was almost six bells, close to three in the morning.

"You work too hard, Zack. It could have waited," Strachan commented, raising his glass.

"Nothing to it, Captain. I like my job, and I'd rather go to sleep knowing my guns will fire the moment I hit the button."

"Commendable. I shall make no secret of my opinion that you're an excellent gunner, and -"

"Thank you, sir."

"And, as I was about to say," he briefly frowned at the interruption, "I intend to have your pay grade raised as soon as we reach Wyvern."

"Thank you again, sir. It's been a pleasure to serve aboard *Shokoten* so far," if he discounted a sadistic bosun who was out to kill him and more questions than a game show. Things on this tub might not be what they seemed, but he had no better offer.

Strachan nodded, slowly rolling his tumbler in his hands.

"Is there anything else I can do for you, sir?" Zack asked, putting a particular emphasis on the word 'else.'

"Not on this trip, Gunner, but thank you for asking."

"Aye, sir." He emptied his glass. "Good night, then."

"Good night. Take the morning watch off. You deserve to sleep in."

*

Captain Strachan kept him busy enough to forget about Pradyn and the first officer over the next few days. While they remained in the badlands, he drilled the crew mercilessly.

Five days out from Pradyn, the rear missile launcher, which was also the hardest to reach of the three, stopped responding to the bridge. Rather than ask engineering to check it out, and get rebuffed by the third officer, Zack grabbed his tool case and made his way into the cramped recesses of the aft compartments.

It was the second dogwatch, shortly after seven in the evening, and most of the off-duty crewmembers were in their messes or cabins. He had a pretty good idea what was wrong. These old launchers had weak control boards. They were originally designed for ground use, but when the Corps pulled them out of service, the company sold them on the civilian market as starship defensive systems.

A good business move, but it didn't do squat for merchants who had no idea how to fix a busted board. Luckily Zack Decker knew all there was to know about this particular piece of weaponry.

The access tube was narrow and cramped, especially for someone Zack's size. Whoever built the launcher into the ship had figured maintenance and reloading would be done from the outside. Going outside while the ship was in hyperspace was the best way to go psycho. The hull shielded humans. Space suits didn't.

Zack pulled the old board and examined it as he lay on his stomach. There, in the middle of the thin plastic sheet, a small but vital part had come loose under the vibrations of the multiple launcher systems and had shorted out its command recognition capability. Decker plugged his AI into the board and quickly reprogrammed the chip to bypass the burnt-out circuits so it could accept commands through its secondary control terminals.

Satisfied he pushed the board back into its slot and smiled when the fire control computer cycled back to life. Then, a loud clang from the other end of the access tube startled Zack. He frowned as he packed away his tools. That could only have been the access hatch.

Not Alers again, for fuck's sake! This time, the little prick will end up in sickbay when I get my hands on him.

Decker crawled backwards, the tube too narrow to turn, and tried to remember where the emergency release mechanism was. Suddenly, his breathing became harder and his body started to feel funny. Decompression. The tube was venting into space.

All compartments could be vented and regularly were to kill off vermin that invariably found their way aboard any spacecraft. But the venting system had triple safeguards and was solely controlled from the bridge. Unless someone could override the safeguards and Alers wasn't smart enough to figure that out on his own.

"Bridge," he gasped into his communicator, "this is the gunner. Stop venting launcher three. I'm inside."

When he didn't receive an answer, he repeated his message, anoxia making red spots dance in front of his eyes. I'm about to die, he thought, after all this crap, I'm about to die of fucking decompression on a freighter, killed by a third-rate moron.

Zack Decker passed out.

— SEVEN —

"He will be all right, Captain."

The voice sounded tinny and distorted to Zack's ears, and somehow he figured it wasn't an angel because they were supposed to emit nothing but glorious sounds. Perhaps he was in Hell, where he'd been wished by many people over his lifetime. If so, then why did one of the minor demons sound like the she-wolf?

"Our Mister Decker is much tougher than anyone would credit." The same silky voice purred near his ear as warm, dry fingers brushed his cheek. His eyes opened a crack, and caught sight of a blurred, crimson-haired, white skinned woman with impossibly blue eyes, upswept eyebrows, pointy ears, and a predator's smile. Yup. Definitely Hell. But somehow, he didn't really mind, if all demons looked like the delightfully dangerous Raisa Darhad.

"Some damage to the blood vessels due to decompression, probably lung damage too, but without proper diagnostic equipment, I cannot find out the extent. We'll find out in the next two or three days if he has sustained severe trauma, but I doubt it. He was not exposed long enough."

"Thank you, Raisa."

Decompression injuries? Zack tried to move his limbs or register feeling throughout his body, but couldn't. Panic gripped him.

"C-can't m-move," he croaked. "C-can't f-feel."

Raisa's warm hand rested briefly on his forehead. "Stay still, Gunner. I have given you a sedative. You have internal damage and your body is covered with bruises. I fear you would moan in pain if you move too much. You will regain full responsiveness when the drugs wear off."

"W-what happened?"

Darhad's face swam before his eyes again.

"You were fixing the command board in launcher three when there was a malfunction in the ship's housekeeping program. After visiting non-human planets, we vent each compartment to make sure we don't bring vermin back. It's an automated function, and it seems the program did not talk to the internal sensors, believing the launcher area was empty. The bridge received your distress call, and we stopped it in time. A few seconds more and you would have died rather messily. I have already examined the housekeeping program and found degradation in the code that caused the malfunction. It will not happen again."

"A-accident?" Decker croaked.

"Yes, of course, it was."

And I'm the Grand Admiral herself, Zack thought sourly through the haze of drugs.

"Accident or not, you'll stay in your bunk until further notice. That's an order." Strachan ordered.

Decker nodded feebly and let his eyelids drop, exhausted. He fell asleep within seconds.

*

When he woke, it was five bells in the afternoon watch of the following day. He opened his eyes and immediately closed them again. The light in the cabin was painful, and his vision was alarmingly red tinged. Then, he felt his body, just as Darhad had promised. It hurt from head to toe.

After a while, Zack opened his eyes, this time for a longer period, and glanced around. He was alone in the small room. Kiani was on duty somewhere else in the ship. Not a single sound of the ship's life penetrated the bulkheads. If *Shokoten*'s engines hadn't been sending their reassuring, almost subliminal vibrations all the way into Zack's brain, he would have thought the ship abandoned. He tried to turn on his side and winced.

His bunk was comfortable enough, but after fifteen hours, he figured he had turned into a feather merchant with bedsores on his bum. A sudden need to urinate overrode all other considerations.

He sat up unthinkingly, swung his legs over the edge of the bed, and grimaced again, this time at the waves of nausea and the pounding of blood in his head. Looking down to regain control of his breathing, he saw his skin for the first time.

"Shit!"

He was a mass of bruises, his body mottled in blue, green and yellow, just as they'd warned when he first woke. Decker frowned. Someone, Darhad if memory served, had said something else that hadn't registered at the time but that now nibbled at the edge of his consciousness.

His bladder sent an urgent signal, and he concentrated instead on getting up before staggering to the heads. He sat down on the cold toilet and winced.

Once he'd made it back to his bed without puking or keeling over, he lay there, unthinking and unmoving, letting his system calm down and return to the dull throbbing from before he stood again.

What was it the she-wolf said?   A glitch in the housekeeping program. Accident.

Not that he believed it for a moment, but there was something else. Oh yeah. She had said he was fixing the launcher's command board. How would she know? He hadn't known the board was down until he pulled it, and all he had done was reset the chip and reroute the command functions. Then he'd shoved it back in its slot. Then the hatch slammed shut, and the compartment vented.

The door opened, and Kiani walked in, her face a mask of concern

"How are you doing, Zack? You look like hell though I understand it will fade away by the time we make port. Are you hungry or thirsty yet?"

Zack grinned.

"A cold beer and a hoagie would be nice, Nihao."

She frowned and wagged her finger at Zack.

"I think not, Zack. No beer or junk food until you are fully recovered. Synthmilk, soyburgers, and hydroponics greens are the only things on your approved menu."

Decker made a face.

"Then I guess I'm well enough to return to duty."

He sat up, earning another burst of nausea and slowly settled down again, grimacing. Kiani laid a restraining hand on his chest.

"No, Zack. You are a very sick man. Catastrophic decompression is not something the body shrugs off in one afternoon. It will take time."

"Can I at least receive visitors?"

"Sure. Do you wish me to send out invitations?"

"Hell, no. Just ask the first officer if she has time to see me."

Nihao frowned.

"You enjoy living dangerously, Zack?"

He shrugged. "I want to find out more about this supposed accident."

"Why supposed?"

"I think Raisa Darhad is wrong. I can't figure why, but she is."

"Perhaps you imagine things. Who would go to such lengths to kill you?"

"Yeah," Decker replied, eyes half-closed in thought, "who?" Alers was who, but he didn't do it alone. Not by a long shot.

*

"You wanted to speak with me, Gunner?" Raisa Darhad stood beside Zack's bunk, hands clasped behind her back. They were alone in the cabin and for once, she didn't try to manipulate the ex-Marine with her pheromones. Even predatory females had enough mercy to give wounded males a chance to recover. She needed to concentrate on his feelings right now, and they were clouded enough with pain that she didn't need sexual arousal as well.

"Yes, sir. Would you repeat what you told me when I woke last night, just after you recovered me from the launcher?"

She nodded and did as asked, repeating her statement word for word. It matched what Zack remembered.

"May I speak frankly, sir?"

"Certainly, Gunner." She could almost smell the skepticism. Decker was no fool.

"Let's cut the crap, Mister Darhad. You know it was a set-up and not an accident, though your explanation was plausible."

"And what makes you speak thus, Gunner?" She didn't seem offended at his tone or words, rather the contrary.

"Something you said yesterday that didn't fit, sir. You said I was fixing the command board when the housekeeping program went overboard. There's no way for you to know. I didn't find out the launcher had a busted board until I got there, and I fixed it on the spot so you wouldn't even notice the job. No spare parts lying around."

She nodded, smiling her predatory smile again.

"Go on."

"Housekeeping programs don't develop unexpected glitches like that either, especially when the systems have triple safety checks. I distinctly remember the hatch slamming shut and the venting start the moment I shoved the board back into its slot. If I had to booby trap the launcher bay, I probably wouldn't have done it any different. Whoever did it rigged the board's I/O feeds to the compartment housekeeping subroutine. The moment the circuit was re-established, puff! It's not very hard to do if you know how."

Darhad arched her eyebrows.

"Impressive, Gunner. That is indeed what I found when I investigated. I realized it was the command board you worked on because that is where your scent was strongest. I did not discover the 'booby trap' as you call it, until this morning, though it is circumstantial evidence at best, and will never satisfy an official investigation. It will not come to that, anyhow."

"Who did it, and why?" Scent? Somehow, the thought of Raisa Darhad literally sniffing around the launcher bay was disturbing.

"I couldn't say. At least not for sure."

"Alers?"

"Possible. But he would not have been able to do it himself."

"Yeah, there's that. The bugger's too stupid. Good only for strong-arming the crew. He must have had help somewhere along the line. So what're you going to do?"

"First, as per the captain's orders, treat this incident as an accident. Anything more and we would open ourselves to an official investigation, at the minimum by transportation safety inspectors from the government. We don't want this as you can imagine. Second, you will stay in your cabin until we reach Wyvern. Considering your state that is necessary anyway. Third, the bosun will be beached at Wyvern. He has become increasingly unstable and is creating more and more chaos on the lower deck. The captain has already radioed ahead for a replacement."

"And what about whoever helped the bastard?"

"Short of interrogating Alers, I have no way of finding out but -"

"Leave him to me, Raisa, leave him to me. It'll be Sonoda for sure."

"As I was saying, Mister Decker," she frowned, reminding Zack that such familiarity was acceptable only on liberty, not on the ship, "I have no way of finding Alers' helpers, but with him out of the way, I doubt we shall have any more problems. The other, ah, suspects don't have reason to act alone. And please keep any accusations against superior officers to yourself. Anything else?"

"Yeah." Zack locked eyes with her. "One more thing. You know little about me, I haven't served with you more than a couple of weeks. Yet you're already taking care of me as if I was an old mate, which is strange since I seem to attract more than my share of trouble. Why?"

"That's simple, Zack. We need your skills," she answered calmly, as if she had been expecting the question, "and value your abilities. You have more experience and discipline than most on this ship, and you have already proven you were trustworthy."

And not only because of your reaction to the contraband, my friend. Your emotions are easy to read. You are open and guileless, almost a cub which is just as rare in this business as a Master Gunner.

"The universe is a dangerous place, especially for merchant ships with our sort of business interests. Few have the luxury of hiring someone like you, and that is a luxury we wish to keep. If you had not been as efficient or as dedicated, we might not have been so solicitous."

Decker nodded. That was an explanation he could accept. It reeked of enlightened self-interest, which he expected from people who lived to make a profitable run. Very well then, he would strive to return their confidence by doing his job well, which he couldn't from his bed. But orders were orders.

"You had better sleep now, Zack. We dock at Wyvern in seven days, and we will need you to perform your duties when we arrive. In the meantime, is there anything I can do for you?"

Yeah, Zack thought, you can strip naked and jump in bed with me now. I'll be feeling better in no time.

He caught an indefinable glint in her eyes as she waited for an answer. A small, wry smile formed on her lips, and Decker had the eerie sensation that she knew what he had just been imagining.

"There is something you can do," he said, looking away, trying to cover his embarrassment. "I wouldn't mind having a reader with access to the ship's data banks, and a channel to monitor my station's activities by remote. That way, if we get in trouble, I can help without getting up."

"As you wish, Gunner," she nodded once, the smile never leaving her face. "But we have crossed back into Commonwealth space and should be safe from marauders."

"Take nothing for granted, sir. That way we'll all stay alive longer."

"So far, you seem to be successful. I shall try to visit you at least once a watch. Would you like that?"

"Very much, sir," Decker grinned.

"Until later then."

*

An alarm siren broke through Zack's unsettled sleep, and his first reaction was to pull his blaster from its recessed shelf above the bunk. But as he woke, he realized it wasn't the battle stations siren. It was the emergency call. Before he could climb out of bed and pull on some clothes, the alarm stopped.

He flicked on the intercom above his head. "Bridge, this is the gunner. What's the problem?"

"Fourth officer here, Mister Decker. There's been an accident in the cargo hold. One of the containers broke free of its magnetic clamps and shifted."

Zack's eyebrows shot up. Two unexpected and unusual accidents within days of each other.

"Anybody hurt?"

"Yeah. The bosun was crushed. He's dead." Gareth's voice held little regret for Alers.

"Thanks. Gunner, out."

Decker slumped back in his bed, lost in thought. Accident or murder? Magnetic clamps weren't supposed to fail just like that. And exactly at the moment Alers was walking by on his daily inspection of the hold? What the hell was happening?

*

Darhad came by a few hours later to check on Zack's condition.

"You heard about the accident, I presume?" Her face was expressionless, and if Decker read Arkanna body language properly, guileless.

"Yeah. Can't say I'm sorry to see the bastard gone. I'll leave the pious hypocrisy to others. How did it happen?"

"One of the magnetic clamps failed in the last day or so. The other one was not strong enough to prevent the container from shifting under the vibrations of the engines. It was unfortunate that the second clamp gave up the struggle just as Alers was passing by."

"Unfortunate indeed," Decker murmured, narrowed eyes watching Darhad with suspicion.

She noticed his reaction and shook her head.

"It was a straightforward accident. I found no signs of tampering. The captain ordered an inspection of every clamp, and we found several more showing excessive wear."

"Convenient. It saves me the trouble of killing him myself."

"As you say, Gunner."

Somehow, he didn't believe the she-wolf. His 'accident' wasn't one, and neither was Alers'. But it solved his particular problem and put the bosun's accomplice on notice, so who was he to dig any further?

*

By the time *Shokoten* skipped out of hyperspace, Zack Decker was back at his accustomed station on the bridge. He still experienced discomfort, but most of the bruising had faded. The intervening week had been very educational for the former Pathfinder. He was now as well acquainted with the ship as her master, if not more so.

"We have contact with Wyvern control," the fifth officer's raspy voice rang out from the navigator's station. "Transmitting approach trajectory now." A few moments later, "course laid in and beaconed. ETA in four hours."

"Thank you, Mister Sladek. Stand down from emergence stations. Please tell me when we have our landing window. You have the con."

"Captain."

Strachan left the bridge and Sladek slipped into the vacated chair, slaving the navigation readout to the small display screen in the chair's arm. Zack decided to try out a few ideas he'd had while he was laid up. He spent the next few hours reprogramming the fire control system until it would do what he wanted.

*

Wyvern finally hove into sight, and the captain reclaimed his chair for the delicate landing procedure. With only fifty million inhabitants, it was still an open, pleasant, and unpolluted planet, and Decker was looking forward to a bit of civilized liberty. But it was not to be.

If the change of cargo had been relatively swift on Pradyn, one of the technobarbarian worlds, it was even more so on an orderly and well-governed human planet.

Robots quickly unloaded the containers less than two hours after touchdown at the busy Draconis Spaceport, and Zack barely had time to run a full check of the hold before the outbound cargo was brought on board. But since Captain Strachan and Nihao Kiani, had business ashore, their departure wasn't scheduled until the wee hours of the morning.

The officers, save for Sonoda and Kiani, ate supper together at the Guildhall's Officer's Club. Only one thing disturbed Decker's brief bout ashore, and that was the annoying sensation of being observed, just as on Pradyn. Though Zack tried, he couldn't see anyone suspicious.

When they returned on board, Decker met the new bosun. She was a no-nonsense woman of indeterminate age with a face hewn from granite. Her platinum blond hair was cut so short, it nearly vanished against her pale scalp, and her gray coveralls looked like they'd been painted on her muscular, short body. She wore a small silver ring through her left nostril.

Bosun Lorena Kader would prove a lot easier to get along with than Alers. She treated Warrant Officer Decker the way a petty officer should: with respect for rank and ability. When Zack wanted three bodies for this job or the other, three bodies would show up, ready and five minutes early. Kader and Decker spoke little beyond pure business, but they were comfortable enough dealing with each other, like any pair of old noncoms.

*

Shokoten lifted twenty-four hours after arriving, this time, headed for Itrul, in the Protectorate Zone, as the badlands wedged between Commonwealth and Empire were known.

"Do you know Itrul, Zack?" Captain Strachan asked, sitting back in his chair. They had jumped to hyperspace a few hours ago and were sailing along smoothly. It would be a long trip, and Zack wondered why their contractors hadn't used a ship and a departure planet closer to the Protectorate. There was enough business headed for the Shield Cluster that *Shokoten* didn't have to go trolling for cargoes, like a tramp, and live on narrow profit margins.

"No sir, not personally. But I've learned enough about the Protectorate and most of the major worlds to find my way."

The Protectorate Zone received its name from the fact that it was under neither human nor Shrehari domination, but covertly patrolled by both. It represented what cynics called the perfect example of the military winning the war and the politicians losing the peace.

At the end of the last war with the Shrehari Empire, the Navy controlled most of the Protectorate. But the Treaty of Ulufan, astonishingly, relinquished all human interest in the zone, in return for two marginal star systems no one wanted or needed.

Now, the Commonwealth and the Empire used the Protectorate to wage covert war by proxy. Detractors maintained the SecGen of the day had given up the Protectorate under pressure from wealthy friends. They could make more money, more tax-free money, by dealing with so-called independent alien worlds than with Commonwealth members.

"Nasty little place, the Protectorate, and Itrul is nastier than most," Decker continued, staring into the amber whiskey at the bottom of his glass. "A lot of Itrulans hire out as mercs and marauders. Not bad either, but fucking ruthless, the kind to eat a vanquished enemy's heart raw, with the enemy still alive and attached to it. I've fought the bastards, and I don't like 'em much. They're unpredictable and very dangerous. What are we doing there?"

"Another special cargo," Raisa Darhad answered.

"You mentioned, a while ago," Strachan said, stroking his beard, "that you had a few ways to disguise a container's contents from a scanner." Zack's head snapped up, and he looked at the captain with suspicion. "Well, now is the time to put that knowledge to good use. The Navy and the Constabulary patrol the Protectorate borders much more than the frontier along the Shield Cluster, and there's a decent chance we'll be inspected."

"What sort of cargo?" Zack asked in a hard tone. It had better not be anything he wouldn't like.

Darhad glanced at Decker, her eyes narrowed as if she were evaluating him. Again, he had the impression she had divined his thoughts. He shrugged off the feeling as the captain spoke again.

"I would rather you find out, Mister Decker." He smiled. "With this." Strachan held up a Mark Nine battlefield sensor. "It will also give you, and us, a chance to verify your camouflage."

Won't do shit for you, Diego ol' buddy. The guys who'll inspect this ship on the Commonwealth side of the border carry Mark Tens, and without a Mark Ten to check my cammo, I can't even begin to guarantee results. Unless, of course...

"You don't look all that happy, Zack," Strachan raised a questioning eyebrow as he placed the sensor on his desk.

"Ah yes, Captain," Darhad murmured, "I believe our dear gunner is wondering how in damnation he is to hide contraband using a Mark Nine as a check, when the border patrols use the new Mark Ten equipment."

Decker started violently and stared at the first officer who smiled, revealing those sharp teeth.

"That's right," Zack stammered to cover his surprise.

How the fuck did they find out about Mark Tens. They're still classified. What the hell am I going to do now? This is another test of loyalty, right? Meaning do it or you'll blow your chances at keeping this berth, and possibly even your life.

"The Mark Nine isn't nearly as sensitive as a Ten," he said, voice steady and unemotional. "But I can boost the Nine's gain to squeeze enough out of it so that in the hands of an expert, it'll be almost as good as a Mark Ten in the hands of your average constable or trooper." Which modifications were illegal, of course. Especially since the gain increase pointed the way towards new technology and that could be called a security violation by your local judge advocate general. But then, Decker shouldn't be able to pull off the trick in the first place.

"Well, Zack, I believe you have work ahead of you. We have a full week before we reach the border area, and another three, maybe four days more before we cross the line. Is that enough time?"

"Sure, Captain. I'll have this baby ready in, say, two or three days. After that, another day and your containers will be as well camoed as I can manage. Not that it'll be perfect," he warned.

"Understood, Gunner, understood." Strachan raised his hand in surrender.

"I'll be off, then." Zack suddenly felt impatient to start on his modifications. "Thanks for the hooch."

"My pleasure, Gunner. Good night."

"Good night, Mister Decker." Darhad nodded.

"Captain. First Officer."

*

"What are you doing, Zack?" Nihao looked at him, and his desk in surprise while the cabin door shut behind her. She pointed at the scattered electronic components, sophisticated miniature tools, and the half-disassembled sensor. "Is it not a bit late for a new science project?"

"I guess," he replied, looking up from his intricate work. "But I couldn't resist. It's a Master Gunner thing. We have this urge to modify and customize every piece of gear we're issued."

"You are a man of many surprises, Zack Decker. What exactly are you doing?"

He briefly debated whether to tell her about the contraband shipment, and his plan to hide it from sensor sweeps, but decided against doing so. He had no idea whether the purser was in on *Shokoten*'s sideline, and she really did not need to know.

"The captain obtained a handheld sensor, for my security sweeps, and I'm boosting the gain. Not exactly legal, but I picked-up a few things that aren't in naval manuals."

Modifying sensors was just one of the skills Zack Decker had accumulated like a packrat accumulated junk. On long cruises aboard patrol frigates, there was a lot of spare time and a lot of boredom for the Marine complement. Most Pathfinder squadrons maintained a training program to upgrade skills, and not only purely Marine skills either. Decker had become a technical whiz of sorts on many non-weapon systems, like sensors, in his spare time aboard *Musashi*.

"Interesting," Nihao replied, in a tone that showed she found it anything but. She undressed, this time not even managing to distract the forcibly celibate Decker and crawled into bed. But the purser spent a long time watching her bunkmate at work, almond eyes narrowed.

*

"Show us your magic, Zack." Captain Strachan swung his right arm towards the container stacks filling the cavernous hold, as he, Decker and the first officer stepped through the large access hatch.

It had taken Zack two solid days of work to boost the Mark Nine. Outwardly, it still looked the same, but its innards would give a Fleet maintenance inspector fits of foaming indignation. The fact that it could be done at all would give Fleet Security nightmares trying to figure out how many former noncoms were turning old declassified sensors into units almost as powerful as the classified ones.

Decker switched the little machine on and slowly walked between the stacks, carefully sweeping each one and scrutinizing the readout on the small screen. He suddenly stopped and aimed the sensor squarely at one of the big plas crates, frowning with concentration.

"Carbine, plasma, military pattern, ten millimeter," he announced. "I can make out three dozen in this container alone."

Strachan gave him an ironic round of applause.

"Bravo, Zack. Well done. I did not tell you that our shipper already takes extraordinary precautions when we bring such a cargo anywhere but into the Shield. Your little machine has done wonders." He bowed. "My congratulations."

Decker shrugged and looked at his readout again. Those were military weapons all right, but they didn't have the usual telltale that identified them as Fleet or Army property, or legal surplus, which meant they had been manufactured without the telltale. It was impossible to remove it without destroying the weapon. And that meant these weapons had been produced primarily for the black market. If they were caught with these beauties, the authorities would not be amused.

He grunted. "To make things short and easy, which containers have contraband, apart from this one?"

"Raisa?"

The first officer nodded and walked down the narrow aisle between the stacks, pointing out random containers to Decker. His sensor detected more, many more carbines, enough to equip a rifle company, along with three dozen light machine guns and the same number of general purpose machine guns, the Marines' beloved gee-pigs.

Other merchandise caught his attention, but he didn't know the restrictions on miniature fuel cells, electronic components and the like, though the Navy was always concerned about state-of-the-art gear ending up in Shrehari hands.

"Someone on Itrul planning to start a war?" Zack asked when Darhad finished pointing out the contraband, taking care to keep his tone and expression as neutral as possible.

"Not our business, Gunner. Ours is but to deliver. I have no idea whether Itrul is even the final destination." Strachan waved his hand in a gesture of dismissal.

"I hope not, sir. Itrulans are mean fuckers, and I'd rather not see them with high-tech like this in their scaly little hands."

They'd have no use for electronics, and Zack guessed the stuff was destined for somewhere else. He wondered how he felt about that. Perhaps he should ask himself how he felt about his continued good health.

"Are you developing scruples, Gunner?" Strachan asked, a hint of steel in his voice.

"No, not really. I like to keep my hide intact, and arming Itrulans isn't a step in that direction." Zack shrugged, discarding his private reservations at the same time. "To hide these buggers, I need a masking field generator, and for that I need parts." He rattled off a list of components from memory.

"Raisa?"

"I believe engineering holds those items. I will ask the third officer to deliver them to Mister Decker's cabin."

"Thanks. I'll write down whatever else I need."

"How long?"

"Probably take me a couple of hours for the first one. The rest will be easier after that. Say three days, sir."

"Very well, Gunner."

*

"There you go, sir, take a look at the readout." Decker handed his souped-up sensor to Strachan and pointed at the first of the contraband-filled containers. It had taken Zack almost five hours to build the first unit and three hours per field generator after that. He finished them all within two and a half days. The precision work drained him and he wanted nothing more than to crawl into a gun turret and fall asleep with his head on the breech.

"I must confess I cannot see anything out of the ordinary. But I'm no combat soldier, versed in the intricacies of scanning."

"Then you'll have to take my word for it, sir. This crate looks like it has only toasters, kettles, and other kitchen delights. The one thing that can sink us is if the sensor tech twigs to the field generator itself. You can pick up residual energy readings that aren't masked by the ship's overall emissions, but you have to know what they are."

"Would your average Marine or constable know?"

"Doubt it." He shook his head. "They don't train the front line people to look for signs like that."

"Good. We can reuse these things?"

"Sure. Just tell me a couple of hours before we land and I can take 'em down."

"Well done, Gunner, well done. You're one hell of a good find for this ship." Strachan clapped him on the shoulder and left the hold.

"As the captain said, Zack, well done," Raisa smiled at him. "He may not appreciate your skill to the fullest extent, but I can read your sensor and understand how good your field generator is."

She stood behind his right shoulder so close he could sense the heat radiating from her body. Her warm breath on his cheek and her husky voice in his ear sent their customary thrills through Zack's body. Then, with no further words, she left the hold, leaving Decker as confused as ever.

*

"Merchant vessel *Shokoten*, this is the Commonwealth Star Ship *Tamerlane*. Please stand by for inspection."

"Standing by. Our shuttle bay is open and ready to receive your boarding party."

"Thank you, *Shokoten*. We'll be coming over in five minutes. *Tamerlane*, out."

"Well, Gunner," Strachan turned and nodded at Decker, "it seems your handiwork will soon be tested."

Shokoten had been intercepted by the missile frigate *Tamerlane* a few light years short the border. A routine inspection, typical for ships in transit to and from the Protectorate Zone.

"Shouldn't be a problem, sir." Zack meant it. He was relaxed, confident even. Over the last few days, he had kept busy fiddling around with his weaponry and running quickie close combat courses for the bosun's people, just in case things turned hot on Itrul. It had kept his worries from intruding.

He stared at the sleek ship displayed on the main view screen. The Liberator-class frigate exuded menace, power, and speed. The vessel was well armed, with missile launchers; gun turret blisters and behind dark squares on the blunt tip of the wedge, four torpedo launchers. Zack felt a pang of homesickness as he examined her. Then Strachan cleared his throat, motioning him to come along.

"No Marines on a missile frigate," Decker commented as he followed the captain. When they were alone in the corridor, he continued. "Sailors usually aren't as sharp as Pathfinders when it comes to sniffing out stuff, so we ought to be okay. They'll not want to waste much time inspecting an honest ship."

Strachan chuckled.

"Honest ship, eh? Is the military naive enough to base its judgment on mere subjective observations?"

"Not exactly, sir, but looks do help." At least with sailors whose experience with starlane scum was minimal.

*

The small, boxy naval shuttle settled down on the hangar bay's deck exactly five minutes later. Its rear ramp dropped and a young officer in dark blue battledress, followed by a party of similarly clad sailors, stepped out of the white craft. The ensign saluted as she saw Strachan and Decker nodded with approval. This kid had enough tact to give a merchant captain the proper courtesies, which spoke well for her.

"Ensign Krasij, frigate *Tamerlane*, sir. My captain's compliments. May I inspect your load manifest and your cargo hold?"

Krasij was a short woman, with copper hair framing a heart-shaped face dominated by high cheekbones and intense brown eyes. Though young, probably fresh out of the Academy, she had poise and sounded as confident as an officer with more experience.

"I have no objections, Ensign. Can you tell me what you are looking for?" Strachan asked, motioning her to follow him out of the hangar bay.

"Contraband mainly, sir," she replied, making a few subtle hand signals at her boarding party. "Things the Commonwealth frowns on exporting to less developed worlds. High-tech weapons, surveillance gear, medical supplies, anything that hasn't been properly cleared."

Krasij's sailors split into two groups. Three stayed by the shuttle, hands hovering near holstered blasters, eyes scanning their surroundings, while the other three, as alert as their brethren, followed Zack.

Strachan and Krasij chatted amiably along the way, the captain using his old Earth charm with consummate skill. One of the sailors, a junior petty officer, quietly scanned the ship as they went along. Decker ignored him though he was tempted to play the outraged security officer. The kid was only doing his job. But he did have a Mark Ten, like his officer.

Once inside the cargo hold, Krasij and the petty officer slowly scanned the containers, stopping at each to obtain an inventory of its contents from the dour-faced second officer.

Zack stood aside and watched the Navy crew work, wondering whether Bowdoin was in on the smuggling operation. The ensign suddenly stopped by one of the stacks and stared at her readout, frowning. She pursed her lips and glanced at the middle container, the one with the gee-pigs hidden among a load of barbeque implements. A stab of fear lanced through Zack's gut.

Of all the rotten, fucking luck, he had to get a shavetail who majored in sensor technology at the Academy. *Any moment now, this little lady will have Strachan pop open the container, and then they'd be right in it. What a way to finish. Zack Decker, retired under a cloud and caught smuggling guns.*

Then, miraculously, she moved on, her frown vanishing. Zack released his breath and tried to keep his relief well hidden. *She must have figured she saw a sensor ghost.*

Another five minutes and Ensign Krasij declared herself satisfied with the inspection. With a warm smile, she handed Captain Strachan a clearance certificate before saluting him formally and climbing aboard her shuttle. With that document in hand, no other Fleet or Constabulary ship would bother them until they crossed the border. Moments later, the boarding party left, and *Shokoten* was home free.

"Thought we were blown for a moment there," Strachan chuckled as he slapped Decker on the shoulder. His laughter sounded tense, almost forced. "But your little gizmos did the trick. Good work, Zack."

As he watched the captain walk away, Decker frowned. *Why did he have the impression there was something Strachan wasn't telling him? He looked a little too uptight for what just happened as if there were more than just guns in the containers.*

He shook off his thoughts and secured the shuttle hangar. Moments after he closed the door, the hyperjump warning blared through the ship. Zack felt the stomach-twisting burst of nausea that accompanied every shift to and from normal space while the lights flickered for a fraction of a second. Then, body and ship settled down as both sailed at many times the speed of light in their own bubble where everything was twisted and distorted.

Next stop, Itrul. Oorah!
Decker grimaced and returned to his cabin.

— EIGHT —

The ship lurched as the battle stations siren erased Decker's highly charged dream of Raisa Darhad doing things a proper first officer shouldn't do.

With a grunt, the gunner dropped out of his bunk and reached for his battledress, instinctively sure that this wasn't a drill. Within seconds, he was dressed, armed and fully awake, the adrenaline already pumping through his bloodstream. He reached down and shook Kiani's bare shoulder.

"Up and at 'em, Nihao. Battle stations and it doesn't sound like a drill."

"Huh?" A sleepy voice grunted.

"It's a great day to die, Mister Kiani," Zack grinned as he gave her a final shake, before leaving his cabin for the bridge.

When he got there, the ship's nerve center wallowed in pandemonium. An FTL torpedo, narrowly missing *Shokoten*, had forced her out of hyperspace. This deep within the Protectorate, there could be only one answer. Decker slipped into his seat and glanced over towards the command chair. Fifth Officer Sladek had the con.

"Where away, sir?"

"I don't know, Gunner," he rasped, fear making his eyes dart here and there. "You have control of all defensive systems."

"Thank you, sir." At Zack's touch, the tactical board came to life.

First the shields.

All six shield generators were operational and at full power. Not bad for a civilian ship. Zack grunted with satisfaction. His status board showed all gun turrets ready and loaded, all missile launchers active and the fire control system standing-by.

The little modifications he'd made were paying off. This was the first time all defensive systems were up without any malfunctions.

Now where was the bastard?

Fingers dancing over the console, Decker reached out across the cold void to find the unseen enemy that had forced them off course. He vaguely knew that the command crew had taken their stations and that the captain was asking for status updates from all departments except gunnery. He knew better than to disturb Decker when the former Marine was hunting.

"Navigation, current position?" Strachan sounded worried beneath his composed exterior.

"Unknown. I have to recalculate our position before we can move. We're not exactly following the standard star lanes."

"How long?"

The fourth officer grimaced. "Fifteen or twenty minutes at least. I need readings off a few major stars and triangulate."

"Damn. Engineering, status."

"No damage, sir," Sonoda's voice sounded tinny and distorted over the intercom. "But I'll want to run a level two systems check before we jump. That torpedo was close."

"How long?"

"Can't tell yet."

"Then get on it."

"Aye, aye, sir. Engineering, out."

"Captain!" Zack's tone was just loud and urgent enough to cut through the hubbub.

"Yes, Mister Decker?"

"I have a contact. Five hundred thousand kilometers off our port bow, turning and closing. Looks like a corvette-sized ship. No friend-or-foe transponder."

"Could it be friendly?" Strachan's tone showed he knew how naïve his question was.

"Not a chance, sir. Military vessels in the sector are too busy chasing the bad guys to bother with a merchant and they'd have a transponder."

"How do you know this is the one?"

"Extrapolation, sir.   Whoever's shooting at us in hyperspace is bound to emerge a few seconds after we do because you never know exactly what your torpedo will do. No choice but to end up being ahead of us. Half a million kilometers sounds about right for a sharp helmsman."

"At least we have time to prepare, and if we are lucky, to escape."

"Perhaps, but I wouldn't count on it." As he spoke, Zack never took his eyes off his scanners. "We're pretty evenly matched. In a slugfest, I'd put my money on us because we'll have better maintained, Commonwealth-built gear. If he has any smarts at all, so would he, unless he's a total fucking newbie who doesn't know an armed freighter from a garbage scow."

"Then why?" Strachan sounded puzzled.

"He isn't alone is why," Decker replied between clenched teeth. His anxiety levels were rising now. He wasn't finding the other ships he knew had to be there.

Where the hell were they? That cocksucker out there wasn't doing this himself. Pirates worked in wolf packs out here. Where?

Then, a sudden thought occurred to him. The fourth officer said they weren't on the regular star lanes. Merchants usually stuck to the marked routes because they're patrolled and because they're patrolled, the scum stays away. That might be why he couldn't find the other ships yet. They weren't near enough. Maybe this beauty here had been the first to spot them. Were they sweeping *Shokoten*'s route by accident, or did they know we were coming? If they knew, what did they want, apart from a good ship? The contraband cargo?

"Three more contacts emerging aft. Two corvette-sized, one smaller. Range four hundred thousand kilometers. We're being boxed in."

"Damn." Strachan slammed his fist against his chair's side. "What are our chances, Zack?"

"Depends on what they want."

"What do you mean?"

"If they want our hull, they'll be real careful to capture us without damaging the ship. If they want our bodies, they'll try to shoot off our engines. If they want our cargo, it could be either way, depending on whether they're in a hurry and whether they have the space in their own holds. I'd rather they want the ship. It gives us more time and chances to escape."

"Incoming message from the ship ahead, sir," the signalman's mate sounded scared.

"What?" Zack and Strachan asked in unison, turning to look at the young woman.

"Put it through," the captain said.

"Most fucking unusual, sir," Zack slowly shook his head, puzzled.

The cruel face of a Shrehari of the Imperial race appeared on the main view screen. His swarthy, ridged forehead gleamed in the low, smoky light of his own bridge. Sharp teeth appeared behind a cruel smile. Scars covered one side of his face, vanishing beneath his long, black hair. His black within black eyes gleamed with malice as he looked at *Shokoten*'s bridge crew.

"Surrender or die, humans." The Anglic words sounded harsh, distorted by the alien's guttural voice.

Decker glanced at Strachan, willing him to reply, to say something insulting and dismissive, and to show no weakness in front of such a dangerous enemy. To keep him talking until they were within firing range. Then he froze.

The bastard was bluffing. He wanted something on this ship, and he didn't want to risk damaging it by shooting. Otherwise, he'd have fired a few shots to disable *Shokoten*.

Zack looked over at Darhad and their eyes met. She nodded minutely as if she had read the gunner's thoughts and agreed. Her right hand danced over her console.

"Sound and vid off," she said, her tone neutral and controlled. "I think he's bluffing, Captain."

"I agree," Decker said.

"Why?" Strachan licked his lips nervously.

"You'd know better than me, sir," Zack replied. "Fact is, pirates never give you a chance to react. They shoot first because they know no one in his right mind will just give up, especially not with a well-armed ship.   Out here, Shrehari aren't regular pirates most of the time, anyway. A lot of them work for Imperial Intelligence.”

“What are our options?” The captain's confident tone sounded false.

“Take a navigation fix and jump. Turn this into a chase. If they're serious about getting *Shokoten* unharmed, we can head back for the patrolled star lanes and pray there's help to be found.”

“Do we have one yet, Mister Gareth?”

“No, sir. Still working on it.”

“Humans, you have thirty of your seconds to drop shields and prepare to be boarded. If you cooperate, we will not harm you.” The Shrehari captain's voice boomed from of the loudspeakers.

“Or we can surrender and hope he's telling the truth,” Zack concluded, his shrug speaking more than words. He glanced at his scanners again. The pirates were staying out of range.   They probably knew what sort of weapons *Shokoten* carried. Decker grimaced. Not a good thing at all.

An idea grew in the back of his mind, something the captain of *Musashi* had tried when a trio of marauders had jumped them.

“Captain, I have a solution that may or may not work. But it's better than just sitting here, or believing that charming asshole out there would actually let us live after we surrender.”

Darhad reacted first. “Speak, Gunner.”

“On my mark, accelerate towards the lead pirate and prepare for a micro jump. He'll be startled enough that we ought to get in a good lick before vanishing. We won't know where we'll emerge, but neither will he. With any luck, by the time he finds us again, we'll have a fix.”

“Unplotted jumps are highly dangerous,” Strachan replied, a hint of fear showing in his voice. “We can end in limbo.”

Zack grinned at the captain.

“Limbo's a tale to scare young navigators in training, sir. The ships who vanished went to an alternate dimension where their crews are living a life of leisure. Is it a go, sir, or do I drop the shields?"

"It's a go. Helm, set course at maximum sublight for the ship dead ahead and place hyperdrive online. Engage at my mark; jump at the gunner's mark."

"Aye, aye, sir. Length of jump?" Gareth sounded terrified.

"Make it ten light minutes."

"Ready."

"Engage."

With a burst of power that surprised even her crew, *Shokoten* accelerated towards the lead ship. Decker brought all guns and launchers to bear, finger hovering over the firing button, waiting to come within can't-miss range.

"Firing now!" Decker released a barrage of plasma and missiles.

"Jump!"

Before he even had a chance to check his salvo's effectiveness, nausea gripped him and broke his concentration. No sooner had it gone that the emergence nausea set in and *Shokoten* winked back into normal space millions of kilometers away.

"Nav, I need a fix. Gunner, any signs of pursuit?"

"Not so far, sir. They're beyond our range. I figure it'll take 'em a few minutes to react, more if I manage a clean hit on the lead ship. I suggest we have another micro jump laid in, so that when they find us, we can vamoose right away. They won't give us another chance to pull this stunt."

"Nav, you heard the gunner. Give us a fifteen light minute jump this time."

The minutes passed with maddening slowness. Apart from Gareth, who was frantically trying to fix their position and Decker, who was scanning space for emergence signs, the others were reduced to waiting with mounting anxiety.

"Four traces seven hundred thousand kilometers off our port side. I can't tell for sure, but one of the ships is leaking radiation. I must have smacked him hard with that salvo."

"How long before they're in range?" Strachan asked.

"Three, four minutes, sir. Enough to last a lifetime."

"A very short lifetime. Nav, if you have a fix, now's the moment to do it."

"I'm trying, sir." Gareth's voice now had a hint of hysteria.

"Incoming!" Decker grabbed his chair's armrests and braced himself. "For what we're about to receive..."

The ship shook as a pair of missiles exploded against the shields.

"I thought they weren't supposed to be in range yet, Decker," Strachan shouted over the groaning of the stressed hull as energy fields fought against each other, bathing the ship in a bright glow.

"The bastards have themselves high-speed, long-range shit, sir. Commonwealth military grade, not Imperial. Someone's been selling 'em stuff they shouldn't have."

Strachan looked at his gunner in astonishment, stung by the accusation underlying his words.

"No damage," Decker continued. "Shields holding at half-power. Another one like that and we lose number five. If you can turn the ship ninety degrees on its central axis, we'll give 'em an undamaged shield for the next salvo."

"Do it, helm." Darhad barked out. "Nav, prepare for micro jump."

"Just another minute, sir, and I'll have a fix," Gareth replied with a note of desperation in his tone. Zack couldn't tell if he was more scared of jumping blind again or of the pirates.

Another hit shook the ship and Zack swore as the feedback from the overloaded shields ran through the ship's electronics, shorting out systems all over the ship.

"Firing a brace of missiles." Then, "starboard launcher's out. So is the subspace commo array."

"Nav, prepare to jump."

"Just a few moments more, sir. Entering course for the main star lanes."

Shokoten shivered again, and again, under the relentless battering of the pirate guns. A part of Decker's mind noted the care with which each burst was fired as if they were trying to estimate the exact moment her shields would collapse and leave her open to boarding.

He shot back, but the freighter's guns didn't make enough of an impression on their shields. *Shokoten* however, couldn't take much more of the Shrehari's pounding.

"Ready, sir," Gareth shouted out, sounding strangled.

"Helm, engage."

A plasma bolt glanced off the front shield, its glow brightening the bridge even through the view screen's filters, as the ship turned to aim at the new jump point. Then, the familiar nausea gripped them again, and they were off into hyperspace, safe for the moment.

Strachan slumped back into his chair.

"Secure from battle stations."

"With all due respect, sir," Zack interjected, turning to face his captain, "they'll pursue. I wouldn't be surprised at another torpedo attack to knock us back into normal space. The buggers want something on this ship and they aren't about to let up."

After a moment, Strachan nodded.

"Belay my last order. Damage reports from all departments."

"Aye, aye, sir."

"Sir, starboard launcher's out. I'll have to go see on the spot. I suspect electronics overload. Apart from that, the shields will recharge as normal. There doesn't seem to be any permanent damage."

"Okay." Strachan stood. "First Officer, Gunner, with me. You have the con Mister Gareth. Pipe the full damage report to my cabin."

When the cabin door slid closed with a soft whisper, the captain headed straight for his small bar, tucked away in a dark firewood cabinet behind his desk. He pulled out a bottle of single malt scotch and held it up, looking at Darhad and Decker.

"No thanks, sir." Decker shook his head. He preferred to stay sober until he was sure they had lost the pirates, which made quite a change from the man who'd crawled into a bottle the day they took away his career. Darhad, whose Arkanna metabolism could handle alcohol a lot better than humans could, accepted a healthy slug.

"Sit." When they were comfortably seated, the captain stared at Zack with cold eyes. "Mister Decker, let us clarify one thing right now. The knowledge about our, ah, special cargo is very restricted, and I wish to keep it this way. You will refrain from speculating openly on the bridge and stick to doing your job, which is protecting this ship. Do I make myself clear?”

His tone raised Zack's hackles. He opened his mouth to reply when he caught Darhad's meaningful glance. She gave him a minute shake of the head. With a shrug, he swallowed his words before they were formed.

“Aye, aye, sir,” he replied instead, looking down at his feet. “Permission to ask a question, sir?”

Strachan didn't smile at the gunner's phrasing.

“Go ahead.”

“Are we carrying anything that could warrant a pirate's particular attentions? Apart from the stuff I know is in the hold.”

The captain stroked his beard, dark eyes boring into Zack's baby blues.

“You're asking a lot of me, aren't you,” he finally said.

“Either you trust me, or you fire me, captain. My job is to keep the ship and its cargo safe. For that, I need to know everything. And if you think I might rat on you, then space me.” Decker held Strachan's stare. “No one in the Commonwealth will cry the day they fish my body out of a deep vacuum.”

“He's right, captain,” Raisa's soft voice intruded on the two men.

“Oh, very well.” Strachan sounded angry. “I have a case of Heyken-Avrilus accelerator chips in my cabin. That's probably what the bastards wanted. They're worth their weight in antimatter in the badlands, especially since the Imperials could never make copies with the same high resonance factor. I'd say the case is worth more to them than our entire cargo.”

“Thank you, sir.” Zack nodded. “Now for the clincher. Who else knew about your case of magic chips?”

“Raisa,” he pointed his bearded chin at the Arkanna, “and the contractor.”

“Then assuming the first officer isn't a pirate mole, I'd say the contractor has a leak. Or he has one hell of an insurance policy riding on those chips.”

“No insurance company covers contraband,” Strachan replied in a flat tone.

"Sure," Zack shrugged, "but even I know a dozen dodges around that. He's covered, believe me. Any chance I could take a look at those chips?"

"Why?" The captain asked.

"Pure, idle nosiness," Decker grinned. "And to check something out."

Strachan clearly wasn't willing, but a nod from Darhad and a growing curiosity overcame his reticence. He opened his closet and pulled out an iridium case with a palm lock, placing it on the desk with exaggerated gentleness.

When he opened the case, Zack leaned over his shoulder and picked up a chip. He examined it under the bright light of the cabin. A knowing grin spread over his broad features. That smile quickly changed into an amused laugh.

"You've been had, captain," he finally told a puzzled Strachan, when his laughter died away. "These aren't Heyken-Avrilus latinum accelerator chips. They're cheap knock-offs that undoubtedly work in low-grade civilian ordnance, but would never suffice for advanced military grade weapons. Even the Shrehari can do better."

"So the contractor set us up." Strachan sounded indignant, which only provoked more laughter from Zack.

"When you deal with sharks, sir, you gotta expect 'em to try for a bite. I've seen this sort of scam."

"He'll pay for it, be assured of that," Strachan growled.

"He won't be there for revenge when we return, sir."

"Oh, I'll find him. He took on the wrong people. I have access to resources he's never dreamed about, nor have you."

"Care to explain, sir?" Decker asked, eyebrows raised.

Strachan hesitated again.

"This information must not be discussed outside my cabin, Gunner."

"Aye, aye, sir."

"Have you ever heard of the Amali family?"

"Yes, sir." Zack nodded soberly. There wasn't a Pathfinder alive who didn't know about the Amalis and their commercial empire, and who didn't hate them with a passion.

They were a political force without equal in the Commonwealth, a force that had corrupted scores of senators and effectively controlled the Secretary General's chair. Rumors also had them as the engine of something called the Coalition. It was reputed to be a shadowy collection of politicos, aristocrats, and financial magnates who wanted a return to the days from before the Second Migration Wars, when the central systems controlled the Commonwealth.

The Amalis were also rumored to have a stake in most of the profitable operations in the badlands, illegal businesses like slavery, drug running, organ farming, and worse. Zack had often fought pirates equipped with human-manufactured high-tech gear. But the Amalis had proven untouchable, thanks to their political influence. Money was the ultimate armor.

"*Shokoten*'s ultimate owners are the Amalis, and they don't take such incidents lightly."

"Yes, sir," Decker repeated, unsure of what else to say, or feel. Or even think. "Sir," he finally said, desperate to be alone, "I have a launcher to fix and a ship to check out. If you'll excuse me."

"Certainly, Gunner. And thank you for that display of tactical finesse. You saved our hides." Strachan was all smiles and charm again.

"Anytime, sir." He grinned as he stood, but felt sick inside. "I wouldn't say no to a performance bonus."

Strachan smiled. "Getting the weapons to our customer will give us all a nice little bonus, Zack."

When Decker was gone, the captain took a sip of his whiskey and glanced at his first officer.

"You know, Raisa, our gunner is much smarter than either of us realized. I didn't know Marine noncommissioned officers were that good. We're lucky to have him, as long as he remains a team player. But I wonder. His reaction to our owner's name was rather strong, though he hid it well."

"I sense no deception within him, Diego. He is curious, yes, and a bit confused, but that is understandable." What Raisa Darhad didn't understand was her sudden decision to lie to Strachan and hide Decker's actual reaction.

*

Zack grunted as he pulled the starboard launcher's power coupling. It was fried. The feedback shielding had been sub-standard crap. After crawling out of the access tube, he went down to engineering to hunt for a replacement part. The senior engineer's mate wordlessly led him to the spares locker and left him to his own devices.

Decker still wasn't liked in engineering, but Strachan had made it quite clear that the gunner received what the gunner wanted. And after today's display, no one in his or her right mind would deny him.

An hour later, Zack slipped a modified module into place. It wasn't perfect, but with his little tweaks, it would do the job as well as a dedicated unit.

He nodded with satisfaction as the launcher's control systems came back online. Now all he had to do before returning to bed was check every remaining launcher and turret. This had been the first time he'd fired them in earnest, and many things could have come loose, but guns were like anything else: the more you used them, the better they worked.

*

By the time he finished his inspection, it was past four bells in the morning watch, yet his mind still gnawed at Strachan's revelations. Nihao wasn't in her bunk when he entered their cabin. He stripped down to his skivvies, climbed into bed and lay there, hands under his head, staring straight at the ceiling.

A short while later, the door opened, admitting the purser who immediately stripped to prepare for her shower. She stopped mid-way and straightened up, hands on her hips, and looked at Zack. Usually, he sneaked a peek at her whenever he could and lately, Nihao seemed to enjoy teasing him. But this time, he ignored her.

"Are you trying to stare a hole through the bulkhead, Zack?"

"What?" Decker broke out of his deep thoughts and turned his head towards her. Then, he grinned. She looked magnificent, like a marble statue, the muscles beneath her dusky skin rippling, her small breasts rising with every breath she took. Before his reaction could become too visible, he turned over on his stomach.

"Just reviewing the attack, seeing what else I could have done. Guess I'm too keyed up to sleep yet." *And you aren't helping one bit, lady. Now either jump me or go away.*

To his disappointment, she vanished into the small lavatory. When she returned, Zack's eyes were drilling through the bulkhead again, and she didn't interrupt him.

Without a word, Nihao shut the lights and went to bed. Her conscience must have been clear because she fell asleep at once. Not Zack. For him, sleep wouldn't come, and he rose to take his regular day watch still as pensive as he had been hours earlier.

*

The coordinates Fourth Officer Gareth had fixed after the micro jump were good and *Shokoten* reached the more densely traveled space lanes without further problems.

Either the pirates had given up, or they could not track them. There was no way for anyone aboard the freighter to tell which. Sensors were limited in hyperspace and useless aft where the 'wake' of the hyperdrive scrambled everything.

In due course, *Shokoten* reached Itrul and dropped out of hyperspace unmolested. She swung into orbit and waited for the primitive spacecon to assign them a landing corridor.

Itrul was close to Earth norm but much drier and warmer. Its oceans were small, and its landmasses broad. The seven major continents, one of which spanned a quarter of the surface of the planet, were arid, especially so in the center where the moisture from the seas never reached. Cloud cover was sparse, revealing a mottled globe, tan or light brown in color, broken by irregular patches of dark blue, or black. Very little green showed from high orbit.

"Looks like a charming place," Zack muttered as his sensors gave him a running commentary on the world below. "Sand, lots of it, and sentient reptiles who'd just as soon kill you as look at you."

"Now, now, Gunner. Don't be so prejudiced," Darhad murmured from the captain's chair. "You know Itrulans only from your bloody encounters with them. They are, on the whole, interesting people. Fierce, yes, warlike too. But they have a strong sense of honor, and they're very, very tough. Evolving on an arid world like this takes good genes."

"Didn't evolve very far until we found 'em, and more's the pity. We should've left the bastards to continue in their old ways. Might have wiped each other out."

"Maybe, maybe not, Gunner. When we land, visit. We will have plenty of time for you to explore. It's not as bad as you may think."

"Not too quick on the cargo handling, are they?"

"They lack the technology, Mister Decker. Everything on Itrul is still done by hand or with animal power. They have only one spaceport, Tanira. The rest of the planet is roughly at Earth's fourteenth-century levels."

"Huh," Zack grunted. "Means that someone's keeping all the goodies to himself."

"Quite correct." Yes, Diego was right, she thought. Our former Marine sergeant was a lot smarter than we gave him credit. "The Akmin of Tanira, the title I believe can be loosely translated as Sultan, is the most powerful of the many feudal rulers on Itrul, and he is the nominal overlord of the main continent. He keeps most of the technology for himself and his household, preferring to give only dribs and drabs to the lesser lords and nothing at all to the people."

"I'll bet he's slowly getting full control of the planet, thanks to the advanced tech we nice spacers sell him. Plus, of course, any Itrulan merc who makes it home in one piece after a few years with high-tech outfits is one hell of an addition to his household troops."

Armed with the marvelous contraband weapons down in the cargo hold, the Akmin was about expand his empire very quickly.

"I always figured there were regulations against fucking up an alien civilization by giving them stuff they aren't ready to have for another couple of centuries."

"Only where the writ of the Commonwealth, or more precisely, the power of the Navy runs. In the Protectorate, there are no rules." Darhad didn't sound sorry. To her, it was just business, a way to make a living and let the hindmost take care of the moral issues.

"Yeah and look where it got us. Same as with the fucking Shield Cluster at the other end of the Commonwealth: sword carrying barbarian pirates in cobbled-together starships preying on anything that moves. Sort of screws up their planet's economy after a while when the bastards think of piracy as a major industry. Once it gets to that point, it becomes impossible to stop short of bombing them back to their version of the Stone Age."

"You have a point, Mister Decker." Darhad nodded thoughtfully, eyes on the dun-colored planet.

"Sir," the signalman's mate called out, "we have a message from Tanira ground control. We may begin our descent."

"Thank you. Nav, check your course and lay in."

"Checked and laid in, sir."

"Helm, engage." She tapped a key on the chair's armrest. "Captain, we are descending to Tanira spaceport."

"Acknowledged. On my way."

*

"They make us land early, then let us wait for days before they unload the cargo. It raises the landing fees considerably." Second Officer Bowdoin's deep, somber voice sounded mournful as he accompanied Decker on his security inspection around the ship. "The Itrulans are not very subtle, but they're greedy. It might be days before we see the stevedores."

"I guess you've been here before?"

"Four times. Repeated visits don't make the place more congenial. I will be glad when we lift."

They stopped at the main airlock and Decker, using his handheld sensor, swept the area.

"That's it then, sir. The ship's as secure as I can make it. There'll be two people on guard here, armed of course, and the other airlocks are hard-wired into the security system. It'll be a different kettle of antimatter when we unload, but with a full security complement."

Bosun Kader would provide the bodies, no questions asked. Just then, footsteps sounded in the passageway and two brawny bosun's mates with plasma carbines of an obsolete but nonetheless lethal model, appeared.

"Morning, Gunner," the elder of the two, a red-faced blonde from Farhaven Colony nodded with politeness. Farhaveners had a special place in their hearts just to hate Commonwealth Marines, but Harris didn't seem to mind Decker, or at least she didn't show it.

"Morning, Harris, Yassa.   You know the sentry procedures?"

"Aye, sir." Both nodded and Harris enumerated the rules before Zack even asked. Another of Kader's changes. She liked to have a taut crew and made sure they did everything by the numbers which was something Decker could appreciate. And did.

"Right. The duty roster's on the computer. Enjoy."

"Thank you, sir."

When Bowdoin and Decker had walked out of earshot of the guards, the second officer glanced at Zack.

"Do you intend to visit, Mister Decker?"

"I guess so. The first officer tells me there are a few things to see and learn, and I'm never averse to a bit of liberty. I have to maintain the tradition."

"Ah yes, First Officer Darhad has an open mind about other cultures and civilizations." Bowdoin's voice was carefully neutral, ensuring that his listener did not think he was criticizing his alien supervisor. But Decker's trained ear detected a hint of well-hidden dislike. Perhaps Bowdoin was xenophobic. Many humans had a hard time dealing with non-human sentients.

"If she recommended you visit, then go, and make up your own mind. But always watch your back. More than one spacer has vanished forever in Tanira's darker alleys. Though I believe you are used to rougher ways."

Zack grinned ruefully.

"In the Corps, you learn to take care of yourself real fast, sir."

"Yes, so I understand."   Bowdoin nodded, "so I understand. Well, as you told your sentries, enjoy."

"Thank you, sir."

*

Nihao Kiani was off on business somewhere in town when Zack returned to his cabin after reporting the ship secure. Probably a human ship chandler's business here too. Pursers had an easy life in space, but when the ship landed they sweated their butts off. At least that's what Zack figured.

He stripped off his battledress and took a quick shower, barely soaking his skin. Then, when he had dried off, he put on his one set of civvies. After a moment's thought, he also slipped on his leather jacket.

It would be too warm, but the tough synth leather would protect him from any 'accidental' knife thrusts, and it would hide his own arsenal. He strapped his fighting knife to his right forearm and, after a moment's hesitation, slipped his blaster in a specially designed inner pocket under his left arm. The ship's data banks on Itrul had mentioned no strict laws or taboos against personal weapons. That didn't mean there weren't any, but Zack's experiences with Itrulan mercs were enough to call for heavy ordnance.

He thrust his hands in the jacket pockets to settle it on his broad shoulders and unexpectedly, his right hand encountered something hard and metallic, about the size of a dress uniform insignia, and he pulled it out, mystified. He opened his hand and looked at the object in his palm, eyebrows shooting up in surprise. It was a metallic, gold colored Marine Corps Master Gunner insignia: a stylized representation of an antique, muzzle-loading field gun with spoked wheels.

How the hell did that get in there?

Zack opened his locker and pulled out his black Marine undress tunic, to pin the badge back on. He couldn't repress a grunt of surprise. The Master Gunner's badge was still there, pinned to the right breast pocket. Last time he checked, he only had one of these little beauties, the one the CO gave him on parade when he qualified. Where did the second one come from?

He turned it around in his fingers, thinking. The last time he'd worn the leather jacket had been on Pradyn. Since the evening he and Darhad had been attacked, he'd had no liberty. Personal closets on the ship had coded locks, so it was unlikely someone broke into his without leaving a trace, to slip the badge into the jacket's pocket. It wasn't impossible. Very few things involving humans were. But why?

And if on Pradyn, when? He would have noticed anyone drop it into his pocket because he hadn't become all that dull yet. The trainees at the Pathfinder School Battalion hadn't called him *The Cat* for nothing. He bet the stupid pickpocket who tried him out in New Aberdeen still didn't have full use of his right arm.

Zack sat down at his desk and shook his head in puzzlement. He examined the badge again but couldn't see anything out of the ordinary. It looked just like the one on his tunic. He pulled his sensor out of the desk's lower drawer and scanned the badge. His first scans showed precisely... nothing. It was solid alloy, even if it didn't read like the same alloy as his real one. Then, he ran a visual check and scrutinized every bit of the badge's surface.

Bingo!

On the back of the insignia, someone had etched a few lines of writing so small they wouldn't show up under the naked eye. A real precision job that could only have been done by a computer-controlled micro laser. After reading the words, Zack sat back in his chair and took a deep breath, struggling to set his thoughts in order.

Why would someone give him a Master Gunner's badge with the motto of the 902nd Pathfinders and the words Duty, Honor, Loyalty etched in letters so small you needed a sensor to read them? And what were 'they' trying to tell him? The Fleet had kicked him out, pensioned him off like a bad bargain.

A knock on the door broke Zack's train of thought.

"Come."

With a soft sigh, the panel vanished into the wall, revealing a black-clad, smiling Raisa Darhad. She wore a skin-tight sleeveless sweater that outlined her high, firm breasts like a second skin, a calf length pleated skirt and high, black boots.

Unless she hid it under her dress, there was nowhere for her to carry a weapon. Of course, she didn't need a gun. Her built-in defenses were enough, as he had witnessed.

Zack barely restrained an appreciative whistle at her appearance, but let his eyes run admiringly over her, not caring whether she noticed. Darhad smiled at him, lips slightly parted and cocked her head. She didn't need her empathic talents to read his attraction.

"I thought you would need a guide in town and since the captain decreed that personnel should go in pairs, and I had no one..." Her voice was inviting, almost seductive, and Decker immediately forgot all about the mystery badge.

"I would be honored, sir," he finally stammered out.

She stepped into the cabin and noticed the shiny little object in his hand.

"What is that?"

"Oh," Decker's rising excitement was pushed aside as he remembered the mysterious inscription. This was not something he wanted to share. "Just my old Master Gunner's insignia. I guess I was getting sentimental." He opened the top drawer of his desk and dropped the badge into a small tray.

"If you have nothing else to do, why not go now?"

"*Avec plaisir*," he replied, grinning.

*

The dry, flinty Itrulan air caught Zack's throat by surprise, and he coughed once, blinking his eyes against the bright, white sun.

"If this is one of their more temperate areas, I'd hate to wander into this place's version of the tropics."

Darhad laughed.

"You get used to it, Zack. It gets better in town."

Decker noticed she'd used his first name, the signal to drop all shipboard formality.

"I sure as hell hope so. If not, I'll blow my pay on cold beer."

"Come." She touched his arm and walked into the sunshine towards the terminal building, her skirts swirling around her long legs.

Itrul had no customs to speak of; they didn't need any.

All off worlders had to sell their merchandise through the Akmin's agents, on pain of death. The lone Itrulan guard in the terminal didn't even deign to notice the human and his Arkanna companion.

As they strode through, Zack caught his first glimpse of the local architecture. Raisa had been right to say this place was still mired in their equivalent of Earth's middle ages.

The terminal building was built of cut stone, and judging by the roughness, the Itrulans had done their cutting with tools considerably more primitive than lasers. Wood beams, blackened with age, supported a slate roof. The windows were glazed, but the quality of the glass was such that it distorted everything beyond recognition. A few technological artefacts appeared here and there, looking like highly uncomfortable grafts on a primitive body. Whatever modern space traffic control and communications gear they had, wasn't displayed for all to see.

They walked along a dusty cobblestone road towards the towering ramparts of Tanira, admiring the barbarous splendor of the city. The heat was oppressive, and Zack sweated beneath his leather jacket. He began to wonder whether being armed was all that necessary if it meant melting to death.

They met a few carts, drawn by thickset, four-legged reptiles with leathery, dun-colored hide. The carters ignored the off worlders, just as they ignored the other pedestrians, Itrulan or otherwise. Covered merchandise filled the awkward wooden wagons, weighing them down enough to make the wooden axles creak in distress.

Other off worlders walked along the road, many of them from races that Zack had never encountered. They either glanced at the tall human with frank curiosity or pretended to ignore him, the latter being the typical reaction of the few Shrehari they met. Raisa Darhad though drew her share of admiring or alarmed looks.

The two spacers stopped at the foot of the giant ramparts, a few meters short of the massive, open gate. Tanira's defenses were massive. The walls, reddish cliffs almost fifty meters high, had been built with blocks of stone as large as a shuttlecraft. Watchtowers, rising even higher, anchored the wall every few hundred meters.

The outer defenses seemed in good repair, and Itrulan soldiers with halberds patrolled the walls, cutting barbarous silhouettes against the bright blue sky. The gate itself was large enough to admit a column of tanks three wide and higher than a battleship's hyperdrives. Metallic, studded doors, nearly a meter thick, lay open before them, recessed into the passage walls on either side.

They stepped into the shadows and merged with the flow of beings entering the city, carried into the depths of the thick walls, past soldiers wearing leather harnesses and carrying spears with strangely forged blades. When they finally emerged on the other side, they entered a fantastic metropolis redolent of an era that lay far in Earth's or Arkanna's past.

Three and four story houses built of multicolor stone were piled against each other on either side of the thoroughfare. Most sported garish signs in a script Decker couldn't decipher, advertising wares he wasn't sure he wanted to identify. Loud Itrulan merchants bellowed across the street, boasting of their wares and trying to attract customers. Exotic smells and unmistakable stenches assailed Zack's nostrils, washing away the dry flint of the open plain.

Here too, members of a dozen or more species moved among the reptilian natives, and for the first time, Zack saw a pair of humans idly haggling with an Itrulan merchant.

An open sewer ran through the middle of the cobblestone street, and Decker quickly averted his eyes from the putrefying mess that filled it. The natives seemed to ignore the stone gulley, deftly stepping over it or using the small bridges built at regular intervals.

He felt long, warm fingers grasp him as Raisa took his hand. Startled he glanced at her.

"Come," she smiled at him, her voice cutting through the buzz of the crowd, "I will show you the Akmin's palace in Tanira's center. It merits seeing."

She dragged him through what seemed like kilometers of crowded cobblestone streets. Tanira was a lively city, more animated than most Decker had seen, and smelly. As they neared the city center, the houses became richer and more gaudily decorated, just as the Itrulans seemed better dressed. But the stench of excrement and rotting meat remained.

Many of the wealthy inhabitants made their way across town on the backs of long-legged, nervous-looking reptiles that bore more than a passing resemblance to Earth's prehistoric velociraptors. Zack also saw Itrulans with steel collars around their necks and dressed in the drab livery of indentured servants. He squeezed Raisa's hand to stop her stately progress through the throngs.

"What are those sad sacks with the collars?" He asked, already suspecting the answer.

"Slaves. The Itrulan economy depends heavily on slavery in many areas, such as mining, forestry, and agriculture. And of course, household work in the wealthier mansions."

"I knew I didn't like this place for a reason."

"Consider it this way, Zack. When your planet was in its Middle Ages, about the same era as these people are, was there no slavery? Were your ancestors not exploiting the labor of others?"

That stopped him cold in his tracks.

"I guess you're right. I'm seeing this place through the eyes of a twenty-sixth-century human, not a pre-gunpowder Itrulan. Lesson well taken, Professor Darhad." He smiled mischievously. "Is or was there slavery on your home world?"

She laughed.

"An Arkanna in captivity is a very dangerous thing." Her talons briefly dug into Zack's hand, reinforcing the point. "No. There never was such a thing. A rarity in the known galaxy, I believe. And before you ask, no, the Itrulans don't use off world captives as slaves. At least not as heavy labor. If there are any, they're kept as pets by wealthy nobles. Most other space faring species don't have the brute strength this planet requires."

They resumed walking and Raisa led him around a corner onto a large plaza.

The Akmin's palace filled Zack's field of vision with gracefully sculpted rose, green, and blue spires, smooth, curved ramparts and pointy watchtowers. A keep within a keep.   But in contrast to the rest of Tanira, the palace exuded an otherworldly grace and culture absent from the typical Itrulan architecture. Zack was impressed and said so.

"I am glad you enjoy the sight, Zack," Raisa replied, smiling. "Unfortunately, we cannot visit the interior which, I am told, is magnificent. The only commoners ever invited inside are those condemned to suffer the punishments of the Akmin's executioner. I understand he enjoys devising and carrying out novel ways of killing off his less desirable subjects. The plaza here is also used for public executions, of which there are several each week. Not today, however."

"Thank God," Decker muttered in disgust.

"The Itrulans don't value life as strongly as you humans. Perhaps it comes from producing so many young to see only a few survive to adulthood. A common problem among egg-laying species."

"Now that we've seen the beast, what's next?"

"I propose we refresh ourselves. It's almost time for the evening meal and I know a comfortable inn where we can spend a few hours of enjoyment."

— NINE —

They went back the way they came, retracing their steps for a few hundred meters. As Raisa led Zack onto a narrower side street, the small hairs on the back of his neck stood up. Someone was watching him again.

Did the unknown watchers have anything to do with the mysterious, inscribed Master Gunner's badge, and with *Shokoten*'s smuggling? He wondered, shaking his head in annoyance while concentrating on dodging the throngs of reptilian humanoids as he followed Darhad, tugged along by her warm hand.

Soon, he found he also had to focus on memorizing the twists and turns they took to reach her 'place of enjoyment.' As on Pradyn, the Arkanna seemed to have an intimate knowledge of the alien city. Whether it was instinct left over from her predatory forebears or simply an innate ability was something Zack couldn't figure out.

After what he figured was almost two kilometers, she stopped beneath a subdued sign in Itrulan that the gunner couldn't decipher to save his life.

"We have arrived, Zack. The Rasstaszykar."

"Sounds like an exotic disease or a Kardati tribesman's sneeze."

She chuckled at Decker's dry tone.

"It means Heaven's Bliss in Itrulan. Come." Darhad pushed aside the bead curtain and led him into the cool, exotic antechamber of the inn with the improbable name. A scent of burning sandalwood, or whatever it was on this planet, tickled his nostrils while his eyes adjusted to the darkness.

"Heaven's Bliss," Decker muttered, shaking his head as he followed her. "Didn't know they had a concept of heaven here. The bastards are all destined for hell, the way I figure it."

They entered a large room already filling with the evening's patrons: Itrulans of all colors and sizes as well as alien humanoids from two dozen Protectorate worlds.

A broad raised dais ran along the room's four walls, enclosing a central wooden floor. Stone pillars rose from the edges of the pit to the dark, smoky ceiling two meters above Zack's head. Large windows, covered with intricately carved wood screens pierced three of the four walls.

The dais was separated into many cubicles by half-height wood panels depicting various scenes of Itrulan life, none of them involving the mayhem and murder Decker had come to expect from the reptilians. Inside those cubicles, large cushions and low settees were grouped around equally low stone tables.

A subdued hum of conversation filled the room, as did a pleasant aroma of cooking food and the unmistakable scent of fermented sugars.

Darhad took him to a side cubicle from where they had a clear view of the door to the outside as well as the one leading to the inn's back rooms. With a graceful yet controlled movement, she settled down on a large, burgundy red cushion and smiled up at him. Zack shrugged, feeling somewhat foolish, sat on the other cushion, at right angles with the Arkanna, and stretched out. Their heads almost touched and Zack inhaled her musky, pheromone-laden scent. She smiled.

An Itrulan wearing a leather apron sauntered up and bared his teeth in a parody of a human smile. He hissed and gurgled a question in his language, looking expectantly from Darhad to Decker. The gunner grinned and shrugged.

"Sorry, pal. I don't speak your language. Not sure I could master those sounds."

Then his eyes widened as Raisa Darhad spat out a lengthy reply in the same hissing, guttural tones as the reptilian. The innkeeper nodded and walked off.

"Impressive. How many languages can you speak?"

"Not that many. I have mastered Anglic and two others among the human languages, and can speak decent Shrehari, Itrulan, Pradyni, and Vorkaz, and understand a smattering of other Protectorate or Shield tongues."

"No shit! When do you have time for fun?"

"Sleep readers helped me quite a bit."

"Lucky you," he replied, shaking his head. "I never could manage the things. They gave me awful headaches every time, and not much to show for it."

"It seems to affect a large proportion of all humans, I believe."

"But not Arkanna?"

"It appears not. But then, I am hardly a representative sample of my people."

Zack bit back a reply he was sure he would regret.

Think talons and teeth.

"What did you order for us?" He asked instead.

"Ah," she smiled, raising a slender, white finger. "Wait and see."

She settled back and let her impossibly blue eyes roam across the room, scanning for possible threats or opportunities.

The leather-aproned waiter returned bearing a wooden tray with two metallic mugs which he carefully deposited on the stone table. He bared his teeth at the Arkanna and her human companion and left. Darhad took one and brought it to her lips.

"Itrulan fire-ale, Zack. Not as good as the best Shrehari brews, but it has a character all of its own. This place serves the best in the city. Your health."

Decker took the other mug and looked at its foamy, dark contents.

"Fire-ale, huh? Sounds interesting. Your health, Raisa." He took a sip, his face lighting up in surprise and delight.

"Wow," he smacked his lips, "this stuff is unique all right. Cold as space and fiery as antimatter. I'd hate to think what it does to your gullet."

Darhad smiled.

"I don't know about human gullets, as you call them, but I know that fire-ale is considered a potent brew by Itrulans, one that rouses the blood."

"Sort of like oysters?"

She frowned, puzzled. "What are oysters?"

"Never mind, Raisa, forget it." Decker grinned and looked away. He took another sip of ale, unwilling to pursue this tack. If she was merely teasing him, it would make things worse. If she was on to something else, he'd rather it happen later than sooner, even if he was finding self-control a much harder business the longer he stayed close to her.

He had made a big dent in his fire-ale by the time the waiter returned bearing a platter heaped with exotic food. The other customers had proven uninteresting after a few moments' observation. Fortunately, Shrehari did not seem to patronize the inn and Zack gave thanks for the small blessing.

He examined the plates covering the table and gave Raisa a questioning look.

"Most of this food should be digestible by humans," she said. "Your metabolism and mine are quite similar, and I know from experience that I don't suffer from any unpleasant reactions."

Decker's eyes narrowed at her comment on the similarity of their metabolisms. When he looked at Darhad again, he caught the same amused smile as before, the one that seemed to mean she knew what he was thinking. If so, he didn't care.

He reached for a spoon and ladled purplish, weed-like vegetable on his beaten bronze plate. It didn't smell unpleasant, rather like seaweed. After a moment's hesitation, he took a bit of everything, trying hard not to speculate what it was, especially the stuff that looked like a mass of small snakes or worms. But the aroma rising from the food was much better than its appearance.

Darhad had already started to eat, chewing each mouthful with obvious delight. Zack closed his eyes as he took his first bite of the purple stuff. Fighting back his gag reflex he bit down and an explosion of sweet and sour erupted over his tongue.

Hey, this stuff is not bad. Now I really don't want to know what it is. Might spoil the fun.

He washed the first mouthful down with a healthy swig of fire-ale, emptying his mug in the process. His eye caught that of the innkeeper across the room, and he raised the cup above his head, in the universal signal for another of the same. The Itrulan waiter did not keep him waiting for long. Fortified by a new supply of drink, Zack tried the other unidentifiable foods with less trepidation.

Between the two of them, Darhad and Decker cleaned off the table, mopping up the last pieces with chunks of thick, nutty Itrulan quasi-bread that tasted something like smoked almonds.

A thin trickle of meat juices escaped Raisa's lips and ran down her chin. Zack, emboldened by the fire-ale, reached over, and wiped off the gravy with his finger, starting at the tip of her chin and ending at her lips.

Her tongue snaked out to lap-up the offered juices. Before he could pull his finger away, she gave him a playful bite with her sharp teeth, drawing blood. Smiling, she licked off the blood and settled back onto her cushion, looking sated. Something at the back of Zack's mind told him he'd just been the victim of an Arkanna mating ritual, and the few drops of his blood on her tongue had tripped a delicate biological switch.

A booming drum broke the spell and Decker turned his attention to the central pit. It now held a small orchestra and a string of veiled Itrulans. The large drum, accompanied by several of its smaller cousins, began throbbing rhythmically, sending vibrations through the gunner's body.

The five veiled Itrulans, Zack assumed they were female although the reptilian humanoids had no visible gender differences he could see, started to dance to the music. They swayed gracefully, arms and legs in unison.

A pair of wind instruments joined the drums, underscoring and enhancing the pounding beat of the dance, mesmerizing the inn's patrons as the dancers moved in more and more intricate patterns.

Astonished at this unknown side of Itrul, Decker discovered an alien beauty in the music and the movements. For a long and heated moment, the gunner forgot his dislike of the species, forgot the bloody battles he'd fought against them and forgot the insults he'd used against their race. This was a side of Itrul no Commonwealth Marine had ever seen.

The pounding rhythm swelled, soared and filled the inn with its magic as the dancers swirled around each other, their speed increasing as they trailed their long yellow veils behind them. Zack glanced at Raisa and their eyes met. The contact was electric.

Her face shined with perspiration in the light of the torches. Her lips parted as her breasts lifted due to rapid breathing. Whether it was the fire-ale or the music, Zack didn't care anymore. He could read arousal in a woman whether Arkanna or human. Reaching over, he touched her smooth cheek with the back of his hand. She took it in hers and brushed it against her parted lips, licking the tips of his fingers. Zack feared another bite, but she kissed his palm, her breath warm in his hand. By now, Decker knew he was beyond the limits of self-control.

She too seemed to have crossed a critical threshold. With the same restrained movements as before, she rose, took him by the hand, and led him towards the back door. None of the other customers paid them any attention.

The pounding of the music followed them through the bead curtain and down the clean, bare corridor, where the scent of burning wood washed away the thick, sensual atmosphere of the main room. Raisa took him up a flight of stairs and, after a quick search, pulled him into a small room, throwing the wooden door shut behind her.

"You seem well organized." Zack's tone was hoarse. "As if you planned this."

"I always plan well when I stalk my lovers," she replied. "You are the only worthy warrior on the ship, the first male I wish to bed in many years."

The gunner didn't have time to reply as she wrapped her arms around his neck, molding her body against his, and kissed him with a passion surprising for the cold, efficient first officer he knew.

Her tongue found his and danced its own mating dance while her hands explored Decker's hard, muscular body beneath his clothes. Finally, she broke loose and undressed him, eyes burning, an unaccustomed blush coloring her cheeks. Zack breathed in deeply as his body responded to the pheromone-laden air. She pushed him down onto the wooden bed, and Zack devoured her smooth, muscular, hairless body with his eyes as she straddled him.

Definitely compatible plumbing.

It was his last coherent thought before he abandoned himself to the moment.

*

Later, when the light of Itrul's twin moons streamed through the open window, Zack and Raisa made love again, but this time with less urgency.

Decker marveled at her smooth, warm skin as he caressed her, appreciating every curve, every nook, and every fold as he ran his mouth over her body, tasting her as he had never tasted a woman before. His fear of her teeth and talons had been entirely misplaced: Arkanna had a built-in reflex to keep them from harming their mates.

They spoke little, and she contented herself with growling Arkanna endearments, or obscenities for all Zack knew, into his ears.

*

The first rays of sunlight tickled Zack's nose, and he opened his eyes, tired but relaxed, at peace. Beside him, the bed was empty but still warm. His eyes focused to take in the room, and he saw Raisa standing by the window, stretching and savoring the clean morning air.

"Good morning, Zack," she smiled, alerted by the change in his breathing as he woke. "I trust you had a pleasant sleep."

"Sleep no," he replied, grinning, "but pleasant, definitely. And I feel more of that coming up."

"I was wondering whether human males liked it in the morning." Still smiling, she climbed back into bed.

*

A short while later, they parted, but Raisa's voice held a tinge of regret.

"Unfortunately, we must leave soon. I have retained the room only for the night, and the captain will expect us on board by noon when our liberty expires."

"And on board ship, no hanky-panky?"

She shook her head.

"It would be inappropriate. We will have to wait until we are on liberty again."

"Too bad. A guy could get used to you real fast."

"The sentiment is mutual. You are the first male I have wanted in a long time, and not only because I am attracted to your body, though it is as fine as any Arkanna alpha's. You have a strong spirit I admire."

"Same here." Zack was surprised to realize that he meant it. Raisa Darhad had been more than just a toss in the sheets, something that happened rarely.

She dressed, putting on blouse, skirt and her over-the-knee black boots. When she was done, she opened the room's wooden door and yelled something in Itrulan down the stairway.

"Breakfast," she said, her eyes caressing Decker as he dressed.

*

Back in his cabin aboard *Shokoten*, Zack Decker smiled as he undressed and examined the bite and scratch marks on his chest and arms. His nostrils still held Raisa Darhad's scent, and he stepped into the shower before the memories of the past night became too vivid.

He was tired but happy by the time he put on his uniform. As he sat by his desk to pull on his boots, he remembered the badge he'd hastily tossed into one of the drawers. The memory dampened his contentment.

Zack disliked mysteries, in particular those that could land him into deep trouble. This looked like one of them. He opened the drawer and took out the insignia, holding it between his fingers, a thoughtful frown on his face.

Then, for a reason he couldn't explain, he pinned the little gold badge to the right breast of his jacket, at the spot he'd wear it on his Marine uniform. He rose just as the cabin door slid open.

"Hi, Nihao," Zack grinned at the purser as she walked in. She wore a simple, conservatively cut suit that fit her like a glove. Her clothes were covered with a thin sheen of reddish dust, proving she'd just come back from a jaunt ashore. But the former Pathfinder's instincts told him she'd not confined her activities to the city. The layer of dust seemed too thick, especially on her boots.

As she came near him, he realized that Kiani stank like a goat which also pointed to more than a night in town. The purser smiled back at him, but without warmth. She seemed tired, irritated and in no mood for a conversation with her bunkmate.

"Good morning," she replied, with a curt nod, before stripping off her long-skirted jacket.

"Had a good time ashore?"

"Huh," she grunted, her back turned towards him. "Always bloody work for me when the ship lands. No fun to be had, in particular on a barbaric backwater hellhole like Itrul."

Zack was taken aback by her tone but understood that she didn't want to talk. Nihao Kiani was a difficult woman to understand. She fell back into the cold detachment of their early days together with frightening ease whenever something irritated her. Other times, she was just like an old pal.

"Glad you had a good time," he replied with more than a hint of sarcasm. Her tone had robbed him of his relaxed mood, and he resented the theft.

"I have to get to work. See you in the wardroom later." Without waiting for a reply, he stalked out of the cabin and headed for the bridge.

*

Raisa Darhad was standing watch, her body a picture of languid repose as she scanned a report on the pad in her hand.

"Permission to enter the bridge, sir?" Decker asked formally, conscious of her delightful presence and her determination to keep their professional and personal lives separate.

"Granted, Gunner," she replied glancing up at him. Her face was solemn, but her eyes twinkled just enough to let Zack know he was still in her thoughts. "We have not yet received word from the Itrulans about unloading, but the captain expects them to move sometime today. With luck, we shall receive an hour or two warning."

"That'll be enough, sir. I'll do my rounds now and brief the bosun's mates."

"Very well, Gunner. Carry on."

*

Captain Strachan had been right. By sundown, several dozen brawny, collared Itrulan slaves, wearing the Akmin's livery, had emptied the cargo hold using only the most primitive of hoists. They did most of the work by hand, forcing grudging admiration for their brute strength even from the ex-Marine, who watched them from the catwalk, his right hand hovering near his gun holster.

He might have enjoyed the bit of Itrulan culture of the previous evening, but that didn't diminish his mistrust. Experience bought with the blood of comrades tended to stay engraved in his mind.

Since this was a one-way freight, *Shokoten* was due to return to Commonwealth space in ballast. Not very profitable for her owners. But, as Zack suspected, whatever profit they made from the hidden cargo on this trip, be it monetary, or otherwise, far outweighed the cost of coming home empty.

*

They lifted the next morning as the rising sun painted the dusty plains blood red. Without a space station to control traffic, *Shokoten* wasted little time in orbit but headed straight back to the Commonwealth, jumping to hyperspace as soon as they could.

"It's over to Mykonos, I hear," Sladek remarked to Zack over lunch in the wardroom.

"Huh," Decker grunted around a mouthful of reconstituted fish cake and rice. Grub was decent on the freighter, but this time around, the time spent planetside hadn't brought fresh food to the galley. Nihao Kiani hadn't made much of an effort, Zack figured, but he appeared the only one to have noticed. Perhaps because few on the ship had bothered to eat a full Itrulan meal and realized they had some good stuff.

"Used to live there."

"Is that a fact," Sladek replied absently as his eyes flitted over to Third Officer Sonoda, who'd just walked in and helped herself at the buffet table. "Not a bad place, I reckon. Provincial, but what the hell. Better than an alien place anytime."

"What's better than an alien place?" Sonoda asked as she sat, her gaze avoiding Decker.

"Next port of call," Sladek said, "Mykonos Colony. Gunner used to live there.

"Backwater hick-planet," Sonoda scornfully replied, dismissing the subject as she bit into a reconstituted poppy-seed bun.

Decker smiled to himself. Whatever he touched had to be lousy in the third officer's eyes. She would never forgive him for standing up to her.

They ate in silence for a few minutes, and then Zack rose to pour himself a mug of coffee from the urn beside the galley door. As he turned, something caught Sonoda's eyes, and she looked at him with a nasty expression.

"Wearing jewelry on your uniform, Mister Decker?"

"It's my Master Gunner's badge, sir," he replied, amused at her hostility. "Didn't know there were formal dress codes in the merchant service. Figured if I was to be the ship's gunner, I might as well look the part."

"Hah," Sonoda snorted contemptuously. "As if a little military bauble will turn a space grunt into a proper starship's gunner."

"He got us out of that pickle with the Shrehari marauders," Sladek pointed out, looking nervous at the rising tension in the wardroom.

"Luck is all," the engineer replied maliciously. "It's pretty easy to shoot blindly and run, but it takes a hell of a lot more to properly fight a ship."

"And you're saying I can't do it, sir?"

"I've seen no proof so far." She replied with a sneer. Before she could say more, the door opened, and Raisa Darhad entered the wardroom.

"Is there a problem?" She looked from Decker to Sonoda. The emotions were as thick as morning fog. She had been passing near the wardroom when she sensed Zack's rising anger. Normally, she wouldn't have sensed him through bulkheads, but their mating had created a bond between them, a one-sided bond, unfortunately, since he was not Arkanna.

"Well, is there?" She repeated when nobody answered.

"No, sir," Zack finally replied, putting his usual mask of studied neutrality in place. He didn't want to pull Darhad into this dispute. Having a superior officer as lover was not a comfortable situation, and he wanted to keep the two separate. Of course, Decker had underestimated her again.

"Do not give me that bullshit, Mister Decker." Zack started at the crack in her voice, and her use of the human slang. "You looked as if you were about to commit murder. And your facial expression is no more congenial, Mister Sonoda. The captain will not have bickering officers on his ship, and it is my duty to make sure this does not happen."

Decker knew his face didn't reveal as much as Darhad had read into it. Over the last few weeks, he'd been teaching himself to keep a better control of his expressions, and he was sure he had made a lot of progress.

"What the hell, sir," Sladek sighed as he sat again. "I might as well tell you myself. The chief engineer and the gunner disagreed on the latter's professional skills as pertains to blowing reivers into the next dimension."

"I suspected as much." She stared at Sonoda with hard eyes. "Well then, Third Officer. You don't trust our gunner's marksmanship. Understandable since he has not been given the occasion to prove himself."

All three officers looked at her in astonishment, especially Zack.

"And it would be nothing more than the truth to affirm that he is out of practice in ship-to-ship combat. Am I correct, Mister Decker?"

"Aye, sir," he grudgingly admitted, avoiding Sonoda's malicious look. "Those Shrehari weren't much of a challenge."

Sladek guffawed but quickly shut up under Darhad's icy glare.

"Very well. I propose a challenge," she continued. "Third Officer Sonoda, you will prepare a combat simulation to be fed into the ship's computer. The captain and I will approve it beforehand, of course. Then, we will all see how good Mister Decker is. Any objections, Gunner?"

"No sir."

"Be warned, Mister Decker, that although the captain and I will review the sim, we will not let it be an easy scenario. It will not be a no-win situation either. You must achieve a clear victory."

Zack shrugged dismissively but remained silent.

"In three days, then. Will that be enough time, Mister Sonoda?"

"More than enough, sir."

*

Word spread fast on small ships like *Shokoten*. There was little in the way of entertainment on board, and a grudge-match was a lot more fun than cockroach races in the biosys section. The crew quickly split into two camps: those who thought Zack would win, and those who figured he was just a washed-out grunt with airs. There were somewhat more of the former than the latter. Decker's rough charm, no-nonsense manner, and hard-nosed skills had won him many friends among the crew.

Betting started on the lower deck and at first gave Zack good odds, which heartened him to no end. Then, as rumors about the simulation made the rounds, the odds started to lengthen, and Zack began to worry in earnest. Master Gunners weren't magicians, and few could claim to be as good as the best Navy gunnery officers. Decker wasn't one of them.

Three days later, at two bells in the afternoon watch, Zack entered the bridge and, after going through the formal ritual, headed for his console.

Captain Strachan and the entire command crew were at their stations and watched him settle in with keen interest. For the occasion, Zack wore his battledress, with the mysterious Master Gunner's badge pinned to it. Maybe the motto of his old outfit would bring him luck. Uncharacteristically, Decker felt nervous, like the day he was married, or the day he took command of his first Pathfinder troop as a young, loud-mouthed, freshly promoted command sergeant.

"Mister Decker," the captain interrupted Zack's mental efforts to calm down.

"Sir?"

"To keep the simulation fair, and give the rest of the crew a good work-out, we shall do a general battle drill. This means you will have access to any personnel or systems on the ship in your efforts to defend it. Anything less and it would not be an accurate test of your abilities."

"I understand. Thank you, sir."

"Be warned, however, that the simulation will be of an appropriate degree of difficulty."

"Yes, sir."

"Number One," Strachan turned towards Darhad, "engage Sim-Alpha and go to battle stations."

"Aye, aye, sir." She bent over her console, fingers flying and the main view screen wavered for a fraction of a second, as a computer-generated universe replaced the real thing. Then, the battle stations siren screeched throughout the ship as the lights dimmed to red.

The sounds seemed to steady Zack's nerves: this was an environment he knew well. Intently, he sent his sensor probes out in an ever-widening circle around the ship to find the enemy that had tripped the proximity alarm. His ears shut out the usual din of a starship's bridge as the captain did what captains normally do when they're about to be attacked.

Bingo!

"One starship on an intercept course emerging nine hundred thousand kilometers on our starboard quarter."

Decker's voice was steady, professional, and cut through the chatter like a knife.

"Identity?"

"Unknown. Refining scan. Power consumption curve consistent with a human-built fast, armed freighter." Then, "Two more emergence traces on our port bow, range six hundred thousand kilometers. Scanning. Same power consumption curve. Definitely human, likely marauders. No honest ship wastes that much power."

Zack grinned to himself. These looked exactly like fast freighters converted to reivers by renegades in the Shield cluster. Like all human tech, they were pretty good, but Sonoda had fallen into the chauvinism trap. If you really want to make life hard for someone in a sim, you don't use human reivers, you use Shrehari. Two Shrehari corsairs of equal tonnage were more than a match for three armed freighters and could really ruin your day.

This wouldn't be a piece of cake, but a lot easier than he thought. Humans were predictable, even renegades, especially sim-reivers programmed by a human starship officer. Had Sonoda used Shrehari, and let the computer set the variable parameters, to better approximate the Shrehari's chronic lack of predictability, there was no telling what might have happened.

An energy spike appeared on the readout of the closest ship.

"Brace for incoming fire," Zack's warning rang out loudly. "For what we are about to receive..."

A string of plasma blossoms erupted from the guns of the lead reiver and sped towards *Shokoten* at a respectable fraction of light speed. A few seconds later, the computer registered an impact on the number six shield, as competing energies clashed. At that range, however, the plasma burst caused no damage to the force field enveloping the ship, but Zack felt an eerie sensation snake through his adrenaline-charged consciousness. By all rights, his mind told him, the ship should be groaning under the pressure of the energy clash.

Then, the developing tactical situation brushed away all other considerations. The battle sim had automatically analyzed the force of the hit and correlated it to the range of the firing ship, a software modification Decker had written himself. Now, the results scrolled on the screen.

Zack smiled. The sim-reivers had shot too early, giving him time to shift his defenses. Quickly, he retuned the frequency of the shield generators to provide maximum strength against the particular energy coefficient of the reivers' fire. It wouldn't make more than a few percentiles difference, but it could easily mean the difference between life and death. The subroutine was another modification he'd done after his stay in the sickbay.

All three marauders closed in on *Shokoten*, in a regular, predictable, and two-dimensional pattern. Zack almost laughed aloud. Sonoda, for all her years on a starship still thought in two-dimensions! She also seemed to think making the attackers come at the freighter at the same speed and evenly spaced would give him a headache. Second-year cadets at the Academy had that sort of lazy thinking beaten out of them fast. As he recalled, Sonoda had washed out of the Academy in her second year.

He turned to look at the captain.

"Sir, I need helm control."

Strachan stared at him for a few seconds.

"Helm, you will take your maneuvering orders from the gunner."

"Aye, aye, sir." The helmsman sounded unsure at the strange order.

Closer, closer, my beauties, Zack mentally chanted as he entered the maneuvering sequence into the computer. There. Now the firing sequence. More simulated hits struck the shields, but Zack ignored them. When a shield was about to go critical, the computer would call it to his attention. He hit the feed button and sent his instructions to the helmsman.

"Helm, confirm course instructions."

"Confirmed, sir, but -"

"Engage on my mark. Three, two, one, mark!"

Shokoten plunged downwards, beneath the ring of encircling reivers and swooped up again. The enemy might be fake, but the ship's movements were very real. Within less than a minute, the freighter had dropped out of the reivers' gun sights and was now coming up straight under the belly of the lead ship, her bows pointing at a spot dead center between the two hyperdrive nacelles.

"Helm, prepare to pull up and clear the reiver's starboard side on my mark."

"Ready, sir."

The bridge crew collectively held their breath as they watched the reiver's keel grow on the view screen. Blossoms of plasma dotted its hull as the pirates fired their small caliber belly guns. Zack didn't seem to notice the return fire.

"Make sure you're not going to ram her," Strachan warned, his voice as tense as if this battle, and the ship filling the screen, were real.

"Then I hope your helmsman is fast off the mark, sir," Decker snapped. "Helmsman, prepare to pull up, three, two, one," the view screen suddenly filled with streaks of light as Decker fired every forward bearing gun and missile launcher, "MARK!"

Shokoten shuddered at the sudden change of course. Just as the reiver slipped off the view screen, it was enveloped by a fireball as the salvo hit at extremely short range.

"Direct hit," Darhad called out, "Number four shield pierced, catastrophic damage to the hull." A pause. "She exploded. Confirmed kill! Backwash degrading our aft shields, down to forty-nine percent. Congratulations, Gunner."

There were a few ironic cheers on the bridge, but all eyes remained glued to the view screen. They knew this was a trick Decker could only use once, and they wanted to see what he would do next.

Zack wasn't listening. His mind was already tackling the next target with methodical cold-bloodedness. First, shift the aft shields out of their arcs of fire. Then...then give 'em the old Raskolnikov Maneuver.

The surviving reivers were slow to react and only now turning to pursue the freighter. Zack fed new maneuvering instructions to the helm and made sure the guns and launchers had cycled through.

"Captain, can you order engineering to release a five-second stream of fuel on my mark?"

"Why?" Strachan raised his eyebrows in surprise.

"Take too long to explain, sir. We can spare it."

"Very well. Engineer, we shall release a five-second stream of fuel. Advise when ready."

As the two reivers finally engaged pursuit, Zack brought the ship back into a very tight loop, keeping the upper shields towards them. He glanced at Strachan with a cocked eyebrow. The captain nodded.

"Prepare to release fuel stream on my mark. Three, two, one, mark!"

A few moments later, he nodded, satisfied that his instructions had been carried out. The ship changed course again.

Zack's finger hovered over the firing button as he watched the readout. At the critical moment, his finger stabbed down and the forward guns coughed out a full spread of plasma.

Come on, come on, Zack silently chanted. Then, the plasma salvo and the two reivers met at the spot where the fuel cloud was expanding. The plasma ignited the volatile crystals and enveloped the ships in a ball of fire brighter than a star. Cries of astonishment rang out.

"Are they -" Strachan asked.

"No, sir. But they'll soon be," the gunner replied, eyes still glued to his console. "Helm come to one-seventy-three mark ninety-seven and accelerate to maximum.

"One-seventy-three mark ninety-seven, maximum, aye."

Shokoten swerved again and pointed her blunt bows directly at the expanding ball of fire. As they neared, it dissipated, showing the outlines of the reivers. Their shields crackled with intense green energy discharges as they fought to repel the last radiation surges of the powerful detonation.

"Helm, prepare to change course to mark one-zero. The moment we're on the new course, pivot her lengthwise one-eighty degrees.

"Aye, aye, sir."

"Firing now," Zack sang out as he launched another salvo at extremely close range. "Helm execute!"

Again, the reivers slid off the view screen just as the plasma enveloped them. When the ship was on her new course, Zack slumped back in his chair and glanced over at

Darhad, sweat trickling down his forehead. He willed his heart to slow its hammering beat as the adrenaline induced high receded.

"Shields have failed on the near reiver. She has exploded." A view of the blast filled the screen as Darhad fed the computer-generated visual to the scanners. She swore loudly in Arkanna, the word sounding like a cross between a low growl and a bark. "The second ship's shields have collapsed. She is helpless." Her head turned towards Decker, eyes glittering.

"Unless the captain has any objections," she said, "I suggest we call an end to this exercise. Two kills and one target wide open to our guns is an overwhelming victory."

"I agree," Strachan replied, after clearing his throat several times. "End simulation and secure from battle stations. Congratulations, Mister Decker. That was one hell of a display."

Zack grinned at Strachan and Darhad in turn. If only they knew how much of a sham the victory truly was. He could never do this against real reivers, considering that it was the first time he had actually taken control of a ship's movements. There wasn't a Navy captain out there who'd have let him do it. This had been one very expensive videogame, nothing more, the stuff spacers played in a starship's rec room.

"I would venture to say your reputation on this ship is now secure, Mister Decker," Strachan said. "I have every confidence that your performance against a real enemy will only be better if such a thing is possible."

Zack gave him an "aw shucks" grin and shrugged. "Only doing my job, captain."

*

Strachan was right, however. The simulation had cemented his reputation among *Shokoten*'s crew for good. Over the next few days, he noticed a new respect in the eyes of ratings and officers alike, except Sonoda and her close familiars.

Only Nihao Kiani seemed unaffected by the change in Zack's status from outsider to member of *Shokoten* family, but the gunner hardly noticed. For the first time in a long time, he genuinely felt at home. And in the euphoria, he dismissed the little mysteries that had been plaguing his imagination and the smuggling that had been troubling his conscience.

— TEN —

Zack stepped off *Shokoten* and grimaced. Autumn had settled over Aramis' northern hemisphere, and Heaven's Gate seemed crushed beneath brooding, gray clouds. Though sunset was still hours away, the lights of the spaceport and the city glittered like tiny beacons of hope, trying in vain to dispel the sense of hopelessness and despair smothering the colony.

He turned up the collar of his spacer's jacket and pulled his brimmed officer's cap down hard, to prevent it from being snatched away by the icy wind's strong fingers. The thin stripes of his warrant rank gleamed on his shoulders as they soaked up the water pouring incessantly from the sky.

Zack shivered as an arctic gust of wind sliced through the insulated coat and chilled his body.

The crew had a few hours of liberty before the ship lifted, and then only because of the long trip ahead. Strachan had wisely given his people time to buy a few things that would make the trip more comfortable, even if their lift-off would be more hectic as a result. The outbound cargo was already on board. Aramis stevedores were an efficient if surly bunch. With this weather, who could blame them?

Raisa couldn't go ashore with Zack this time. She still had to clear the ship through interminable layers of bureaucracy. Not that it mattered. The only thing Decker wanted to do was pay Tren Kinnear a short visit, to let him know he was doing okay, and then visit a few shops to stock up on hooch, cigars, and a few other little luxuries. His next time alone with Darhad would be weeks and hundreds of light years away. Tough, but that was a spacer's lot.

Dodging puddles on the grimy tarmac, Decker headed for the terminal building, shoulders hunched against the cold, hands shoved deep in his pockets, and eyes narrowed against the stinging spray of rain.

A small trader lifted from runway twelve, the usual ear-shattering roar of thrusters muffled by the thick, wet air. Zack turned to watch the ship lift on a rapidly dissipating pillar of steam.   The traders roaming humanity's outer reaches belonged to a small tribe, and he'd seen the sleek freighter several times before.

By the time Zack entered the terminal, shaking the rain droplets from his cap and jacket, the small ship had been swallowed by the dense clouds.

The waiting room was grimy, like all things at the working end of a spaceport.   But it was warm, dry, and more importantly, had a public box that didn't charge for calls to taxi services.   He waited alone in the cavernous room, eyes staring at the street through dirty windows.   No one else was dumb enough to wander outside in this weather, and most of the crew had already gone ashore.   Apart from *Shokoten*, there was no other freighter on the ground now that the small trader had boosted out.

A battered taxi, shiny under a slick coat of freezing rain, careened to a stop and Zack hurried out, shoulders hunched, and climbed aboard.

"Where to, Mac?" The driver, a genuine human driver, asked as he leaned over the back of his seat to glance at Zack.

"To the *Dragon's Tooth*. Know it?"

The driver pushed his flat cap away from his forehead and cackled, a sound more like an aborted cough than an actual expression of amusement.

"Shit, Mac. Ain't worth being a taxi man 'round here if you don't know the best spots in Spacetown."

He grinned, showing a row of crooked teeth, and then turned his prizefighter's mug toward the front, gunning the taxi's four turbofans. With a stomach-turning lurch, the hovercar sped off into the gloom, its driver humming a tuneless air punctuated by soft snorts.

Human taxi drivers weren't very common, except on low-tech colonies. Zack would have thought Aramis had come far enough, at least in the larger towns. Not that he minded having a breathing, sentient being at the controls, but an AI would probably have been safer.

With a whine of overstressed fans, the taxi screeched to a stop in front of a door that spilled an inviting square of warm light on the cold, gray sidewalk. Above, lit in garish colors, the caricature of a leering, Shrehari reptile invited patrons to enter.

"Here you are, Mac. That'll be three creds fifty." The driver turned around in his seat and grinned at Zack again, his small eyes nearly vanishing inside the deep folds of a face that had seen one fist too many.

Zack handed over four one-cred chips.

"Keep the change, buddy. Thanks for the ride." He didn't know whether the price of the trip was high, low, or just right, but right now, he didn't care either way.

"Thanks, Mac. If you need a ride back, just call the dispatcher and ask for Larry. I'll be there in a flash, as long as I don't have another fare."

"I'll do that." Decker nodded and stepped out of the cab. The door slid shut behind him, and Larry sped away with his habitual recklessness. Zack shook his head and walked into the welcoming warmth of Tren Kinnear's inn.

The noise and heat, along with the smell of beer and food washed over him like a wave as he crossed the threshold. This close to suppertime, the inn was filling with locals in search of a square meal and a pint of ale.

Zack took off his brimmed cap and unfastened his pea jacket as he made his way to the bar. He received a few uninterested glances but attracted no other attention. Merchant officers were a common sight in Kinnear's establishment, and simple warrant officers merited little notice, even those who stood almost two meters tall, with seamed, hard faces and shoulders to match.

"Good evening, Mister," a young barmaid chirped, smiling in welcome. Short, with curly blond hair and a pert nose, she looked like someone's younger sister. She hadn't been around the last time Zack had seen the place. "What'll it be?"

"A pint of your best bitter and tell the owner of this place that his old buddy Zack's in town." Decker sat on a high stool, dropped his coat over its neighbor, and set his cap on the bar.

The girl looked at him for a few seconds, surprised at the request, then shrugged and expertly drew a large glass of amber liquid from the antique beer-pull. After carefully placing it in front of Zack, she turned around and stuck her head through the door connecting the bar to the kitchen.

"Mara, merchant officer named Zack wants to see the boss."

Tren's wife shouted back something unintelligible. Seconds later, her large body thrust aside the door. She stared at Zack with raised eyebrows.

"My, my. 'Tis Mister Zachary Decker, as I live and breathe. And looking mighty fine too, in that merchant officer's uniform. I'll go pull the old bugger from of his cave. He'll be glad to see you." Then she vanished again.

Zack sipped his drink as he turned around to survey the inn. No other uniforms in the place, but plenty of men and women who looked like their day jobs didn't involve eight hours behind a desk. No obvious villains or cops either though Decker doubted that his unfortunate encounter with the corrupt Spacetown detective still sat on someone's to do list.

"Hey, Decker, you old fart! You're looking good, my boy, looking good."

He turned around at the sound of the familiar voice and grinned broadly as he put down his beer. Grasping the proffered, meaty hand in his own, he shook it enthusiastically.

"Tren, you slimy purveyor of diseased goods, still short-changing the clientele, I see."

"No other way to make a profit, buddy. So how have you been?" Before Zack could answer, Kinnear walked around the bar and grabbed his upper arm. "C'mon, let's sit down comfortable-like. Sissi!"

"Yeah, boss?"

"Serve Zack another of what he's having, get me a pint of dark and both of us a plate of whatever the old girl's cooking back there."

They sat in a corner booth and grinned at each other.

"I'm glad to see you well, Zack. How's your job on *Shokoten* working out?"

"Better than I expected. It isn't the Corps, but it has its moments. I owe you for getting me the berth. I've done more traveling in the last while than ever before. You wouldn't believe the places I've been and the stuff I've seen." He stopped as Sissi brought them food and drink, and then went on to tell his old friend about his travels, omitting any mention of Darhad or contraband.

"An active life," Kinnear said, popping a bread crust soaked with gravy into his mouth. "Not that I'm envious, mind you," he continued, chewing between words, "I have all I need here, but you're doing fun stuff too. I'm happy you found yourself a place. You were none too nice a sight when you first crawled in here. Now look at you: warrant officer in a merchant ship, gunner no less." He pointed at the badge on Decker's right breast.

"Nice they let you wear the old pin. Brings back memories, don't it? Back in the good old days when we were jumping out of perfectly good shuttles flying in low orbit. I miss them sometimes. A man knew what he was fighting for and who he could trust."

Decker didn't know why, but Tren's brief trip down memory lane, just after noticing the mystery pin, gave him mixed feelings. His face lost its smile, and he stared down at his plate, toying with his utensils.

"Yeah. Good old days they were, Tren." His voice sounded false even to him. Suddenly, he felt a burning need to return to the ship, get away from Kinnear, and back to the life he'd made for himself aboard *Shokoten.* "So how's the inn doing?"

"Fine. Just hauling in the creds, we are." If Kinnear had noticed Decker's sudden change of mood, he gave no sign. "Nothing much has changed."

"Whatever happened to the girl I brought in?"

Now it was Kinnear's turn to drop the smile and glance away.

"Hell, Zack. Was nothing we could do. Little fool decided she was safe to take a walk one night, a couple of months ago. Didn't much look like the whore you brought to us that night. She was off drugs, booze, and sex, working regular hours in the place every day. Mara pretty much decided Ellena was the kid she never had."

To his surprise, Zack could see tears forming in the corners of Tren's eyes.

"Anyways, one night she wants to go to the movies, see the latest flick. We said she'd better not because there's no guarantee she won't be recognized. But she had cabin fever, I guess. Short of tying her up, there was nothing we could do. We couldn't leave the place so she went alone. I asked one of my buddies to keep an eye on her, and he did. Up to a point. At the flicks, she went into the little girl's room and never came out. When my friend became nervous, he asked one of the lady attendants to check. Not a fucking trace of Ellena. They found her two days later, lying in a ditch outside town. She'd been stripped, tortured, and raped before being killed." Now Tren was crying openly.

"The fucking bastards waited for her after all," he continued. "Yeah, it was the pals of the guy you killed. Wanted revenge. I heard the message loud and clear. Won't be hurting anyone now though. I have other friends who don't like seeing young gals be murdered. Those crooked cops are now pushing up daisies, and the local head cop's launched an internal investigation that's shining light into the shittiest corners of the Spacetown precinct. Don't worry, they won't stumble on your name. Took care of that when you first ran to me."

"Shit!" Decker felt like someone had hit him with a battle cruiser's main guns. The sharp edge of depression had nicked him earlier. Now, he felt his spirits hit rock bottom. The only thing he could think of was getting away from this place and the memories that kept intruding into his new life.

"You said it, buddy." Tren wiped his tears away with a meaty paw and drained his beer. "So, you here for long?"

"Nope. We lift tonight on a long haul towards the core. Just came by to say hi. Still have to buy personal supplies for the trip. Be about time I leave now."

"Don't you worry about personal supplies, Mister Warrant Officer Decker," Kinnear replied, a smile returning to his face. "I'll fix a package before you leave this place.

Have another brew, and I'll see what's in stock. You still like single malt? Cigars?"

"Yeah on both counts." Now Decker felt uneasy as if he were taking advantage of a friend with whom he hadn't been entirely straight. Or to be more precise, a friend with whom he had shared a belief in values he had forgotten lately, values he had, admittedly, trampled on by helping Strachan carry out his business.

Sissi brought him more ale while Kinnear foraged around his back room for what he'd called his 'care package.' About ten minutes later, the older man came back with a tightly bound bundle.

"Here you go, Zack." He placed the plastic-wrapped box on the table. "Three bottles of my finest Caledonian single malt, a box of Romeo y Julieta cigars, a few cans of fancy meats, caviar and preserved fruit, and a bottle of my very own homemade digestive liqueur," Kinnear grinned with pleasure.

He slapped Decker on the shoulder. "When you're back on Aramis, you can tell me how you like it. And tell me about this long haul of yours. Not too many folks head that far out."

Zack drained his beer and stood. "Thanks, Tren. Thanks for the brew, the supper, and the package." He held out his hand. "I'm glad to know there's a place I can always come back to and find a friend."

"Anytime, buddy, anytime. I'm always happy to see you. Have a safe trip and watch out for those alien babes. You don't wanna leave little Zacks on all the planets in the fucking galaxy on top of every stinking colony in the Commonwealth, do you?"

"Don't worry about that, Tren." Decker managed a small smile, but just because his mind flashed a picture of his very own alien babe. He let go of Tren's hand and put on his pea jacket.

"Any chance of calling a taxi?"

"Don't you worry about that neither. Just follow the guy standing by the door there. He'll take you back to the port. A friend of mine headed the same way."

Decker glanced over at the tall, bearded man by the door and nodded. Larry, the taxi driver, wouldn't be driving Zack back, and for that, the ex-Marine was thankful.

"'Bye, Tren."

"Take care, you young bugger." Tren gave Decker a bear hug. When the older man released him, Zack put on his brimmed cap, grinned briefly, and followed the bearded man out of the *Dragon's Tooth*.

Kinnear watched his friend leave and shook his head. He'd noticed Decker's rapid change of mood, the doubts written large on his open face, the hesitations and evasions in his account of his time on *Shokoten*, and especially his reaction to Tren noticing the Master Gunner badge. But he couldn't afford to dwell on Zack's situation, lest he developed doubts of his own. He returned to his place behind the bar just in time to greet an old customer.

"And how are you tonight, Jenny? Business still good?"

*

Zack hurried across the wet tarmac and up the gangway, rain trickling down his collar. The outer airlock opened at his touch, and the bosun's mate of the watch grinned as the gunner shook himself dry.

"Wet one, sir?"

"That it is, Veelan. Dirty fucking weather."

"We'll soon be off this mud ball, though, aren't we?"

"Yup. A few hours and we lift. Have a lovely evening."

The kid snapped to attention. "You too, sir."

Decker's short conversation with the young spacer had done much to raise his flagging spirits, and he caught himself whistling a tune by the time he reached his cabin, after meeting what seemed like half the crew in the passageways. Yup, *Shokoten* was home all rights, rough crew, contraband cargo and all.

*

"Heaven's Gate control to *Shokoten*, you are cleared for take-off as number one. Be advised of small craft traffic near your authorized flight path up to ten thousand." Zack raised his eyebrows in surprise at the announcement. They must be crazy to fly at night and in this weather. "Report to orbital control when passing thirty thousand. Have a successful trip."

"*Shokoten* to Control, thank you and goodbye," Captain Strachan replied, "Nav, confirm course is laid in and has been accepted."

"Confirmed."

"All systems green, sir," First Officer Darhad chimed in from her console to Strachan's right.

"Helm, keel thrusters on. Increase gradually until you have neutral lift."

"Aye, aye, sir."

A rumbling ran through the freighter's hull as the atmospheric thrusters powered up. Pillars of steam rose from the runway, shrouding *Shokoten* and cutting off her view of the city. She lurched a bit, and Zack knew the landing struts had left the ground.

"Hovering at two meters, sir," the senior helmsman said in a tense voice.

"Take her up to one thousand, stand by aft thrusters."

"One thousand, aft thrusters online, aye."

This time, they felt the change in motion as the ship rose vertically, leaving a column of steam behind and giving the crew a last glimpse of Heaven's Gate before the low cloud cover swallowed them.

"Nine hundred."

"Aft thrusters on."

"Aft thrusters on, aye. Passing one thousand. We are on the plotted lift course, sir."

"Thank you, helm. Well done."

*

Lift-off was always difficult for a ship the size of *Shokoten*. A sudden, strong wind shear when she was still close to the ground could spell disaster. But, as Zack learned, Strachan's bridge crew was good at its job.

As they sailed upwards out of Aramis' troposphere, into her stratosphere and beyond, where the blue of the sky gave way to the black of space, the gunner amused himself by tracking the planet's defensive setup. He played little mind games on how he'd outwit them, should he need to land *Shokoten* unseen.

Like most human worlds, Aramis had its own defense force independent of the Fleet. And like most defense forces, this one was competent but not enough for a Pathfinder. By the time *Shokoten* left the planet, released by orbital control, he had figured out not one but four possible infiltration routes.

*

"I think we need to stay at a higher level of vigilance from about ten light years before the border until we're well past Kardat and the rest of the marauder hideouts." Zack pointed at the star map on Strachan's desk. "That means the gun systems are live, the shields are up at all times, and the crew lives in battledress. Plus, we keep a qualified hand on the sensors at all times."

"It will require expanding the watches to fill the added tasks," Darhad noted, "but I have no problems with the gunner's suggestion. It makes eminent sense to be prepared."

"Agreed. Raisa, post the orders and re-jig the watches."

"Aye, aye, sir."

"I wish to discuss another matter, while I have both of you here." Zack and Raisa nodded. It had become Strachan's habit to take Decker into his confidence alongside the first officer, and such a statement no longer surprised him. "I have received sealed instructions from our owners that supersede the instructions given at the Guild exchange."

Decker raised his eyebrows in surprise. There was little doubt Strachan meant orders from their real owners.

"We are no longer stopping at Rhada, our original destination," Strachan continued, "but sailing on towards the core for a planet called Ventos Prime, about fifty light years beyond Rhada on a direct flight path."

"Why?" Zack was curious. It tacked another week or more to their trip. He had never heard of Ventos Prime for that matter.

"No idea. Seems the deal they had on Rhada fell through. I guess it's a bit of luck that they found a new buyer and seller relatively close by." Strachan sounded unconcerned about an even longer trip beyond the borders of the Commonwealth.

Zack carefully schooled his expression, but his mind was filling with questions. Ventos Prime was a distant destination for a cargo of low-grade tech. Who knew what they'd be hauling back from a planet few had ever heard about.

Darhad caught his mental agitation but refrained from commenting. Instead, she asked, "Will we resupply along the way? That distance will strain our stores. We are not a survey cruiser."

"I've been told that someone on Ventos Prime can provide us with enough perishables to keep an adequate safety margin for the return trip."

This time, Darhad raised her eyebrows, merging their upswept tips with her crimson hair.

"I had not realized Ventos Prime had a ship's chandlery business equipped to deal with humans."

"All I know is that I have my orders," Strachan replied, eyes hardening. His tone brooked no further discussion, and that surprised Decker as much as anything else had. He normally treated his first officer with much more tolerance, at least in front of his gunner. The captain didn't seem overly pleased with this trip. Was it the distance, or was there something else?

"That will be all."

Decker and Darhad rose, acknowledging the dismissal.

*

"What's eating him?" Zack asked her when they were alone in the passageway.

"I believe our captain is most unhappy about the change in orders. I also think his secret instructions contain much more than he has told us. Maybe we shall find out when we arrive, maybe not. Put it out of your mind, for there is nothing we can do."

Zack smiled at her resigned tone and briefly touched her. He hurriedly dropped his hand when Nihao Kiani appeared. She gave the two of them a strange look before she vanished into the captain's cabin.

"There's someone who will be just as unhappy about this news," the gunner chuckled. "She won't like the thought of dealing with supplies on a planet we've never been to. Heck, make that a place most humans have never seen. Do we have anything on the place in our data banks?"

"I shall verify. But I doubt it. Data costs creds and we don't have the cash to spare for exotic bits of information, such as a planet that far from the regular trading routes. All we likely have are the coordinates and basic contact instructions."

"Huh." Zack frowned. "How the hell will we deal with people about whom we know nothing?"

"Perhaps we'll be met by a human or at least an agent hired by humans, whose role is to handle the transactions. We shall find out when the time is ripe, no doubt. I must conduct my daily inspection now. Until lunch." Her lips briefly twitched as she blew him a discreet kiss.

*

Shokoten sped on, coming out of the hyperspace currents every so often to recalibrate the hyperdrives and plot the next jump. They passed the border without incident and without sighting a patrol ship. The Navy was hard pressed in this sector, and their frigates were widely dispersed to cover as much space as possible.

Then they passed through the Badlands: pirate havens, techno barbarian kingdoms, and assorted riff-raff with the pretensions to high tech status. The Shield Cluster was the Fleet's nightmare and a treasure trove of illegal profits for anyone with the means to exploit them. Slavery was rife and skilled humans fetched the highest prices; the drug trade flourished, and markets for plundered goods of all kinds abounded.

A ship like *Shokoten* was an attractive target even if she was well armed, and it paid to be prudent. Decker slept easier when the worst of those worlds were far in their wake. Marauders tended to operate between the Cluster and the Commonwealth where high-end shipping was densest.

The length of the trip, however, began to tell on the crew by the time they passed the Rhada system. They were not used to such long runs without setting a foot ashore, and life in the cramped quarters of a ship without recreational facilities became tedious. More than once, Zack had to break up arguments that got out of hand, but he could do nothing to ease the underlying cause, which was boredom and acute cabin fever, mixed with knowing they were very far from home.

He kept himself busy with physical training when he could no longer find any duties to keep his hands and mind occupied. With Strachan's permission, he converted a small, unused cargo hold in the upper hull into a gym, scratch building the exercise gear, and tinkering with the room's gravity. Word spread, and soon, Nihao Kiani, Raisa Darhad, Fourth Officer Gareth, and the bosun joined him whenever they could.

*

"You know," he said one afternoon, when he and Nihao were alone in the mini-gym, "the one thing I miss is the martial arts sessions we used to have aboard *Musashi*. Pumping iron and skipping rope in high gee is fine to build up muscle, but doesn't do shit for reflexes."

He laid down his improvised barbell and wiped the sweat from his brow. Nihao glanced at him with her usual bland expression and, never missing a stroke, kept on skipping as she replied.

"I can offer you with an adequate sparring partner in judo, tae-kwon-do, karate, and aikido."

Zack ran his eyes over her tall, muscular body and nodded, a grin spreading on his face. She looked tough enough to give him a decent fight.

"Okay, kid. What and when?"

"When is now. What is whatever you wish."

"Aikido?"

"Agreed." She stopped skipping and coiled up the rope. "I suggest you bring the gravity back to normal, or we may inflict permanent injury on each other."

They cleared out a fighting space in the center and laid out a thick rubber mat normally used to cushion fragile cargo.

Standing at opposing ends of the mutually agreed arena, they came to attention and bowed stiffly at each other. Then, they took up a fighting stance and circled, looking for an opening. Nihao's eyes never left Zack's, and the gunner found himself forced to judge his moment by trusting his peripheral vision. And whatever he could read in the purser's impassive face, which was absolutely nothing.

She struck first, throwing Zack off balance and sending him crashing to the ground. He rolled, absorbing the punishing fall, but didn't rise fast enough. Nihao's bare foot came out of nowhere and slammed down towards his throat, stopping within millimeters of crushing it. Zack conceded the point.

They faced each other again, circling, and Nihao attempted a similar trick, but this time, Zack was ready. He blocked her move and then used her momentum to put in one of his own. With a grunt, Decker threw her down and pounced as she tried to roll away. Catching her with his right arm, he struggled to establish a chokehold. Kiani let out a fighting yell and threw him off with surprising strength.

They scrambled up and resumed the slow dance, wise now to each other's abilities. Zack tried a lightning attack and completed half the movement, getting his body into position near her to deliver a disabling stroke, when she lashed out with a leg. He would never have been able to see it coming: she had such absolute control over her body and eyes.

The foot connected with Zack's solar plexus, slamming the air out of his lungs. He fell backwards and landed badly, both the kick and the fall stunning him. Nihao was on him in a flash, her strong right arm tightening around his neck, and there was nothing he could do.

Black dots danced before his eyes, and he slapped the mat in the universal signal of surrender, but her grip didn't loosen. His vision blurred, and he heard a ringing in his ears.

Finally, just as he was about to pass out, she released him, letting his head drop on the mat. Another face replaced Kiani's sweaty brow

"Are you all right, Mister Decker?"

Zack blinked once or twice, and Raisa Darhad's worried frown swam before his eyes.

"Okay," he croaked. "Just a friendly bout."

"I would suggest Mister Kiani needs to learn a bit more about setting the right limits," she replied, speaking in a louder tone for the benefit of the stone-faced purser. "Martial arts are as much about control as they're about fighting. Or do I have a wrong idea about your human practices?"

"No, sir," Kiani replied.

"Let it be," Zack said as he rose, rubbing his chest and neck. "I was outclassed by someone who is obviously sensei. That'll teach me to assume a civilian spacer isn't as highly trained as a Marine."

"Well met, Nihao." He bowed. After a few moments hesitation, as if she suspected him of sarcasm instead of taking the words at their face value, she returned the bow.

"You must teach me how you manage not to telegraph your moves. I didn't see that kick coming. You could've killed me right there and then, had this been for real."

She bowed slightly again, an ironic smile playing on her lips. "I could have killed you, had I not exercised self-control."

Darhad's lips tightened, but she held her peace.

Zack picked up his towel and wiped his face.

"This did me a lot of good, even if it hurt like hell." He grinned at the two women. "We must do this again another time, Nihao. I'm always ready to learn from my betters." He nodded at Darhad. "If you'll excuse me, First Officer. I think I'll go lick my wounds in private now."

*

Later, in the shower, Zack watched a large, purple bruise spread over his chest and remembered her chokehold.

She'd been a lot rougher than usual in a sparring match, and could easily have killed him had she held on to his neck for much longer. That thought brought on another, less pleasant one.

Did she let go because she knew it was time, or because Raisa walked in on them? He did tap the mat a few times. And why would Nihao Kiani want to harm him, if that was the case?

His train of thought broke when Kiani stuck her head into the small shower cubicle.

"Don't take all day in there, Zack, or I shall throw you out."

"Come in and join me."

"Very well." She opened the door and stepped in.

The stall was so small their bodies filled it almost completely, and Zack couldn't avoid touching her, with the expected results. To his astonishment she grabbed him and guided him in, releasing a soft sigh as they joined. Her lips crushed his, and their tongues met. She was utterly different from Raisa: heavier, stronger, wilder, and more demanding.

Where the Arkanna shared with Zack, giving and taking, Kiani only took greedily. But she felt good nonetheless. Until that is after they climaxed, and Zack remembered that he had a previous engagement with one Raisa Darhad.

I guess I can always say that I was raped by Nihao, he thought, feeling weak-kneed. He disentangled himself and grinned at her.

"Thanks for that unexpected bout of the post-combat sport. For what it's worth, I'd rather do this than fight you. Anytime you want a rematch..."

She smiled back, but the smile didn't quite reach her eyes.

"I suggest we rinse off and head to our appointed duties," she replied, all business again.

And I love you too, kid. Zack felt irritated at her off-hand tone. He didn't expect declarations of undying lust, but somehow, she had made him feel used.

Without another word, they washed and returned to the cabin. For the rest of the day, Kiani acted as if nothing had happened. Zack, however, on closer reflection, wondered about her. Did the bout of martial arts turn her on, or was it the sight of his and Darhad's growing intimacy? They made no secret of their relationship, even if they kept it off *Shokoten*.

Whatever it was, he realized that he would be better off without a repeat performance, no matter how deprived he became. Something about Nihao was definitely bothering him.

Soon enough, Decker had more pressing issues to deal with. During the night watch, *Shokoten* came out of hyperspace in the Ventos system. Less than twelve tense hours later, the freighter slipped into orbit around the distant, alien world.

— ELEVEN —

"It's pretty close to Earth norm, Captain," the gunner reported, a hint of doubt in his voice. "But there are trace gases and pollution in the atmosphere I don't like. Plus, there are a lot of radiation hot spots on the surface, more of them and warmer than you'd expect to occur naturally."

That wasn't all Decker had seen from orbit, using the ship's scanners. Ventos Prime was hot, dry, its two huge landmasses parched.

It also showed evidence of multiple nuclear strikes, small ones to be sure and mainly concentrated on one of the two large continents, but enough to poison the atmosphere and the ground for centuries. He couldn't tell how old the strikes were, but he was willing to bet it would still be a long time before the craters down there stopped bombarding nature with stray gamma rays.

"Looks like the natives enjoy lobbing tac nukes at each other," he continued. "Have we received landing coordinates? I'd like to take a closer look for anything that might make our hair and teeth fall out. This isn't a healthy place if you ask me."

"Nothing yet, Gunner. You'll be the first to know," Strachan replied with an irritated frown. Darhad threw Zack a warning glance.

Decker shrugged and returned to his scanners. Tweaking their output beyond the manufacturer's specs, he focused on a major center of life on the most bombarded continent, which he had called, for lack of a better name, Continent One. Frowning, he fed the results through *Shokoten*'s computer and waited. His frown deepened when the machine spat out its analysis.

Life, definitely, but it isn't humanoid. Not even close. Nothing in the data banks match. And there's a hell of a lot of 'em. Over two million within a single square kilometer. That can't be right! Ah, I see. Multi-layered underground city. Sort of like a hive.

He mentally shivered as his imagination conjured a nightmare of giant creatures mindlessly crawling through miles of dark tunnels, feeding the likes of Zack to their young. Then he had another thought.

He turned his instrumentation on the bomb craters and sent the scans deep underground. The computer cycled through another analysis, leaving Zack to twiddle his thumbs with impatience.

The captain, struggling to control his own anxiety, ignored his gunner and stared at the planet on the viewscreen as if regretting this run. Raisa Darhad busied herself with minor tasks, shutting out the growing feelings of uncertainty and worry from the rest of the bridge crew.

Here we go. Zack focused his attention on the readout again. *Just as I suspected. Remains of tunnels similar to those of the bug city, under the nuke craters. Shit, when did I start thinking of the aliens down there as bugs? They could be anything. Bad to develop preconceived notions, Pathfinder.*

But Zack couldn't wipe the picture of hives from his mind. He was ill at ease, much more so than at any other time since joining *Shokoten*. The remainder of the crew seemed to be as well, if he was any judge of moods. It seemed like a damn strange place to be shipping household tech.

He turned his attention on the other continent and was surprised to find an environment dissimilar from the first one. The continents were at nearly opposite ends of the globe, separated by thousands of kilometers of ocean, but even then there shouldn't be that much difference. Few nuclear explosion craters pockmarked the surface, and only near the water's edge as if someone or something had used them to drive off an enemy landing.

Continent Two also had more vegetation and more signs of sentient life, widely scattered in above ground towns. The life signs too differed from the earlier ones. Sure, the basic patterns looked similar, but that was normal if both species evolved from the same earlier, more primitive life forms. Somehow, Zack wasn't surprised when he found no underground warrens, but he suspected that the nuke sites near the water's edge might have obliterated embryonic hives.

The more he saw of Ventos Prime, the less he liked it. It was no wonder the standard navigation data banks or the Guild's Better Business catalog didn't list this place as a vacation destination. Now he *really* wanted to find out what they were doing here.

He entered his observations in the ship's log but put his own comments and deductions under password lock in his personal files. No need to alarm the crew, and maybe, just maybe, Strachan would prefer him not to be quite so observant or smart. Especially smart.

Raisa had told him Strachan was often surprised to find that former Marine noncoms were a lot brighter and more knowledgeable than he thought. And Zack's instincts, for reasons he'd rather not dwell on, told him he shouldn't push things.

"Mister Decker!"

Zack's head snapped around when he realized he'd been lost in thought and had missed Strachan's orders.

"If you're still with us," the captain said, with uncharacteristic sarcasm, "you might wish to scan the coordinates nav has fed to your console. We've already wasted enough time up here."

"Yes, sir," Zack came to attention in his seat. "Right away, sir." A few moments later he turned his chair towards the captain again. "The coordinates are near a large city on Continent Two." At Strachan's raised eyebrows, Decker explained that he'd baptized the two largest continents on the planet.

"Radiation readings are within tolerable limits, but I suggest all personnel who'll come into contact with the air down there wear filters. It'll sift out the most noxious airborne dust particles. We ought to be fine for about an hour or so of continuous exposure. I wouldn't recommend shore leave here." Nor would he recommend resupplying in this place, he thought, remembering Strachan telling them they'd get the pantry topped up on Ventos Prime.

"Thank you for that editorial comment, Gunner," the captain snapped. "Nav, confirm course and lay in."
"Confirmed, sir."
"Helm, engage."

*

The filters might have kept pollutants from searing his lungs, but they didn't keep out the choking smell, and Zack grimaced as he stepped out of the airlock.

The red sun hurt his eyes, and he cursed all cheap civilian filters without self-polarizing facemasks. But the fiery, giant orb hanging over the horizon did more than just hurt his eyes. It turned the gray, chemical and radiation filled atmosphere into a churning smog-tinted an unhealthy shade of brown.

The alien town shimmered in the distance, its dun-colored walls, and spires merging with a monotonous plain devoid of vegetation. Billowing pillars of smoke grew from muddy stems on the town's outskirts, adding to the crud hanging over Ventos Prime.

Far away to the north, a purplish mountain ridge reared up against the dirty sky like the rotting teeth of an antediluvian creature. The ship's scanners had shown high concentrations of heavy metals in the ground, an underground aquifer so polluted that a single sip of the water would kill a human being, and heavy traces of cancerous chemicals in the air. One heck of a vacation spot for would-be mutants.

Zack took in the scene with one sweep of his watchful eyes, but strange and worrisome as the planet was, the ship beside which *Shokoten* had landed worried him even more. Sleek, pointy, with many dark scars, and welded-on patches, it looked like nothing other than a marauder, a renegade ship. He searched its hull in vain for a registration number, a name, or a homeport.

Its belly ramp was down, and a pair of fierce Kardati humanoids stood guard, their plasma rifles slung over their shoulders. Deep-set red eyes had glanced at Decker with disinterest, cataloging him as nothing more than a civilian spacer, potential prey.

A cloud of dust rose at the foot of the town's walls and grew as it neared, accompanied by a loud, irritating sound that set Zack's teeth on edge. Soon, the cloud resolved itself into a column of ground vehicles, each carrying several standard containers, each belching clouds of dark fumes from rusty tubes behind the cab, and each making enough noise to wake the dead. The stench from these trucks was indescribable, and several of the bosun's mates with Zack swore as they fingered their guns.

A set of feet made the decking of the ramp vibrate. He glanced behind and saw, to his surprise, that Captain Strachan was coming down to join them, wearing one of the lightly built breathing masks.

"Sir." Zack nodded.

"I see our cargo has arrived. Please make sure that none of the natives climb aboard. I must speak with the agent. I believe that's him coming now."

A swarthy skinned, black-clad figure stepped off the other ship's ramp and, accompanied by one of the guards, made his way towards *Shokoten*, seemingly oblivious to the racket of the ground convoy.

As Strachan stepped off the ramp to meet him halfway, Zack motioned one of the mates to follow the captain. If the reiver was going to have a bodyguard, so was Strachan. As an added gesture, Zack loosened his blaster in his holster, making sure the gesture wasn't lost on the strangers. They gave him a cold, uninterested glance and then looked away dismissively.

The captain and the mystery man held a quiet conversation on the dusty landing field between the ships while a group of natives waited patiently by their trucks. They weren't on a real tarmac. This looked more like a combat LZ than a spaceport: no tower, no ramps, no terminal, and no communications array. In fact, nothing broke the uneven sameness of the beaten ground. It probably meant the natives didn't have spaceflight technology yet, and that meant the humans shouldn't be there.

Commonwealth law was clear about contact with pre spaceflight civilizations. Nobody wanted a repeat of the near disaster caused by first contact with preindustrial cultures in the Shield Cluster. Within a few years, unscrupulous traders had sold Shield races such as the Kardati, enough tech to let them jump to a spacefaring society without accruing the benefits of civilization.

Ever since, the Shield had been a nest of reivers, pirates, buccaneers, slavers and worse: feudal cultures with high tech, techno barbarian, as the Fleet called them. The only way to stop them after a few generations of violent living would have been to bomb them back into the Stone Age. Even the hardest of hardliners would have balked at those measures.

Decker studied the Ventosans with eyes narrowed against the glare. They were not humanoid by any stretch of the imagination, looking more like six-limbed, tailless lizards with long eyestalks and gray-brown skin. The center pair of limbs appeared to function as feet or as hands, depending on the owner's whim. The eyestalks could swivel independently and did so with dizzying speed as the natives anxiously glanced at both intruding vessels and their strange crews. With the capacity to produce nuclear bombs, they certainly weren't preindustrial, but what they had done to their planet put them far down the scale of civilization.

Strachan finished his exchange with the agent and returned to *Shokoten*, his face a neutral mask. The other man headed for the cluster of natives. A few moments later, the trucks, still belching their noxious fumes, formed in a single file and made for the ship. Zack repressed an overwhelming desire to run for the clean, scent-free air of the ship's interior and dispersed his mates to cover the approaching aliens.

The Ventosans parked their empty, wheeled trucks directly beneath the ship's fully deployed gantry. With the help of the second officer's crew, the inbound freight was quickly unloaded and driven away. Just as rapidly the outbound containers were hoisted aboard from the backs of the remaining trucks.

None of the ship's crew spoke with the aliens, and all communication was done through basic hand signals that the aliens seemed to understand well enough. In less than an hour, *Shokoten* had exchanged its battered containers for those supplied by the natives, and the crew was busy strapping them down for the return trip.

Decker saw Kiani slip out of the freighter and vanish into the other ship. She returned half an hour later with a scowl of disapproval on her face, but with a string of grav pallets, driven by the other ship's crew, behind her. The pallets held standard foodstuff crates, marked with the logo of one of the Commonwealth's larger chandleries.

As he read the markings, only to discover they were getting soy-based rations, Zack made a grimace of distaste, causing the nearest Kardati to laugh derisively. But Nihao, who seemed to be in an atrocious mood, snapped out an order in a tongue Decker didn't understand, and the spacer lost his look of merriment.

With Ventos Prime's sun setting the horizon on fire, *Shokoten* closed up, pumped out the polluted air, and prepared for liftoff. Zack had made sure every crewmember who had exposed himself to the atmosphere went through a decontamination routine in a specially prepared airlock. Some, like Nihao, grumbled but cooperated when the gunner showed them a list of the crud they were carrying on their dust-covered bodies.

Later, when *Shokoten* was buttoned up, and Zack sat at his station on the bridge, he kept a close, but surreptitious eye on the other ship. As it powered up to leave the planet, he took scans of its emissions.

That pretty much kicks it. No honest trader has that much power in her thrusters. Eats up too much fuel to be profitable.

But he didn't dare run an active scan. They'd be bound to detect his interest, and that might not be good for his continued health. By the time *Shokoten* broke out of orbit, the mystery ship had vanished, boosting out on powerful engines to destinations unknown.

Zack returned to his quarters, lost in deep thought, the moment they went FTL. Something smelled to high heaven. He was sure the secret lay not in what they'd delivered, but what they picked up. Standard Commonwealth-style containers on a distant, pre spaceflight world meant more than just simple smuggling, and Zack's gut instinct gave him severe pangs of discomfort.

He had to scan those containers without being caught. Doing it openly was out. When he asked Strachan whether he should camouflage them, the captain shook his head, acting just too much on the anxious side of irritable, and that had raised the former Pathfinder's sensitive bullshit detectors even further. Beans to bullets Strachan didn't want Zack to find out what was in the containers.

Nihao Kiani, when she finally joined him in their cabin, remained silent and ignored the gunner in her old, cold manner. Judging by the temperature in the room, nobody could have figured they'd made the beast with two backs in the shower less than forty-eight hours earlier.

That night, Decker's sleep was plagued by nightmares where monsters conjured by his overheated imagination pursued him down claustrophobic tunnels lined with silvery cocoons. More than once, he woke in a cold sweat only to repeat the experience the moment he fell asleep again. Even if his conscious mind couldn't pinpoint the origin of his discomfort, his subconscious was on to something.

*

It took Zack a few days to plan and prepare his unauthorized visit to the cargo hold. As chief of security, he had many access possibilities, but it was a given, at least in his mind, that anything he did would be double checked by someone else. The Marine Corps trained its Pathfinders to assume the enemy was at least as competent as they were, and the former sergeant wasn't about to chuck that oft proven bit of wisdom out the nearest airlock.

If this were something beyond mere smuggling, Strachan would watch him closely for any signs of disloyalty. Or, as Decker saw it, signs of his old loyalty to the Corps resurfacing.

Gun turret number four was below the hold and its access tube also had emergency hatches into the hold itself. On freighters, where space was at a premium, systems that could be combined often were. Of course, the access plates were all wired into the security system, so his first move was to reroute the detectors into a closed loop.

Then, he needed an excuse to spend time working on number four, which meant a controlled malfunction that would look real to anyone but a gunner. Finally, he needed a way to keep random security checks from detecting him in the hold while simultaneously showing him in the turret. That required a delicate rewrite of the control software, a modification that would only kick in when Zack wanted it to.

As he spent hours on his secret work, Decker felt more like a Fleet agent out of a low-grade action show, than a merchant gunnery officer, and that brought his mind back to the inscribed Master Gunner's badge that had been slipped into his pocket.

*

Five days out of Ventos, the mood on the ship was at its lowest ebb. Strachan's tension had trickled down to the lower deck and added to the crew's underlying nervousness at the long light years between *Shokoten* and the safety of home space. There was also something indefinable in that atmosphere, something that had started on the alien planet and had grown, as if evil had slipped aboard and was waiting in a dark corner of the ship, biding its time.

Zack had never experienced a sensation quite like it. Infected by the mood himself, his own paranoia grew as he worked on his plans for a private visit to the cargo hold. He was disturbed to find he didn't even trust Raisa, although the Arkanna seemed just as uneasy as everybody else did, and had been cut off from Strachan's usual confidences along with the gunner.

Decker sat at his console during the final hour of the afternoon watch, alternately checking his security net and scanning the surrounding hyperspace bubble for drive wakes. The bridge was quiet, each member of the watch keeping to him or herself. Below decks, the off-duty crew was quiescent for once, most either sleeping or playing games. Raisa had the con and sat in the captain's chair, eyes alert, observing the crew and their stations. Her body seemed relaxed, but Decker knew it was filled with coiled power, energy that couldn't find an outlet.

His plan was ready, and he wouldn't have a better chance than now, near the end of a watch, with Raisa in charge. He ran a full check of the weapon systems, triggering the carefully placed subroutines. These, in turn, created a malfunction in turret number four, started the feedback loop, and set the scan foiling routine to standby mode.

"Mister Darhad?"

"Yes, Gunner," she replied, stretching as she walked over to his console.

"I've detected a malfunction in turret four, probably nothing more than an end-of-life breakdown in one of the components. But the guns aren't going to fire until I fix it. Permission to carry out repairs? It's near the end of the watch anyways."

She glanced at the screen over his shoulders, giving Zack's nostrils the chance to get reacquainted with her scent, and lightly laid her hand on his shoulder.

"By all means, Gunner."

"Thank you, sir." Decker glanced up at Darhad and forced a smile. "I'll give you a report when I've seen the damage."

She removed her hand and stepped back to give him room to rise. As he unfolded to his full height, their eyes met. Her brows furrowed minutely as if she had seen or sensed something unusual, and Zack suddenly feared she had somehow sensed his purpose. He smiled again and winked though his insides were in turmoil and his throat constricted as if he were about to jump into battle.

Without a backwards glance, he left the bridge, stopping by his cabin only long enough to change into coveralls and pick up his tools. Nihao Kiani, stretched out on her bunk, reading, ignored Zack.

*

The dark access tube was as claustrophobic as the hive tunnels of his nightmares and Zack shivered as he closed the hatch behind him. Crawling slowly, he passed the access plate leading to the cargo hold above him. Upon reaching the turret, he pulled the command module from its socket. That simple act broke a computer-monitored loop and set in motion his scan-masking routine, which would show him to be in the turret and not in the hold, no matter where he was. Of course, it wouldn't foil a handheld unit independent of the ship's systems. But as far as he could tell, he had the only one within light years.

He crawled back to the access plate and carefully broke the magnetic seal holding it in place. With a grunt of effort, he caught it and slowly put it on the tube's floor, taking care to make as little noise as possible. Vibrations carried far.

Decker pulled himself through the opening and onto the cargo hold's cold floor, emerging between two stacks of battered containers. He remained motionless for almost a minute, heightened senses reaching out to listen and smell for anything that shouldn't be there. Then, he pulled out his sensor and flicked it on.

The first two containers, marked as having originated on Rhada, registered nothing usual beyond complex polymers, trace minerals, and what looked suspiciously like massive amounts of hardened clay. Certainly nothing to pay for a long trip. Not knowing what he was looking for, Decker kept his sensor's settings broad and general, and he almost missed it the first time around.

There. A slight blip on the readout. He frowned as he narrowed the focus and tried again, slowly running through the spectrum.

If he didn't know any better, he'd have said those were organics. The clay compound in the container was just similar enough to the composition of whatever it was to hide it, but he had seen something close to that organic sequence before, on Ventos Prime. There were about three dozen separate organic things inside, each about the size of a basketball.

He shook his head in puzzlement, and with an inexplicable fear slowly worming its way down his spine, Zack scanned each container in turn. When he was finally done, twenty long minutes later, he slipped back into the access tube and put the hatch in place, activating the magnetic seal.

He crawled back to the gun turret and stopped his camouflage programs. The interruption wiped the hacked lines of code through a simple, self-destructing virus. Then, he stretched out in the confined space and put his arm under his head.

They had ten containers with each holding three dozen of the organic things, which a routine Fleet or Constabulary inspection won't find since they can't make the difference between the clay and the 'melons,' not without having seen a scan of the Ventos Prime ecosystem.

Another five containers each held two high-tech artefacts that were way beyond what Ventos Prime could produce. If he believed his sensor, those were stasis boxes. And why not believe his sensor? He calibrated it himself.

The law said you weren't supposed to import organics into the Commonwealth without a license, especially from a pre-spaceflight planet where they weren't meant to be in the first place.

And where did that leave him? There was no way to figure out what these things were, and he sure wasn't going to ask Diego Strachan. Not if he wanted to live to see the end of this trip.

Zachary Decker was a realist. He understood his only course of action was to make as if he had no idea what they were hauling and wait for a chance to find out more about Ventos when he could reach a library terminal. Such as find out what that primitive, probably interdicted planet had that would attract a merchant freighter belonging to a company which belonged to another company which was owned by the corporation which belonged to one of the richest families in the Commonwealth.

What if he found something the Fleet needed to know? More to the point, what if it was something enough that someone might decide he was a security risk after all?

He quickly downloaded the scan onto a thumbnail-sized chip that he then encoded for added protection. The chip vanished into his toolbox, hidden among the bits and pieces in a side compartment. As a final measure of security, he wiped the sensor's RAM and made sure its internal storage memory had no trace of the scan.

A few minutes later, he had set the turret to rights, changed a few strategically chosen, worn-out modules, and fooled the computer into believing he had run a full spectrum post-repair test. That would account for the time he spent down there.

*

Raisa Darhad must have known something preoccupied Zack. She gave him searching glances whenever they were alone in the wardroom. It heightened the Decker's paranoia, especially since he now strongly suspected she was an empath of sorts. But how much she knew, and how she would react to his findings remained an open question.

A few days after the malfunction in number four, Darhad invited Zack to a sparring session in the mini-gym, making sure they'd be alone and undisturbed. It wasn't an unusual occurrence, now that the sinking morale among the crew had whittled down their training group.

Decker and Darhad met at the appointed time and stole a quick kiss before stretching their muscles to prepare for the bout. They made small talk only, the gunner carefully weighing each word.

They fought for a few moments, sizing each other up and making a few practice throws. Then, the Arkanna moved like a flash and tossed Decker to the mat, grabbing him in a tight hold once he was down. Instead of letting him go right away, so they could resume combat, she placed her lips against his ear.

"Zack, why did you go into the cargo hold a few days ago?" She asked, whispering. "Don't worry, no one else knows."

For a few heartbeats, Decker was struck dumb at her words and his gut tightened in fear. The rational part of his mind took over, however, and he realized that she had maneuvered him into this position to question him without that fact being apparent. Which could only mean she didn't want to harm him.

Raisa let go and rose to her feet in a graceful motion. They squared off again and this time, Zack threw her to the mat. When he had her in a tight hold, he bent his head down and pressed his cheek against hers, speaking more softly than she had. Arkanna hearing was vastly better than a human's.

"Something strange about this trip. Had to know what we picked up on a planet we shouldn't have visited." She grunted in question. "Yeah, I found something. We picked up organics on Ventos. They're well hidden among crap that wouldn't start to pay for the voyage."

Zack released her perspiring body, and they rose to square off yet again. This time, the two combatants locked into a standing hold, each trying to unbalance the other.

"Do you have any ideas?" She whispered.

"None I'd care to explore right now. We need to discover what on that planet is so attractive. The first chance we have, we must find a library terminal with nobody knowing." Pause. "Are you in on this with Strachan?"

"No. The captain has not confided in me since we three last met. Our cargo is unknown to me, but, like you, I'm overcome by unease."

"How did you find out I snuck in?"

"You left your scent in the cargo hold. I checked the day after, as I suspected you would be interested, and the malfunction was too convenient."

"Damn!"

"I'm the only one on board who could do it, and then only because you and I are intimate. I would have helped." She sounded disappointed.

"Fair enough," he replied ruefully, "I should have trusted you."

"When we reach a human planet, we will learn more."

And somehow, hearing her say it with such conviction, Zack knew they would. When they separated and bowed to each other, signaling the end of the bout, the gunner felt much better about his predicament. He was no longer alone.

"Thank you for the fight. I should be pleased to meet you again in this arena, at your convenience."

"The pleasure is all mine, First Officer." *Damn right it is, you splendid, screwy, unpredictable she-wolf.*

*

The purser walked into the cabin and ran her watchful eyes over Zack's sweaty body as he stripped to prepare for his shower.

"Did you have a good fight with our first officer?" Kiani asked in a neutral her tone.

"Yeah," he replied, trying to sound nonchalant. *Keeping an eye on me, Nihao? How did you know I was with Raisa in there?* "She doesn't have your ruthlessness, but she gives a good workout."

"Not ruthless?" She laughed sharply. "Beware Arkanna women, Zack."

He narrowed his eyes and stared at her. "Why?"

"They're treacherous and selfish creatures. They're empaths and can manipulate any male they want for their own ends. Did she tell you how she came to leave her world?"

"Yeah, sort of, but treacherous and selfish? C'mon. Aren't you laying it on a bit thick?" Zack didn't know how to react. What was it with her? Was the strain of the voyage uncovering a hidden streak of jealousy?

"Am I? Our dear First Officer Darhad is a murderess on the run from her own people. She did not tell you," Kiani nodded knowingly when she saw Zack's astonished face.

"She killed her pack matriarch out of jealousy and murdered two more Arkanna as she fled."

"You found out about this how?" Decker asked, anger taking over.

"Pursers have their own intelligence system. One hears much on alien worlds, and Darhad's story eventually reached my ears. Arkanna in human service are unusual. She could not have gone to the Empire: they would have handed her back to her people. Yes, Zachary, your lover has murdered three of her own, and at least one human. Did you know she had a predilection for gunners? Your predecessor found out when he became ensnared in her web. He tried to break free, but in the end, he lost. And she killed him for it."

"What the hell's your problem? Is it because you and Lokis had a thing too?" Zack lashed out at her, harsher, in his confusion, than he had intended to be.

"Yes we had, damn you, and no, I'm not blackening her simply for revenge." Her eyes blazed with anger and pain. "The bitch stole him from me out of spite." Her chest heaved as she fought to control her emotions.

"Listen, Zack, when they found Lokis, his body bore marks that looked much like those inflicted by talons or claws."

"If you're convinced she killed him, why didn't you tell the captain?"

"Because she has influence over him as well and because I have no evidence that will stand up in court. But I'm sure she's a murderous bitch who has no heart for anyone. Lord only knows what she wants of you. Apart from the obvious that is."

"I find this hard to believe. I've killed before. More than she has."

"But you did it in the line of duty. Beware, Zack, she will tire of you. I know I've not been easy to deal with or shown you much concern of late. My duties are demanding. But I do like you and wish you well. I don't want you to end like Lokis, in a gutter with your throat ripped out."

Zack shook his head as he tossed the towel on his bunk.

"Here look!" Nihao had pulled a holo out of her desk.

He took the image and stared at it, stomach heaving in horror. On it, a human male, approximately forty years old, lay on a litter-strewn, cobblestone alley. His throat had been ripped out with great force, and the visible parts of his body were lacerated with parallel slashes.

"Lokis?"

"Yes. The Pradyn Guard gave us this." Her voice trembled, and she seemed on the verge of tears.

Raisa could have done this. He had seen her do it to the Pradyni muggers on their first shore leave together. Then again, this picture could be forged, but why would anyone do that?

A quiet sob broke his train of thought, and he looked at Nihao. Tears ran down her cheeks as her shoulders shook. Instinctively, Zack took her in his arms to comfort her, forgetting his nude state. He felt her sob against his shoulder, her breath on his neck and her hands on his back. It aroused him. It also aroused her. She lifted her head and looked him in the eyes, sending a thrill up the gunner's spine.

With his help, she stripped off her uniform in record speed and pushed him down on her bunk. Straddling his hips, she guided him inside her. Zack's last coherent thought before his senses overloaded was that manipulation took many forms. And males of all species were putty in the hands of determined females.

— TWELVE —

Zack spent a long time in the shower scrubbing off Nihao's scent, but he couldn't wash away her ugly accusations. How she slipped from cold and distant to hot and passionate had done much to throw him off kilter.

Unable to figure out what he should do, Zack tried his damnest to stay away from situations where he was alone with either woman. It was easy enough with Raisa: duty kept her busy, and it wasn't too hard to make sure they exercised when someone else was in the gym. Nihao was another matter.

Sharing a cabin became a distinct chore. He tried to make sure he came off watch when she was already in bed, but sometimes, she either waited for him or woke, and then would seduce him with frightening ease. Marines were often accused of thinking with their gonads, and Zack Decker did the Corps proud.

*

Shokoten soon neared the Shield Cluster and Captain Strachan put the ship on heightened vigilance. He was even more nervous than on the way in, and Zack decided that the ship's owners attached a lot of importance to the cargo they were bringing back. Knowing who they were, he could understand Strachan's anxieties. Failure was a capital sin on Pacifica.

On the other hand, the heightened vigilance kept Zack out of Nihao's clutches by giving him an excuse to work twenty hours a day either standing watch, drilling the crew or keeping the ship's armaments in peak condition.

It also brought back him in closer contact with Raisa, and his deep-set guilt at cheating on her. If the Arkanna sensed his confusion, she hid it well and asked no probing questions, though he sometimes caught her looking at him with unspoken worry in her eyes.

*

A few light years short of Commonwealth space, but still in the badlands, *Shokoten* emerged for a routine hyperdrive recalibration and so the navigator could plot the next jump.

While the engineer's crew worked with unusual speed, Zack scanned the surrounding area most carefully, a sinking feeling in the pit of his stomach making him very uneasy. They were in the prime marauding country, just out of reach of a Fleet constrained by law. Why Strachan chose this spot to emerge for course corrections was beyond Decker's understanding.

The bridge buzzed with quiet activity, but Strachan's fingers danced impatiently on the arm of his chair as if he were expecting something.

Suddenly, Zack's eyes were drawn to the lower corner of his tactical screen.

"Captain," he called out, voice calm but loud enough to break through the hubbub of the bridge. "I have an emergence trace about a million kilometers behind us."

"Identify."

"Still too far out, sir."

"Very well, Gunner," he replied, calmer than Zack had expected. "Go to battle stations and keep me advised of developments."

Zack turned his attention back to the interloper, leaving Strachan to egg on his navigator and engineers. The unknown ship was on a direct intercept course, and its speed matched that of an over-engined pirate. Decker had little doubt about its intentions. When it was about three-quarters of a million kilometers away, the other ship fired.

"Captain, they've just put two missiles up our wake. At that range, assuming she hits us, it'll only rattle the shields. Must be a new crew out there, to fire so early and give themselves away."

"Thank you, Gunner," Strachan nodded, still calmer than he should be. If Zack hadn't known any better, he'd have sworn the man relaxed when he heard the reiver had fired. "Nav, are your computations final?"

"Aye, sir. Ready to go."

"Engineering had given the all-clear," First Officer Darhad reported.

"Helm, lock in the course and engage."

The stars blurred as the hyperdrives took *Shokoten* beyond light speed. A familiar nausea rose in Zack's throat but it vanished within seconds as the ship's speed stabilized inside its bubble. He searched for signs of pursuit, but in vain. The distortion of the hyperdrives blanked out any signals.

They ran for an hour, then two in silence. Eventually, near the end of the watch, the navigator announced that they had entered Commonwealth space again, an announcement that brought subdued cheers and broad grins from the bridge crew. They weren't quite home yet, but at least they now sailed where the Navy's writ protected merchant ships.

The relief proved to be short-lived. A distant explosion rattled the ship, and they tripped back into normal space, giving the crew an unexpected dose of disorientation. Zack swore over the whoop of the alarm siren and searched for the reiver's emergence trace on his tactical display. He didn't see the small smile play on Strachan's lips. Darhad, however, did, and she sensed a kind of tense amusement in him.

"Got him," Zack broke through the din of voices. "Eight hundred thousand kilometers off our starboard bow. Turning towards us. All our weapons are powered up and ready to fire when he gets within range. I suggest nav plot an emergency micro jump."

"Thank you, Gunner. I will take your suggestion under advisement."

Decker looked at Raisa, surprised by the reply, but she shrugged, as mystified as he was. He returned his attention to the attacker and prepared to repulse him with all *Shokoten* had.

"Signals — send out a distress call on all frequencies," the captain continued. "Helm, prepare for defensive maneuvering. Mister Darhad, ask our engineer to move as fast as she can on recalibrating the drives."

"Aye, sir."

Zack studied the reiver's cautious approach, frowning. He was too slow and too prudent as if he were afraid of something. Pirates working within patrolled space struck fast and hard. They had little time before a Navy ship might appear.

It turned out to be the same ship that had fired on them earlier but this time, its captain waited to come within range before opening up with his guns.

Shokoten's helmsman made rapid course corrections, trying to throw off the reiver's aim while Zack replied in kind. A few shots struck the shields without causing damage. For a moment, he had the strange notion that they were fighting a sham match, one of those bouts where both boxers were careful not to injure each other.

Of course, it could be that the reiver had a lousy gunner, but that seemed unlikely. Pirate crews whose performance displeased their captain rarely had long careers.

The battle soon turned into a stern chase as the reiver kept taking pot shots at *Shokoten* while Decker tried as best he could to hit him back with his turrets slewed aft. It fast became monotonous. The pirate shot and struck. Zack fired back and struck. They'd both cover another hundred thousand kilometers or so and shoot again, without causing appreciable damage to each other's shields.

Then, a third ship appeared, plunging out of hyperspace towards them. Decker let out a crow of triumph as he identified it.

"Captain, we have a Navy missile frigate off our port side! Five hundred thousand kilometers and closing fast."

Shokoten shook with a final salvo, and then the reiver abandoned the chase and jumped, unwilling to relinquish the role of hunter to the frigate.

"Freighter *Shokoten*, this is *Garibaldi*, Captain Bezan commanding. Are you all right?"

Cheers echoed through the bridge as the face of a dark-haired officer appeared on the main screen.

"This is Captain Strachan. Thank you for your timely intervention. We've suffered no damage, except to our nerves."

"Glad we could be of help, Captain. It doesn't happen all too often that we arrive in time to scare away the bad guys. Not often at all." Bezan frowned, his dark eyes watching Strachan with palpable suspicion as if he thought something was funny about this incident. The gunner could relate. He smelled a rat too. A big, fat, rotting rat.

"I suppose we were lucky," Strachan was looking uneasy, though he still tried to ooze his slickest brand of charm. "It likely helped that I have a good gunner who held the pirate at bay long enough."

Bezan raised a skeptical eyebrow. The merchant service wasn't known for the quality of its weapons' officers.

"I would like to congratulate this martial paragon if I may, Captain Strachan."

Strachan motioned Zack over.

"Warrant Officer Zachary Decker," he said, "is a former Marine Corps Master Gunner and has proven to be quite an asset."

Zack nodded at the screen. "Sir."

"Well, well. The universe is small, isn't it, Sergeant, or should I say, Mister Decker? Glad to see you again. And equally happy that you landed on your feet."

Zack managed to contain his surprise only by a tremendous effort of will. He knew about Bezan from serving aboard *Musashi,* which patrolled the same area of space as *Garibaldi* but he'd certainly never met the man in person.

"Glad to see you again as well, sir," he stammered out, hoping he didn't sound puzzled. It could have been his imagination, but he seemed to detect a sign of approval from Bezan.

"Captain Strachan, with a man like Decker behind your guns, I can believe you gave the reiver more to contend with than he would have thought. Tell me, Mister Decker, how does it feel to be on the receiving end of piracy?" Bezan smiled, but the smile had a dangerous edge to it.

"If all reivers are like the one you ran off, I don't figure it's much of a problem, sir."

"Easy mark?" That hint of suspicion was back again, if it had ever left. Strachan glanced at Zack, his eyes betraying anxiety at what the gunner would say.

"Not easy sir, but it wasn't an experienced crew or captain, I'd say. What with the cleanup of the area last year, the reiver clans must be building up from scratch. At least this guy knew enough to break off when the odds shifted." Zack sensed rather than saw Strachan relax. He shrugged. "Luck's always in the game too, sir. Guess we were lucky this time around."

"I suppose you were," Bezan sounded thoughtful. He rubbed his chin. "Where are you headed?"

"We're bound for Pacifica with a cargo of assorted minerals, luxury items and samples from Rhada," Strachan replied, dismissing Zack with a flick of the fingers. The gunner had played his part and was no longer required.

"A long trip."

"Indeed. But a ship like ours goes where the contract stipulates. If our owners wish to open trading in exotic items with a far-off planet, then who are we to gainsay them."

"Sounds familiar," Bezan chuckled. "And here I thought you merchant types were free to roam the star lanes. I guess I'm an old romantic. Anyway, you should be all right from now on. Things have been quiet in the sector. Have a nice trip, *Shokoten*."

"Thank you and please thank your crew for the rescue."

"All in day's work. *Garibaldi*, out."

Strachan looked like he wanted to sigh with relief when Bezan's face faded from the screen.

"Nav, plot a course for Pacifica. I don't think we'll have any more problems."

"Course laid in and ready."

"Helm, engage."

Strachan turned towards Zack and smiled.

"Well done, Mister Decker. Stand down from battle stations. I believe we shall encounter no more troubles."

The gunner nodded and powered down the guns, shields, and launchers. But his mind was elsewhere. Did Strachan mean well done for the fight, or for snowing Bezan? When he got right down to it, that reiver was shamming, and Bezan could smell the ruse.

A signal on his console caught his attention, ending that particular bit of speculation. One of the aft turrets had overheated during the stern chase and needed his immediate attention.

By the time he'd completed a thorough check of the ship's ordnance, he was too tired to think. Even Nihao left him alone that night after taking one look at his drawn face.

*

The next day, Zack reviewed his log entry of the incident and, on a hunch, checked the reiver's power curve. Each ship had its own emissions signal, distinct even from a ship of the same class and type, launched by the same shipyard on the same day, a starship fingerprint of sorts. These could be faked, just like real fingerprints, but Zack didn't think it was the case here. The power curve of their mysterious attacker was so close to that of the ship that had met on Ventos Prime that Decker was convinced they were the same.

It only reinforced his belief that the whole attack had been a setup, designed to fool a patrol ship into dispensing with the usual customs check. And it had worked like a charm. Except for one thing. Why did Bezan pretend he knew Decker personally?

Zack found no satisfactory answers to any of his questions and the rest of the trip to Pacifica became an exercise in frustration and patience. His mood did not lighten when *Shokoten* finally slipped into orbit.

"Captain, we received a message from the surface."

The signalman's voice broke through Zack's bad mood. He perked up to listen. They had been circling the planet for close to six hours, a long time for a developed world that depended on trade, and he wondered why.

"A flight plan, landing coordinates, and authorization to land," the signaler continued. "Feeding to nav now. There's also a private message for you."

"Thank you," Strachan nodded.

"Sir," Gareth turned from his navigation console, "the coordinates are not for a spaceport." He sounded puzzled. "They're on an island in the South Ocean. The computer lists it as privately owned."

"Your point being?" The captain asked, unusually sarcastic. Before the young officer could reply, he continued. "Just enter the flight path and take us down there. If our owners want us to land on a private island, we will land on a private island."

"Aye, sir."

"Engage." Then, Strachan left the bridge for his cabin, a move that made Darhad raise her eyebrows in surprise as she slipped into the captain's chair. *Shokoten*'s cautious master usually liked to oversee landings himself. He returned a few minutes later and glanced at Zack with a frown, but declined to comment.

*

The island slowly grew on the main screen, and Zack watched with interest. It was approximately kidney-shaped, about fifty kilometers from tip to tip and maybe half that at its widest. The indentation of the kidney looked like a decent natural harbor, with clear blue waters and sandy beaches. A low range of wooded hills ran along the island's spine, ending with an extinct volcano at the southern end. Along the bay's shores, someone with a lot of money had built a sizeable landing strip, surrounded by many low buildings.

When *Shokoten* had settled on the plascrete pad, its hull pinging and groaning as it cooled down, Strachan rose from his seat.

"Mister Bowdoin, prepare to offload. Container carriers will arrive shortly. We will not load outbound cargo here. Zack, you're with me. There will be no need for your security detail this time."

They stepped down the gangplank into the bright sunshine. Natural heat and light hit Decker like a sledgehammer after endless weeks cooped up inside the ship. Sweat immediately formed on his brow and ran down his back. He took one glance at the magnificent scenery and whistled.

"Nice resort, Captain."

Strachan grunted in reply as he set off on a flagstone path bisecting a beautifully manicured lawn. Zack, Pathfinder instincts aroused, examined his surroundings, trying hard to look nonchalant. Guards, dressed in light green battledress and billed caps, carrying short carbines, were patrolling the area. They looked tough, professional, and military. Mercenaries.

The buildings were two-storied and, while the smaller ones had large, polarized windows, the three larger ones presented only blank walls. An antenna array poked out of the palm-like trees further inland, and Zack recognized a sophisticated communications system with satellite uplink. Another array came briefly into view and the gunner nearly stopped in surprise.

Now, why would a private island have an aerospace defense command and control system?

He looked for hidden sensors, automatic weapons, and other defensive arrangements and it didn't take the former reconnaissance trooper long to find well-placed and well-hidden military-grade ordnance. There were likely much more he couldn't see. Either the owners of this island were paranoid, this far inside the Commonwealth, or they had something here worth the expense.

If the island belonged to the Amalis, it made little sense. They were said to own most of Pacifica, and what they didn't own, they controlled through others. Even the Fleet had no business on this planet.

Strachan led him off the main path, and they headed towards a sprawling, flat-roofed villa reeking of luxury. It was covered almost entirely with polarized glass that kept out the glare of the sun while affording the people inside absolute privacy.

Carefully trimmed shrubbery surrounded it, as did extensive flower beds and exotic statuary. The rose quartzite walkway ended at a recessed porch flanked by two crouching, life-sized jade tigers that probably cost as much as a small warship complete with crew. A black door silently slid aside at Strachan's touch, and they entered the house. The cool dimness momentarily blinded the gunner.

A servant in green livery greeted them in silence and led them down a carpeted hallway lavishly decorated with modern artwork, energy fountains, and slowly undulating, potted pseudo-shrubs in full bloom.

At the end of the corridor, another black door slid aside, and they stepped out onto an enclosed patio. An ornate fountain burbled merrily in the center of the flagstone-covered area, the beautifully sculpted mermaid at its top spouting blood red water. Comfortable looking chairs were arranged in small groups around tables hewn out of single blocks of blue stone.

A tall, slim man of indeterminate age rose and smiled at their approach. He held out his hand for Strachan.

"My dear Captain. I am most pleased to see you back in good health from your long and strenuous trip. I trust all went well." He spoke with an educated Pacifica accent, his voice deep and pleasant.

"Very well, sir. Very well indeed." Strachan looked like he was about to fall over himself with obsequiousness. "May I present Warrant Officer Zachary Decker, *Shokoten*'s gunner? He is in no small part responsible for the well-being of the ship."

The man with the patrician nose turned his gaze on the former Marine and examined him from head to toe. Zack returned the look measure for measure, noting the rich cut of his clothes, his perfectly set blond hair, carefully manicured hands, dark tan, and cold eyes.

"So this is the man you were telling me about, Diego. Mister Decker, I am Walker Amali, head of the Honorable Commonwealth Trading Corporation. You may know it as ComCorp. I own *Shokoten* through one of my holding companies." He said it without affectation. The man who controlled the richest private company in the Commonwealth seemed utterly unimpressed with his own power.

"Sir." Decker snapped to attention and nodded.

"Your captain has reported many good things about you. He thinks you are an asset to his ship and our business interests."

Zack didn't know what to answer, so he remained still.

"A man of few words, I see," Amali continued, still smiling, but the smile never reached his watchful, cold eyes. "I forget myself. Can I offer you gentlemen a drink? It will be some time before we finish offloading your ship. Scotch, Gunner?"

"Thank you, sir." *Good guess. Or do you have a detailed file on me, Mister Amali?*

A few moments later, another liveried servant brought a tray of drinks. When he had left, Amali raised his glass.

"I would like to propose a toast, to a successful voyage."

It could just have been Decker's imagination, but there was a hint of jubilation in Amali's tone.

The scotch was excellent, of an age and mellowness a mere warrant officer could never afford. Zack relished every drop, yet he remained uncomfortably conscious he was drinking with one of the Fleet's most elusive and corrupt adversaries, a man whose family had proven they would stop at nothing in their pursuit of power and profits.

He could lash out now and kill the man with a single blow, doing more damage to the Amali empire and the Coalition than entire battle groups had done in years. Of course, his own death would follow soon thereafter. He mentally shrugged. As one of his former commanders had often quoted, 'Ours not to reason why, ours but to do and die.' Unwilling to die just yet, he sipped in silence.

Walker Amali looked at him strangely, and Zack suddenly feared he had let his thoughts show in his eyes. He looked up at the clear blue sky and emptied his glass, smacking his lips.

"One hell of a scotch, sir, if I may say so."

"Indeed, Gunner. Do you wish another glass?"

Almost before Zack could answer, the servant was back with his tray and a full tumbler of the amber liquid.

"Tell me, Mister Decker, that is a Master Gunner's badge on your uniform, is it not?"

Zack felt an irrational stab of fear and tried to cover it by shrugging.

"Aye, sir. A little souvenir of my time in the Corps."

"May I see it?" Decker knew it wasn't a request but an order.

With a leaden hand, he removed it from his tunic and handed it over. Amali turned the golden insignia in his fingers, examining it with interest.

"Very nice, Mister Decker. I believe it represents a nineteenth-century field piece."

"Yes, sir."

Amali nodded, his eyes locking with Decker's for a moment.

"A most appropriate award for a man who can outwit and out-gun pirates with a mere merchant vessel." He handed the badge back.

They spent the next few minutes in idle conversation, and Zack studied his host with half-closed eyes, trying hard to look like a tippler enjoying an excellent drink. He doubted that it fooled Amali, and was relieved when the magnate called a servant to lead him back to the door. Amali wanted to speak with Strachan in private.

*

Zack took a few deep breaths when he stepped out of the house and tried to shake the alcohol fumes from his head. The scotch had been potent, more so on an empty stomach, and Amali's servant had given him generous servings.

Eyes narrowed against the glare, the gunner wondered again about the extent of Amali's little colony. His instincts told him that this was a well-planned, easy to defend installation. It reminded him of nothing so much as a luxury version of a Marine outpost. Even then, Marine outposts weren't blessed with so much modern equipment. He slowly walked back to the landing strip, forcing himself to memorize everything he saw.

Armed guards watched him with the same interest as bodyguards showed a potential threat, and Zack knew that if he walked off into a direction other than the ship, they'd make sure he changed course.

When he turned the corner around one of the windowless buildings, *Shokoten* came into full view. Ground effect flatbeds were busy hauling the containers off to a hangar at the far end of the bay. There, they vanished down a ramp, confirming Zack's impression that at least parts of the structures were underground.

He could see no other crewmembers on the tarmac, not even on the belly ramp, getting a bit of fresh air. Zack wasn't surprised, when he climbed aboard, to find that all outside cameras had been switched off, on orders from the captain. Someone didn't want the entire crew to see what was happening. Why then, did Walker Amali ask the one crewmember who was ex-Fleet, into his home?

He must have known Zack was the only one aboard the freighter who could take a quick look at his setup and figure out it was more like a fortified camp than a rich man's private resort. Curiosity perhaps.

Twenty year Marines who helped their new civilian employer flout the law weren't common. In the mind of a wealthy sociopath like Amali, it either made him a scumbag without morals, or an infiltrator. A Fleet infiltrator. For the first time, Zack wondered about the exact circumstances of his enlisting aboard *Shokoten*.

The thought gave Zack a shiver as if someone had walked on his grave. The peril of his position suddenly became apparent. Amali had only to believe he wasn't merely a senior noncom who had retired under a cloud to seal his fate.

He returned to his cabin and pulled out the data chip on which he'd encoded his findings in the cargo hold. If Strachan found out, Zack was a dead man.

Decker stared at the chip for what seemed like an eternity, unable to decide. Then, he changed into coveralls, grabbed his toolbox, and crawled into turret three's access tube. Once inside, he started the self-diagnostic routine, hoping the electronic activity would make him look busy.

He slipped the data chip into his sensor and turned it on. Then, calmly and in a logical sequence, he described Amali's island, drawing a plan of the enclave, marking each building, in particular the one that had swallowed the containers. With that, there was no turning back. This chip would mark him as a spy, no matter what.

He still didn't know what he would do, but meeting Walker Amali seemed to have triggered something within him.

Nobody questioned his twenty-minute stay in turret three, though Raisa sensed something new in Zack when they met in the wardroom for a belated lunch. She didn't pry but made sure, with glances and keywords that she felt something had changed. Zack didn't know whether to feel scared or reassured.

They left the island later that afternoon, headed for Hadley Spaceport, the planet's main terminal. Nihao Kiani, as usual, was the last on board and seemed disinclined to give an account of her activities.

The trip was short and uneventful, and they berthed near the massive Hadley terminal building. Strachan gave the crew liberty until they loaded the cargo for their next trip.

Zack was changing into his favorite civilian clothes when Kiani walked into the cabin. She had spent the time since landing at Hadley closeted with the captain.

"Going out, Zack?"

"Yeah. I thought Raisa and I would take a breather in town. It'll be good to step off the old tub."

"Be careful. I mean it." Their eyes met, and Zack thought he read genuine concern in hers. Her warning, well-meaning as it seemed, irritated him.

"I will. Nothing on Pacifica's going to get me. I don't intend to visit the wrong spots."

"You know what I mean."

Decker shrugged and closed the door to his locker.

"See you tomorrow."

*

He met Raisa at the head of the gangway. She looked ravishing in her long black skirt, high, sleeveless red blouse, and carefully done crimson hair. Darhad smiled at him, bloodless lips parting to show her white, pointy teeth.

"It has been a long time, and we have much to discuss."

She took him by the hand and led him out of the freighter. The late afternoon sun bathed Hadley with indecently lurid shades of red and orange. An acrid tang seared the back of Zack's throat as he took his first breath of city air.

Around the spaceport, buildings crowded out the horizon. Towers of glass, steel and concrete reared up high, higher than on any other human world except Earth itself.

But the man-made beauty of the skyline hid another reality, as Decker well knew. Slums, tenements, and welfare islands clustered around the prosperous business center of the city, ghettos where many Pacificans lived a dull, mind-numbing existence of entertainment, drugs, and destitution.

Pacifica and the other worlds controlled by men and women such as the Amalis represented the Commonwealth's rotting core. Zack hated this place with a passion. He only stepped ashore to be with Raisa and to find answers to his questions.

When they had left the spaceport behind and walked down a street teeming with cars and people, a street that nestled among the tall buildings like a river at the bottom of a canyon, Zack thought it safe enough to speak.

"We have to find ourselves a public terminal that'll give us info on Ventos Prime. I have to know what the hell we brought back to Amali. The bastard's up to no fucking good. Not with that setup of his on the island."

"Old Marine instincts resurfacing?" She asked, her right eyebrow raised in question. He glanced at her for a few moments, but she wasn't mocking him.

"And what if they are?" He finally replied, remembering Nihao's accusations.

"Nothing wrong with that, darling," she murmured. "As I have said before, we are bonded, and I will fight your battles at your side."

Her eyes searched his expressionless face.

"You are confused." She sounded hurt. "You have been confused since we left that accursed planet."

"You can sense it?"

"Yes." The admission held no regret or anger.

"Why didn't you tell me you were an empath?" Zack's tone was sharper than he wanted it to be.

"I did not wish to frighten you. Very few people know about my abilities, which incidentally are natural among Arkanna females of mating age. I have never tried to influence you. Read your emotions, yes. Mated Arkanna females are sensitive to their mates' moods. It's instinctive." Her face and voice expressed sincerity, and Zack desperately wanted to believe her. Especially now.

"Nihao Kiani knows."

Raisa's eyes flashed with anger.

"Our dear purser seems to know too much. She should be careful."

Zack's heartbeats thudded in his ears. He felt helpless to prevent his next words.

"She also told me you killed Lokis."

"What?" Raisa stopped and grabbed his right forearm with her strong left hand.

"Nihao told me you had an affair with Lokis and killed him when he tried to break it off."

Instead of laughing off the accusation, she looked Zack in the eyes and frowned.

"Why would she say such a thing?"

"You tell me."

"Zack. I never touched Lokis. He was a secretive man who seemed to be interested only in Kiani. Nor was he my type, to be frank. There was something about his manner that I did not like. In any case, I was on board the ship the night he disappeared."

"Nihao showed me pictures taken of his body by the Pradyni Guard. He looked slashed to bits by someone with fangs and talons."

"Do you really believe I would kill someone in a manner that could be traced back to me? Am I that stupid in your eyes?"

"People do stranger things when they believe themselves wronged or are enraged."

"True," she nodded. "But you must believe me. I had nothing to do with Lokis' death. Whatever Nihao Kiani told you were lies. If anyone wishes you harm on the ship, it is she. You and I are mated, and I could no more harm you than harm myself. Understand, Zack, that when I say Arkanna females mate for life, it is an absolute."

The Command School axiom came back to Zack: wrong or right, make a bloody decision. He went with your gut instinct.

"I trust you, Raisa. I have to because I love you."

He pulled her into the shade of a litter-strewn alley and quickly told her everything Nihao had said. When he confessed to letting himself be used by the purser, she stroked his cheek and kissed him.

Then she gave him a sad smile.

"I forgive you, Zack. Kiani is a redoubtable adversary, and you are an innocent in her hands. I know you're mine, not hers. Now let us find what we both want. An answer to the mystery of *Shokoten*."

*

With her unerring sense of direction, she led him into the seedier part of Hadley. The less fortunate citizens of Pacifica gave them only a passing glance. Decker, leather clad and stone-faced looked too much like one of the toughs who owned the slums. Though Hadley had no open sewers like Tanira, the stench of the streets was just as powerful, if less barbaric.

They entered an unmarked doorway set in a grimy, concrete high-rise that looked abandoned in the waning light of the day. Raisa took a flight of stairs down towards a dim red light and the odor of rotting cabbage. By now, Zack knew what to expect. The Arkanna seemed to know all the hidden clubs in this arm of the galaxy. Why she did so, he preferred not to speculate.

A huge bouncer passed them through a sensor gate before letting them enter the underground club. The opulence of the place did not surprise the gunner. Patrons were ensconced in the many cubicles lining the walls. He didn't see a bar, but human waiters of both sexes, soberly dressed, seemed to serve a steady stream of food and drink.

The quiet buzz of conversation meshed pleasingly with the subdued music. Two other doors pierced the far end of the room, light glimmering between the velvet curtains that covered the openings. A woman in her late thirties, hair cut fashionably short, led them to an unoccupied booth. After taking their order, she disappeared.

"Nice club," Zack commented, eyes taking in the layout of the place, "but I don't see a computer terminal."

"This is Pacifica. The ruling families wish to keep their control over the planet, and that means control of information. If we walk to the nearest public terminal and ask for a download on Ventos Prime, we would not return to the ship alive."

"Damn!" He swore. "Good point. And to think I figured you were dumb enough to slash Lokis." But Zack smiled to turn his words into a self-deprecating joke. An apology of sorts. "It seems I'm the dummy."

She smiled back and took his hand in hers, kissing his fingertips.

"And I love you too, Zack. To answer your unspoken question, this is, as you may have surmised, not quite a licensed establishment. It serves those who hold power and wealth through other means than the ones approved by the upper classes."

"Criminals," Zack said in a flat tone, disapproval written all over his face.

"A relative term," she replied, eyes twinkling at his almost naïve sense of propriety. "On this planet, the ruling families aren't much different from organized criminals, other than they either legalize what they want or pay others to do it for them. You would be hard pressed to find a place of amusement that was not controlled by someone with dirty claws. For our purposes, this place is suitable."

A throaty chuckle escaped her lips. "One could argue that this club is probably cleaner than many licensed ones."

"And how is it you know about a club run by the local mob?"

"I have not always been a merchant officer, Zack. There was a time in my life, soon after I fled Arkanna when I had to do less than palatable things to survive. Since then, I have kept my contacts, as a safeguard, in case I ran into trouble I could not handle. Please do me a favor and ask no further questions. I'm not very proud of those days."

Decker realized it was a matter affecting her personal honor, and he tactfully changed the subject of conversation. Trust had to be absolute, or it wasn't trust.

"So how are we going to obtain what we want?"

"Wait."

When the waitress came back, Raisa whispered a few words in her ear. The woman nodded and vanished through one of the doorways. She returned a few minutes later and beckoned Raisa. Zack made to follow her, but the Arkanna shook her head.

She was gone for almost half an hour. When she returned, she slipped into the booth and smiled.

"A friend will make inquiries and put us in touch with someone who can access the information. In the meantime, I have arranged for us to enjoy some privacy."

Taking his hand as she rose, Darhad led him through the other doorway into warren of carpeted hallways paneled in dark wood. A short flight of stairs took them to a luxurious private room with a large, round bed, a deep roman bath and a mirrored bar containing every form of liquor known to humankind.

There, they made love as if the universe didn't matter.

It was over all too soon when a discreet knock at the door and a whispered message brought a sad smile to Raisa's face.

For a moment, Zack had the awful premonition that this had been their last time together, but he shook off the sensation and grinned.

"We have a bite?"

"Yes. Get dressed." She sounded almost as wistful as he felt as if unwilling to leave the warmth and safety of their private world. "I have the address of a hacker who my contact sometimes uses. It will cost us a few creds, but I have been assured he is worth the money."

"You never cease to amaze me, Raisa."

— THIRTEEN —

Decker and Darhad left the underground club by a dingy back corridor that opened on a garbage-strewn alley. Full night had fallen over Hadley, and the moonless sky held nothing to ease the gloom, save for a smattering of stars bright enough to pierce the polluted atmosphere.

Raisa's sensitive Arkanna eyes found the way without hesitation and, holding Zack's hand, led them to a street lit only by grimy light globes long due for an overhaul. The teeming city never truly slept, and a low buzz filled the air, a mixture of distant hovercar fans, snatches of music from late night bars, police or ambulance sirens. Drunken shouts rang out now and then as human beings beyond hope quarreled simply to feel alive. Distant coughs sometimes ended a dispute when one of the participants used the ultimate argument.

They changed direction several times, passing through small side streets that stank of urine, hopelessness, and despair. Zack was preternaturally alert to danger. Hadley's slums were not a healthy place: dark shapes, hidden in the shadows, watched them with hungry eyes as they passed by. The gunner didn't have his blaster in its usual place under his left arm. Pacifica frowned on private weapon ownership, for reasons that had nothing to do with the sky-high crime rate. That didn't mean no one had guns. Only that honest citizens didn't. Then again, honesty was a relative term on Pacifica.

More than once, the small hairs on the back of his neck rose in alarm, as a sixth sense told him they were being followed. He also thought he heard footsteps behind them the few times they stopped while Raisa took her bearings.

For some reason, Hadley's concrete canyons unnerved him more than any guerrilla-infested jungle ever had. Marines didn't like cities. The tall office and apartment blocks could swallow an entire division and spit it out piecemeal. Far better an open battlefield on a sparsely populated world.

A beggar wearing a dirty, tattered suit stumbled across their path, drugged to the gills. His dilated pupils saw reality through a meth fog, and he ignored the two spacers. Zack shook his head in a mixture of pity and disgust. By morning, he would have been mugged and beaten, perhaps several times, as the lowest scum tried to feed on what was left of him.

They turned onto a street lined with abandoned apartments. The pavement was crazed and split from a continued lack of maintenance and hardy native grasses grew through the cracks. A partially disassembled hovercar sat on the curb, its fans and fuel cells long since stripped off and sold, leaving gaping holes in the dented, discolored chassis.

Zack sensed a human body inside the wreck, watching them. On the opposite street corner, a trio of hunched junkies warmed their hands over a fire burning in an empty fuel drum. They gave Zack and Raisa a passing glance and returned to their whispered conversation.

Decker had seen war zones with more personality than Hadley's slums, and he wondered how the poor could live like this without revolting. He asked Raisa as she scanned a row of decrepit, windowless tenements.

"Secret police, Zack," she replied distractedly. "Any hint of rebellion is crushed without mercy, and in complete secrecy."

Decker shook his head in disgust.

"I thought we were supposed to be the good guys, with sentient rights for all."

"Welcome to Pacifica. It and the other Coalition members are the modern wave of industrial feudalism. Come, I have found our destination."

When they reached the scarred steel door, she pushed the call button and waited.

"Yeah," a raspy, hostile voice asked from a wire-covered speaker.

"Friends of Harrah, coming to see Korden."

"You the she-wolf?" The voice asked.

"Yes." Raisa spat out a single word in Arkanna to confirm her claim.

"All right. Take the stairs down and turn left at the bottom."

The door clicked once, and Zack pushed it inwards. It closed behind them with a snap that sounded final, as if it were the door to a prison cell, or to Hades.

A low murmur of voices rose from the darkness, like demons of the deep crying out in torment. Raisa took the lead once more, her eyes glowing eerily as they saw the way.

A strong stench of urine and cheap soy grub assaulted Zack's nostrils, and he grimaced with distaste. His right hand reached instinctively for the absent blaster under his left armpit, and he swore, both at his own ingrained reflexes and the stupid laws that ensured only criminals had guns on this cesspool of a planet.

The stairs proved to be much longer than Decker expected. But by the time they reached the bottom, several meters below ground, he had other things to wonder about. They passed a sound baffle on the final landing, and a wave of noise washed over them.

Where they expected a basement, or a hidden setup like the club, the gunner and his mate found an underground casbah, alive with activity.

Wide corridors went off in all directions while small stores and stalls spilled into the walkways, selling wares of all description, most of which, Zack figured, were stolen. A mouth-watering mix of food smells hovered over the crowd, making Decker's stomach rumble.

Bars, brothels, and amusement places for all tastes filled the spaces between the stalls, painting the walls with pulsating lights, and throbbing music. A few seemed tame, but others made him turn his face in disgust.

Peddlers tugged at their sleeves for attention, offering everything from discount stims to vibrablades to forbidden sex.

"Do you think the government knows about this place?" Zack asked Raisa, as they passed another intersection teeming with sellers, buyers, and their often-compliant victims.

"Probably and making a healthy profit in taxes. A lot of money changes hands down here every night."

"This sort of place will give you political trouble one of these days. All it takes is a flaming revolutionary to turn the casbah into a fucking guerrilla hidey-hole."

"It's not our problem, Zack."

"It will be, one day. People will not stand for this sort of life forever, and when they're fed-up, watch out."

"Then we shall try to be far away when the day comes."

"Yeah."

They stopped in front of a narrow storefront advertising custom electronics and, pushing aside a bead curtain, walked in. An acne-scarred, sallow-faced man in his late thirties sat behind a counter littered with appliances. Most of the gizmos were in various stages of disassembly and had seen hard use. Decker recognized several items that were illegal on most planets.

The man looked up at them with washed-out, tired eyes, brushing his shoulder length hair out of the way. When he saw Raisa, his eyes widened almost comically, and he dropped the small palm pad he'd been examining.

"You the she-wolf?"

Raisa nodded.

The man glanced at Decker and turned his attention back to Raisa. Clearly, her dangerous, alien beauty fascinated him. He ran a trembling hand through his greasy hair while a tic tugged at his right cheek, giving him a manic cast.

"I'm Korden. What can I do for you?"

"We need information about a certain planet outside the Commonwealth, a place that is probably not in any general access database. And we need that information with nobody knowing we're interested."

"Right," Korden nodded. "That's why you came to me. I can pull anything out of the Pacifica net, including stuff the Families, the military and anybody else thinks is secure."

Net-freak, Decker decided, after running a critical eye over the man, one of the people who spend their lives hooked up to computers and knew how to navigate the data streams. It was like a drug. They forgot to feed or care for themselves properly, and their nerves became brittle. Until they finally died. Or their consciousness merged with the net. No one had ever been able to tell.

"My price depends on how hard it is to obtain the information you want. I can only tell you that once I'm done." He blinked nervously, eyes still fixed on the Arkanna.

"Fair enough," Raisa gave him a predatory smile. His Adam's apple bobbed a few times beneath his stubbly chin.

"C'mon to the back." The net-freak led them into a room even more cluttered with electronic junk. A debris and tool covered workbench occupied one wall while an unmade bed was pushed against another. The aroma of unwashed socks and stale food seemed almost like a physical presence.

Korden dropped into a chair facing a terminal and placed a metallic band over his head. Small connected with metal ports set in his skull, hard-wiring his brain to the computer. Contact with the machine seemed to infuse him with renewed energy, and his voice was steadier when he asked, "What's the name of the planet?"

"Ventos Prime."

The man nodded once, then his face muscles went slack and his eyes lost focus as his mind merged with the net. Data began to stream across the screen at high speed

Feeling edgy, Zack wandered around Korden's place, poking into dark corners and examining the technological debris the net-freak had accumulated. The sounds of the casbah filtered through the curtain and created a backdrop of white noise that grated on the gunner's nerves.

He didn't enjoy playing spook. Some Marines entered that line of work and transferred to Fleet Intelligence, from where they never returned to a line unit. Not Zack Decker. He preferred the direct way of doing business, with a gun in each hand, and a troop of armored Pathfinders behind him.

Zack's peripheral vision caught a movement on the other side of the grimy window. But when he turned to look, the face was gone. He couldn't be sure of what he'd seen because there was simply too much activity in the alley. Yet he couldn't shake the idea that someone had been watching him.

"Zack!" Raisa's call shifted his attention back to the net-freak in the back room. He joined her behind Korden.

"He's broken into Amali's classified systems and discovered a dense data pack on Ventos Prime. Look." She pointed at the screen.

As they read the scrolling words, Zack's heart sank into his stomach and bile rose in his throat. What he saw on the screen just couldn't be real, but his own sensor had shown him the evidence in *Shokoten*'s cargo hold. It all fit. And it imperiled the very survival of the Commonwealth.

"My God, Raisa," Decker sounded hoarse as he whispered. "What have we done?"

"We could not know. When smuggling becomes second nature, we forget to think about the consequences of our actions. The important question is – what do we do now?"

"Damn if I know. Who the hell will believe this crap? And more to the point, how the hell will we find someone to tell it to?"

A sound behind them made Zack turn and drop into a crouch, hand reaching again for the non-existent blaster.

"I believe I can solve that dilemma for you," a very familiar voice said from the shadows of the doorway.

"Aw, shit!" Zack swore as Nihao Kiani stepped into the room, a large bore blaster pointed at them. She wore a simple black outfit of trousers and high-collared jacket that blended so well with the background, Zack knew it had to be stealth cloth. In the low light of Korden's back room, her cruel smile and narrowed almond eyes twisted her features.

"Please move to the side." Kiani motioned them over with the gun's thick, heat-blackened barrel. The net-freak, still plugged into the data stream, was oblivious to the sudden drama in his shop. His slack face still stared through unfocused eyes at the glowing screen.

When Kiani had a clear bead on Korden, she pulled the trigger twice. The first shot took off the top of the hacker's head, plasma vaporizing his skull along with the headband. Grayish-pink matter splashed against the wall with a sickening sound in a wide fan of droplets. Before his body had time to slump, the second shot burned through the terminal and fried its electronic innards, producing nothing more spectacular than a few sparks.

"Why the gratuitous murder?" Raisa Darhad hissed, talons and fangs bared.

"Oh, not gratuitous, my dear first officer," Nihao's smile was mockingly cruel. "And neither will your deaths be. Not that anyone would care down here. Pacifica, and in particular Hadley, has one of the highest murder rates in the Commonwealth. Three more corpses in the morning will disturb no one. Nor will the police care much. They're of the opinion that anyone who risks the casbah and dies there got what he or she deserved."

Kiani seemed to relish the situation, the awful odor of charred human flesh and voided bowels, and the anticipation of more death. Her dark eyes glinted with a madness Zack had seen before, in Pathfinders who took too much pleasure in killing. Men and women like that had always given him the creeps, but no one as much as her. The change from when he last saw Kiani was too radical. He shuddered.

"You will understand that my superiors cannot afford to let anyone who knows about Ventos Prime live," she continued, "to tell the Navy."

"Why are we a danger to you and your masters?" Decker asked sharply. Anger flared within him and his fight-or-flight reflex took over, leaning heavily towards the fight option. Marines never ran from a confrontation.

She laughed with delight.

"So naïve, Zack, yet such a good agent. The Fleet chose well in you. So much better than Lokis."

"Hah," Zack snorted, "that's where you have your wires crossed. I haven't worked for the Fleet since they pensioned me off."

She stopped laughing abruptly.

"Then why are you pursuing this?"

Decker shrugged. From the corner of his eyes, he saw Raisa move slowly away from him, preparing to rush Kiani.

"Since you'll shoot me anyway, why not tell me what this is all about," he suggested, more to distract her and give Raisa an opening, than to satisfy his curiosity.

"The villain telling his victims all about the plan before attempting to kill them works only in cheap spy novels, Zack." Kiani seemed amused. "Where you're headed, the knowledge will be of little use. So why waste my breath?" Her eyes snapped over to Raisa, and she smiled again.

"Ah, I see. Sorry, but it won't work."

"If you intend to kill us, then do it," Raisa growled back at her.

"Soon, you alien bitch. But I wish to enjoy myself a bit first. Incidentally, you may be pleased to know that I will miss Zack as much as you will. He is quite a lover though I believe he prefers human women to alien animals."

"I beg to disagree. He has a weakness for females, but his acts with you were only normal physical reactions from a healthy, heterosexual male."

"So our gallant gunner has told you." Kiani's smile grew in size and cruelty. "But you're wrong about his motivation where I'm concerned."

"No," Decker replied, voice low and menacing. Pure rage was building within him. He could no longer stand her attempt to hurt Raisa by rubbing his betrayal in her face.

"I may be a dummy, but I've figured out you have one hell of a talent for manipulation, Nihao. You thought I was a Fleet agent, so you needed a way to ensnare me. It didn't take a fucking genius to see that Zack Decker is a horny bastard with an eye for the ladies. You wave it in my face long enough, and I'll bite. But that's all. And since I'm not a Fleet Intelligence type, your bedding me was wasted. It was sex, mediocre sex at that, nothing more."

He glanced at Raisa and saw a profoundly moving look in her eyes. Something soft, adoring, brushed his mind. It was the other half of Raisa's talent, something he felt for the first time. The sensation filled his eyes with tears because of the intensity of her love for him and because he knew they would not consummate that love ever again.

Kiani smirked.

"How touching. The tough Marine and the murderous Arkanna going soft over each other. Perhaps you'll meet in Hell if the demons have a tender spot for lovers."

Something else brushed Zack's mind, an idea of coiled power, of animal rage, and he understood Raisa was preparing to pounce before Kiani shot them. She wanted him to keep the purser distracted for just a few seconds more.

The combat veteran in Decker wanted to obey. A slim chance was better than no chance at all, and someone had to tell the Navy. But the part of him that had become joined to Raisa knew she would die in the attempt, die trying to save his life. Kiani was too tightly wound to be caught unprepared. And at this range, she couldn't miss.

"Tell me one thing before I die, Nihao. For who do you work? The Amalis? This seems a bit too big even for them."

Kiani frowned, apparently expecting another maneuver from either or both of them. Then she shrugged.

"All right, because you were such a good little boy in bed and pleasured me so well, I'll tell you. I work for the *Sécurité Spéciale.*"

Decker opened his mouth to ask what that was when Raisa Darhad pounced like a wild beast, like a female protecting her mate. The gunner saw a flash of black silk and gleaming talons, then the bright flash of a plasma shot illuminated the room. Raisa's momentum brought her down on Kiani, and both women fell to the floor. By the time Zack put his brain and limbs in gear, she had sunk her fangs into the purser's throat and buried her talons in her face.

Kiani let out an anguished, burbling howl of pain, arms and legs thrashing about, but she couldn't shake Raisa off. Zack saw a clear opening and kicked the purser in the side of the head with his steel-toed boots, caving in her skull and ending her suffering. The stench of blood and death became overwhelming.

Decker dropped to his knees and gently took Raisa by the shoulders.

"You got her good, you crazy she-wolf," he whispered. Blood from Kiani's torn throat flowed into a dark pool beneath her head as her lifeless eyes stared up at the grimy ceiling.

He turned Raisa over and cradled her in his arms. The front of her skirt was stained russet with blood where Kiani's shot had pierced her pelvis. Zack knew it was a fatal shot, had seen it even as she took down the purser. A fully equipped starship sickbay could have saved her, but down here...

Her impossibly blue eyes focused on him and he sensed her gentle mind brush again. This time, he cried openly.

"Tell them...," she whispered, the life force oozing out of her with every breath.

"Yeah," he sobbed, "I'll tell the Fleet and stop the bastards. I swear it!"

A smile briefly appeared on her lips. "I... am... pleased... my mate."

Then her body relaxed as her eyes rolled up. She was dead.

Zack screamed with a rage and a sense of loss he had never experienced before, holding her head against his chest as he rocked on his knees.

*

He lost track of time as he knelt by her body, tears running down his cheeks, oblivious to the life teeming just a few meters away in the Kasbah. The only woman who had genuinely loved him, and who he had truly loved since his wife left him so long ago, had died saving his life. No, not only saving his life, Zack realized as shock set in, but also giving him the chance to warn the Fleet.

He turned numb as his mind shut those mental functions that kept him from moving fast and staying alive. It was something that happened every time death surrounded him. Emotions locked away behind the need to survive, Zack rose and took stock after gently depositing Raisa on the floor.

No one had heard the brief fight, or if they had, they'd wisely ignored it. He was alone with three corpses in a shabby shop, in one of Hadley's underground Kasbahs, an illegal playground for every crook, pervert, and hopeless slum dweller in the city.

He picked-up Kiani's blaster, popped the magazine to check its load, worked the receiver to make sure there was a round in the chamber, and then stuffed it into his jacket's inner pocket, after making sure the safety was on. Then, he rifled through the dead purser's pockets, ignoring the bloody shreds of her torn throat, but careful not to stain his boots or pants with the blood thickening on the floor. His search yielded a packet of chips containing almost a thousand creds, two spare magazines for the blaster, a pocket knife of good steel and little else of use.

He crouched by Raisa's body. She looked peaceful in death, and a twinge of pain tugged at his heart, but his sharp survival instincts crushed the resurgent anguish of loss. Still, he couldn't just leave her there, to be found and used in who knew what fashion. Zack took the money she carried in a skirt pocket, and the combat knife hidden in a slit on the outside of her left boot.

By the time he was done, he had figured out a way to dispose not only of her body but of the others as well. Face set in granite, he left the shop and waded through the packed alley to a small shop he'd noticed earlier, thrusting aside the merry-makers with his powerful elbows. Those who looked at his eyes and the set of his jaw moved aside to let him pass without protest.

A shifty-looking man with a receding chin, greasy hair and a twisted nose looked up at his imposing bulk with calculating eyes when he walked into the gun shop. He was alone in a room empty except for a counter built from scrap plas sheets.

"I need a molecular disruptor," Zack stated in a matter-of-fact tone.

"Those things are illegal on Pacifica, buddy," the weapons merchant replied, eyes looking everywhere but at Zack. "What makes you think I'd be dumb enough to sell any?"

The gunner leaned over the counter and grabbed the little man by a grimy shirt collar, lifting him off his feet and away from whatever weapon he was about to use. Face a few centimeters away from the merchant's weasel-like features, Zack stared him straight in the eyes.

"Listen, fuckhead. If you can't get molecular disruptors, you aren't worth shit as a dealer and the people running this place wouldn't let you set up shop. Now show me a fucking disruptor. I'll pay a fair price for it." Eyes promising death, Decker's hold tightened.

"Okay, buddy," he finally replied in a half-choked voice. "I'll go look in my stockroom if I have any." The man's breath was as foul as his appearance, and probably his morals.

Zack shook him.

"If you have a stockroom, I'm the fucking grand admiral. You have a list of your inventory in that piece of crap you call a brain. Now do you want to make money, or not?"

Something in the dealer's eyes told Decker he'd rather make the money by killing him than selling him a disruptor, but he nodded anyway. Without gentleness, the gunner let him drop to the floor. Weasel Face picked himself up and vanished behind a grimy curtain. He was back a few moments later with a dented and scarred metal box. Depositing the box in front of Zack he smirked.

"That'll be two thousand creds, plus another hundred creds for each power pack you want."

"You're selling me this," he opened the box and pulled out, as he had expected, a battered, ancient and probably broken Shrehari disruptor, "piece of shit for two thousand, without power packs?"

"Hey," he licked his lips nervously as he glanced over Zack's shoulder, "disruptors are hard to get, bud. Take it or leave it. You won't find anyone else selling."

The dealer's eyes widened slightly, and his lips parted as he stared behind Decker. With a smooth, practiced movement, the gunner pulled out his purloined blaster and whirled around, falling into a crouch.

The leather-clad tough guy, a local enforcer for whatever mob controlled this Kasbah, brought up his gun as he stepped into the room and squinted at Zack. He never finished his motion. Decker's blaster coughed once, drilling a large hole through the bravo's forehead and flash-boiling his brain. With a thump, he fell to the floor, face down, the back of his skull gone. A dark stain appeared on the bravo's trousers as he voided his bowels and bladder in death, filling the shop with a nauseating stench.

Weasel Face made a retching sound and spilled his dinner on the floor, adding to the poisonous reek. Ignoring both the dead enforcer and the gun seller, Zack holstered his blaster and picked-up the disruptor. He'd handled this type before and stripped it with ease, examining each part. It was clapped-out, as he'd figured, but there were still a few shots left in it.

"Hey asshole," he snapped at the merchant, still on his knees, retching, "I need a power pack for this piece of junk and I need it now."

Weasel Face looked at him in terror. When the words sunk in, he nodded and climbed his feet, wobbling.

"Don't go calling any more tough guys, shithead," Decker warned, "or I'll blow *your* fucking brains out too." The dealer took one look at the corpse by the door and retched again before doing Zack's bidding.

Within seconds, he was back, an old, but fully charged power pack in his trembling hand. Zack took the palm-sized rectangle and slapped it into the disruptor's pistol grip. A red light on the receiver winked. The gunner raised the weapon and pointed it at Weasel Face.

"I figure I need to test this baby first, don't you think, considering you've already tried to screw me."

"N-not m-my f-fault," he stuttered, looking like he was about to die of sheer fright. "B-boss m-man wants to know 'b-bout people wanting illegal g-guns. 'S-specially o-off worlders."

"Sure," Zack smiled cruelly, the shadows transforming his face into a grinning skull.

Weasel Face fell to the floor with a loud thump, face first in his own vomit. He had fainted.

Decker pointed the disruptor at the enforcer's body and pulled the trigger. A short, dull blue beam of energy lanced out and struck the body near the waist. Flesh and bones dissolved under his eyes as the disruptor charge broke the complex molecules composing a human body into their constituent atoms. It was as if someone with a giant, invisible eraser was rubbing out the corpse. An eraser with a crackling blue edge of energy. A few seconds later, all that remained was a small pile of dust gently settling on the dirty floor.

Zack pulled out his wallet and dropped five hundred creds on the counter. It was a fair price for a gun that had only a few more shots left, even if Weasel Face had called the mob on him. The gunner grinned again. Now he'd have two organizations after him: Kiani's bunch, and the local mafia, who were sure to check out whatever happened to their man. No doubt they already had a summary description of him. When Zack Decker got himself into trouble, he did it right.

No one had entered Korden's shop while he was gone, and the three bodies were still in their individual poses of death, slowly stiffening. Zack pointed the gun at the Net-Freak and pulled the trigger. He might have been a computer addict who had probably helped many crooked people, but he didn't deserve to die like this.

When Korden's body had vanished, he shot Nihao Kiani and watched her disappear too, blood pool and all. Kiani would have earned whatever fate the Kasbah's scum reserved for the newly deceased, but Decker couldn't bring himself to leave her body to the vultures.

Only Raisa remained as beautiful in death as she'd been in life. Surprising himself, Zack offered a prayer to the God he had long ago abandoned, asking him to make sure her soul joined those of her kind, in whatever heaven collected Arkanna when they passed on. Then, with a death howl, he pulled the trigger and watched his mate's body vanish forever, leaving him alone. When it was gone, his iron control reasserted itself.

The computer was destroyed, the information found by Korden irretrievable. But Decker had it memorized. Not that it mattered. Those at Navy HQ, who would want his information, knew all about Ventos Prime. What mattered was the data encrypted on a much-used data chip, hidden away in his toolbox on board the merchant starship *Shokoten*.

He glanced around the room, making sure he left nothing incriminating behind and shoved the disruptor in another of his jacket's roomy cargo pockets. If the Hadley fuzz caught him with it, he was fried.

Heck, he was fried on Pacifica, anyway. Kiani had said she belonged to a secret organization that worked for the likes of Amali. Which meant, unless she was a lone wolf, that this *Sécurité Spéciale* not only knew of her suspicions about Zack Decker but also knew where she was tonight, stalking him in Hadley's slums. She may have a backup agent somewhere.

First order of business, return to the ship and grab his stuff. Second order of business, find a way off Pacifica. Overriding consideration: stay alive until he could talk to someone at Fleet Intel. Zack nodded to himself, it was a plan, even though it was damn sketchy. He'd have to do a lot of improvising. Good thing Pathfinders were trained to think on their feet.

As he stepped out of Korden's shop, he let his eyes roam in a one hundred and eighty-degree arc, searching for anybody who seemed to pay him too much, or too little attention, anybody who didn't look like a drunk, drugged, or fucked-out reveler. Someone who looked like he, or she, worked with Nihao Kiani.

Nobody. Which meant nothing, since Decker wasn't a spook, with spook training.

Head rearing above the throng, the gunner made his way to the stairs leading back to the real world. His eyes never rested, and his body remained tense, ready for action, ready to kill. Something within him had snapped with Raisa's murder, and he had turned into one of those Pathfinders with the dead eyes and the casual love of death, the ones who had frightened the hell out of him because they had lost their souls.

*

Decker walked out into the night, unmolested, and took a deep breath of fetid air. His mind's eye saw the way back to the spaceport and set off, ears and eyes alert. He turned into a garbage-strewn alley smelling of rotting fish a few blocks down and saw a gang of six youths smoking a stinking weed. As he passed them, they whispered among themselves and followed him.

"Hey, man," one of them said in an arrogant drawl, "you gotta nice jacket there, dude. I think you'd like to give it to me, because I'm a nice guy."

The other youths, three boys, and two girls tittered at their leader's words.

"Yeah, hey," one of the girls chimed in, her high-pitched voice echoing between the walls. "Fedor'd look great in that jacket, and you don't. If you make him a nice present, I won't rip off your balls."

Without stopping, or changing pace, Zack replied over his shoulder, "Why don't you piss off and go to bed like good little kiddies. Maybe then, I'll leave you alive, even though you shitheads are a fucking insult to the gene pool."

"This man's not nice." The leader of the gang, the one called Fedor, sounded sorrowful. "I figure we're gonna hafta kill him for insulting' us." He closed the distance with Zack.

This time, Zack stopped and turned around, drawing his blaster in the same movement, pointing it at Fedor's forehead. The youth stopped, mouth hanging open.

"One more step, fuck-face, and I'll put a nice hole right between your eyes. I'll be doing humanity a favor by making sure you don't pass your shitty genes to another generation of dickheads. It's up to you: do you want to die tonight?" Decker's face and voice were frighteningly cold.

"Hey, take it easy, man," the girl made to step closer, fear dancing in her reddened eyes, "we were just joking' like, you know."

"Yeah right," Zack didn't take his eyes or his aim off the Fedor. "Stay where you are, little girl and no one gets hurt."

"Do it, Gabbi," Fedor's choked voice was barely audible. The acrid stench of urine suddenly banished all other odors as the gang leader pissed himself.

"Sure, man," she backed off, hands held chest high, palms outwards.

Decker, moving faster than the kids could follow, switched the gun to his left hand, and belted the leader on the mouth with his right fist. The youth's feet lifted off the pavement as he sailed backwards and landed on his butt, blood spurting out of his smashed mouth. He screamed in pain at his broken jaw, shattered teeth, and ruined pride. The others, in fear of the big, black-clad maniac with the gun, ran away into the night, abandoning their leader.

Zack holstered his gun and grinned at the gang banger.

"Next time, pick on someone your own size, kid. You're damn lucky to be alive. Usually, I kill shitheads like you. Ask the two I killed less than an hour ago."

Without a backwards glance, Decker continued on his way, wiping the incident from his mind. They'd had youth gangs on his native planet. But those didn't go around offering to kill strangers for a leather jacket. At worst, they'd help an old lady across the street.

Fucking Pacifica shit!

*

The main thoroughfares near the spaceport were just as empty and abandoned at two o'clock in the morning as the slum streets. A few hovercars sped by, late night revelers returning home, cops on the prowl or high-class escorts heading off to work. The sky had vanished behind a thick layer of clouds, and a suffocating blanket of humidity weighed down on the city, making Zack sweat.

The horizon lit up as an electric storm rippled through the night south of Hadley. Then, as he turned a corner, rain pelted down, soaking his hair, streaming off his jacket, and washing off the grime of the city. But Hadley would never be clean, no matter how many rainstorms poured down. Not while Walker Amali and his like controlled Pacifica.

He was dripping with water by the time he reached the deserted freight terminal, slick and shiny under the rain and the intense arc lights. The dusty lobby was deserted. An arrivals and departures screen flickered forlornly in one corner, ignored by the dying rubber plant whose roots poked out of the parched earth of its pot. Food wrappers littered the floor, as did discarded, onetime porno vid chips. The blue screen gave Zack an idea, and he went over to read the words scrolling by.

He disregarded the scheduled passenger flights. Emigration controls were too tight on those to slip through. Pacifica's government had a nearly paranoid aversion to letting any of its less fortunate citizens off the planet. They preferred deporting their undesirables to one of their less healthy colonies. Those who could work but couldn't afford the bribes for an exit visa had to stay.

As the list of freighters scrolled by, one name caught Zack's attention: *Demetria*, a free trader with a one-woman crew. He remembered the sleek ship from a dozen spaceports along the distant border, even though he had never spoken to her dour captain.

She was due to leave at daybreak for Santa Theresa, a Pacifica colony on the outer rim of the Commonwealth. It wasn't great, but it would get him off the planet.

All that remained was to convince her skipper, Captain Avril Ducote, to let him board. The beauty of *Demetria* was that with only her as crew, he could easily hijack the ship, should she prove less than cooperative. The screen listed her berth as only two down from *Shokoten*.

He crossed the rain-swept tarmac and strode up *Shokoten*'s gangway, the metal ramp vibrating beneath his feet. When he reached the top, he touched the controls, and the outer airlock door hissed open. Stepping in, Decker shook the water off his head and clothes.

"Evening Gunner," a cheerful voice greeted him with affectionate respect. "Wet night for it, eh?"

"Oh, hello Veelan," Zack forced a smile. "On duty again?"

"Drew the short straw." He shrugged. "Is the first officer also on her way?"

Decker shook his head. "No. She remained in town. I've come to pick up a few things before going back."

If Veelan noticed the gunner's change of mood or unusual explanation, he gave no sign. Zack patted him on the shoulder before stepping through the inner airlock. The bare passageways were empty and cold at this time of night, matching Zack's mood. He met no one on his way to his cabin.

Once there, he ripped open his locker, pulled out his duffel bag and stuffed his belongings into it. He exchanged Nihao's blaster for his own and dropped the newly acquired weapons in with his clothes. Then, he opened his toolbox and recovered his souped-up sensor. No use leaving it to a bunch of crooks.

He dug inside the parts bin, looking for the data chip and felt a tendril of panic grown in his gut. It wasn't there. Impatient, he pulled the tray out of its housing and spilled in out on his desk. Nothing. He repeated the same procedure with the rest of the toolbox. Still nothing. An ugly thought wormed its way through his mind. Had Kiani searched the toolbox and found the chip? Was that why she came after Raisa and him? There seemed to be no other reasonable explanation.

Swearing, he searched the late purser's desk, locker, and bed, ripping everything open and tossing her belongings on the deck without care. He found money, which he kept, and some specialized miniature tools, which he also kept. But no data chip. It was gone.

Zack looked at his timepiece. *Demetria* lifted in two hours that meant her captain would be coming back from her obligatory face-to-face with the port duty officer soon. A final check of both cabin and bathroom proved he had all his stuff. He left what had been his home and locked the door behind him. It would be at least twelve hours before someone missed him, enough time for *Demetria* to take him to the nearest jump point and into hyperspace.

As he passed the main corridor junction on his way to the airlock, a door opened on his right, and a tousle-haired head poked out of the opening. If Zack's memory served, that was bosun Kader's cabin. Then why was he looking straight into the face of Third Officer Sonoda?

The woman smiled maliciously as she took in Decker's waterlogged appearance, his duffel bag, and his quick pace.

"Jumping ship, Gunner? I thought you enjoyed life here, what with being the captain's pet and the first officer's toy boy."

Zack shrugged, feeling no anger at the cruel jibe.

"And what if I am? It's no skin off your butt, which," he stopped and poked his head inside the cabin, chuckling, before she could react, "is flabbier than I thought. A bit more exercise would do you good. Bye, bos'n Kader. Was nice serving with you. But I deplore your choice of lovers."

The woman shrugged.

"You take what you can. Have a good one, gunner." She stood up still sweaty from their lovemaking and wrapped her arms around the robed third officer's waist. It was more to make sure the infuriated engineer didn't go after Zack than a gesture of affection.

She pulled a protesting Sonoda back into her cabin and closed the door. Zack knew he could count on a good hour before Kader let her warn anyone, which was more than enough. If that is, the third officer even bothered to tell anybody Decker had deserted. She'd be only too glad to see him go.

Veelan gave him a cheery 'see you tomorrow,' as he signed Decker out again. Standing in the rain, the gunner had a last stab of regret at leaving the ship. He'd been at home in *Shokoten*, had respect and a purpose in life, even if he was involved in smuggling. If truth be told, he had been involved in smuggling in one way or another ever since he discovered Shrehari ale long ago.

Dismissing nostalgia and regret as senseless, Zack headed for the service bays, where a covered walkway would lead him to *Demetria*'s berth. Within minutes, he reached the security gate protecting the free trader and rang the ship. When he received no answer, he nodded with satisfaction. The captain wasn't aboard yet. That meant he had a better chance of convincing her. It was always harder to turn someone down face-to-face than over a vidscreen, especially if the convincing required a gun. He hid in the shadows near the gate and waited, ears alert to the sound of footsteps.

The wait was short. A few moments after his arrival, a cloaked female shape came down the walkway and stopped in front of the gate, unlocking it. The moment it opened, Zack sprang out and gave the woman a slight shove, pushing her into the secure area. The gate snapped shut behind them.

Captain Ducote's reflexes were good. She whirled around, cloak flying about her shoulders, arm outstretched and fist clenched to strike her attacker. Zack blocked the blow by grabbing her right forearm and twisting it down. She was a strong woman, stronger than the gunner expected, and tried to dance out of his grasp. It took all of Zack's might to hold on as she slammed him into the security gate, using the gunner's own weight to unbalance him. Zack's head rang as it connected with the cold steel tubing.

She raised her left fist and drove it towards Decker's face. Without letting her go, he shifted to one side, and she struck his shoulder instead. He grunted at the force of the blow. Had Ducote landed it on his jaw, Zack would have enjoyed a taste of the pain he'd given the youth a few hours earlier. While the captain gathered herself for another strike, breathing heavily, Zack stuck his blaster in her face. She stopped struggling at once.

"Please, Captain Ducote. I mean you no harm. Let's stop this and talk."

"At gunpoint?" She snarled. "Fuck you." But her body relaxed and Zack let her go.

"Thank you, Captain."

"Okay. You have the gun. So tell me, what the hell do you want?" She asked, pale cheeks flushed, eyes blazing. Her left hand rubbed her right wrist where Zack had held her in his steel grip

"A berth off Pacifica, Captain Ducote."

She laughed without humor. "You have a funny way of asking, mister..."

"Decker, Zachary T. Decker. Formerly gunner on the freighter *Shokoten*, before that, command sergeant in the 902nd Pathfinder Squadron." He sketched a little bow, but his gun never wavered.

"And why, pray tell, would I accept? You obviously are on the run from something. The law perhaps?" Her voice dripped with contempt. She was a proud woman, unused to this sort of treatment and robust enough to take care of herself. Zack wondered whether he'd made a mistake.

"I could say," he replied, "that my gun is reason enough, but I have it out only to make sure you listen." She snorted in disbelief. "If I don't leave Pacifica, I will die. I have very dangerous people on my tail. I shook 'em off for now, but they'll find me if I stay here. And then, it's goodnight Zack."

"Assuming I even believe you, who are these people, and why do they want to kill you?" Her expression made it clear she wasn't prepared to take his word.

"Ever heard of the Amali family?" She nodded. "They own my last ship, and they're up to something evil, something I found out on the last trip. I must get somewhere away from here and contact Fleet Intelligence. The bad guys know it's what I intend, and they don't want me to talk. They've already tried to kill me once tonight. But my mate stopped the killer."

Something in his tone and face gave her pause, and she looked at him with a curious expression, her smooth forehead crinkled into a frown.

"Your mate?"

"Yeah. Her name was Raisa. She jumped the bitch who wanted to kill us before she could shoot me and took one in the belly. Died in my arms."

Zack's voice wavered just for a fraction of a second as his guard slipped, but it was enough for Avril Ducote to take a fresh look at her assailant. Something about him rang true.

"She must have been quite a woman."

"Yeah. That she was." Again, a glimpse of pain that vanished almost before it appeared. No one could fake that.

"What is this thing you have discovered?"

"You probably won't believe me, Captain. I'm still not sure I believe myself and they even took the only concrete proof I had, but someone's willing to kill to keep the information secret." He held her eyes, willing her to believe him. "It's not like I want a free ride. I'll pay you what you ask and do whatever work you want. I'm pretty good with weapons, shields and can turn my hand to most engineering jobs."

Her face hardened again. "What proves you'll not rape me in my sleep, or hijack my ship?"

Decker shrugged and flipped the blaster in his hands so that he held it by the barrel. He offered the gun to Ducote.

"You can do what you want with me, Captain." He had no more arguments to offer, and this was his last gamble. "If you want to turn a Mykonos Colony boy over to Pacifica scum, go ahead. There are two more guns in my bag and two knives in my pockets."

"A real walking arsenal, aren't you?"

"Let's just say I collected them along the way. Only this gun and one of the knives is mine."

Ducote took the blaster and pointed it at him as if she knew how to use it. Zack raised his hands, palms outward.

"I'm still not sure whether the smart move would not be to hand you over to the local police, Mister Decker."

"It is, Captain Ducote," an arrogant voice replied behind Zack, on the other side of the security gate. "He's a very dangerous man, a killer wanted by the government. He killed an agent of the Commonwealth and two innocent citizens tonight, and has committed serious assault on another, a mere child. I would appreciate your handing him over so I can make sure he faces the law.”

Without turning around, Zack said, “Funny guy, aren't you. My tally isn't nearly as impressive as you make it out to be. I don't know if the *Sécurité Spéciale* is a government agency, but if it is, it has strange loyalties and even more bizarre ideas about what's good for the Commonwealth. From where I stand, your agent was a murderess herself. She shot an innocent computer freak right in front of my eyes. She probably also killed my predecessor aboard *Shokoten*, Harwan Lokis, and she killed my mate, Raisa Darhad. In my book that makes her a ripe target for retaliation. So I gave Nihao Kiani the deathblow. She was going to die anyway after Raisa sank her claws into the bitch. The only guy I shot down was a mob enforcer who was about to do me in from behind. As for the child,” he laughed humorlessly, “he direly needed disciplining.”

Decker’s eyes bored into Ducote’s as he said, “You have the choice, Captain. Believe this creep and you condemn me to death.”

As he spoke, Zack had loosened his knife in its forearm sheath and tried to pinpoint the voice's position behind him. If Ducote saw his movements and the knife, she ignored him.

“My, my,” she commented caustically, “two different stories. Which one will I believe? Why not join us, Mister? If you work for the government and have official identification, I think we can come to an agreement.”

Her right hand kept the gun pointed steadily at Zack's midriff while she moved sideways to the security gate. Before she could reach it, the other man did something to the gate's keypad and unlocked it, easy as you please. He swung the metal barrier aside and took one step forwards, pointing an ugly plasma pistol at Zack's back, while an unpleasant smile distorted his otherwise bland features.

“This is the end of the line, Decker. You'll pay for Kiani's death and your meddling. Just keep your paws up. I know your tricks. Captain Ducote,” he glanced sideways at the frowning woman, “I believe you have Mister Decker's gun in your hand. I need it as evidence. Please give it to me.”

"What? So you can kill her too," Zack interjected, "just in case I told her too much."

"Silence," the agent snarled. "The gun, please, Captain Ducote." He glanced over at her.

"Don't do it Captain!" As he yelled out his warning, Zack whirled around and threw his dagger at the agent. The blade had barely left his hand when he dove to the side, narrowly avoiding death. As Zack had expected, the agent pulled the trigger a fraction of a second after he moved, but the plasma only grazed his left thigh.

The dagger, however, found its target and the force of the throw buried the slim blade into the killer's neck, severing his carotid artery. The agent collapsed, bleeding to death. It was as clean a kill as Zack had ever made with the knife.

Ducote, startled, cursed as she stepped backwards, the gun no longer pointing at Decker. The security gate slammed shut with a clang as the man, still pumping blood, slumped to the ground.

"I guess that makes two deaths this evening if I believe your story, Mister Decker."

Zack picked himself up, grimacing at the burn mark on his leg. It hurt like the devil but was nothing more than a flesh wound. He glanced at Ducote and grinned when he saw her aim the blaster at him again.

"You realize you'll have serious questions to answer when they find the body here."

"I do, Mister Decker, and I don't think I'll thank you for them. Right now, I wish only to rid myself of your troubling presence and leave."

She frowned and stared at the agent's lifeless body.

"Would he have killed me?" Ducote sounded dubious.

"Better believe it, lady. These people have one hell of a thing going and can't afford a single peep out of anybody. That little cocksucker didn't know whether I had told you anything or not, but he couldn't take that chance. You'd have died moments after me. You either take me in your ship or shoot me right here and now because my life isn't worth a rat's ass on Pacifica. They'll catch me in a matter of hours, and I'll probably end as human game for a pervert's hunting party after they squeeze me dry of everything I know. That or I'll become a living organ bank."

Zack's voice had taken on an edge of harshness that made her look at him again. She made a snap decision, based on what her confused instincts were telling her.

"Very well, Mister Decker. I shall take you, but on my terms. And if you give me any trouble, I shall not hesitate to space you. I'm not a killer as you are, but I've had my share of troubles and know how to handle them." Her eyes strayed to the agent's corpse. "Have you any idea how to dispose of this body?"

"Sure," Decker replied. "The solution's right in my bag. A Shrehari disruptor."

"But that's illegal!" Ducote sounded shocked.

"Yup," Zack grinned, clearly unashamed and relieved now that he had a way out of this mess. "But there's no better way to remove damning evidence. If it makes you feel any better, I bought it only a few hours ago, to make sure my mate's body didn't fall into the hands of people who'd show it less than proper respect. I wouldn't dream of using it on a living person."

"Once again, Mister Decker, I wonder whether I believe you." She kneeled down and rummaged in Zack's duffel bag, always keeping the blaster aimed at him.

"It this it?" She held up the battered weapon.

"Yeah. Just aim it at the scumbag's body and pull the trigger."

She looked at him with suspicion.

"Perhaps I will use it on you afterwards. That way I have no problems at all."

Zack shrugged.

"Suit yourself, lady. With Raisa gone, I have little to live for, except getting my information out to the Fleet. But if you're going to spare me, can you retrieve my dagger before you zap the bastard, please? It's a souvenir from my time in the Corps."

She looked at him for a few heartbeats, as if debating whether to tell him to sod off or not, then squatting by the body she yanked the knife out of his throat, wincing at the wet noise it made as it broke free. She wiped the blade clean on the agent's clothes and dropped it in the duffel bag.

"Thank you, Captain."

Without replying, Ducote disintegrated the corpse, and then dropped the disruptor back into the bag with a grimace of distaste.

"An efficient machine, Mister Decker. Now listen carefully because I won't give you a chance to correct mistakes. You will walk on board the ship ahead of me and do everything I tell you. I will lock you in a cabin where you will stay until I decide to let you out. If you try anything funny, and I mean anything at all, I will space the cabin, and you will die. Understood?"

"Sure, Captain. Though spacing the cabin won't do much for the interior decorating."

"No attempts at humor, please. I'm in no mood for forced levity. Keep your hands in sight at all times. Turn around and walk towards gangway."

"Thanks, Captain. You've saved my life."

"Just do as I tell you. I would rather not regret my momentary folly," she snapped back, unhappy with her choice and wishing Decker would vanish into thin air.

— FOURTEEN —

"Strip."

Zack gave Ducote a crooked grin, his hands still held up at shoulder level, palms outward. The trader did not smile back. Though outwardly calm, her washed-out blue eyes betrayed anxiety and irritation. Decker had ruined what should have been an entirely normal lift and thrown her life into turmoil and she resented him for it.

"Why, Captain, we barely know each other," he replied.

"To borrow one of your expressions, Mister Decker — funny guy. Now strip so I can see you have no hidden weapons." Her voice was as hard and sharp as freshly hewn quartz.

"And put me at a psychological disadvantage. A stark-naked man with his privates flopping about will feel embarrassed, humiliated, or just plain uncomfortable, which from your point of view is dandy. Good move, Captain."

"Indeed, Mister Decker. I'm glad you approve."

Her sarcasm bounced off Zack without leaving a trace.

After climbing aboard the ship, she had steered him down a narrow and short corridor to a tiny cabin aft of the cockpit. Everything seemed small aboard *Demetria*, except her cargo holds. From what he had seen, the ship's living area was smaller than an average bungalow. But she looked to be in good repair and was spotlessly clean, for all that she showed signs of wear and tear on her bare metal bulkheads and decks.

As he undressed, Zack examined Captain Ducote. A tall, strong-boned woman, she was handsome rather than pretty, with a square face, strong chin, hawk nose, and pale skin. Her long, straw-colored hair was pleated and draped into a crown at the back of her head. Pale blue eyes sat beneath eyebrows so light they seemed bleached. She wore clean, dark blue coveralls that molded her body like a second skin.

Noticing his speculative gaze, she snapped, "Make it quick, Mister Decker. I have a lift window to meet, and you're delaying us. Remember what I said. Disobey me once and I space you. Or down here, throw you to your enemies."

He knew she didn't mean it. For all her coldness, she didn't look like a killer. But Zack knew she would kill to defend herself, and with the same sangfroid, she had shown so far. He obeyed, dropping his clothing, item by item, into a small pile at his feet, until he was stark naked. The bare decking felt cold under his feet, but he repressed a shiver, standing nonchalantly, as if his nakedness in front of a strange woman didn't matter. Decker grinned again.

"Like what you see, Captain?"

She made a face. "I've seen much better, Mister Decker."

Zack shrugged. "Then you're a lucky woman."

Ducote ignored the reply as she picked up his clothes, the gun still pointing steadily at Decker. When she was done, she stepped back into the corridor.

"You should lie down during lift-off. *Demetria* is much more maneuverable than *Shokoten,* and I enjoy piloting her. I shall bring you food once we've left orbit."

With that, the cabin door hissed closed. Zack didn't bother trying it. He knew Ducote would have made sure it was locked. He shrugged and stretched out on the bunk, oblivious to the chill and discomfort.

The immediate danger had passed and now, like a proper Marine, he took his rest while he had a chance, and fell sound asleep, his body, and spirit exhausted by the events of the long and tragic day.

*

The cabin door whooshed open. Decker, who was lying on his back, hands behind his head, glanced over and smiled.

"Had a decent lift-off?" He had woken briefly, while the pressure of climbing out of Pacifica's gravity well had tried to mash him into the bunk, but had fallen asleep again when Ducote had switched to artificial gravity. It had been a smooth departure, professionally executed.

She tossed him a bundle of clothes.

"Get dressed, Mister Decker. I've decided I would rather risk losing the psychological advantage I hold over you than seeing you naked all the time."

Zack bit his tongue, repressing a smart comeback that would not have endeared him to the dour woman. But his smile grew larger.

"Thank you, Captain. And you can call me Zack."

"I think we should forego familiarity, Mister Decker. After all, your recent behavior has not given me any cause to consider you friendly."

He gave her an amiable shrug. "Suit yourself." Without further comment, he pulled on the clothes under Ducote's watchful eyes and unwavering blaster.

He checked his trouser and shirt pockets. Ducote had emptied them. When she noticed his gestures, she said, "I will return your property when I put you ashore, minus, of course, the price of your passage."

"And when will that be?"

"On Santa Theresa; or if you fear for your life there, at the port of call after that one. A free trader lives on a narrow margin, and I cannot afford to make a detour only to drop you off."

"It'll be a long trip, under the circumstances, keeping a virtual prisoner under watch and under lock. I'm not about to hijack your ship because I wouldn't know how to sail her. I'm just a Marine gunner with some naval skills, and I don't go for rape. If a woman doesn't want me, there are always others who do."

Ducote cocked a skeptical eyebrow at him.

"You have a high opinion of your charms, Mister Decker," she said in a dry tone. "Come. We will break our fast. The ship is on autopilot until we reach the jump point."

"Listen, Captain, not that I'm impressionable, but could you stop pointing that gun at me? It'll help lower the tension in here and help my digestion."

She glared at him with her cold eyes and then glanced down at the blaster. With a shrug, she tucked it into her coverall's cargo pocket.

"I suppose you have a point, Mister Decker. You will have to tell me how you came to own an Imperial Armaments fifteen millimeter in such good condition."

Zack grinned. "You seem to know your guns pretty well. I'm impressed. Few people would recognize Shrehari hardware."

"One sees many things as a free trader and hears much more. Perhaps that's why I agreed to take you off Pacifica because your story didn't sound as far-fetched to me as it would to the master of a company ship. However, my opinion could change when you tell me more over breakfast."

Ducote led him next door to a small galley and told him to squeeze his bulk between the table and a bench fixed to the bulkhead. She might have put the blaster away, but in the time it would take for him to get out of his tight seat, she'd have a chance to empty the gun's magazine into his body.

She shoved two plastic covered packages into an autochef and programmed it. They did not speak in the minute or two it took the machine to produce a healthy, nutritious, and to Decker, bland meal. He ate with appetite nonetheless, savoring excellent coffee served in battered tin mugs.

"Thanks. That hit the spot something fierce."

He pushed the empty tray away and slumped back against the bulkhead, sipping the black, bitter brew. Ducote grunted in reply, chewing on the last of her soyburger. When she was done, she cleaned off the small table, refilled their coffees, and sat down, hard eyes on Zack's face.

"Story time, I believe, Mister Decker. What is this danger that has you turned into a fugitive?"

"Well," he started, "I guess it all began when they threw me out of the Fleet..."

*

"...and then I figured your ship was my best chance off Pacifica." He concluded. "The rest you know."

She had listened to him in silence, asking few questions. Ducote now stared into the dregs of her coffee, digesting Zack's tale. He had told her everything because he needed her help, and she could feel that he had been entirely truthful. Or at least told her the truth as he believed it to be, which could differ from reality. What had touched her most was his expression and tone when he spoke of Raisa Darhad, his dead mate. If nothing else, that small, vulnerable part of Zack Decker had convinced her to keep an open mind.

"Have you ever thought, Mister Decker," she said, frowning, "that you might have been maneuvered into *Shokoten* by Intelligence? That your friend Tren Kinnear has not completely retired after all?"

He looked thunderstruck at the idea. Then, he chuckled. But the sound was far from amused.

"You know, Kinnear always was an operator. By the gods, but that would explain a lot, including my predecessor's death."

"A Fleet agent who they unmasked."

"Who Kiani unmasked. And to think she tried to make me believe Raisa did it." He shook his head in disgust. "So the Fleet took advantage of my situation by putting me in Lokis' place, hoping I'd be loyal enough to the old Corps to pass the word if something looked really wrong. Boy, if I ever get my hands on Kinnear, I'll fucking kill him for sending me in blind. We always used to hate the Navy brass who did that to us when we were both in the Pathfinders."

"Assuming you're right," Ducote asked, "how will you prove it? You no longer have your data chip with the sensor readings. Somehow I doubt the Fleet will try an operation against the Amalis based on your say-so, even if they put you on *Shokoten* to ferret such a thing out."

"You have a point," Zack said in a resigned tone. "With my record, no officer in his right mind will take me at my word. But before I even try to convince someone, I have to contact the right people. I can't just walk onto the nearest base and tell them my story. They'd either throw me out on my ass or take me into protective custody as a nut case, especially without proof. What a mess."

He fell silent and stared off into a corner of the galley, trying to control his frustration. Ducote observed him in silence and wondered what to do with him. Extraordinary as it seemed, his story was so smooth and logical that it was believable.

She had always prided herself on her ability to make quick personal judgements. It was a vital asset to a free trader whose livelihood depended on her negotiating skills. Her guts told her she should trust this man, and help him as much as she could.

"Okay, Mister Zachary T. Decker, although I don't understand myself for once, I've decided to take you at face value," her features hardened for a moment, and her voice took on an edge of steel, "for now. I will drop you off at any port you choose, provided it's on my route. Though I will take your money for the passage, I can use another pair of hands around here. Free traders have no room for idlers. You say you know your way around a starship. I shall give you occasion to prove it."

Zack nodded.

"Deal, Captain. I'd rather keep busy anyways. It'll keep me from brooding." Again, she saw a flash of pain and loss in his eyes. It touched her in a surprising manner.

"That being said, you can drop the 'captain' nonsense. We'll be living cheek-by-jowl for the next few weeks, and the formality will drive me crazy. Call me Avril."

"Please to meet you, Avril. I'm Zack."

He thrust his strong, callused hand over the table.

She took it and squeezed hard, testing him. Her hand felt as well-worn and hard-worked as his and that pleased him.

"Welcome aboard *Demetria*, Zack."

*

"Try it again." Decker's voice echoed down the short corridor connecting engineering to the cockpit. He was wearing borrowed coveralls, now grease-smeared and stained, like his hands and forearms. His broad frame fit snugly inside the belly turret's access tube, and he had to fight a twinge of claustrophobia every time his mind had more than a few moments to think.

Everything was small on the ship, cabins, passages, engine room, cockpit, guns; everything except the cargo hold and the drives, which was just as well. The popguns she carried wouldn't have fought off a pleasure sloop, let alone a reiver. But, if Avril's pride in her ship was warranted, she could outrun just about anything in space.

Zack's first move, after a guided tour and a long discussion about her abilities, had been to study her schematics and figure out a way to boost the guns' power. Ducote didn't seem overly thrilled about the notion, preferring to rely on speed, but she didn't stop him. It gave her a chance to test his skills without jeopardizing a vital function.

After crawling into the first turret, he grimaced in disgust. Avril had said a free trader lived on a tight margin, and she hadn't been kidding. Her maintenance expenditures had been limited to the vital systems, and the guns looked like hell. Lubricants had dried up and hardened, freezing many moving parts. Command modules had died from simple neglect, and vibrations had worked some of the wiring loose and shorted out the more sensitive controls.

The ordnance was the only part of the ship that lacked maintenance, but Zack needed three days of full-time work just to bring the guns back to their original state. Meanwhile, Ducote had gained a new appreciation of his competence. A pleasant side effect of her growing respect for him was a thaw in her manner. She now smiled more and seemed more willing to talk about personal things. But the trader still didn't trust Zack enough to leave him in the cockpit alone.

"Power output is ten percent above nominal," Avril yelled back.

"Good. Now keep an eye on the readout and tell me when I reach twenty-two percent."

He fiddled with the interlink, swearing as sweat ran into his eyes.

"Twenty-two percent!"

"Is it stable?"

"Yes."

Zack shoved the module back into its slot and locked it in place. He crawled backwards out of the tube and turned as he rose.

"That ought to do it," he commented, wiping his hands on an old rag. "Still won't win you first prize in a slugfest with pirates, but it'll keep 'em well enough occupied while you run. What you need is a good defensive missile pod. Now that'll call for some respect."

She shook her head in exasperation.

"I can't even afford a decent evening gown, Zack. How do you expect me to pay for a missile pod?"

Decker grinned sheepishly. When he wasn't thinking about Raisa and the secret he carried in his head, he could almost believe he was enjoying himself. There was something satisfying about his work aboard *Demetria*.

"I suppose you're right," he replied. "Anyway, that takes care of what little you have. What do you want me to do next?"

"Eat supper."

As if in reply, Zack's stomach gurgled, causing him to chuckle with embarrassment.

"Traitor," he muttered as if scolding the offending organ. "Okay, boss. What's on the menu?"

"You'll see, Zack. Come." She vanished into the small galley. Decker shrugged and made a quick stop in his cabin's washroom to relieve his bladder and wash the last of the lubricants from his thick fingers.

*

"You do seem to know a lot about starships. For a Marine, I mean." Avril was putting away the large meal at the same rate as Zack, which was unsurprising, considering she was almost as big as he was. "Manning guns is a given, at least for an ignorant civilian like me. But pulling full maintenance and goosing up the output seems more in the realm of naval engineering."

"Nothing to it." He wiped his mouth with the fancy napkin she insisted on putting by their plates at every meal. "When you go on your advanced gunnery training, and then the Master Gunner's course, you learn not only to shoot everything that shoots, but also to repair it, strip it down and, hell, even how to build it from scratch if you have to. We received the whole theory and all. From there, it's a small enough step to learn the same for starship guns. Not a hell of a lot to do on long patrols, and I figured expanding my horizons would keep me and my brain happy."

"I'm impressed."

"Hey," he grinned, "you haven't seen anything yet."

"Oh," she looked at him skeptically under raised eyebrows. "Do you know anything about shields?"

"A bit. Why? You have a problem?"

"Not that I know. But I thought you might reassure me."

"Shit, Avril. I have nothing else to do."

"So I've noticed," she said dryly, before tucking away the last of the rice stew. "I'll keep you busy, Zachary Decker, have no fear. We Reformed Dutch Calvinists have this thing about work."

"Yeah, so I heard."

*

"Santa Theresa doesn't appeal to you?" She raised her pale eyebrows in question. They were seated in the cockpit, she in the pilot's chair, Zack beside her at the co-pilot's console. The planet in question, one of Pacifica's colonies, was growing on the screen as they approached her on a straight course.

"Not really." He made a face. "The only Fleet outfit on-planet is a battalion from the 2nd Regiment. If I go to them, it'll be like going to the Pacifica government, and that means Amali's flunkies. Those Palace Guard fuckers can't be trusted worth shit. Best if I don't show my face off the ship." He paused. "They don't do customs here do they?"

"Not if we're coming straight from the mother world. As long as you don't leave the spaceport, there will be no ID check."

"Don't you have to give a crew manifest?"

"Yes, but I can always list you as someone else. Care to pick a name?"

"Jeez, Avril," Zack shrugged, "I don't -"

"Jeez Avril?" Ducote asked with a straight face, though her eyes danced with mischief. "Strange name for a big man like you."

Zack snorted.

"That's the problem with you Reformed Calvinists: too bloody literal. Must be the Dutch ancestry. Why not list me as Tom Brown. An innocuous name that could fit anyone."

"Very well. Thomas Brown you shall be."

"Good. With any luck, the scumbags won't know I've left on your ship, and won't twig to your new crewmember. That means there's a good chance I'm home free."

"I don't know about that. If anyone cares to check back with Hadley spaceport, they will see that Tom Brown could only have come aboard on Pacifica."

"Yeah, there's that." Decker seemed deflated. "But it'll take them a couple of days, and that might just be too long to bother.

*

Rosalito spaceport was typical of the outer colonies: a stabilized earth tarmac with a simple, prefabricated terminal building and minimal traffic control gear. *Demetria* set down near a tramp freighter, a battered, ancient thing that was holding together only by its captain's willpower. Avril stepped ashore to meet with the port officials and arrange the unloading of her cargo, luxury items that fetched a high cost on frontier worlds.

Zack spent the time in engineering doing post-flight maintenance checks. In due course, Ducote returned, leading a string of cargo carriers bearing the logo of a ComCorp subsidiary that held the monopoly on imports to Santa Theresa. During unloading, Decker had stayed out of sight in the cockpit, in case one of the stevedores was really a *Sécurité Spéciale* officer looking for him.

A few hours later, while they waited for news of their outbound cargo, the airlock alarm buzzed insistently. Avril entered the cockpit and turned on the external camera.

"Yes?"

The bland face of a colonial official appeared on the screen. He smiled ingratiatingly.

"Santa Theresa traffic control, Captain. I'm sorry to disturb you, but your ship has been selected for a random safety inspection."

"Rather unusual, no?" Avril let just the right amount of annoyance creep into her voice, masking the sudden surge of fear.

"As I said, Captain," the inspector's smile never wavered, "I'm sorry about this, but I have my orders. Too many ships with serious safety problems have called here, and the Santa Theresa authorities are anxious to avoid accidents."

"One moment, please." Ducote switched off the camera.

"Quickly now, Zack, climb into access tube three near the main reactor. There's a niche halfway down. It used to hold a plasma converter before the ship received a newer model fusion plant. The niche has a hinged bulkhead plate you can open with a magnetic spanner. When you're inside, seal it with your laser welder. The residual radiation from the reactor should cover your life signs. I shall let you out later. You ought to be safe for an hour or so."

"But doesn't the guy know you have an additional crew member?"

"The question never came up at the port authority, and I didn't submit a crew list."

"Why?" What Zack really meant was why Ducote took the risk of hiding him from the authorities, thereby endangering her livelihood, and possibly her life.

She read the real question in his eyes but instead of wasting time with an elaborate reply, she tapped him on the shoulder.

"Later, Zack. Go."

*

It was uncomfortably warm and cramped in the niche but effective. The smiling inspector took one look down the tube and compared it with ship's blueprints that still showed a plasma converter in Decker's hiding place. He also took a sensor reading that was effectively fogged by the stray emissions from the reactor.

When he glanced into Zack's cabin, Avril had a momentary surge of panic. But Decker, through force of habit, had cleaned it up that morning and stowed his gear. Thankfully, the inspector didn't ask to see the contents of the tiny closet. He left an hour later, still smiling, but Ducote could read a hint of frustration in his eyes. She freed Zack from his confinement and ran her medisensor over his sweat-soaked body.

"You took some radiation, but nothing threatening, though I suggest you visit a hospital for a dip in a regen tank."

"When I can stop running and hiding," he replied with a sour grimace. Then, realizing he was doing her an injustice, his features softened. "Sorry, Avril. You're right. Thanks for hiding me."

"It was well that I did. The inspector was not looking for safety violations."

"*Sécurité Spéciale*?"

"Could be." She shrugged. "But he obtained no satisfaction from his little charade."

"Say," Decker suddenly remembered, "you told me you didn't put me on your crew list. Why?"

A cold smile tugged at Ducote's lips.

"The port captain was a bit too anxious about my trip this time around. I felt it was best not to mention my new first mate."

"That was quite a risk." He frowned. "Not typical of a Reformed Calvinist to lie so much in one day."

Avril blushed and gave him a playful punch on the arm.

"God will understand. It was for a higher cause."

"Thank God for me," Decker looked heavenwards.

"I already have," she replied, eyes twinkling.

Before Zack could explore the meaning of her double entendre, the communications console screeched for attention. It was the port authority with her outbound cargo.

"It seems that they've given up on finding you aboard, Zack. We shall sail for Dordogne in a few hours. Maybe, this time, we are safe."

"Yeah, let's hope." But Decker sounded dubious.

They lifted off at sunset, with the best wishes of the port captain. Unnoticed by either, the old tramp followed them an hour later, her thrusters pushing harder than her appearance would have credited.

*

"Dordogne next, then." They were sharing an evening meal in the galley while the ship headed for the jump point on autopilot.

"Yes. My hold is full of rare oils destined for the Diogenes cosmetics factory."

"Good."   Zack   nodded.   "The   Treizième   Regiment d'Infanterie de Marine, the 13th Marines for you civilians, is stationed there. If I can find the regimental intelligence officer, I may have a chance. The Treizieme's a good outfit. Fought with us on Hispaniola."

"Just a word of caution, Zack, I shall not be landing on Dordogne. The Diogenes operation is in a zero-gee habitat trailing the Deveaux orbital station. You must find your own way down to the planet, or over to the naval orbiter."

"Forget the Navy station, Avril.   Only those with authorization can board a shuttle to the place. It must be dirtside if I want to talk to Fleet personnel."

"Are you going to manage all right?"

He grinned.

"Hey, kid. You're talking to an old Pathfinder. I'm used to going places where people don't want me to go. Getting from the Deveaux station to the barracks of the Treizième will be a snap."

Ducote didn't reply. Instead, she studied the dregs at the bottom of her coffee mug. The minutes ticked by in silence as Zack cleared off the table and poured more of her excellent coffee. Finally, she looked at her companion.

"Listen, Zack. I'll be on station for several days. If you cannot conclude your business on Dordogne or if the Fleet no longer requires your presence..." She left the rest of the invitation unsaid.

"Thanks."   He laid his callused hand over hers and squeezed. "I'll try. I have nowhere else to go."

Before the ensuing silence could deepen and lead to things for which Zack was not yet ready, he left the galley and climbed into the cockpit. Usually, he never fled a developing situation involving an attractive woman, but Raisa's death was still too fresh in his mind. Later, maybe, after settling this business and extracting his revenge. Provided he was still alive.

The thought of death pushed his mind into a new direction, and he switched on the ship's scanners, to satisfy his growing paranoia. He had tweaked the delicate sensors and thanks to his careful tinkering he picked up the other ship almost immediately.

It was behind them, on a parallel course, well beyond normal scanning range, near the limits of his boosted gear's capacity. Frowning, he fiddled with the controls to obtain a clearer readout, but it remained fuzzy as if its emissions were jammed.

"Avril," he called out, "come look at this."

"What is it," she asked, leaning over his shoulder, hand on the seat back. Decker inhaled a whiff of her fresh, flowery scent.

"We may have picked up a tail. He's on a parallel course and jamming his emissions so we can't get a clear reading. Did the port authority give you any kind of traffic advisory?"

"No. We are the only scheduled ship today."

"That settles it. This guy can't be clean." Zack called up a polar view of the system on a side screen and traced *Demetria*'s flight path on it. "Do you think you can maneuver the ship through this gas giant's magnetic pole and then slip into orbit, shutting everything down?"

"Stealth mode, Zack?"

"Yeah. You heard of the tactic?"

"Used it before, when a reiver tracked me in the badlands. No problem."

She slipped into the pilot's seat and took the ship off autopilot. Skillfully, without making the course change seem too abrupt, she nudged *Demetria* towards the planet, aiming for its south pole.

The huge ball of gas slowly grew on the screen. Flashes of light rippled beneath the clouds as electric storms wider than an Earth-sized planet screamed their fury, generating enough power to keep a large colony happy for years.

Periodically, Zack checked their pursuer and became puzzled when he didn't change course to match. His gut told him it was a tail. So what was the unknown captain doing?

"Damn!" Decker climbed out of his seat and headed for the corridor.

"What is it?"

He didn't reply. Instead, he went to his cabin and rummaged in his duffel bag. Decker returned holding his souped-up sensor.

"I have to visit the cargo hold."

"Why?"

"I think your cosmetic oils aren't all oil."

Understanding lit up her eyes.

"Take the main hatch. I'll switch off the lock override."

*

Decker slowly walked across the hold, between the container stacks, letting his sensor scan through the entire electronic spectrum. When he had done it once, he carried out the whole process again. His patience was finally rewarded when a brief blip appeared on the readout. He stopped moving and pointed the machine at every container around him in turn. At the fourth try, he found it.

"Avril," he called through the open hatch, "we have a clandestine electronic passenger."

"What is it?"

"Shielded phase-shift beacon. I'll bet it works in hyperspace as well. That's why the bastard behind us didn't change course to match. He knew he could find us easily."

"That's assuming the other ship is a pursuer."

"Trust me, he is. No other explanation. I can feel it in my bones."

"So what now?"

"Can we dump the container?"

Her head poked through the opening.

"With great difficulty. And I would have to explain to the Diogenes shipping people why I'm one container short of the manifest."

"Hmm." Zack looked at the scan again, wondering whether he could disable it without ditching the valuable oil. Then, something else on the readout grabbed his attention.

"We may not have a choice," he said, voice flat and unemotional. "This isn't just a beacon."

"What?" Her eyes widened in understanding. "No!"

"I'm afraid so. My guess is they want to capture or destroy us somewhere in deep space because your act down on Santa Theresa didn't convince them. They'll blow a hole in your cargo hold with this baby and wreck us. Then, all they have to do is reel your ship in, take us off, and blow *Demetria* into the next dimension. You ship will be written off as another mysterious loss."

"Then we must dump the container."

"Not so fast. It might have an anti-tamper device. We have to remove the one on top before anything else."

"Easily done." She disappeared into an alcove near the hatch and rummaged around. A few moments later, she reappeared, wearing an exoskeleton. Large arms with clawed ends hung from the top of the construct.

She maneuvered into position, sweating under the weight of the machine, and used the powerful mechanical arms to lift the upper container and deposit it to one side.

"Thanks, Avril. I need you to hold my sensor for me now."

"Sure, hang on." She struggled out of the frame and placed it against a bulkhead, out of the way. Perspiration ran down her pale forehead and matted her hair. Kneeling beside Zack, Ducote took the proffered instrument.

"Keep it pointed at the thing. I'm going to open it, and this baby will hopefully warn me of any anti-tamper shit before I trigger it."

She nodded though her eyes filled with worry.

"Go ahead."

With excruciating care, Zack snapped off the shipper's seal and snapped the latches open, glancing at the sensor's screen every few seconds. Sweat ran into his eyes, and he swore at the sting but didn't stop working. Ducote, seeing his discomfort, pulled a soft bandanna from her leg pocket and gently sponged the perspiration from his face.

He lifted the lid millimeter by millimeter, searching for evidence of a booby-trap. During his career, he'd seen many types and knew he had to look for the unexpected.

"There!" He glanced at the sensor, then into the narrow opening between lid and container.

"What?" Avril's voice was steady, but he could hear her fear.

"A laser-reflector anti-tampering device. Looks like it's hooked to a magnetic circuit. If I have this right, the moment the container leaves the metal deck, the magnetic field holding the reflector in place breaks and the reflector slips away. The detector no longer gets a bounce-back and kaboom," Zack explained. "Very slick."

"Can you do anything about it?"

"Yeah. First thing, though, is move the lid out of the way."

"Is connected to anything?"

"Yes, it is. A simple wire detonator. There." He pointed at a hair-thin, shimmering strand in one corner. "Be a dear, Avril, and fetch the little gray plas package in my duffel bag. It contains tools that might be useful."

"Sure." She rose. "Zack, how long will this take? We will pass through the gas giant's Van Allen belt soon."

"Damn! Reset the course. No knowing what'll happen when we enter a strong magnetic field. This thing may go on its own, or the bastard may simply send a detonate command if he loses track of us."

"On my way, but won't our pursuers know we've found something, now that we change course for the second time within an hour."

"Can't be helped."

*

Ducote returned a minute or two later carrying the small package.

"We're back on course to the jump point. Our friend is still following at the same distance."

Decker nodded. He carefully replaced the container lid and opened Kiani's miniature tool collection. He studied the half-dozen instruments in silence.

"You know," he remarked, "when I took these out of Nihao's locker before I jumped ship, I had no idea what they were for. I'm still not sure I do, but something tells me they're good for EOD work."

Ducote reached over and picked one of the tools up. She examined it, frowning.

"If I might hazard a guess, Zack, this could be a negative field inducer." Without waiting for a reply, she twisted the lower handle and waved the wand-shaped instrument in front of the sensor. "I was right."

"Good. Keep it handy. I think I know what to do."

Carefully, Zack lifted the lid again and examined the detonator at the end of the monofilament thread.

"Inducer."

Ducote slapped it in his palm. Slowly, Decker slipped it into the opening, aiming its business end at the detonator.

"Scanner."

With one hand, he adjusted the sensor's controls and looked at the readout.

"So far, so good. Please cut the thread and remove the lid. Be careful not to touch the inducer or my hand. If the negative field fails, the detonator will blow."

She complied, and when Zack had a clear view, he grinned.

"That was the hard part. I need a plasma welder."

A few moments later, she held up another of Kiani's tools.

"This is a precision instrument, Zack, a beautiful piece of workmanship."

"Good. Now come around to the side and I'll show you where to cut."

Avril nodded, unsure of her role in disarming the detonator, but she complied.

"See those sheathed fiber optic wires down there? They connect the detonator to the bomb. The bomb itself is hidden below the oil packages. Normally, I'd be afraid that cutting the wires will trip a dead man's switch and blow the thing, but we all have to die eventually, so it won't matter." He grinned at Avril's expression.

"Just kidding. EOD man's humor. Fiber optics are too sensitive for a dead man's switch. If it were hard wiring, I'd think again, but the plasma welder will fry the optical receptors. I'd do it myself, but I can't afford to move the inducer by a millimeter."

"Okay." She still sounded unsure but was unwilling to show fear. Within seconds, she had sliced through the wiring. Nothing happened, and Zack slumped down on the deck, leaning against the container as he wiped the sweat from his face.

"I wouldn't exactly say explosive ordnance disposal is the most stressful work in the galaxy," he commented wryly, "but it's right up there with antimatter bottling. I could sure use a cold beer."

"Okay," he continued after a few moments of silence. "The biggie now." He leaned into the box and examined the laser reflector setup, muttering to himself. Finally, he straightened up, looking grim.

"The bad news is it's hardwired."

"And what's the good news."

"I have none." He wiped his hands on his trousers. "Can't cut the connection with the bomb."

"So what's the solution?"

"Slide it out the door and down the ramp, then give it a mighty kick into the void, hoping it isn't powerful enough to tear up the hull from the outside."

She looked at him incredulously. "And who will do the pushing?"

"Me."

*

The hatch swung shut behind Zack's suited back, and a red light began to blink in his helmet's overhead display as Ducote started pumping the air out of the compartment. He felt his suit expand to its working girth as the air inside fought against the vacuum.

"Ready and waiting."

"Stand by." Her voice sounded tinny and small in the helmet's earphones.

Vibrations ran through the metal deck as the rear cargo doors opened and the ramp slid out. Decker stared at the magnificent star field for a few seconds, drawn to the void like a man on a cliff is attracted to the edge. Then, he put his weight on the container and slowly pushed across the deck, grunting with effort, muscles straining to the breaking point. He didn't dare use mechanical help for fear of accidentally lifting the container up, even if only by a millimeter and for a fraction of a second.

Slowly, strenuously, he moved the bomb across the hold and onto the edge of the ramp. Battling his fear of the void, he clipped on a safety line and resumed his painful progress. By the time he reached the end of the ramp, his guts were turning to water. The ship may have been moving at a respectable velocity, but it seemed stopped in relation to the immensity of space.

This would be the tricky part. Decker unclipped two personal spacewalk devices from his suit's belt and attached them to either side of the container, jets pointing towards the ship. Then, because he hadn't found a better way, he unrolled two strands of string, each attached to a nozzle trigger. Carefully, he backed into the ship.

"Ready."

"Be careful, Zack."

Decker pulled on the strings as hard as he could, triggering high-pressure nitrogen thrusters. They erupted in clouds of crystallized gas, momentarily masking the container. Then, a bright, silent explosion blotted out the stars as the bomb exploded, its magnetic anti-tampering device no longer restrained by the metal surface of the ramp.

Decker felt something hit his suit, punch through and dig painfully into his leg. Air escaped in a puff of white ice.

"Pressurize the hold, Avril. I've been hit by shrapnel," he shouted into the commlink. "My suit's holed."

Zack struggled to pinch the fold of material around the puncture and stop the flow of air while the cargo doors ponderously slid closed. Time seemed to ooze by like molasses while he waited for the telltale in his helmet's display to show the hold was pressurized again, his leg feeling the cold of space seep in through the hole.

A light blinked green in the corner of his eye, but it took his brain a few seconds to realize he was out of danger.

"Zack," an insistent voice rang in his ears, "are you all right?"

"Yeah, Avril, yeah." Decker slumped against the nearest container and breathed in deeply, his adrenaline rush crashing. "How's the ship?"

"Fine, except for the ramp. Half of it is gone."

"You weren't going fast enough, kiddo."

"Huh," she snorted. "Any faster and we would have had relativistic problems. Good work, Zack. You saved our lives, and my ship."

"Why is it, Avril old dear, that I have the impression saving your ship is a notch above saving our hides?"

"Because without the ship, we would have to walk to Dordogne."

For some reason, that absurd statement was hysterically funny, and Zack collapsed with laughter. After a few heartbeats, Avril joined him, the tension of the last hour flowing out.

"Or," he fought for breath, "we could always hitchhike. Maybe the guy on our tail will pick us up."

Decker sobered up at the thought of their pursuer.

"Speaking of which, we're not out of this yet. I'll be up in a sec."

Two dull explosions rang through the hull and stopped him in his tracks.

"Are we under attack already?"

"No, of course not." He could hear the amusement in her voice. "Those were the explosive bolts holding the ramp. With its lower half gone, there was no point in keeping it. If there is any justice in the universe, it will float into the other ship's path and make a big hole in her hull."

"I think we used up our daily ration of luck just now."

*

"The pig behind us has increased speed," Ducote announced as Decker limped into the cockpit, a bandage around his thigh beneath red-stained coveralls.

"See?" Her finger traced his trajectory and power curve on the left screen.

"He knows we disposed of the bomb and beacon. Now all he can do is intercept. How far to the jump point?"

"Ten minutes. We will reach it before he does and then I will program a circuitous path. He'll lose our trail after our second jump.   Assuming he finds our first emergence point."

"Good tactics, but I'll bet the bastard knows that too. Can you divert power to the guns?"

"Sure, but is he not too far away?" She asked dubiously.

"He won't be in the last minutes before we go FTL, and that's when we want to blind him, but I'm more worried about missiles right now. He will try everything he can to stop us from jumping."

"Right." Ducote nodded as her fingers danced over her console. "You have all defensive systems on your panel, with power at your command."

"Roger, Captain."

The minutes ticked by in silence until...

"There!" Zack pointed at the tactical screen. "Four missiles. By their speed, I'd judge military grade, human. Expensive bastards, but effective. Computing intercept..." Then, "Firing solution confirmed. Come to papa, little birdies."

A low whine rang through *Demetria*'s hull, then another and another, as her guns shot bursts of pure energy into the path of the oncoming missiles. Like a calliope, the eight barrels pumped out shot after shot, in quick succession, saturating space between the two ships.

Zack whooped as a bright flash briefly flared in the distance.

"One down, three to go!"

"Power use is affecting our jump drive spool-up, Zack," Avril warned, her eyes fixed on her controls.

"Yeah, I know. But the only way to stop missiles is to pump as much energy into their path as you can. Our speed won't matter shit if one hits us in the ass."

The guns whined ceaselessly as Zack cycled them through the firing sequence without pause, and a second missile exploded in a brilliant display of fireworks. Then, a red light blipped on the gunner's board.

Zack swore.   "Shit!   We lost number two turret. Overheated."

He had lost twenty-five percent of his firepower, and his chances of destroying the two remaining missiles had dropped by the same factor. An amber warning light told him number three turret was about to follow. And the missiles were fast closing the range.

"How long before the jump?"

"Ninety seconds."

"Can you make it sixty?"

"Our emergence might be off by a wide margin."

"And our lives by an eternity if we don't. I'm about to lose the second turret, and with only four barrels, I have little hope of stopping the other two. They'll hit in a minute."

Ducote remained silent for a few heartbeats, and then reached for the controls.

"FTL in five," hyperspace shutters closed over the cockpit windows, "four, three," Zack aimed his guns at the other ship, "two, one, JUMP."

Nausea came and went, leaving a feeling of relief that made Avril sigh as she slumped back in her seat.

"That was close."

"Naw. I've seen a lot worse." He grinned at her. "We make a pretty decent team. That was a high power reiver on our tail, and there aren't too many who can claim they escaped their sort. I wouldn't wonder if it was the junk heap we saw on the ground. I thought she looked a bit strange for a tramp freighter."

Ducote smiled back and nodded.

"We do make a good team. Zack, you have a berth on *Demetria* when this is over if you want it. And I mean that. I can use the help and the company. It's not a rich life, but I travel a lot." She placed her hand over Zack's and squeezed, her eyes meeting his.

"I accept. When this is all over." He didn't add *if I'm still alive.* But she saw the thought in his eyes.

*

The massive spindle shape of Deveaux Station hung several kilometers ahead of *Demetria* as they waited for the tug to lock on and pull them to their berth. They were out of danger for now, under the guns of an orbital defense platform.

The trip to Dordogne took more than two weeks. Avril had plotted a circuitous route with unexpected course changes to shake off the other ship. It had worked, though the days were tense, as Decker and Ducote took turns standing watch for any signs of pursuit.

Somewhere on the other side of Dordogne, out of sight and unreachable for a retired Marine noncom, was Starbase 26, the military station. The only Marines on board would be a military police company, but Zack still felt a twinge of homesickness at the thought of its nearness.

"Wouldn't it be simpler to have you offload at the Diogenes facility?" He asked more to derail his depressing train of thought than out of real interest.

Avril laughed, her alto sounding delightful to Decker's ears.

"They have stricter security than most naval installations. No one except the company's own shuttles dock at the orbiter."

"You've handled stuff for them before."

"Yes. They're most generous in their payments for a fast and safe delivery. I have a standing offer with them. Ships of *Demetria*'s size rely on high value, luxury items for their survival, and Diogenes' raw materials, as well as their products, are about as high value as they come."

"Means you can't afford their perfumes, eh?" Zack grinned crookedly at her.

"Go jump into a black hole, Decker." Ducote made an obscene gesture and grinned back.

"*Demetria*, this is Deveaux control." The radio crackled to life. "Stand by for tractor beam lock-on. You have docking bay number seventy-two."

"Standing by," Avril replied. Then, when the sensors showed positive tractor beam lock, "You have us, Deveaux control."

"Welcome to Dordogne, *Demetria*, and enjoy the ride."

A few minutes later, a muffled thump resonated through the hull as the ship mated with the wide airlock. Grappling arms held her hull fast and, essentially, she became one with the station.

"There we go. If you'll excuse me, I must see the representative to arrange offloading."

"Alright. I'll go book myself a shuttle trip down to the Toulon spaceport, then."

"You'll need to show your ID on the way out of the docking area. Let me do it. It'll be safer that way."

"Thanks, Avril, but I don't think anyone will be doing me in on this station. I won't leave the public areas, I promise. See you later."

"I hope so, Zack."

"Hey, I'm leaving my stuff here, aren't I?"

*

The freight docks took up a full third of station, alternating between cavernous inner docks for large bulk carriers and smaller outside moorings, for ships like *Demetria*.

Zack took a rim corridor to the wide feeder passage that led to station's core. The passage, fifteen meters wide and ten meters high, showed heavy use. Arc lights at regular intervals banished all shadows though their intensity hurt Zack's eyes at first.

Conduits ran along the unpainted ceiling and walls, color-coded in a system that only the designers could understand. Warning signs in a dozen languages were the only decoration. The smell of hot lubricants, cold metal, and honest sweat permeated the passage.

Zack kept to a pedestrian strip marked off by a double yellow line on the deck, merging with the flow of stevedores, technicians, and merchant sailors. High-speed container carriers caromed by on repulser fields, transferring goods from deep space haulers to cargo shuttles headed for the surface.

The pedestrian strip eventually split in two, the left half continuing to the other side of the station. A string of security gates shut the right half and Zack headed for a booth marked 'new arrivals.' He slipped his ID into the reader slot beneath a flat screen displaying the logo of Deveaux station, a crowing rooster wearing a red Phrygian bonnet.

The face of a strikingly beautiful blonde woman replaced the capped fowl. She smiled at Decker, and he smiled back even though he knew she was just a computer sim.

"Ship?" She asked in a softly accented Anglic.

"*Demetria.*"

"Thank you, Mister Decker. I must inform you that the Merchant Guild register still shows you as a warrant officer on the MV *Shokoten.*"

"I changed ships on Pacifica and haven't changed my status."

"Be sure to visit the Guildhall then, Mister Decker, and have your files updated. It's to your advantage. The Guildhall is on level fifty-two green." Zack's ID card popped out of the slot, followed by a blue gate pass. "Have a pleasant stay on Deveaux Station."

"Thanks." The beautiful apparition vanished, leaving the holographic rooster to pose in its ridiculous manner.

Zack had no intention of visiting the Guildhall on Deveaux, or on Dordogne. The fewer people who knew where he was, the better. Except that now, to exit the docking area, his name was swimming in the station's data banks, but that couldn't be helped. He could rig guns and sensors beyond their legal limits, but he couldn't forge ID.

A bank of lifts and a holo map of the station beckoned a few steps from the gate. Zack called up the location of the passenger transport brokers. It was on level forty-six red, right beside the station's shop district. He stepped into a lift and punched in his destination. It disgorged him on level forty-six within moments.

The shop district was humming with activity, even though it was late in the station's night watch. Nothing commercial ever closed on Deveaux, which, like all other busy stations, lived twenty-four hours a standard day. He let the crowd flow by on either side of him for a few moments as he took his bearings, then set off to the right.

The variety of bars, stores, and restaurants was huge, catering to all budgets and tastes. Tantalizing smells hovered over the broad avenue and Zack's stomach rumbled with sudden hunger. Dordogne was renowned for its superb food, and even the blatantly commercial Deveaux was said to monitor the high standards of its restaurants.

The gunner lingered in front of a few shop windows, both to admire the elegant fashions and to look for a tail. Several stunning dresses caught his eye, and he wondered how Avril would look in them. But the prices kept him from speculating too much. That wasn't the case when he passed a lingerie shop, and it took a certain amount of willpower to corral his wandering thoughts.

At that moment, he had the eerie feeling of being watched again. It had been a while since the last time and now, with the memory of the recent past still fresh, he felt the small hairs on the back of his neck stand up straight.

Zack angled off the main concourse into a smaller boulevard on his left, intent on either spotting or shaking his tail. The crowds were much thinner here as the shops catered to a more specialized clientele, those with money burning in their pockets and tastes far removed from the mainstream. His worn leather jacket and plain black trousers made him stand out like a sore thumb among the richly dressed pleasure sailors looking for a good time.

He came to a bend in the corridor, where a floor to ceiling safety mirror had been set at an angle to prevent traffic accidents. Zack's eyes met his own worried reflection, and then he saw a man and a woman coming up behind him fast, pistols only half-hidden inside their jackets.

When they saw they'd been spotted, the man drew his gun and fired. Zack's finely honed reflexes saved him as he jumped aside and searched for a way out. The guns made no noise. A tinkle, like broken glass, drew his eyes back to the mirror. Small shards tumbled to the floor after hitting the hardened glass.

Needlers, his mind absently registered, shooting thin slivers of polymer ice. Silent and deadly. Assassins' weapons.

He sprinted down the corridor, shoving protesting merrymakers out of the way. Though he didn't dare look back, Zack knew his assailants were following him, and gaining. There was little doubt in his mind that these were *Sécurité Spéciale* agents. How they had found him so fast raised ugly questions about the organization's reach and resources. His name had surfaced in the data banks only minutes earlier, yet they had found him on a crowded commercial level, one level among fifty open to the public, within that time.

He veered around another corner and headed for a broad staircase leading downwards. The further he went, the fewer people he saw, which was bad, very bad. His feet rang on the fake marble steps as he took them two at a time.

The stairs abruptly ended on a grassy surface. Zack looked around, feeling worried for the first time. He had managed to go to the one place he should have avoided at all costs: the terrarium.

A cavernous chamber filled with vegetation, the terrarium was a fixture on most stations, to give spacers and station dwellers alike a taste of nature. To make it more natural, the light cycle in the terrarium followed that of the station's notional day and night watches, which meant it was dark right now, with only a smattering of fake 'stars' covering the ceiling.

There was another stairway at the opposite end, and Zack jogged down a flagstone path towards it, ears straining for the sound of his pursuers. He breathed in the fresh smells of nature: cut grass, flowers in bloom, apple trees. Muted moans came from a cluster of shrubs to his right and Decker grinned briefly.

Then, a figure suddenly appeared in his path. Though he couldn't make out features, he knew it was the woman who'd pursued him earlier with her male friend, who seemed conspicuously absent.

"Hide and seek time is over, Mister Decker," she said, her voice rough and husky.

Zack gathered himself for a desperate lunge at the woman, but she and her companion were pros. While the man had followed him, she had taken a shortcut. Now he was caught between the two.

"Good night, Mister Decker," an amused male voice softly chimed in from behind.

He felt the sting of a dozen mosquitoes on his neck and numbness filled his body with frightening speed until his legs gave out.

Zack Decker crumpled to the ground in an untidy heap, unable to do more than grunt. After that, his universe turned black.

— FIFTEEN —

Decker slowly opened his eyes and closed them again when pain lanced through his brain. It hurt enough that he decided he was still in this universe, and not in some mythical hell.

He remained still for a few heartbeats and took stock of his situation. For one thing, he was alive, still wearing his own clothes and lying on a bunk. A quick test proved that he had the use of his limbs though any movement made his head pound. He sensed an all too familiar subliminal vibration —hyperdrives pushing a ship in its own FTL bubble.

Zack remained still and kept his eyes shut as he reconstructed his last memories. He saw the pursuit in Deveaux station's commercial district, the wrong turn into the night-time terrarium, a woman popping out of the shadows in front of him, barring his way, and dozens of pinpricks as she, and the man behind him, emptied their needlers. Not poison but sedatives. His last memory was of falling on the cultured grass.

He opened his eyes again and sat up, wincing in pain. After a few heartbeats, he swung his legs over the edge of the bunk, simultaneously wishing he hadn't done so. Nausea rushed up his throat, making him retch. His breathing became labored as he fought the sickness. Whatever sedative they had used, it left nasty after-effects.

In time, the compartment stopped spinning, and his stomach settled down in an uneasy truce with his brain. The cabin was small, bare and not unlike the one Avril Ducote had given him on *Demetria*. A small ship then, perhaps a space yacht or a courier. Squinting against the glare, he looked around and quickly spotted the video pickup in one corner.

Next question, how long had he been out? Zack glanced at his wrist, but it was bare: they had taken his timepiece.

Standard procedure. Never give a prisoner something that could help him order his life. Zack absently rubbed his chin and encountered stubble. His last shave had been four or five hours before docking, and this seemed like a full day's growth. That meant he'd been out fifteen to eighteen hours. Time enough to leave orbit and jump. His bladder suddenly sent him urgent signals and confirmed his estimate.

He stood on unsteady legs and staggered to the small toilet, sighing as he relieved himself. That business taken care of, the beginnings of hunger gnawed at his insides. He grinned again. Zachary T. Decker didn't stay down for long. He glanced up at the surveillance module on the ceiling and waved.

"If it isn't too much trouble, guys, I wouldn't mind a bit of grub and some water."

Then, he settled on the bunk again and put his hands behind his head. A few minutes later, the cabin door vanished with a whisper, and a mean looking blaster filled the opening. Behind the blaster, Zack recognized the male part of the deadly duo that had netted him like a rookie. He looked as bland and unassuming as before, someone you wouldn't notice in a crowd, as long as he wasn't pointing a gun at you. Come to think of it, he and the inspector on Santa Theresa had that blandness in common. Maybe it was a requirement to join the *Sécurité Spéciale*. Two small objects sailed into the cabin and landed with a thunk on the deck beside the bunk.

"Enjoy, Mister Decker." His Anglic was accent-free, his voice unremarkable. The door closed again before the gunner could ask any of the questions burning on his lips.

Sitting up slowly this time, Zack leaned down and picked up the two packages: a military-issue emergency ratpack and a zero-gee water skin. He couldn't repress an automatic grimace at the sight of the ratpack. Nourishing and life sustaining, but unappetizing, the slab of protein, vitamins and minerals tasted salty-sweet and gooey. It was the subject of more jokes and put-downs among ground pounders than any other matter, including the General Staff. But right now, it was food for a big man who hadn't eaten in almost a standard day.

Zack unwrapped the bar and sniffed, nodding. It smelled just the same whether hidden in a cave on Hispaniola or on an assault shuttle skimming the treetops on Ganesh. He briefly considered the possibility that it had been adulterated or poisoned. There were ways of doing it without leaving traces on the vacuum-tight wrapper. He knew of at least a dozen and had tried several himself, giving hungry guerrillas a bad case of gastroenteritis on New-Tasman. The results hadn't been fun to watch, but it had worked.

On the other hand, if his hosts had wanted to poison him, they could just as well have killed him on Deveaux and dumped his body into the garbage compactor. It didn't take a genius with four years at the Academy to figure that one out. He took a bite of the ratpack and chewed as he considered his situation.

First, he was on his way back to Pacifica, to Amali's hideaway. That was so sure a bet, he was willing to use his left nut as collateral. Second, the reason they were taking him back instead of just killing him was that they wanted to find out how much he knew, and who he had told. Third, once they'd squeezed the information out of him, Zack Decker would vanish forever.

He had no illusions that he'd resist interrogation. Everyone talked, eventually. The only ones who didn't were those with conditioning, and they died instead. But while he was alive, he had a chance. Never count a Pathfinder as dead until you've seen the body, and even then make damn sure.

Another thought occurred to him, and he almost choked on his last bite. One way or the other, they'd find out Avril knew, and that meant she would die too if it wasn't already too late. Nothing kept another team of *Sécurité Spéciale* agents from snatching her off *Demetria*.

He emptied the water skin and stretched out on the bunk again. The hours passed, but he felt no ill effects from the food. Which either meant it wasn't tainted, or they had given him something slow acting, like tailored biologicals, that would kill him at a predetermined time when he least expected it. Nothing inconvenient happened to him either, like artificially induced diarrhea or nausea, just for fun and games. Perhaps the *Sécurité Spéciale* didn't go for laughs.

The trip, judging by his beard growth, took four ratpack-filled days with no chance at a shave and a shower. By the time the usual, momentary emergence nausea overcame him, he was going out of his skull with boredom and strongly suspected he smelled like a goat.

Ratpacks, with their highly concentrated proteins, gave a human body flavoring and aroma than would repel a hungry tiger. Only man-eating Tasman targos found it appetizing and used to home-in on Marines who'd been eating the stuff for days. New-Tasman was the one campaign where the brass had given them decent food to eat, and that only after a few troopers had become late-night ratpack-flavored snacks.

He sensed rather than heard the changeover from sublight drives to atmospheric thrusters and somehow knew they hadn't spent the usual time in orbit waiting for a landing window. When you're working for the Amalis, who owned Pacifica as if they were medieval dukes, you didn't have to go through the same procedures as ordinary mortals.

His fight-or-flight adrenaline dispenser keyed up his system to prepare for whatever lay ahead, quite uselessly, a more rational part of his mind remarked. The guards he'd seen the last time would not let him simply walk away from the ship. Not that he'd have anywhere to go. Amali's island was thousands of kilometers from the nearest mainland. And even that probably belonged to the motherless shit.

Zack Decker, though having no particular religious beliefs, seriously contemplated the need for a miracle, like the ability to walk on water, or be raised to the heavens on a beam of divine light. The thought made him grin, but to any observer, it would have looked more like a rictus.

The pressure of gravity increased as the yacht decelerated through the final hundred meters of descent. He felt as if someone had placed a heavy slab of plascrete on his chest.

Then with a muffled thump, the downwards motion stopped, and the pressure lifted. They had arrived.

He listened to the ship's groaning and pinging as the superheated hull cooled down after re-entry. Another low hum signaled the opening of the belly ramp. Zack stood, straightened his clothes, hand absently brushing the spot where he'd worn the duplicate Master Gunner badge before his abduction. They'd taken that from him, along with everything in his pockets, before he woke.

The door whooshed open again, as it had every day since leaving Dordogne, and the same blaster, held by the same face, replaced it.

"The trip is over, Mister Decker. I recommend that you avoid doing anything stupid. Mister Amali's mercenary guards are good shots and have orders to kill you the moment you try to escape. Not that you'll get past me, of course. Come."

The barrel of the gun pointed aft and Zack had no choice but to comply. He gave the man one of his patented grins, satisfied at the brief look of distaste on the other's face as he wrinkled his nose, courtesy of Zack's five days without washing. They walked down the steep ramp into the Pacifica sunshine.

The heat and light of the tropical sun hit him hard after weeks in an artificial environment, and he stopped, momentarily blinded. An impatient prod from the blaster had him moving again.

As his eyes adjusted to the glare, he saw that they had indeed landed on Amali's island and that the same competent looking guards patrolled the property, carbines carried at the ready. A six-man patrol met them halfway across the tarmac and formed a box around Decker. Amali wasn't taking any chances, and Zack didn't know whether to be flattered.

The gunner perspired freely, wiping beads of sweat from his forehead before they could run into his eyes. Dense, sweet flower smells assaulted his nose and reminded him of jungle patrols on a dozen planets. The path they followed was familiar. It branched off towards the manicured lawn richly planted with flowery shrubs fronting the black, opulent mansion.

"Off to see the head man himself, eh?" Zack asked, turning his head towards the agent with the blaster.

"If I were you, Mister Decker, and thankfully I am not, I would find nothing to smile about."

"Hey, isn't that great? You can speak in full sentences."

The sarcasm earned him a painful jab in the ribs with the blaster, but the man's face didn't lose its blank expression.

"Mister Amali has asked to see you. He did not specify whether you should get there on your own two feet."

"No sense of humor, eh?"

"No." But this time, the agent grinned, a cruel grin that did more to worry Decker than anything else so far. Throughout the exchange, the six guards had remained stone-faced and alert, ignoring the tense banter. They might have been mercs, but that didn't mean they were stupid. Not with the sort of money Amali could pay.

They took him to Amali's manor and through the plush hallway to the enclosed patio. As they approached the gurgling fountain in the center, Walker Amali, looking as urbane and polished as ever, stood. The attractive peroxide blonde who'd been climbing all over him moments earlier rose at a flick of his fingers and walked away, bare breasts bouncing. She glanced back at the new arrivals before vanishing and Zack gave her his best Marine leer, just for form's sake. After all, old Pathfinder noncoms had a reputation to uphold.

"Mister Decker. What a pleasure to see you so soon again. You will forgive me if I don't offer you any refreshments, but..." Amali raised his manicured hands, palms upwards, in apology. His nose twitched when he caught a whiff of Zack's aroma.

Decker felt lightheaded, like a man who had nothing to lose by a little defiance.

"Can't say the pleasure is mutual, Amali, but then, you're a slimy bastard, and I don't like those. Though I wouldn't mind getting to know that bimbo of yours. Does she give good head?"

The magnate's eyes tightened. He took a step forward and slapped Decker across the face.

"Uncouth and impolite to the last. The flower of Fleet Intelligence."

Two of the guards pinned Decker's arms back before he could return the blow. Instead, the gunner laughed with open contempt.

"Is that the best you can do? A five-year-old old has more strength, and for your information, I'm not Intelligence. Never was. You have the wrong guy."

"Mister Decker," Amali replied, a dangerous tone in his voice, "as they say, you can fool some people some of the time, but you can't fool all people all the time. I must admit you had me fooled during your last visit. But only just. As the leopard cannot shed its spots, a Marine cannot change his loyalties."

Zack snorted. "There's all kinds in the Corps, asshole. If I had you fooled, as you say, that's because you're one of the biggest fucking congenital idiots in the known galaxy. Especially if you think you'll get away with whatever you're planning."

Amali laughed.

"Brave words, Mister Decker. I must say that I find your courage admirable. You are the first agent who penetrated my organization so deeply."

"Would that be the *Sécurité Spéciale*, by any chance?"

"No, Mister Decker. It belongs to the SecGen, as you well know. I have their use in matters involving the Coalition's interests. I handle my commercial interests with other, more direct means. But come, let us drop the charade. You are a Fleet operative as the delightful Miss Kiani established."

Zack snorted.

"If your mind's made up, Amali, then believe I work for the Fleet. Wouldn't be the first time someone's mistaken me for something I'm not. But if I'm a hotshot spy, then why hasn't the Navy dropped in on you yet? I had four weeks to pass the information to my supposed employers. While we're at it, why would I let myself be captured so easily? You'd think a trained spook is good enough to ruin Smiley's day." He jerked his head towards the agent who caught him. Smiley didn't like his new nickname and jabbed Decker hard in the ribs with his blaster.

Amali clasped his hands in the small of his back and stared up at the deep blue sky. Zack didn't think for even a second that he believed him. Not faced with the evidence he had left in his wake.

"Hmm, be that as it may," Amali shrugged, making a small moue of languid disinterest. The aristocratic, disdainful expression on his smooth face made Zack want to wipe it on hard concrete. "I do know that you are much too familiar with my affairs. Your recordings show an interest that does not correspond to your supposed status as merchant ship gunner. Yes, Mister Decker. I have had occasion to read your findings and deductions. Fantastic. Miss Kiani brought them to my attention the evening after your departure from my little island. By the way where is she? We have not been able to contact her since her last report when she transmitted the contents of your data chip."

"Dead, Amali. Her body disintegrated by my hands." Zack chuckled. "A shame too. She was one hell of a good lay. Probably better than your bimbo, even if her tits weren't as big, or as artificial.

Amali raised his eyebrows and tsked, refusing to be baited again.

"Pity. But she has served her purpose admirably. I suppose you also killed her partner that same evening?"

"Yeah." Zack let a shit-eating grin spread across his face. "Your fucking *Sécurité Spéciale* isn't worth crap if a retired Marine noncom can wipe 'em off the face of the universe that easily." He received another painful jab in the kidneys from Smiley's blaster.

"I'll take care of you too, sonny," the gunner muttered over his shoulder, "just mark my words."

"Ah, but you see," Amali replied, ignoring the exchange between agent and prisoner, "I don't believe you are a retired Marine noncom. The Navy placed you aboard *Shokoten* to replace their dead officer, Lokis. But this time, they succeeded. Good cover story. It took Nihao Kiani nearly half a year to figure it out though she suspected you from the outset. I didn't approve of her attempts to kill you without proof, but it would have saved us much trouble had she succeeded when you first joined the ship."

Zack barked out an incredulous laugh.

"You trying to make me believe you have scruples? I might not be the brightest guy to come out of the Corp's Command School, but I'm not that fucking dumb."

"Believe what you will, Mister Decker. Your opinion matters less to me than bird shit on the hood of my speeder," Amali replied. "I did not bring you here to trade insults, though a non-entity like you can scarcely touch me, but before you join your unfortunate predecessor in whatever hell is reserved for failed spies, I wish to know how much you found out, and whom you told. Then, I have a very special finale for you."

The magnate's languid, bored tone managed to wear down Decker's self-control. If the mercs weren't holding him in a grip of steel, he'd have slammed the heel of his palm into Amali's nose, driving the cartilage into the brain and killing him.

"One last thing before you go, Mister Decker." Amali reached over and pinned something to his jacket, patting it into place. "Your Master Gunner's badge. A beautiful piece of miniature script work. I like that. Unfortunately, the sappy words Duty, Loyalty, Honor, will be of cold comfort to you in a few hours. We wondered whether it was a special device. You see, Miss Kiani noticed that you did not have it when you first came aboard *Shokoten*. I can only assume that it was a reminder from your friends in Naval Intelligence as it is nothing more than an unusual alloy. Maybe it will bring you luck, though where you are going, you will need more than just luck." He chuckled. "Take him away, but make sure he can still play his part."

Before the guards roughly turned him around, Decker spat at Amali, landing a thick gob of saliva on his cheek. The magnate flushed in anger.

"You will regret that, Decker. You will beg me for mercy."

As they took him away, Zack laughed. In the end, he had made the goddamn creep lose his temper. But at what price? The man who controlled ComCorp had nothing to fear from the law and could make him suffer any torment he desired, and if Walker Amali was half as cruel as his father Peterson was rumored to have been...

The mercs led him to half-buried, windowless building near the tarmac. A short flight of stairs brought them down to an armored door that opened on a sterile, white corridor.

They shoved him into the first room on the right. It was equipped like a dentist's surgery but with a few refinements. Now real fear wormed its way through Zack's gut. He recognized the sophisticated interrogation equipment and knew he would tell them everything. No training could help him now.

The guards strapped him down in the reclining chair and took up position along the wall, silent as ever. A technician appeared from another doorway and deftly shaved Zack's head. As soon as he was done, he vanished again.

A few minutes later, a wizened, white-haired man appeared. He wore a light green medical smock and looked for all the world like a kind cleric, with a wrinkled, red face, bulbous nose, and twinkling eyes.

"Good day, good day, Mister Decker," his head bobbed as he smiled absently at the prisoner, displaying crooked, yellowed teeth. "I'm Doctor Hans Cantos. We will get to know each other intimately over the next hour."

Cantos broke off and giggled, bobbing his head again.

"At least, I will get to know you intimately, so you will understand if I drop all formality and call you Zachary. In return, you may call me Doctor." He giggled even harder at his little joke.

"Do you know what this equipment is, Zachary?"

The gunner inhaled a whiff of the doctor's bitter, cloying scent, like that of orchids and burning tealeaves. Cantos was a shimmer addict. Zack knew enough about the drug to know that Cantos was hooked without hope of ever shaking it. The only way shimmerheads escaped the weed's grasp was through death. And that came soon enough for heavy users as the active ingredients slowly burned away their nerve endings.

"Yeah, Doctor Shithead. A mind probe." Zack felt a small measure of pride that his voice was steady and his tone insolent although he his fear was mounting.

"Tsk, tsk, tsk. So impolite. I dislike rudeness."

Cantos shook his white mane as he placed the shining dome of the probe on Decker's head. Long, needle-like tendrils formed on the inside of the hemisphere as its surface prepared to establish a direct link with the gunner's brain. Tendrils crawled across his bare scalp as they moved into position and he shuddered with horror.

Then pain exploded from a dozen spots on his skull as the probes drilled through skin and bone to touch his very being. He screamed. Cantos merely continued to smile, bobbing his head, as he manipulated the probe's controls.

"Pay attention now, Zachary," he leaned towards the gunner, his fetid breath warm and sickening on Zack's face. He sounded like a benevolent schoolmaster.

"F-fuck y-you."

Cantos tasked. "I've already told you I dislike rudeness. Now, I shall have to make you suffer for it. You see, the probe can also directly stimulate the brain's pain centers. Quite marvelous, I think."

He touched a button on the control panel, and a surge of incredible pain lanced through Zack's body. It was as if all his nerve endings were on fire. He screamed with enough force to bruise his vocal cords. All of his muscles twitched in a single, unified contraction, making his body arch against the chair, pulling painfully at the restraints

The pain suddenly vanished, but its phantom remained as a lingering memory, a tingling that would never die and would always promise to flare up in agony again.

"How do you like my little nerve inducer?"

Decker gasped. It had shot through him for only a second or two, but it had seemed like an eternity.

"I-I'll k-kill y-you, runt."

Pain surged again, drawing out his last reserves of strength. He no longer heard his own screams, but his mind refused to shut down, to drown out the agony in unconsciousness or death. The probe kept him awake, making him endure every microsecond of soul-searing hell.

When it stopped, Zack's muscles relaxed their tetanic spasm, and he slumped into the chair, sobbing, only half-aware of his surroundings. Cantos's stinking breath brought him back to a semblance of rational thought.

"If you insist on being impolite, I'm afraid I shall have to insist on using the inducer again. Believe me, I dislike causing so much suffering."

"Now," he said with a sickening smile, "I shall ask you a few simple questions, to calibrate this delicate machinery. Please answer truthfully. I will know if you are lying and shall use the inducer again. If you hope to make me hurt you enough to send you into a coma, disabuse yourself of the notion. The machine knows your exact tolerance at each moment, and will make sure you stay conscious. Now, what is your full name?"

"Walker Amali. Ahhh!" Zack's voice filled the room with an unearthly wail that made even the merc guards shudder in horror.

"Let us try again." Cantos sounded resigned, even sad at his lack of cooperation. Decker knew he was only delaying the inevitable, but he couldn't give in without a fight, even though it hurt like crazy.

"What is your full name?"

"Z-Zachary T-Thomas D-Decker."

"Excellent. What is your planet of birth?"

"Mykonos Colony." Zack's voice was weak and hoarse, his vocal chords badly bruised by his screaming.

"Thank you. What unit did you last serve with?"

"The 902nd Pathfinder Squadron."

"Excellent, Mister Decker. You see how easy it is." Cantos beamed at him, like a proud father. "You will be pleased to know that I have calibrated the probe to your brain patterns, and you have nothing more to fear from the inducer. Just sit back and relax."

Intrusive, incorporeal fingers began to sift through his mind, reaching out from the probe's metallic spikes. They caressed his thoughts, his memories, and his soul like the fingers of an obscene lover, exploring, sifting through his memories, revealing Decker's innermost being. He tried to fight the horror but in vain. Nothing could stop the tendrils.

Part of him screamed in rage and terror though his throat remained silent. Through open, staring eyes, he saw Cantos smirk and bob in front of his screen, seeing in full color and detail that which made up Zachary Decker's being — his experiences, his loves, and losses. His life. Cantos was a voyeur of the soul.

Instead of merely homing in on the memories Amali wanted, the doctor spent a long time in his degenerate pursuit of titillation. All of Decker's sex life paraded on the mind screen: his wife, Raisa, Kiani and the others. Then, his moments of deep pain joined the good memories: Darhad's death, his forced retirement, and the many miseries of a long life on the frontier. Nothing remained hidden.

Finally, to his ultimate horror, Zack felt Cantos extract all he knew about Amali's operation, and the memory of telling Avril Ducote everything, condemning her to death. Suddenly, as if Cantos had tired of the peepshow, the insubstantial fingers vanished, leaving the cold metal spikes behind.

"There we go, Mister Decker. That wasn't very difficult. And you'll be glad to hear that I've done it without damaging your psyche. Unfortunately, most of my customers do experience permanent damage." He sounded almost comically wistful. But Zack wasn't in a position to appreciate the humor. He was trembling with anguish and self-loathing, his soul violated and dirty.

"You appear to have led a fascinating life. So varied." Now, the dwarfish doctor sounded envious.

"Jealous, y-you f-fucking eunuch? Sh-shiimmer already robbed you of your balls?" Zack's voice held so much agony that the few guards who hadn't looked away a long time ago now turned their eyes upwards and studied the ceiling, wondering how they ever came to serve here.

"Oh Mister Decker, and just when I thought we had established such a good working relationship."

An eternity of nerve-fire hit Zack again, but no sounds came from his abused throat. It was as if the violation of the soul had robbed him of any connection with his flesh.

When the last twinges from the inducer subsided to a dull ache, Cantos apologized. But looking at his crazy eyes, Decker knew he wasn't sorry at all. He enjoyed his job very much. Too much. He was very near the edge of permanent drug-induced insanity. The gunner knew that if Amali hadn't ordered he be kept in working condition, the doctor would have slowly twisted his whole being into a single mass of endless pain.

At a command from Cantos, the metallic tendrils of the probe slipped out of his skull and merged with the helmet's shiny inner surface. Moments later, the helmet itself lifted, leaving a dozen tiny blood spots behind. Cantos, with a tenderness that surprised even the brutalized and half-conscious gunner, applied medical paste to fill the holes in his skull. When he was done, he smiled at Zack.

"Goodbye, Mister Decker. Maybe we shall meet again. But I doubt it."

When the guards untied him and pulled him to his feet, Zack found that his legs no longer obeyed the commands of his brain. The brawny mercenaries had to drag him through an underground passage before throwing him into a bare cell.

They brought him food, trays of real food, not ratpacks or reconstituted stuff but the guards didn't speak, and Zack didn't have the energy to try, though he ate with appetite.

He had no idea how long they left him there. The meals came regularly, and his strength returned as the last physical traces of the pain inducer faded into an indelible memory, but the agony of the mental rape would not go. That soiled, hateful sensation remained vivid and unyielding, and would stay for a long time. Perhaps forever. Nightmares haunted him mercilessly, ensuring the experience remained engraved on his neurons.

*

After nine meals or three days by Zack's reckoning, the same six guards returned and escorted him to a cold, clean lavatory, ordering him to shave and wash. They gave him nondescript coveralls to wear once he was clean, disposing of his old clothes, including his beloved leather jacket. One of the mercs, his face twisted by an expression of cruel irony, pinned his Master Gunner's badge to the coveralls' right breast and patted Zack on the head, to the laughter of his friends.

"There you go, little Marine cocksucker. Now you can keep on impressing us peasants."

Decker joined in the laughter but when they were distracted, he belted the merc who'd patted him on the head, sending him crashing in a shower booth, blood streaming from his nose and mouth. Zack's fist hurt like hell, but he had heard a satisfying crunch and knew he'd broken the other man's jaw. He would be eating through a straw for a good while.

Two of the guards grabbed him as the others went to pick up their stunned comrade, muttering angrily, but Amali's orders were that Decker be presented in good health, freshly washed, and shaved.

They took him through yet another underground tunnel. The hum of environmental machinery filled the silence as they neared their destination while a dry, acrid scent, faint but unmistakable grew along with the hum. His memory twitched at the odor, but his broken synapses weren't making the connection.

The mercs stopped at a smooth, white door set in the right-hand corridor wall, a few meters short of a pair of armored hatches. It whooshed aside with a faint sigh.

They dragged him inside and shoved him into a metal chair. Restraints slapped over his wrists and ankles, pinning him down. Then, the hired guns backed off and took a position against the walls of the lounge.

The room was plush, as Decker expected from anything surrounding Amali. It was the size of a typical citizen's living room, about ten meters by ten meters. Three of the four walls were a muted beige, while the fourth, the one Zack faced, was the milky opaque of a polarized window, currently shut.

Smooth blue carpeting covered the floor, complementing the exquisite period furniture with its tones of turquoise and lavender. Several loungers were grouped around table hewn from a single crystal. Abstract paintings from old Earth Masters covered the three solid walls.

They waited in silence as the minutes ticked by. Zack wished he could work off his rising anxiety by throwing wisecracks at the mercs, but he fought to keep silent. The last thing his pride would let him do was to show those rent-a-troopers that an old Marine noncom was scared. This was obviously the start to the promised finale.

After almost half an hour, the doors sighed again, and Zack caught a whiff of Walker Amali's expensive scent.

"Good morning, Mister Decker. I trust you've recovered from your little session with Doctor Cantos. An exceptional scientist, our doctor, do you not think so?" Amali came into Decker's field of view and smiled at his captive. He wore an expensive white tropical suit of shimmering silk, which absorbed perspiration without a trace. A platinum chain glittered around his neck, nestled below a strong chin.

Zack, for want of anything better, smiled back, peeling his lips from his teeth in imitation of an Arkanna challenge. The gesture was lost on the human.

"A pity he is slowly sinking into madness," Amali continued, "but he does good work for me, and I must reward him as he wishes, with the finest quality shimmer."

He sat down on the sofa, his gestures elegant and restrained.

"Somehow I feel I must thank you for having provided me with such a wealth of information, Mister Decker. Shame that you were telling the truth about not being a Naval Intelligence agent. Had you kept your nose in your own affairs, you would have had a pleasing career on my ships. I can always use Fleet-trained material. A pity too that your meddling has cost a competent first officer her life. Darhad was destined for her own command in one of my shipping firms." He smiled sadly at Zack.

"Bastard," Decker spat. "You won't put the blame for her death on me. She was an honorable woman, who did what she believed was right. It was your whore who killed her!"

Amali's sad smile broadened into a delighted grin. Zack could read the 'gotcha' spelled out in large letters on his face, and to his surprise, the realization calmed him.

"You know, Amali, I can't figure why I let a sniveling little coward like you get my goat," he said, voice low and even, though it remained hoarse. "You wouldn't last a minute in a man-to-man fight. But then, I forget. You're not really a man, are you? Tell me, was that bleached blonde of the other day actually a woman, or was she just for show?"

Walker Amali's grin froze, and his nostrils flared minutely, but he did not otherwise react.

"Insult me all you want, Decker. You can prove what a man you are very soon." He snapped his fingers at his attendant, whom Zack hadn't noticed until now. The woman, a small, pale-skinned, and thin creature of indeterminate age and pinched countenance scuttled forward.

"Yes, Walker?" Her voice was soft, weak, and her use of Amali's first name sounded stilted, uncomfortable. She wore a white lab smock over a tan pantsuit and kept her agitated hands in the coat's pockets.

"Sit, Ellenah." As she complied, Amali turned his attention back towards Zack. "This is Professor Ellenah Rocheford, late of the Pacifica Institute of xenomedical research. Among her many degrees and accomplishments, she is an expert in alien neurosciences. Ellenah, meet Mister Zachary Thomas Decker, late of the merchant vessel *Demetria*, which, you'll be interested to know, Decker, we are actively hunting down." Again that cruel grin flashed across the magnate's face.

But Zack felt an inner jubilation. They hadn't found Avril yet. By all appearances, she had escaped and Amali had made a mistake telling him. Now, the gunner could let himself relax.

"Mister Decker will assist us by acting as a test subject," the aristocrat continued. "I think it is appropriate that he receive a full briefing before we begin the experiment, purely in the interests of fairness."

Yeah, I'll bet, Zack thought disgustedly. *You want to be fair to me like a reiver wants to tango with a fully armed Pathfinder commando. More like enjoy a bit of psych torture before you let me have it.*

"Ellenah will be pleased to explain everything and answer all your questions." He nodded at the woman. "You may begin."

"Yes, Walker. Mister Decker, have you ever heard of a planet called Ventos Prime?"

"Yeah. Been there, seen the nuke strike craters, scanned the eggs on board *Shokoten* and the stasis boxes that contained, no doubt, a couple of mature ones. Now you want to surprise me by announcing that you have a matched set of Quas on this island."

"Ah, so you know. Good, that will make my explanations much simpler." She seemed to take Decker's familiarity in stride.

"Sure Ellenah, but you'll tell me why, aren't you?" Zack smiled his patented Decker smile at her, but the old charm was gone. Or the Professor was immune.

"Why not start from the beginning." Amali's silky voice intervened.

As if Zack had suddenly inherited Raisa's empathic talent, he knew this briefing was important to Amali, that the gunner was the first outsider to see the extent of his plans and accomplishments.

"Yes, Walker. A Navy survey ship discovered and charted Ventos Prime twenty years ago. They found a remarkable example of dual evolution that produced two quite distinct species, constantly at war with each other. The Qwallor, six-limbed reptilians, developed on one of the two largest continents and attained sentience approximately thirty thousand standard years ago. They evolved rapidly and have reached the rough equivalent of Earth's early atomic age. The other species, the Quas, are six-limbed insectoids who evolved on the other main continent, in total isolation from the Qwallor. A hive society, the Quas are at best semi-sentient and in the estimate of the Commonwealth's best xenologists, will likely remain so. However, the Quas are very prolific, highly aggressive, and very, very expansionistic. Their soldier subspecies has terrifying strength, speed, and endurance. The expanse of ocean between the two species has kept them apart for millions of years, until sometime recently, within the last millennia, a storm washed a young queen and a few drones across the water on a natural raft. Or at least that's what Qwallor scientists believe. The newcomers immediately tried to establish a colony, starting an interspecies struggle that still goes on."

"The Qwallor soon found that the only weapon in their inventory that could destroy a hive was a nuclear device. They wiped out the abortive colonies on their continent and then built long-range bombers in an attempt to bring genocide to the Quas lands, with very limited success. Under ideal conditions, a single surviving queen can spawn as many as fifty new hives in the space of a hundred standard years. That, Mister Decker, can mean up to fifty million adult Quas, consuming everything organic in sight, even each other when nothing else remains."

"Shit," Zack interrupted, laughing. "You want to seed Outworlds with these bugs and watch 'em eat up whole colonies? It won't work, Amali!"

"Silence, Decker," the magnate snapped. "And listen."

"You are correct. Such a project would not be viable. Though incredibly resilient individuals, the Quas' reproductive cycle slows in conditions too different from their home world. They would not spread fast enough on Earth-norm planets to achieve critical mass and overwhelm them. It would take very long to breed them to adapt to Earth-norm, however, in a controlled environment, the queens will thrive."

"Then what are you doing with the things?"

"Patience, Mister Decker. The Qwallor have the Quas under control on their world though they're slowly poisoning it with radioactive fallout. After discovering the Quas, the Navy interdicted Ventos Prime, correctly deducing that the insectoid species represented a grave danger if taken off-planet, a disease that could devastate any life-bearing world. They continued their studies under strict secrecy, however, recording a significant amount of valuable information. Nevertheless, importation of Quas eggs or queens is a serious offense. Walker," she motioned to her boss, "found out about the Quas and immediately saw the potential in them. He hired me to study his plans and develop a way to turn these semi-sentient beings into something humans could control."

"You wouldn't," Zack gasped, suddenly realizing where the Professor's monolog was headed.

"We already have, Mister Decker," she continued, unemotional as ever. "We have implanted control circuits into Quas brain stems and can control their actions through neuroelectric impulses."

"Think about it, Decker," Amali chimed in, unable to resist crowing at the climax of Rocheford's story. "A hive of Quas, with a queen at the center, a queen producing eggs like a munitions factory produces artillery shells, and every two out of three shells, soldiers, almost two meters tall, bodies covered with their own natural armor, fearless, ruthless, and unstoppable. A private army under my control."

"And the bugs just let you do it?"

"No," Rocheford shook her head. "They're semi-sentient and don't recognize such concepts as cooperating with other species. For Quas, there is either their own hive, or prey, but we found that short of killing them, one thing will incapacitate Quas without harm: a particular ultrasound frequency. We disable them with the sound and while they're stunned, bore into the chitin at the base of the neck, connect the box, and close the opening. It will be easier with the hatchlings, which we will implant at the pupa stage while the exoskeleton is still forming. So far, we have harnessed the adults that came from Ventos Prime, except the queen, of course."

"Just an idle question, Prof. How come the Qwallor obtained bugs for you? I thought you said they nuked 'em on sight."

"I shall answer that, Ellenah," Amali's smooth, cultured voice stayed the Professor's reply. "You see Mister Decker, we offered them an irresistible price for their cooperation: the disabling ultrasound frequency. It will not do them much good, as they don't yet have the technology to produce it at a sufficient energy level to do more than simply repel the creatures. Nor, do I think, will they ever attain that level. I fear their world is doomed to perish under the weight of environmental poisoning. The Qwallor part of their world that is. Quas can absorb radiation and other poisons without problems. They can survive where no human can. Who knows, maybe they will mutate into something even fiercer."

Amali rose and approached the milky polarized window. With a sweep of the arm, he gestured towards the impenetrable barrier.

"Mister Decker, prepare to meet the future terror of the Marine Corps. An army of soldiers who don't question orders but execute them, even if it means their own lives; soldiers who take six months to hatch and six more to reach adulthood, with all the fighting instincts built-in. Compare that to the eighteen years or so it takes to make a Marine from a single ovum and spermatozoid. With my one queen, the good Professor assures me I can have a regiment within two years, even under the less than ideal conditions we have here. A regiment that will renew itself completely every twelve months, a regiment that needs no logistics tail because it will live off the land. A cheap, renewable, and highly efficient resource." There was a light of madness in Amali's eyes as he spoke.

"The Quas soldier can be taught to use suitably modified plasma weaponry, simple to be sure, but deadly enough. And failing that, he can tear a human of your size and strength in two with his forelimbs just as easily as you can pass wind. His exoskeleton is equal to the armor your Marine friends wear, and a simple plasma rifle will not be enough to stop the soldiers. Not by a far cry. Consider them six-limbed, single seated tanks if you will. Tanks that will overwhelm even the bravest Marine regiment in the blink of an eye."

"You're fucking insane, Amali." If Zack wasn't scared before, he was now.

"No, Mister Decker, I'm merely desirous to solve the Commonwealth's endless bickering and problems for good. Since Grand Admiral Kowalski's day, the Fleet has been a law unto itself, flouting the rightful authority of the SecGen and the Senate, often in favor of the upstart colonies who style themselves the Outworlds. My army, which I will place at the SecGen's disposal, will sweep away anybody foolish enough to stand in the Coalition's way. If your Grand Admiral Connor fights our rightful leadership of the Commonwealth, millions of Outworlders will suffer. You cannot reason with Quas soldiers. They eat the ones they defeat in battle."

"You're mad," Decker whispered. But his words died stillborn as the window opened to reveal a nightmare world.

An embryonic Quas hive, in the heart of the Commonwealth.

— SIXTEEN —

"Behold, Mister Decker." Amali's glee knew no bounds and for once, Zack was too horror-struck to make a smart remark.

On the other side of the window, a grotto bathed in dim red light cut a picture of the Hell foretold by so many human faiths. A hell populated by man-sized, six-limbed demons with huge composite eyes.

The Quas were much more hideous in person than their pictures on Korden's computer screen could convey. Insectoid down to every detail, their reddish-brown exoskeletal bodies looked like those of giant ants. On some of the creatures, the lower segment tapered into a short, powerful tail ending with a long stinger, a refinement Amali and his tame academic had forgotten to mention. It didn't take Zack long to realize that these were soldiers.

The most horrifying feature of the Quas was its head. A flattened ovoid that sat on the upper segment like a malicious tumor, it sported two huge, multi-faceted eyes, eyes that never closed, never blinked, and never showed emotions. Beneath the eyes, a mouth like something out of a nightmare glistened. Its jaws were able to open wide enough to swallow a small pig. Blackened pincers as long as Zack's forearms framed the mouth and long, thin antennae grew out of either side of the head.

They walked on the rear two limbs, but the other four could be used as additional legs for climbing and running. Each arm ended in three sharp claws.

In the grotto, drones and soldiers skittered around, their limbs scraping across their chitinous bodies. It sounded eerily like the rustling of dead leaves. They chattered among themselves in a language that resembled the high-speed clicks of a beetle, if it had been fed amphetamines, but alien as they were, Decker could see that they belonged to a structured, disciplined and organized society.

What most held his attraction were the rows of pulsating, semi-translucent white globes: Quas eggs, hundreds of them.

"What do you think, Mister Decker?" Amali leaned languidly against the window, arms crossed, a look of intense satisfaction on his face.

"You have a producing queen," the gunner replied, mind still reeling from the sight of the Quas hive.

"But of course. You helped bring it back here."

He touched a key on a hidden pad by the window frame. The milky whiteness returned, only to dissolve into the image of a small cavern. In the middle of the chamber, gross, distended, and nightmarish, a Quas queen wallowed in a nest built out of a vaguely aspic-like substance that pulsed every time she moved. Her distended, lumpy egg sac filled most of the space, glistening and shining with an inner light of its own. As Zack watched, mouth hanging half-open, another egg slid out of the sack, sticky and gelatinous.

"Another soldier, Mister Decker," Amali smirked. "Two out of three eggs are."

A drone picked up the egg with loving care and skittered out of the queen's chamber, chattering away in its clicking tongue. The image faded as Amali fiddled with the controls. It reformed, this time showing a honeycombed cavern of indeterminate height. Each alcove contained a whitish, fibrous mass, held into place by thin filaments. The masses moved and writhed in their nests.

"These are the pupa hatched from the eggs you brought back from Ventos Prime. All are doing well. I have twenty new soldiers, ten drones and," Amali's voice dropped to a whisper, "one new queen."

"She will be ready for impregnation in less than a year," he continued, "a ritual I shall be most interested in watching. You see, the drones compete for the favor of a single moment of sex, but at what cost, Mister Decker, what cost?" His eyes gleamed with perverse pleasure. "I shall tell you what cost: the queen eats her mate after the act."

Decker snorted.

"I know a few human females who'd do the same thing, given half a chance. Like your whore, Nihao Kiani. Who knows? You might meet one like her soon, and good riddance."

"You are mouthy for a man about to undergo the ultimate test, Mister Decker," Amali snapped irritably.

Zack snorted. "Oh? And what would that be, asshole?"

"Laugh and insult me all you want, Decker." Zack noticed that Amali's urbane politeness had vanished: he no longer rated the 'Mister' in front of his name. "But before you have too much fun, watch this."

The window faded to white again before opening on yet another view of the hive.

"Unfortunately, we must make do with a recording. I would have liked to show you a live example of Quas feeding, but..." He let the rest of the sentence hang. It didn't matter. Zack felt sick to the stomach as he realized what he was about to see.

A human, disheveled and gaunt, filled the center of the screen. Dressed in simple gray coveralls, like the ones Zack wore, he was tied to a stake with a chain that wrapped around his waist. The chain had maybe two meters slack. Zack recognized the prisoner and his nausea intensified.

"Failure must be dealt with swiftly and harshly, *pour encourager les autres*, right Decker?" Without waiting for a reply, Amali continued. "It was Captain Strachan's misfortune to hire you aboard *Shokoten* and jeopardize my plans, the second time he has made the mistake of taking on Fleet infiltrators. He will not make that mistake again. Another good officer lost because of your meddling, Decker. Oh, have no fear; he is alone in paying the ultimate price. Your former shipmates, whom I cannot blame as they don't even know they serve me, are alive, and still aboard *Shokoten*, under a new master."

"Still, Diego Strachan gave me one last instance of usefulness, by 'volunteering' as our first test subject, just as you will be our next." Amali's voice was flat, unemotional.

Zack glanced over at the Professor and saw she mirrored her patron's blank expression.

A Quas soldier appeared on the screen and the gunner caught a flash of patched chitin at the back of the head.

"The specimen you see is under the direct control of Professor Rocheford."

She nodded absently, her dead eyes staring at the view without seeing it.

"Now," Amali's cruel smile reappeared, "the Professor will release the soldier from her control and let it act naturally."

It was as if a connection had been severed, or more accurately, re-established. The creature's composite eyes focused on the helpless Strachan, who screamed. In a flash, it closed the distance to the human and its four upper limbs grabbed him, drawing blood where they punctured the skin. Black jaws slid out of the skull and homed-in on Strachan's head. Antennae twitched in a macabre dance as the mouth pincers took hold of his ears.

Then, the stinger whipped around and impaled the prisoner through the back, its length piercing right through to gleam redly in the middle of the chest.

Strachan's screams ceased abruptly as he died. The creature's jaws opened wide and engulfed the bearded head. They closed with a snap, severing the neck. Blood gushed, splattering the Quas' shiny body. But the bug didn't seem to care.

It methodically tore the arms and legs from the torso, snapping them as easily as Zack would snap the wings off a broiled chicken. The limbs followed the head down its maw. All that remained was the bloodied trunk of what had been, moments earlier, a living, breathing human being, who for all his faults and crooked transactions, didn't deserve such a fate.

Zack felt fury rise in him, a rage that burst through his self-control, smothering all of his other emotions.

"You'll die for this, Amali," he hissed. "I'll make damn sure of that myself. And so will you, Professor."

He turned to look at Rocheford and was astonished to see her sit rigidly, like a statue, eyes unfocused and lifeless, tears streamed down her cheeks, trembling hands clenched in her lap, the knuckles white.

"You must forgive the good Professor," Amali's silky voice insinuated itself through the layers of Zack's fury. "She is somewhat sentimental."

"Maybe it's because she has a fucking conscience, you sickening shit." Decker's shout echoed across the room. "But then, I suppose you wouldn't know what a conscience was if it bit you in the ass. You'll pay for that poor sod and everyone else you've murdered. That's a Pathfinder's oath."

Amali laughed with derision.

"You'll make me pay? I seriously doubt that Decker, unless, of course, you find a way to return from the dead and haunt me." His laughter was rich, melodious and filled with contempt. "What you just saw, my oh-so-tough friend is your destiny: food for a hungry Quas soldier, a soldier in the future Coalition Auxiliary."

"Then get it over with, asshole," Zack snarled.

"Not so fast." The magnate's face became serious again, though a dark malice burned in his eyes. "We must still conduct many tests before I can field my army, and one of those is to see how effective Quas soldiers are against Marines. You, my uncouth friend, are a heaven-sent means to test this: the best of the best, a Marine Pathfinder."

"A hand-to-hand fight with that? You won't enjoy the experience. The bug has me cold with his fucking stinger."

"No, no, Decker." He shook his head. "Something more enjoyable: a manhunt. Quas hunting Marine. On this island."

Zack tried to shrug, to hide the terror gnawing at his innards, but the restraints turned his movement into a spastic jerk.

"What's my motivation? If I survive, you'll give me my life?"

"Of course not. Your life is forfeit either way. But you have the choice to die like Strachan, without a struggle, howling in terror." He waved at the screen. "Or you can die like a Pathfinder, fighting to the end. The Quas will kill you, no matter what you do. I'm counting on your survival instinct and that unreasonable belief you Marines have of fighting against any odds. Like your spiritual forebears on Farhaven. Interesting that your Marine Corps' most important moment in history is a bloody defeat. Yes, you will fight, Decker. You may even kill a Quas or two.”

“You're right. Give me a chance to fight, and I will.” Zack snarled. “Marines never surrender. I don't fucking expect you to understand, but your bloody monstrosities don’t have me yet, and neither have you.”

“Ah, Mister Decker.” Amali shook his head again, smiling. “Brave to a fault. If only I could find a way to distil your spirit and inject it into the sorry excuses that pass for soldiers on Pacifica, I wouldn't need the Quas.”

“If you were hoping to swim off this island,” he continued, “disabuse yourself of the notion. The seas are infested with a fish resembling Earth's sharks. Only these are more vicious. You will not pass the reefs surrounding the island. Assuming, of course, the Quas are not after you. They can survive under water for short periods. As I said, they're the ultimate soldiers. Perhaps you may hope to sneak into my little colony and steal a ship or weapons or who knows what.”

Amali shook his head. “Please disabuse yourself of the notion. A fence able to prevent Quas and humans alike from entering surrounds the estate. Of course, sensors cover the island so I will always know where you are. So, Mister Decker. Are you game?”

“Fuck you, Amali.”

But the target of the profanity was already turning his attention to the mercenary guards.

“Take him to his cell. Make sure he eats well tonight. Give him anything else he wants, within reason, of course: whiskey, holovids, pen, and paper to write his will.” Amali chuckled, pleased by his wit. “Tomorrow morning, Decker. Until then.”

*

That night, Zachary T. Decker, late command sergeant in the 902nd Marine Pathfinder Squadron, fought off despair by trying to convince himself that Amali's Quas manhunt would turn into a Marine bug hunt.

Don't count a Pathfinder as dead until you've seen the body, and even then make damn sure.

But try as he might, Zack couldn't find a way out. Amali had this place sewn up. The guards won't let him make a single step sideways while he was within the compound and once out in the island's jungle-covered hills...

The only question was how long he could stay alive out there. He knew more than just a handful of dirty tricks, but nothing about his opponents, apart from the fact they had one hell of a built-in weapon, could shrug off small caliber plasma, and ate their vanquished enemies.

His only consolation was that they hadn't found Avril Ducote yet. Otherwise, Amali would have thrown the fact in his face, or changed his perverted little game to give Zack even more incentive to fight. The gunner tightened with fury at the thought of her in Amali's hands.

His last meal was excellent and came with a glass of vintage red wine and a snifter of Dordogne brandy. Amali had a strange sense of humor, wasting the talents of his chef and the contents of his expensive cellar on a smart-ass ex-Marine who was about to die.

Decker slept, after a fashion. But it was a rest tormented by dreams of chasing Quas soldiers, and each dream ended with a long, black stinger piercing his body.

*

The mercs came for him as a dazzling tropical sun washed away the last of the night's chill, painting the island's hillsides with vibrant primary colors. For all that Amali despised Decker, he took no chances this morning.

His escort numbered eight silent guards, each carrying his carbine at the ready. They clamped a thin steel collar around his neck and took him through an underground warren to a large, plascrete walled room. It was unfurnished but sported a wide ramp sloping upwards. At the top of the ramp, sliding doors had opened on a rich tableau of native vegetation. A soft breeze strummed strangely shaped leaves in multiple hues of green, turquoise and blue, stirring scents of sweet life and dark decay. The sounds of the living jungle made a pleasant backdrop to the grimness of what would be Decker's last morning in this life.

Amali, dressed in expensive, tailor-made fatigues, waited at the foot of the ramp, hands joined in the small of his back. He was alone.

"Good morning, Mister Decker." He nodded. His politeness had returned overnight, though he looked tired, with red-rimmed eyes. For a moment, Zack wondered whether the man wasn't a junkie himself.

"I trust you are ready to, as they say, 'show your stuff.' Did you enjoy last night's supper? My cook is such a splendid artist."

"Does your cook have a nice, peachy butt too, Amali? Or are you that impressed by his ability to use an autochef?" *Ave Amali. Those about to die smart-mouth you.*

Zack's fear had given way to recklessness ever since waking, and that sense of recklessness kept growing. It was the feeling of a man who had nothing left to lose, and therefore nothing more to fear.

"Spirited to the last. Superb, Mister Decker. You will give us a grand show, I'm sure." The magnate smiled, but it didn't reach his narrowed eyes.

"The rules are very simple. You shall have an hour's head start. The entire island, except the estate, of course, is your battleground. You may use whatever you find to defeat the Quas. As long as you stay alive, the game will continue, even if it takes days, which I doubt." He paused, trying vainly for dramatic effect with a man who didn't care anymore.

"And for each Quas you kill, I will release two more."

"Any weapons?" Zack's voice was steady, even bored.

"No, Mister Decker. They say a Pathfinder's body is a finely honed weapon. So is a Quas soldier's body. Any other questions?"

"Yeah. In case I don't get the chance to ask later, do you want me to bury you on this island, or feed your body to the fishes?"

Amali laughed.

"Excellent, Mister Decker, keep up the spirit."

He pointed at the jungle.

"I will start the clock the moment your feet leave the ramp. It opens outside the fence, right into the forest. One last thing, Mister Decker, just so you know I do have a healthy respect for you. That collar my men have placed around your neck is not only a transponder that will permit me to keep track of you, but also an explosive device. Should you, by some miracle, leave my island, it will detonate the moment it no longer receives its telemetry signals, which will happen approximately five hundred meters from the shoreline. The charge will sever your neck cleanly, I'm told. Like a twist of detcord." He paused, looking at Zack as if for the last time.

"Goodbye, Mister Decker. It's been an interesting few days."

Zack gave Amali the rigid digit salute and walked up the ramp. He wore the same gray coveralls as before, with a pair of sturdy combat boots on his feet. And that, with light underwear, was the total of his possessions. No, not quite. A slanting ray of sun glinted off the gold Master Gunner's badge pinned to his chest, briefly catching Zack's eye.

As he stepped off the hard surface of the ramp and onto the spongy carpet of tropical decay, the armored doors slid closed. The timer had started to tick on his one-hour head start.

Decker remembered the aerial view of the island from his first visit. With the rising sun as a guide, he headed for the saddle between the two hills dominating the center of the landmass, trying to put as much distance between himself and the compound. The jungle was thick, and he struggled to make headway.

When the undergrowth finally thinned as the ground rose, his hands were scratched and bloodied. His boots were already soaked through, thanks to a short stroll into an overgrown slough. It had occupied the center of a minuscule clearing, and Zack wanted to take advantage of the open space, no matter how small. It was a mistake he wouldn't make again. Thumb sized leeches had attached themselves to his legs as he crossed the stagnant water and their bite had stung.

Along the way, his trained eyes spotted small receptors mounted in trees. They were simple, passive devices, good only for getting signals from his transponder, but they could come in handy if Amali lets him steal a few. He had said Zack could use anything he found, but men like him had no sense of honor.

The hour's head start passed quickly, judging by the sun's climb into the dark blue sky. Temperatures also rose, and the jungle became a sweltering steam bath that soaked Zack's skin and painted irregular patches of sweat on his coveralls.

Perspiration ran into his eyes, and he swore at the salty sting. He removed his t-shirt, ignoring the myriad insects fighting for a bite of his bare torso and, with a savage gesture, tore the khaki fabric into strips, tying one around his shaved head as a sweatband. He tucked the others into his pocket after pulling the coveralls' upper part back over his arms and shoulders. They might come in handy later.

The jungle had cleared sufficiently to give him a decent line of sight and let him move fast. He would be able to hear and see the bug approach early enough to run. Though where exactly he would run was a question to which he found no answer.

Going through the motions, Zack took a short stroll in the middle of a narrow fresh-water stream that flowed between the two near hills, just in case the Quas could track him by smell, though he doubted that was one of their built-in strengths. They had no visible nose, or ears. But whether they didn't have good hearing or a good sense of smell depended on what those antennae did.

One thing was sure, with eyes like that, they likely saw much better than Decker and into the extremes of the visual spectrum too, such as infrared. Which meant the bugs could probably track him and pin him down by the heat his body gave off, and there would be little he could do about it.

He reached his chosen battleground and turned his attention to weapons. Rocks and sticks were out, for obvious reasons. He needed something more, preferably a twenty millimeter rocket rifle, or a light Gatling gun. And while he was at it why not ask for a full Pathfinder squadron with all the trimmings?

Another of the passive receivers caught his eye, and he decided to investigate. The native tree's bark was rough and the climb among its turquoise fronds easy. When he reached the fist-sized oblong, Zack saw it wasn't connected by wires and grinned. It had to work on internal fuel cells. He braced himself and slammed the heel of his hand into the device's side sending it plummeting to the ground. Zack jumped after it, landing smoothly on the carpet of rotting vegetation.

He picked up the sensor and examined it. It was of the disposable type, with a simple plas shell and mass-produced innards. Finding two flat stones, he held it sideways on one of them, and carefully hammered the shell with the other, hoping to crack it at the seam between the two halves. It split open on the fourth hit. Zack grinned. For all his riches, Amali had skimped on quality.

He examined the inside and nodded, satisfied. It would be an easy job to cross-circuit the fuel cells and set them to overload. If the cells held a sufficient charge, the sensor could blow like any decent hand grenade, sending shrapnel in all directions. Whether it would do anything to a bug was another question, but homemade grenades were better than bare hands any day.

Zack stripped the connectors, ending the sensor's incarnation as tracking device. Somewhere on Amali's estate, a merc guard must be wondering why this unit suddenly went dead, just after reporting good old Zack Decker near it.

A circuit overload was seldom, if ever, instantaneous. Even a starship's antimatter reactor took a few moments to go from a short circuit to a big bang. That time delay would be his fuse, and if perchance the buggering things didn't behave like typical power units, then it didn't matter whether he killed himself with a jury-rigged grenade or a barehanded attack on a Quas soldier. Dead was dead, on any planet and in any language.

Ducking behind a large boulder, Zack slapped the shell halves together, leaving two exposed strands of wire hanging out. With a quick wrist movement, he twisted the wires together, counting the seconds from the moment they touched, and threw the sensor over the rock. It bounced off a tree and landed with a muffled thud.

At the count of thirteen, the fuel cells exploded with a loud bang that echoed between the hills. Shards of plas, superconductor and metal, flew in all directions, slashing through the leaves.

"Hot damn! Those fucking bugs are going to experience some serious indigestion from my homemade bombs. And all I have to do is pick 'em off trees, like little red apples."

Zack collected five more devices in the immediate area, clearing out the wide space between the two low hills, and quickly transformed them into hand grenades.

Then, pockets bulging, he turned north and climbed to the summit of the higher knoll, which was as bare as a monk's tonsure, or his own skull for that matter. At least three hours had expired since his release, which meant a bug had been hunting him for two, and if Amali was vectoring the thing onto him, it should show up soon.

Decker slipped between the quartet of large, black rocks that crowned the hill, taking advantage of the natural cover and the vantage point that gave him a clear view of the slope. He lay down on his stomach, facing the estate and, making sure his throwing arm had room to swing, stacked his grenades within reach, careful that the exposed wires didn't touch by accident. Now, all he had to do was wait, and that was the hardest part.

*

The minutes stretched out as the sun beat down on his exposed scalp. A headache began to throb in sync with his heartbeat. Perspiration soaked him from head to toe while the pebbles beneath his body dug into his bruised flesh. He was preternaturally alert, eyes searching the dark tree line, adrenaline keeping his body at peak readiness.

After a wait that seemed to last an eternity under the unrelenting tropical sky, the sound of rustling leaves reached Zack's ears, the sound of a Quas' limbs rubbing against its chitinous armor. The opening round was about to be decided. He picked up a grenade and prepared to join the wires.

The Quas burst through the tree line twenty meters below Zack and stopped, head swiveling, antennae quivering. It chattered softly to itself, its deadly tail swishing through the low vegetation. Then, like an anti-tank missile on terminal guidance, its cold, dead eyes locked onto Zack's hilltop hideout.

Decker twisted the exposed strands of his first grenade together, counting down the fuse delay time.

Six, five, THROW, three, two, one.

The grenade exploded three meters to the bug's right, and Zack raised his head to look. He swore at the sight. Shards of shrapnel stuck out of the thing's body, but it seemed to treat them as annoyances, brushing them away as if they were lint specks. He primed another grenade and held it until the last moment. Then, he reared up and threw, shouting in defiance.

The goddess who watched over all reckless old Pathfinders had a light workload that day. By an incredible chance, the jury-rigged grenade blew in mid-air, less than a meter in front of the Quas, at the height of its head. Jagged shards of hardened plas and metal sliced through the bug's composite eyes and penetrated its brain.

The creature let out a bone-chilling scream and keeled over, bluish ichor flowing from multiple gouges. Zack shivered at the sound and absently brushed a sting from his cheek. His hand came back bloody, and he realized he'd caught shrapnel from his own grenade. A few centimeters higher and he would have lost an eye himself.

Like a man hypnotized, he watched his alien hunter twitch and thrash on the rocky slope as its autonomous system refused to follow its higher functions into oblivion. Decker stayed at a healthy distance, lest he was caught by the long stinger as it swept the ground with a horrible rasp. The Quas soldier took a long time to die.

"Good guys: one. Bugs: zero," Zack whispered, stunned at his own success. "So now I know your weak spot, you bastards. Aim for the eyes and you kill the Quas."

With a last look at the dead creature, Zack turned to pick up his three remaining grenades and stuffed them in his pockets.

"Time to make tracks, Decker, you're about to have two of the critters on your tail."

*

"You're sure it's dead, Professor?"

"Yes, Walker," Rocheford replied in a dull voice. "It suffered massive trauma to the head and died within minutes."

"And we have no idea how he did it?"

"No, sir," the mercenary tech replied from the sensor console. "The guy busted every receiver in the area. Six in all went down right after he came within range."

"Why would he want to do that?" Amali wondered, frustration replacing his earlier good mood. Then, an ugly thought made him frown even more.

"Captain," he turned to the mercenary commander, "can those sensors be used as weapons?"

The stocky, flat-faced man scratched the side of his head

"Anything with fuel cells can be made to blow, if you know how," he replied in his low, raspy voice. "Those little things wouldn't generate much of an explosion, but if it's strong enough, you have yourself a grenade. It could be enough to kill the beasties with the shrapnel."

"Would a man like Decker know how?"

"Marine Corps Master Gunner and Pathfinder to boot? If anyone can, he'd be the one to bet on, sir."

"But to kill a Quas soldier?" Amali shook his head in disbelief. "It has to be a fluke. Professor, release the next two soldiers. Captain, put a pair of drones in the air and find Decker. If he's using my instruments as weapons, I want to know, preferably before he causes any more damage. You shouldn't have any problems vectoring on his position. Just wait until the next unit goes offline."

"Yes, sir."

"Once you've found him, make sure you don't lose him. I want the Professor to steer the Quas to his position. Then, I want to see how he killed a soldier."

"Sir," the tech turned his head towards Amali, "we have him again! He's backtracking towards the estate."

A small red blip appeared on the schematic of the island.

"Good." The magnate smiled, eyes narrowed in malice. "That will make life simpler for us. Tell me, Captain, do you think he intends to use his new-fangled weapon to penetrate the estate?"

"It would take more than a grenade, sir," the merc replied. "I don't -"

"Another receiver down," the tech interrupted. "He's off screen."

The red blip had disappeared again. And this time, it didn't come back. After a wait that seemed to stretch for hours, Walker Amali's anxiety grew and he began to fidget. Zack Decker had already killed one alien warrior. What else was he capable of doing?

The drones couldn't find Decker through the thick foliage; the Quas couldn't find him either, and the sun was setting. Somehow, Amali got a mental picture of a grinning Zack thumbing his nose at them all. It wasn't until the captain gave him a strange look that he realized his hands were gripping the back of the tech's chair so hard he was shaking.

*

Hunger gnawed at Zack's innards as he slipped back into the saddle between the two hills. Pacifica's sun was kissing the horizon, turning the ocean into a fiery sheet of molten lava, and it would be night soon, with the abruptness so characteristic of the tropics on any planet. The darkness would enhance the bugs' biggest advantage, the eyes, while it would blind him. He had heard the two new soldiers move through the trees, talking to each other, searching for their prey. He had also spotted the dangerous drones. They were looking for him, and once they found him, the Prof would vector the bugs to his position. Amali wasn't playing fair, but the gunner hadn't expected him to do so.

Zack had spent the afternoon exploring the area, secure in the knowledge that his captors could not know where he was, and what he was doing. Had Amali invested in better gear, things might have been different, but he figured he'd earned a break.

Decker crawled into the little tunnel he'd found hidden beneath a bush, just a stone's throw from the stream. It was narrow, barely big enough for a Quas soldier, but not big enough to let the bug swing its tail. And it had a smaller exit, which Zack had enlarged just enough to make a human sized escape hatch, at the price of bloody, torn hands.

He made a final check of his dispositions, and then tossed a bloody rag, a strip of t-shirt with which he'd cleaned his hands, out of the tunnel. The drone couldn't help seeing it if it came over the spot before full darkness and if the tech at the other end was alert. Many ifs. With luck, he'd be able to take a break in the underground warren, sleep all night if they didn't find him, but the first sound of chitin against stone would wake him in a flash.

It was infiltration training all over again. Except the Corps' Pathfinder School didn't use human-eating Quas as opposing force.

The sliver of light at the mouth of the tunnel vanished as the sun set, plunging Decker into blackness. Now was the time at which Quas composite eyes became an asset no human could match unless he wore a Marine battle helmet, with built-in night vision gadgets. He chuckled at the thought. If he had a battle helmet, he'd have the rest of the armor suit too, and a plasma rifle, and a whole damn troop of Marines, while he was at it.

Soon, he fell into a light sleep.

*

Decker's eyes popped open as alarm bells went off in his head. He knew instinctively it was late, well past midnight. A faint rustle of dead leaves had woken him. He strained to listen again, heart racing, blood pounding in his ears. The small hairs on the back of his neck stood up in fear, and he shivered. Quas raised a primal terror within him, now compounded by the obscurity.

There it was, in front of him, near the entrance to his tunnel. He groped for the grimy, rubber-sheathed wires he'd found near the estate earlier, part of an older system. The long wires were connected to a grenade tied to a stick wedged into the tunnel, at what he judged would be the level of a crouching bug's eyes.

Zack listened, trying to decide whether the creature had entered his burrow or whether it was still screwing around outside, trying to figure out what the bloody rag on the ground meant. Then, he heard it: a scraping of chitin on rock. But it wasn't coming from the front. It was coming from the back, from his emergency exit.

Panic closed his throat at the thought of being boxed in by the bugs, to be torn apart underground without seeing the stars one last time. He tried to breathe in and couldn't. His fear rose further when he heard what sounded like strong claws tearing at the rock and dead coral, widening the hole. Then, a slithering from the front made him turn his attention back again. The bug was in the tunnel. He could smell it, sense its mindless, evil presence, its instinctual desire to kill and devour. Closing his eyes he asked for the intervention of a deity he had long ago abandoned and joined the two wires.

The grenade blew after only three seconds and Zack's first, irrelevant thought was short fuse!

Then the horrible screech of the wounded Quas drove out everything else. He had to exit the tunnel.

Amali would know his little insect friend had taken a hit, know where he was. A new duo of bugs could be here in an hour or less.

The scrabbling and anxious chattering behind him reminded the gunner he had no way out. Grabbing his three remaining grenades, he screwed up his courage and headed for the front entrance, thankful that he couldn't see the damaged face of the Quas. When he neared the ambush site, he turned around so he could go out feet first. Within moments, his boots touched something sticky, wet, and crunchy: the bug's ruined head. Its body blocked the entrance, arms twitching in death, scraping against the rock.

The stench of the dead alien made Zack nauseous, and he gagged, thankful that his stomach was empty. If it hadn't been for the live soldier behind him, he might not have been able to keep up his courage. Steeling himself against what he was about to do, Zack kicked the Quas' body with both feet to drive it out of his way.

His boots sank through the shattered eyes and into the creature's primitive brain. Ichor splashed all over the enclosed space, spattering his exposed skin with something that burned like a slimy acid. He retched again, tears flowing out the corner of his eyes from the stinging ichor mist. Zack stomped the dead body over and over, swearing and cursing in more languages than he could remember

Finally, the body rolled away as it popped out of the tunnel. Decker scrambled out behind it, sobbing as he saw the stars. He took several deep breaths of fresh night air to calm his racing heart. This was as close as he'd ever come to losing it. Not even the worst on Hispaniola had ever made him panic like that.

The bugs had been smarter than he thought, much smarter. He doubted that the drone had shown them the way. No, the Quas must have found his bloody rag and made the correct deductions, exploring the area and cooperating to corner him. That realization frightened him all over again.

A loud rustling drew his attention back to the here and now. The second bug was about to burst out of the shaft. Zack armed a grenade and tossed it in. Then, without looking back, he ran into the jungle, intend on reaching the shoreline on the other side of the island.

Smart as the Quas were, the second bug didn't recognize the grenade for what it was. A muffled bang and a loud screech marked its passing.

"Good guys: three. Bugs: zero," Zack muttered to himself as he pushed through the dense foliage, feeling his way through the darkness, ignoring the thorns tearing at his skin.

"Now it'll be four against Zack. The odds are getting even."

Decker knew it was just bravado. Without food, he was weakening fast, and with four of the things on his back, cooperating in a way he hadn't expected, his improvised grenades would no longer suffice.

If the next team of Quas didn't end his illustrious bug-hunting career, then Amali would. He wasn't the type to continue the game for sport with losses climbing so fast. At least he'd have shown the bastard that Marines died hard.

*

Zack reached the pristine beach on the far side just as the first light of dawn brightened the western horizon. He washed off the dried, caked-on ichor in the shallow waters, leaving red burn marks behind, his tired eyes were alert for any sign of Amali's killer fish.

By now, he must have passed at least one operational receiver, which meant they knew where he was. The next batch of bugs would be along soon.

He stretched, causing his muscles to protest in pain. His stomach rumbled in protest again, and Zack did his best to ignore it. The cold light reflecting off distant clouds made the reality of his situation frighteningly clear. He had nothing to eat, no way out and no hope of survival. All he had was his damned pride and an unquenchable desire to go down fighting.

For lack of a better plan, he returned to the tree line along the black beach and slowly made his way to the southern end of the island where an extinct volcano towered above the jungle. He had a vague notion of drawing the Quas into a wild chase through the crater if only to make a change from the jungle hunt.

Along the way, Decker took down three sensors, which he modified as he walked. The sun soon rose but cast an ominous, dull red glow behind the low clouds and growing haze.

With detached fascination, the gunner watched roiling, black thunderheads form an unbroken carpet of darkness that threatened to occlude the newborn light, giving the day a sick hue. High waves broke against the coral reef as surface currents fought the onrushing storm.

Sudden gusts of wind tore at the palm trees, threatening to topple them. Then, a steady gale slammed into the island and snatched the breath from Zack's lungs. He withdrew deeper into the forest, but the elements found him nonetheless, drowning his hearing in white noise, the rain stinging his eyes.

A palm tree toppled across his path, almost crushing him under its weight. Even the jungle had turned against him.

He burst through the tree line back towards the shore, right into a driving, dense rain. Lightning flashed in the distance, blinding him for a moment. Straining to take each step, Zack walked into the ocean, in a half-baked attempt to blur his trail, even though what little remained of his rational mind knew it would be useless.

He needn't have bothered. On the spit of land ahead, four reddish shapes broke out of the undergrowth, tails swishing. They spread out and moved in, struggling against the chaos just as Zack was doing. The gunner stopped and tried to pull a grenade from his pocket. A wave toppled him over, and he went under, losing the plastic package.

When he came up for air, spluttering and wheezing, the Quas had come closer. The salt burned his eyes, and he tried to rub it out, but only made things worse. Tears streamed down his face to mingle with the downpour.

Zack could no longer escape. He knelt in the shallow water to keep his balance and pulled out another grenade. A blinding, suicidal madness grew out of a dormant part of his soul, pushing aside his rising panic. He raised his fist at the soldiers.

"Come on, you fucking bugs," he yelled, the force of his shout searing his throat. Howling winds snatched his words away, and anyhow, the Quas couldn't understand him. "Come and die with Zachary T. Decker, Command Sergeant, Commonwealth Marine Corps, retired. The first of those who will wipe you out."

He twisted the wires of his grenade together and counted down the fuse delay. At four, he threw it with all his might at the leftmost Quas. The grenade blew in mid-air, driving a spray of shrapnel into the creature. It staggered and was knocked over by a tall wave that almost drowned the human.

Coughing, retching and fighting the raging surf, Zack pulled another mini-bomb from his pocket and prepared to arm it. Just then, the water around the nearest soldier erupted in a violent boil. Decker nearly dropped his grenade in surprise.

"You can forget the heroic last stand, Sergeant Decker." A loudspeaker-amplified voice behind and above him momentarily drowned out the tempest. "Stand clear and prepare to climb aboard."

He didn't dare look for the source of the voice. Two bugs remained standing and were still advancing on him like automatons. The plasma cannon erupted again, spitting a flash of super-heated matter on the next Quas, vaporizing it and a lot of seawater around it. While the gun cycled, Zack armed the grenade he was holding and tossed it at the last Quas. The bomb exploded as the cannon spoke again.

"Good guys: seven. Bugs: zero. Eat your heart out, Amali." Only the wind heard him, but it was enough.

Now, Decker could look at his mysterious savior. He turned just in time to see a sleek assault shuttle, unmarked but liberally streaked with black from hard use, land in the pounding surf. A forty-millimeter cannon poked out of its nose like the beak of an alien bird of prey. Heavily modified and camouflaged, Decker nonetheless recognized the naval Warthog attack boat, with its swept back fuselage, stubby wings, and graceful engine pods.

A hatch beside the cockpit opened, and a black-clad arm beckoned him inside.

"Hurry, Sergeant. Their air defense system spotted me on the way down. They don't know what I'm about, but they'll put two and two together fast enough now that we've killed their tame bugs."

Stumbling through the surf, blinded by the rain and his tears, Zack Decker reached the shuttle just as legs were about to give out in sheer relief. He was about to climb aboard when he remembered the collar around his neck.

"Hang on," he yelled at the woman in the pilot's seat. "I gotta take this crap off me, or I'll make a bloody mess in your ship the moment you lift off. It has a dead man's switch."

She nodded and pulled a small tool case out from under her seat. "I've seen these things before. They're a variation of the ordinary slave collars," she shouted at Zack as she opened the case and selected her instrument. "Hold steady."

Reaching out, she did something and the collar snapped open. Zack tore it off his neck and tossed it into the surf.

"Thanks!" He climbed into the cockpit, dripping water everywhere.

She shut the hatch behind him, cutting off the roar of the storm. In the ensuing silence, Zack slipped into the co-pilot's seat and, with her help, he strapped in, hands trembling. Shock at his unexpected rescue was beginning to numb his senses.

The woman turned her full attention back to the shuttle and lifted it out of the waves. Moments later, buffeted by the wind, yawing and tossing, the Warthog rose towards the black clouds at a steep angle. Gravity and speed pressed the two humans into their seats. When they broke through the clouds, high up in Pacifica's atmosphere, the sun caressed Zack's face through the thick cockpit window, and the abrupt change from storm to calm snapped his mind back to the present.

He glanced at the woman beside him. She was tall, slim and long-limbed, but wiry, judging by the strong tendons in her hands and wrists as she gripped the shuttle's controls. Her black hair, cut just below the ears and swept back, showed strands of silver at the temples. The lines around her mouth and crow's feet in the corners of her dark, deep-set eyes marked her as mature, a few years older than Zack, but not by much. Definitely military, he decided and not only because she wore an unmarked battledress that had seen a lot of use.

Attractive, the gunner thought, his mind seeking refuge in the irrelevant and innocuous, *but in a tough way. Sort of like Raisa. Officer, if I know my old Navy.*

"Thanks for the rescue," Zack's voice, worn out by the effects of his harrowing experiences, was no louder than a harsh whisper.

"You're welcome, Sergeant, though I apologize for taking so long." Her voice, now that she wasn't shouting, had a rich alto timbre.

"Huh?" Decker frowned in puzzlement as the use of his former rank and the apology finally cut through the fog in his brain.

The woman chuckled.

"Sorry, Sergeant. Let me introduce myself. I'm Commander Hera Talyn, Naval Intelligence. We've been looking for you ever since you vanished on Deveaux station. It's a minor miracle they let you keep the Master Gunner's badge."

"Why?"

"It's what we used to find you. Actually, keep track of you for the last year or so."

"Amali had it checked, and it was just a piece of metal alloy. Otherwise, he wouldn't have let me keep it."

"Our dear Walker was only partially right," she replied, amusement plainly visible on her lean face. "That alloy has an unusual characteristic: close to a human body's energy field, it becomes a beacon that a properly tuned sensor can spot at one hell of a distance. We were glad you decided to wear it after our operative slipped it to you on Pradyn. It made our jobs a lot easier."

"So I was set up as a dupe to infiltrate Amali's organization?" Zack countered angrily. The force he put in his words strained his vocal cords, and he coughed.

"It was not quite that easy, Sergeant. I'll explain everything once we're back on the ship and away from Pacifica. By now, I suspect Amali has discovered you've left his island and has scrambled his resources to stop us."

"Damn!" Zack shook his head. "Next time a buddy sets me up with a job offer..." Then, "Say, Commander, what sort of ship is waiting for us? A frigate?"

"No, Sergeant," Talyn smiled again. "*Demetria*. Captain Ducote will be overjoyed to find you're alive and well."

"Damn!" Decker repeated, a slow grin spreading on his battered face.

— SEVENTEEN —

Commander Talyn handed control of the Warthog over to the AI and pushed her seat away from the console. With a sigh of relief, she stretched her limbs and grinned.

"Unless our friend Amali has also bent Pacifica Aerospace Control to his every will, we're safe. I'd give my next month's pay to see the bastard's face when he realizes you slipped out from under his multi-million cred defense umbrella."

"And out of the grasp of his fucking bugs," Zack replied in a voice that was half whisper and half gravel. "But he isn't the sort to stop his plans over one retired Marine if I read the scumbag right."

"You have, Sergeant." She looked at Zack, and her grin vanished, replaced by a frown as she saw his state clearly for the first time. Her trained eye immediately recognized the traces of the mind probe, and she groaned.

"One thing about Amali: he never falls short of my expectations. Cantos?"

"Yeah." Zack looked away. "He said I suffered no permanent damage." But his tone belied the words. Decker's neurons might still fire in proper sequence, but the thing that defined Zachary T. Decker had been damaged.

"I'm sorry," Talyn whispered. "I'm so very sorry."

The silence deepened in the cockpit, and she felt an unaccustomed sense of guilt. Working for Naval Intelligence's special operations section often meant compromising one's values for the greater good. But the moral balance sheet calculated in the safety of a sterile operations room meant absolutely nothing in front of a man who'd gone through the worst sort of hell because of one cold-blooded decision.

Zack broke the silence first, shutting his feelings away with the other miseries he'd collected over the last few weeks.

"If I remember rightly, Commander, the proper procedure after a mission is a debriefing while the memories are still fresh." His eyes remained fixed on the star field beyond the cockpit window.

Talyn didn't respond. Her gaze was still transfixed by the small dots of healing flesh on his scalp. His matter-of-fact tone had stayed any further apology or explanation. He didn't want them.

"Yes," she finally said, "yes, you're right, Sergeant. A debriefing."

For the next two hours, Talyn skillfully extracted things from Zack's memory that even he had forgotten. She questioned him as she would question any trained Pathfinder after a mission, not like a civilian, or even a soldier who'd gone through an ordeal that would destroy most people. Decker wouldn't appreciate a gentle treatment. His self-respect and inner balance had been badly shaken, if not irretrievably ruined. Treating him like damaged goods would only make things worse.

"You show the recall abilities of a trained agent, Sergeant. I'm impressed. Your report completes the spotty picture we have of Amali's hideaway, though I can't help wishing he had shown you the hive in person rather than through a vidscreen. It would make the follow-on force's job a lot easier." Zack still stared through the window as he had ever since Talyn had noticed the probe scars.

"It wasn't just a vidscreen, sir, but an actual window," he replied, his voice devoid of emotion. "The first view, that of the egg chamber, was direct. I'd swear to that. Which means the queen's chamber and the nursery aren't far away."

"Yes, you're probably right. Amali's psych profile makes him out to be the kind who prefers live demonstrations of his power."

"I'm sure showing me a tape of the bug eating Strachan, instead of me seeing it live, put a damper on his enjoyment.

But since the asshole offered me a starring role in the sequel, maybe it didn't matter."

He turned to spear Talyn with hard eyes.

"Speaking of Strachan, what happened to *Shokoten*? Most of the crewmembers were good, honest spacers. Nothing to do with the shit the captain was doing."

"Still sailing the star lanes, as far as I know. The Amalis, whatever else they may be, aren't wasteful. Only Strachan suffered the brunt of their displeasure. He vanished in Hadley three days after you took off in *Demetria*. We had always presumed him dead and now you've confirmed it. There's a new captain aboard *Shokoten*, and I'm pretty sure that she won't be doing anything illegal for a long time. The ship's usefulness as a cover for smuggling expired when you ran."

Decker shrugged and looked outside again. The Warthog was about to enter the system's inner asteroid field, and Talyn turned off the autopilot, taking the controls once more.

"That's good. I felt at home on *Shokoten* once Alers was gone. So what happens now? Will anyone take care of that fucking psychopath?"

"First," Talyn gave Zack a quick glance, "we park this thing aboard *Demetria* and head for the rendezvous with the follow-on force."

Talyn pointed out the window. "And there she is."

"*Demetria*, this is Falcon One, over."

"Falcon One, this is *Demetria*. How's the weather planetside?"

"Humid, with a storm brewing," Talyn grinned briefly at Decker.

"Password," she whispered.

"Any luck, Falcon One?" Avril Ducote asked, anxiety coloring her normally steady voice.

"Scratched, bruised and wet like a dishrag, but otherwise unharmed, *Demetria*," Talyn replied, deliberately avoiding any mention of the real damage Zack had suffered.

He wouldn't want her to tell Ducote, out of shame. But Avril had to know, and would, when the two women managed a moment alone together, preferably soon.

"He's looking forward to a big shot of anything alcoholic you may have on board."

"I was about to ask whether you picked up the right one, but if it wants booze, it has to be an ex-Marine called Zack Decker." Something in the way Avril spoke drew Zack's attention, and he frowned for a moment. "The cargo hold is open for your landing, Falcon One. And the celebratory whiskey is ready and waiting."

*

The Warthog's thrusters died away the moment the assault boat settled on the bare deck of cargo hold number one. Zack climbed out of the comfortable co-pilot's seat and stretched his limbs out as far as the small cockpit allowed. His entire body felt like a single, massive bruise. Every muscle had stiffened during the flight from Amali's island, and he hurt like hell.

Jumping out of the open cockpit door, he landed on the deck with a hollow thump, sending a renewed wave of pain up his legs and spine. Across the hold, the access hatch swung open with a metallic clang.

Through it strode Avril Ducote, Valkyrie-like in battledress with a sidearm, her long blonde hair swinging down her back in a thick braid. A smile of pure pleasure filled her face, piercing through Zack's dull ache like a thin shaft of sunlight through a carpet of storm clouds. She stopped in front of him, so close that they nearly touched and her eyes looked searchingly into his.

"You're alive," she whispered, as if in disbelief.

"Yeah, so Commander Talyn tells me."

"You don't know how happy I am, Zack." Now he could see tears forming.

"Somehow, I think I do." It was clear to Decker, even in his current state, that Avril Ducote had fallen for him. He didn't know how he felt about that because he didn't want to touch any of his emotions right now, except hate, but his resolve faltered for a few seconds. His hard, blank stare softened, and some of his inner turmoil and pain shone through.

"For what it's worth, Avril, I'm damned happy myself to be back on your ship, and not only because that means I've escaped from bug island."

She nodded, smiling shyly.

"Then I'm even happier."

"Sorry, Avril, Sergeant, but we must go," Talyn's gentle voice intruded and drew them apart. Though the agent really was in a hurry, her primary concern was getting Zack out of a situation she knew he couldn't handle yet. Not until his mental wounds had scarred over.

"Of course, Hera," Ducote replied, blinking away the excess moisture in her eyes. "Come, Zack. First a shower and a shave, then clean clothes. There will be a hot meal and a glass of whiskey waiting for you in the galley."

*

"So, what happened after I left the ship at Deveaux Station?"

Zack glanced at Avril and Talyn in turn. Though he still looked like hell, the shower, and fresh clothes had gone far in improving his appearance, but he wasn't the same Zack Decker who'd left *Demetria* only a short while ago.

The intervening days had given his eyes a haunted look. A look that gave Ducote a jolt of despair every time she saw it, because she feared the Zack she knew, her Zack, was gone.

While he had showered, Talyn had given her a brief run down on his encounter with the mind probe, and its effects. Avril had tightened in fury at the revelation, and would have strangled both Amali and Cantos on the spot. But she also understood Zack's state, and the fact that things might never be the same again.

They were in the small galley, he drinking scotch, they coffee. *Demetria* had jumped to hyperspace ten minutes earlier, on her way to a rendezvous Talyn, irritatingly, refused to explain.

Zack had given Avril an account of his time in Amali's hands, sparing her no detail. His hard, brittle honesty had astonished Talyn, but she realized that Zack Decker was a remarkable man. Too remarkable for the way he'd been treated by the Marine Corps.

"Maybe Avril should start, Sergeant," Hera raised an eyebrow at Ducote.

"Why do you insist on calling Zack 'sergeant', Hera?" Avril asked with a hint of asperity.

"Military courtesy," the agent shrugged. "He's a retired command sergeant with twenty years honorable service and is entitled to the rank."

Zack snorted in derision, the first sign of the old, hard-assed Pathfinder he'd shown so far, but she ignored him.

"Unless he prefers I call him something else."

"Try his name. It's Zack."

"No need, sir," Zack chuckled at Avril's reaction. "'Sergeant' suits me fine. It's a damn sight better than what I've been called lately. And I guess I came by the title honestly, which I can't say about a lot of other things."

"And why does he call you 'sir'?" Avril was openly disapproving now. "You people kicked him out of the Corps."

Avril's defense of his free, civilian status made Zack smile with enough warmth to give her pause.

"It's the way things go, Avril," he gently replied, before the discussion went any further. "She's a commander and outranks me, so I call her 'sir,' same as she calls me 'sergeant.' It wouldn't feel right to do otherwise, even if I'm retired. Now can we talk about what happened, please?"

Avril sighed but held her peace.

"As you wish."

She settled back and stared down into her coffee mug.

"About ten minutes after you left the ship at Deveaux, Hera showed up at the gangway, asking to speak with you..."

*

"Excuse me, Captain Ducote. I'm looking for Zack Decker."

"And why should you look for this Decker person on my ship?" Avril eyed the tall, dark woman with suspicion, determined to cover for her friend and shipmate.

"My name is Commander Hera Talyn, Naval Intelligence." She showed Ducote an official-looking identification card. "It's vital I speak with Decker soonest. He's in great danger from people who want to silence him."

"How do I know you're not one of the people who wish him harm?"

"So he's on board?" Talyn asked.

"I've not said so, Commander. Please tell me why I should trust you. Anyone can flash a cute little ID card."

"You're right, anyone can. But to prove my bona fides, we'll need to agree that you know Decker, and do it quickly. If he's already left the ship, I must to find him before the opposition does."

Avril stared at her for a few seconds and then shrugged.

"Somehow, I don't think you would simply walk up and ask if you were one of the *Sécurité Spéciale* scum. Their methods seem to lack subtlety."

"Not always." Talyn's eyes never left Ducote's. "But if it means anything to you, I'm the case officer who led Decker into this pickle, and I'm trying to extract him in one piece."

The agent could read Ducote's indecision her eyes, but refrained from pushing any further. Then, the look vanished, and her face tightened.

"He left the ship about ten, fifteen minutes ago to book a shuttle flight down to Toulon. He wants to try contacting the Marine Regiment's intelligence officer down there and give him the information he uncovered."

"Damn!" Talyn swore, slapping her right hand against the airlock hatch in frustration. "I had hoped to reach him before he went ashore. The *Sécurité Spéciale* has a hit team on the station. Unfortunately, we don't know what they look like. Decker is in great danger."

"Will they kill him?" Ducote's face had gone white with fear.

"I doubt it. They'll want to know how much he found out, and to whom he spilled the beans. Then, they'll kill him."

"Zack told me everything." The trader's voice was nearly inaudible.

"Which means you're next on their list. Don't leave your ship. Let no one aboard, and if you own a sidearm, keep it handy. I'll try to intercept Decker before the *Sécurité Spéciale* team does."

Talyn turned on her heels and left the ship, heading for the station's core. Ducote, now thoroughly frightened, closed the airlock and retrieved Zack's old Imperial Armaments blaster from her cabin.

*

Talyn returned three hours later, with a grim look on her face.

"He's gone."

"What?"

"Station security traced his movements. He last appeared in the shop district along with the two *Sécurité Spéciale* agents tailing him."

"I thought you didn't know what they looked like."

"No, but they made the mistake of moving like a team of hunters, which marks them as trained agents. We spooks can recognize each other. The training's the same. After that screen capture, nothing. I'm sure he's off the station by now. A private yacht left an hour after the last sighting, and that was no coincidence. The pilot of the ship looked like the male half of the *Sécurité Spéciale* duo on the harbormaster's screen when he filed his flight plan."

"Where is the yacht headed?"

"Pacifica."

Avril nodded. Then, she frowned.

"But Commander, these *Sécurité Spéciale* people sound like professionals. Why would they leave such a trail on the station's security system? You took little time to find them. Is it a red herring?"

"Good question," Talyn smiled tightly. "But I doubt it's a false trail. The *Sécurité Spéciale* wants Zack Decker, and that means no complex operations. A simple snatch and grab before the opposition can react. And it worked. Once they reach their destination, they're home free. The Fleet has no jurisdiction on Pacifica, and no one there will lift a finger to help us.

"What now?"

"My people are combing the station, just in case, and I'll put some additional resources on his tail, but frankly, I don't think we can intercept the yacht in deep space. You know how hard it is to find a ship that doesn't want to be found. That's if I can even move the resources into place fast enough. I don't have a ship nearby to do it myself." She glanced at Avril, a thoughtful look in her eyes. "It occurs to me that since he told you what he knew, the information he collected isn't lost."

Ducote's face hardened.

"If I tell you what he told me, you no longer have a reason to save him."

"I could force you. There are methods," Talyn replied with a shrug. When Avril's face tightened in anger, she continued. "But, before you kill me with your bare hands, I won't. He clearly means a lot to you, and to be frank, I feel an obligation towards him. I dreamed up the plan that placed Decker on *Shokoten* as an unwitting plant. A Pathfinder major reminded me, not that long ago, that there are values beyond winning or losing, and we forget them at our peril, or we become no better than our enemies. He was right, and this is one of those times where the values come first."

Ducote stared at Talyn warily.

"Your ship can take us to Pacifica," the agent continued. "We may have a chance if I can arrange for a Fleet transport to meet us on the way and deliver a specially modified assault shuttle. You realize it may not work."

Avril Ducote nodded once, but her face plainly showed relief mixed in with the anguish. Surprising herself, Talyn reached out and squeezed Ducote's hand.

"Our chances are fair. The *Sécurité Spéciale* is good, but no bogeyman."

"And what is it?"

"Bad news, Captain."

"Call me Avril, please." She held out her hand.

"And I'm Hera."

"The *Sécurité Spéciale* is a civilian intelligence agency that answers only to the Secretary General of the Commonwealth. It replaced the old Special Security Bureau wiped out by Grand Admiral Kowalski years ago.

That's one hell of a story in itself, by the way. The problem with the *Sécurité Spéciale* is it doesn't actually serve the Commonwealth as a whole, but the SecGen and the Coalition, a bunch of people just as nasty as their agents."

"I've heard the name of the Coalition whispered before, but who are they, and what do they want? Or is that classified?"

"It is, but only so they don't find out how much we know. The Coalition is a grouping of senators, planetary politicians, military officers, and businesspeople like the Amalis, who dream of turning the Commonwealth into an Empire, with themselves at the center, as a new aristocracy. They want to return the Outworlds to their subsidiary status as they were before the Migration Wars. These days, the Navy has its hands full trying to make sure no one takes the first step towards something we'll all regret. At least the part of the armed forces based in the Outworlds. The others, well, you can imagine."

"That sounds appalling."

"You better believe it. If you ask me, this old Commonwealth of ours is headed for the biggest shit hole since the last Migration War, and that's why I'm in this crappy line of business. I'm not saying all that justifies what I did to Decker. But it worked where all our earlier efforts didn't. With the kind of stakes in this game..."

*

Demetria left Deveaux Station within the hour, her offloading and departure miraculously smoothed by Talyn's connections. At the minimum safe distance, she jumped into hyperspace towards a rendezvous point, halfway between Dordogne and Pacifica.

Their meeting with the unnamed spy ship didn't delay their flight by very much. Yet, by the time *Demetria* released the modified Warthog in the Pacifica system's inner asteroid field, the fast yacht had gained several days on them.

Though trying to keep up hope, for Ducote's sake, Talyn privately doubted she'd be able to retrieve Decker in time, if she even found him. Masquerading as a courier, the

Warthog slipped into low orbit, timing her descent so it was night over the island. The shuttle sailed down, all systems off, in full stealth mode and Talyn searched for a sign of the special beacon disguised as a badge on Amali's private island.

When the Warthog was low enough to track the beacon and pinpoint Zack's location, a dawn storm was already blanketing the area. Talyn had to switch back to full power to slice through the tempest, alerting the island's guardians in the process. Fortunately, that same storm screwed with their systems just long enough...

*

"...and then I dropped out of the cloud cover, just in time to see the heroic tableau of Zack Decker's last stand in the pounding surf. The rest, as they say, is history." Talyn allowed an ironic smile to tug at her thin lips.

"If you had showed up a few minutes later, you wouldn't have found a Zack Decker anymore. But I'd have given the bastards one hell of a case of indigestion, I can tell you that." Zack downed the rest of the whiskey and looked at Talyn with suspicion.

"Tell me, Commander, how the hell did I get mixed up in all this. I was just minding my own business on Aramis, crawling into a bottle every night, and blowing my pension on booze."

There was more than a hint of anger in Decker's voice, a subtle warning he wouldn't accept bullshit. Avril squeezed his hand reassuringly as Talyn looked at them in turn, clearly deciding how much she could say.

"The Navy's been keeping a close eye on all Amali activities since we shut down one of the Coalition's covert programs last year. Success has been hard to come by because the Amalis and their cronies enjoy the full support of *Sécurité Spéciale* resources. On the off-chance, we placed undercover agents on all of Amali's ships, including *Shokoten,* which was a special target because it was fast, well-armed and good for solo runs into the badlands."

"Harwan Lokis," Zack said in a flat tone.

"Yes, though that wasn't his real name. He was a Navy lieutenant, and a good operative. The *Sécurité Spéciale* was on to him pretty fast and murdered him on Pradyn."

"It was Nihao Kiani."

"We suspected as much. Thank you for confirming it, Sergeant."

"Don't bother looking for revenge, sir. Her body is dust in a Pacifica Kasbah."

"You?"

"Raisa and me. And a Shrehari disruptor."

Strangely, the thought of the formidable Arkanna and the sound of her name didn't give him anything more than a quick twinge of pain and emptiness.

"Thank you again. That saves me an assassination." She took a sip of her coffee. "After Lokis' death, we were without a mole on *Shokoten*, and that made us nervous, since she was the most likely for any covert operations, especially now that the Amali's tame reiver clan is history. If you believe in fate or the gods, then it was preordained that a solution to our dilemma would walk right into our hands."

"Me."

"Right again."

"So Tren Kinnear works for you, does he?" Zack growled, eyes narrowing in anger. "The slimy bastard. He'll feel my fist on his face when I see him again."

Avril squeezed Decker's hand, as much in support as to contain his rising anger.

"Kinnear is a casual, not an operative. He runs a popular tavern at a major spaceport, so he hears and sees things. And he passes those things on to us."

"Out of sheer altruism, right?" Zack's words dripped with sarcasm.

"Mostly, yes," Talyn replied, ignoring his tone. "At first, Tren Kinnear came to us on his own with information, out of a feeling of loyalty and duty. Since then, he's been a valuable asset. And before you ask, he's never accepted a single cred in payment. He's a very proud man."

Zack grunted in disbelief.

"When your little problem with the police happened, and Kinnear took you in, he told us about it and asked us to help keep things quiet, as a return favor for his work. That's when I pulled your personal file and had a brainstorm." Talyn smiled sadly. "Sergeant, I think by retiring you early, the Marine Corps cut off its nose to spite its face."

Decker glanced away in embarrassment.

"Thank you, sir."

"Since the *Sécurité Spéciale* had uncovered Lokis, I figured someone who wasn't an agent but with the brains to work things out on his own might do the trick. You fit the profile and would make an excellent merchant ship gunner. I instructed Kinnear to set up your recruitment aboard *Shokoten* the next time Captain Strachan came in and to make both you and he believe this was merely one ex-Marine trying to do a favor for another. I had hoped that if you found something dangerous to the Fleet or to the Commonwealth, you'd feel it was your duty to pass it along, and that you'd know danger when you saw it. Kinnear wanted you to be fully briefed and not sent in as a dupe."

"Yeah, right," Zack muttered, shaking his head, "and I'm a Verdanian hermaphrodite."

"Then don't believe me, if you like," Talyn briefly glanced at the ceiling, as if praying for patience. "But I vetoed that idea. If you went in as an agent, the *Sécurité Spéciale* would have you marked within days, and we'd be back where we were."

"So you sent me a trinket to remind me of my oath to the Corps. Once a Marine, always a Marine."

"Something like that, yes, and to give us the means to track you. We had an agent watching at every port, ready to reel you in if you gave signs of wanting to speak."

"Except Pacifica, the night we went into the Kasbah."

"Yes. How did you know?"

"I can tell when I'm being watched, a sort of sixth sense."

"I'm impressed. That night in Hadley, our watcher vanished. He was probably caught in the net the *Sécurité Spéciale* was closing around you."

"How did you guys plant that badge on me anyways?"

"I slipped it in your pocket in that rowdy bar on Pradyn, just before *Shokoten*'s first officer joined you."

"You?"

Talyn smiled.

"I was the Ungaran spacer beside you."

"I'll be damned," Decker shook his head with grudging admiration. Ungarans were the most human-like of all Shield races, but still... "You're good, sir."

"Does that mean you're no longer pissed-off at me?" Talyn raised her eyebrows.

"Yeah." Zack shook his head slowly. "When all's said and done, your plan worked. Knowing what I now know, I'd do it all over again. That fucker Amali is just too damn dangerous."

"Spoken like a true Pathfinder."

Decker acknowledged the compliment with a wry smile.

"After twenty years, it's damn hard to break some habits."

"I'm glad to hear it, Sergeant because I must ask you to do something else."

"Yes, sir, I'll do it, sir. I'll lead in that follow-on force you mentioned."

"Thank you, Sergeant. That will be a great help."

"Hey, Commander, I know the difference between a mission based on a briefing and one that's guided by someone who's actually seen the target up close."

"No!" Avril Ducote's voice stilled the others. She glared at Talyn indignantly.

"Zack has already done more than enough for you. He's no longer a Marine. Why should he go risk his life again? Let your follow-on force do it without him." Then, her tone dropped to a whisper. "I don't want to risk losing him again."

Decker took her hand.

"This is something I must do, Avril. If it saves a single Marine's life, the risk will be worth it, and I have a promise to keep. I told Amali I would kill him myself."

"You hear the sound of the bugles, and you have to go? Once a Marine always a Marine? Go then, Zachary Decker, and be damned. Just don't be surprised if I don't wait for you."

Then, before tears overwhelmed her, she fled the galley.

"Sorry, Sergeant."

"Don't be, sir. I can understand why she's upset. Me, I can look at this mission and not think about whether I'll be coming back or not. It isn't in my nature; otherwise, I'd never have made it as a Pathfinder. So I don't look at it as a chance to die, only as an opportunity to make the scumbags die. Avril will come around.”

“I hope so, Sergeant, for she and her ship will have a role to play in the operation.”

“I figured as much. So who's the follow-on force?”

Before Talyn could answer, emergence nausea overcame them.

“We're at the rendezvous,” she said when it passed. “Let's head for the cockpit and see if they've arrived,” she replied instead, a sphinxlike smile on her face.

Avril was behind the controls of her ship. Without turning around to face them, she said, in a savage tone, “We're here, Commander.”

“Whatever happened to Hera?” the agent asked.

“I can’t be friendly with the woman who blew on the damned bugle, knowing my shipmate would respond like a hunting dog to the hunt master's call.”

Zack placed both hands on Avril's shoulders and squeezed.

“Hey, take it easy, girl. I'm doing this because I want to, not because a spook manipulated me.” He glanced at Talyn, eyes apologizing for the unflattering description. The agent smiled back.

“Anyway, I won't be going in alone, like last time. If I survived on my own, imagine with a full strike force.”

“Promise you’ll come back?”

“Hey, I promised when I left the ship at Deveaux. I came back didn't I?”

“Yes,” she finally replied, grudgingly, “with a bit of a delay.”

“Not my fault, Avril. Complain to Walker Amali. Or shall I give him your compliments when I put out his lights?”

“I don't care, Zack. Just come back.”

He was about to reply when a flash of light out in space caught his eye.

“Ship emerging, Commander. And damn close too. Either they have a good sailing master, or the captain's a hot-dogger.”

“Both, Sergeant. That's them.”

They waited in silence, watching the growing spark off their port bow. As the ship neared, Zack could make out its shape.

"Hey, that's a bloody patrol frigate." His heart beat faster as he recognized a ship just like the one he'd called home for several years. Happy years.

"It's the patrol frigate *Charles Martel*."

"The 251st," Zack said in a low voice.

"Indeed. They're the follow-on force. The 251st has been doing jobs lately that never officially happened."

"A spook commando?"

"Something like that. Unofficially, they work for my bureau in Naval Intelligence. Do you know them?"

"Some. Like their sergeant major. Most of the other noncoms too. Corps' a small place."

"So I hear, and the Pathfinder community even smaller. Not to throw aspersions on your old unit but the 251st are the best of the best. That's why they get the prize missions."

Zack nodded, only half hearing Talyn. His mind had returned to the days when he wore black battledress with the six silver stripes and crossed swords of his rank. When he had lived on board *Charles Martel*'s sister ship *Musashi* and led the thirty Pathfinders of Third Troop, 902nd Pathfinder Squadron. The days when he felt alive and happy, respected, known as a master craftsman in his chosen profession. He'd give his everything to return to that life.

If he hadn't accepted this mission before, he would now. A chance to finish off Amali by being a Pathfinder for the best Pathfinder outfit in the Fleet was enough to give him goose bumps.

*

"*Demetria*, this is the Commonwealth Starship *Charles Martel*, Simon Dubois commanding."

Zack snapped out of his reverie and looked at Avril. "They're calling you."

"Oh, right," Ducote replied, sounding as if she too had lost herself in contemplation. "This is *Demetria*, Avril Ducote commanding."

"Is there a Commander Talyn on board?"

"Yes. Hera," Avril pointed at her commo console, "go ahead."

"Talyn here, Captain Dubois. Everything's good. Sergeant Decker is with us, and he's agreed to go with the squadron. I suggest we dock *Demetria* with your ship."

"Agreed. Stand by for tractor beam lock, Captain Ducote. We shall pull you in and mate the ships at our keel airlock. When we have you, please cut all engines."

"*Demetria* standing by."

With a smoothness born of long practice, the frigate's crew gently took the small trader into their tractor beam's embrace and mated her to the underside of the bigger vessel with barely a shudder. When the airlocks were pressurized, Talyn touched Avril's arm.

"I shall need you both at the briefing."

She looked at Zack with a critical eye. His cuts and bruises were still livid, but he still looked the part of a tough ex-Marine, in his old, black battledress with the Imperial Armaments blaster on his hip. The only insignia he wore was the Master Gunner's badge, but nobody would fail to recognize him as a combat-hardened noncommissioned officer.

Talyn in the lead, they climbed the ladder to the upper airlock. The hatches opened smoothly, and Zack inhaled the achingly familiar smell of a warship under sail when they left the trader and clambered aboard the frigate.

Zack barely noticed the figures waiting by the hatch as he stepped into the ship. Snapping to attention, he saluted first towards the bow of the frigate where in the days of ocean-going ships the national ensign had flown, then the officer of the deck who happened to be the captain himself.

"Permission to come aboard, sir."

"Permission granted, Sergeant Decker. Welcome." Commander Dubois shook Decker's hand after returning the salute.

Another officer stepped forward and held out his hand. He was tall, almost as tall as Zack and a few years younger, but his weathered face and old eyes hinted a long time spent on the frontier. Pale hair, blue eyes, with a hawk's nose and a firm chin, he would have looked intimidating to a civilian, but to Decker, he looked like one of his own.

"Major Kal Ryent, CO of the 251st. Glad to have you along. I understand you saw the inside of the target."

"Yes, sir. And I'll be glad to guide you in."

"Good. My sergeant-major has told me a lot about you when we found out you'd be joining us."

"Knowing Vanlith, everything you heard was bad, right sir?" Zack grinned.

"Right, Sergeant, which means you'll fit right in." He smiled.

When Decker saw Ryent's pale eyes shift, he suddenly remembered his manners.

"Sir, I'd like to introduce Captain Avril Ducote, of the trader *Demetria*. I owe her a lot."

"Pleased to meet you, Captain." Ryent shook Avril's hand, appraising her. He liked what he saw. Ducote seemed steady, capable, and experienced.

"I suggest we head for the briefing room," Talyn said once the introductions were over.

"Right, Hera," Ryent replied, flashing the intelligence officer a quick smile that, to Decker, seemed more than just a greeting between casual friends.

As they walked down the all too familiar passageways, Zack asked Talyn in a whisper, "You, and the major old friends, sir?"

"You could say that, Sergeant," she replied in the same tone. "We've done a few missions together."

Zack nodded, a knowing smile briefly playing on his lips.

The lift deposited them on the bridge deck, by the ship's briefing room and as the gunner stepped through the door, a deep, vibrant voice stopped him dead in his tracks.

"Well, well, well, if it isn't Zachary T. Decker, Command Sergeant, retired. Who left the airlock open and let you on board a perfectly respectable ship?"

The speaker, a stocky, broad-shouldered noncom in his late forties stood by the conference table, fists on his hips. He wore the starburst insignia of a sergeant major and the gold jump wings of an expert Pathfinder.

"Vanlith, you old bugger," Decker shot back, grinning broadly. "I see the Corps finally fucked-up and made you respectable."

Avril Ducote was surprised to see the two men embrace.

"Speaking of fuck-ups," the weathered sergeant-major said when they let go of each other, "the Corps made a real doozy in your case. How's retirement?"

Zack grimaced.

"Shitty, Gus. Don't take it if they offer. The first thing you do is crawl into a bottle. Then, you get yourself into more trouble than a gaggle of recruits on shore leave. And then you end up on a fucking frigate, wondering how the hell you volunteered to jump into shit with a bunch of certifiably crazy Pathfinders. Civvie life is nuts, man."

He punched the older man in the arm.

"Gus, I'd like to introduce you to Avril Ducote, the captain of the ship I'm working on. Avril, this is Augustus Vanlith, the only reprobate in the Corps to make sergeant major after getting busted down to private not once, but twice. He's one hell of a Pathfinder."

"Captain," Vanlith shook Avril's hand, "I can only express my admiration at your fortitude. Zack can be one hell of a nasty customer. And I wish you all the happiness you can find in this shitty universe."

"Thank you," she replied shyly, wondering how he knew about their budding relationship.

"Sergeant, Captain Ducote," Major Ryent interrupted with a smile, "I'd like to introduce the rest of my people."

For Zack Decker, it was old home week, a return to the life he had loved. He either knew all the 251st's senior noncoms or knew people who knew them. The Corps was indeed a small place.

"... and if we can finish with the tearful reunion," Ryent's command voice called everybody to order, "I suggest we turn to planning the mission. Take your seats please." He turned to Zack.

"Sergeant Decker, the floor is yours. My battle captain will project aerial views of the target on the vidscreen on request."

Zack went over to the white screen.

"Okay, Pathfinders, Uncle Zachary will tell you a sweet bedtime story, and when I'm done, you'll want to slice Walker Amali's balls off yourselves."

*

For the next hour, Decker described the island and Amali's operation in excruciating detail, including his own ordeal. Talyn supplied information she'd obtained through her intelligence sources, but it was essentially Zack's show.

"Thank you, Sergeant," Ryent nodded when Decker finished his briefing. "It'll be a tough nut to crack, especially since we'll violate the Rules big-time by mounting an unauthorized op on a member planet. Hera, what are our mission parameters?"

"Simple, Kal." Talyn let her hard eyes roam around the table, meeting the others' square on. "Kill all Quas adults, especially the queen, all pupas and destroy all eggs. In intel words, terminate with extreme prejudice. Not that it'll be difficult, after Sergeant Decker's speech. Once you've done that, destroy the labs, data banks and anything associated with the hive."

"Dibs on the interrogation room," Zack interrupted.

Ryent looked at him for a few heartbeats and nodded. Anyone who had suffered a mind probe was entitled to demolish the gear that had raped his mind.

"What about the humans?" The major asked.

"If it shoots or resists, kill it. If it runs and hides, let it be. Ideally, I'd like a few survivors to spread the word that the Fleet has the cojones to violate the Rules when the Coalition goes beyond the pale. And that's why you're going in under your own colors, not as a covert force."

"Good." Ryent and the Marines nodded with satisfaction. They disliked fighting under a false flag, even if politics and secrecy made it necessary. "And Amali?"

"Mine again, sir," Decker interjected. "I promised him I'd see him dead."

"If we catch him, he's yours, Decker," Ryent replied.

"If." Talyn sounded dubious. "He probably has a foolproof escape route only he knows about. And at the first sign of danger, he's gone."

"Leaving his people on their own," Zack's voice dripped with acid. "Fucking coward."

"Any other constraints?" Ryent asked.

"Yes. It'll be a light infantry op, using Warthogs instead of the Typhoons and combat cars, and we can't afford to put *Charles Martel* in Pacifica orbit. Too obvious. If Captain Ducote agrees, we'll use *Demetria* to bring you into launch position, and retrieve you after the mission. Her ship is large enough to carry the gunboats, and can slip into orbit without attracting as much attention. Your descent will be in full stealth mode, not only to deceive Pacifica Aerospace Control, but also Amali's private AA artillery."

"I'll do it," Avril Ducote said, voice steady. But Zack wasn't deceived. Her pallor had increased, and he could see she was frightened. But gutsy.

"Okay." Ryent stretched his arms and rolled his shoulders as he stood. "Hera, Mo, Sarn't-Major, Sergeant Decker, Captain Ducote and Sergeant Takahashi, please stay behind. We'll work on the mission plan. The rest of you can start preparations. We'll hold orders in two hours. Sergeant Ikeda, get a full issue of combat gear ready for Sergeant Decker, minus, I believe, a pistol. You seem to own a well-maintained Imperial Armaments specimen, Decker."

"Aye, sir. Took it off a reiver near Koramshar. My first Fleet Pathfinder op."

"With the 902nd, right? I heard about that one when I was at the School. An excellent piece of work."

"Thank you, sir."

*

Three hours later, Vanlith took Zack down to the locker room to draw his kit. Along the way, Decker breathed in the atmosphere of a warship's Marine barracks and felt the loss again. He belonged here.

Word about him had spread fast, and the Pathfinders preparing their armor and weapons nodded in greeting as he passed. Ikeda waited for them beside an open locker which now bore the name Decker, Z.T.

The armor fit like a glove and Zack reveled in the feel of its protective weight. He was pleased to see that they'd put command sergeant stripes and swords on it.

"Sorry, I couldn't find a crest of the 902nd, Decker."

"I think I still have a few hidden away. Hang on." Decker dug into an inner pocket and grinned as his hand came back with several plasticized insignia. He slapped a crest on each sleeve, above the rank stripes.

"A lot better, Zack," Vanlith nodded. "Why not go the whole hog?" He took the remaining two crests from Decker's fingers and pressed them on his battledress.

"Welcome back to the Pathfinders, Command Sergeant Decker."

Vanlith reached into the locker and pulled out a fifteen-millimeter carbine. He tossed it at Zack, who caught it and expertly worked the action, performing the approved Marine Corps weapons safety check.

The carbine felt right in his hands, natural. A beautiful piece of machinery lovingly maintained and which he would lovingly use. Soon.

"Lock and load, Zack, because we're going on a bug hunt."

— EIGHTEEN —

Demetria, now bearing the name, hull number, and transponder of a free trader called the *Beryl Zephyr*, sliced through Pacifica's night sky, pitching and yawing as Avril Ducote fought the high stratospheric winds. On a planned approach to Eisener City, a minor spaceport in the tropics, the disguised ship would overfly the island group that included Amali's retreat.

Hera Talyn, sitting in the co-pilot's seat, kept watching the excruciatingly sensitive stealth generators they'd installed on the ship's hull. They were essential to the mission since they disguised the fact that the *Beryl Zephyr* looked exactly like a ship the Amali family and the *Sécurité Spéciale* desperately wanted.

They also concealed the unusual cargo in its hold: four Warthog assault boats loaded to the gunwales with a squadron of Marine Pathfinders, armed, and equipped for a deadly night raid.

Should the incursion go wrong, there was no doubt in anyone's mind that an official inquiry by the Adjudicating Authority would lead to a severe political crisis and heavy pressure by the Senate to disband the 251st and its sister squadrons. But every mission lately carried the same risk. Special operations commandos didn't exist for simple strolls in the park. Major Ryent and his troopers knew they were deniable and expendable. If they were caught, the Grand Admiral would disavow their actions and throw them to the wolves. The same went for one Commander Hera Talyn, of Naval Intelligence.

These thoughts were far from Talyn's mind as she double checked the ship's planetary positioning system and flicked on the intraship radio.

"Raider-Niner, this is Mother Two, launch in five minutes. Opening doors."

Down in the cavernous cargo hold, the four sleek gunboats waited in silence. Their black hulls seemed to absorb what little light the red emergency lamps provided.

Within, the four assault troops of the 251st sat patiently in well-ordered rows, the troopers joking in low tones as if their voices could give them away. This would be, for most of them, just another in a long string of combat jumps.

Zack Decker was dressed like the others in black scout armor and wore the standard utility belt loaded with grenades, spare magazines for his carbine, detcord, and a fighting knife. He sat half way down the outboard bench, wedged between a pair of troopers. Ryent had assigned him to Raptor Three. It would be the first to jump and the first to land. Its mission was to destroy the hive.

Just like everyone else in the craft, Decker was feeling the old pre-jump jitters turn his stomach into a seething nest of angry hornets. He had hundreds of jumps under his belt, but he still felt anxious before each one, which was just as well. When fear vanished, mistakes happened. At an altitude of five thousand meters, those mistakes were often fatal.

"Raider-Niner, this is Mother Two, launch minus sixty. Counting down. Have a good one, Pathfinder."

"Raider Team thanks you, Mother," Ryent's ironic voice crackled over the general net, "and promises to come home for supper. Out to you. Raptor Leader, stand by."

At launch minus thirty, the Warthog pilots started their gunboats' thrusters for the short burst that would free them from the trader's hold. At the word 'go', Raptor Three sprang through *Demetria*'s rear cargo doors, quickly followed by Raptors One, Two and Four.

The gunboat pilots, inertial guidance systems pointing their shuttles at the target, made final course adjustments, hoping they were still within the ship's stealth field, and then turned all systems off.

"Okay, Avril," Talyn grinned at Ducote, looking eerie in the green glow of the instrument panel, "prepare to make the thrusters look like goners."

"Ready." If Ducote was nervous, she gave no sign. Talyn admired her calm, a rare thing in an untrained civilian thrust into a military operation.

"Hit it." Almost at once, the ship began to buckle as the atmospheric thrusters malfunctioned.

"Eisener control, this is the *Beryl Zephyr*." Talyn's voice sounded suitably fearful. "We have a malfunction in the atmospheric thrusters. Switching to sublight drive and aborting descent. Request parking orbit so we can fix the problem before trying again."

"Eisener control here," a bored voice replied. "Roger your last. Go to two-seven-four mark three-five. Contact orbital control once you reach two-hundred thousand." The controller's tone seemed to suggest he expected this sort of incident with free traders.

Ducote punched in the course and flicked on *Demetria*'s sublight drives. Immediately, the two women were pushed back into their seats by the increase in thrust. The ion stream from the sublight drive wiped out any trail the Warthogs might have left.

"Roger, Eisener control, we'll try again later. *Beryl Zephyr* out."

"So far, so good," Talyn commented through clenched teeth.

*

Invisible gliders, the gunboats slipped through the clouds on a shallow descent, their sharp beaks aimed at Amali's island. No light reflected off their black skins, no sensor wave bounced back to betray them. At best, with the most sophisticated gear, an experienced tech would mistake them for a flock of birds or sensor ghosts.

The Pathfinders, silent and contemplative now that they'd left the safety of the ship, dealt with the coming battle in their own way. In the semi-darkness of the jump bay, the armored Marines looked like eerie cousins to the semi-sentient insects they were about to destroy. No sound but the wind whistling along the fuselage disturbed their peace.

Some prayed to the God or gods of their childhood, some thought of the enemy below and drowned their fears in a rising tide of bloodlust, while others meditated, focusing on inner harmony. Veterans all, the Pathfinders had learned to channel their fears away long ago.

Two bright red lamps switched on: the signal for ten minutes to jump. In Raptor Three, the jumpmaster rose and stood below the lights. He extended his arms in front of him, hands flat, and palms facing upwards. Slowly, he raised them.

"Stand up."

The Pathfinders unbuckled their seatbelts and stood, facing the rear of the shuttle. Automatically, the seats folded back into the bulkheads, freeing up space for the bulky troopers. The jumpmaster hit his chest with both fists, just below the shoulders, where the parachute straps joined the harness.

"Check your equipment."

In pairs, the Pathfinders checked their altimeters, manual release handles, parachute covers, and harness buckles. The 'chute taken care of, they made sure their small packs were strapped on, their rifles, carbines, rocket launchers and machine guns were secured against their chests, but ready to use with a single tug, and their various pouches and pockets sealed, so nothing fell out five kilometers above the ocean.

The jumpmaster raised his hands to the sides of his head, palms facing the troopers.

"Sound off for equipment check."

From back to front, each Marine slapped the shoulder of the trooper ahead of him and yelled "Okay."

When the signal reached the jumpers at the head of the four files, they gave the jumpmaster a thumbs-up signal. Any Marine, who wasn't okay, would have stepped out of line and left the stick.

The jumpmaster then placed his right hand on his helmet visor, at the level of his mouth

"Go to internal."

With a flick of the hand, the troopers buttoned up their suits and began breathing the stale, canned air that would keep them alive until they reached the lower altitudes.

The JM raised his hands to his ears again.

"Sound off for breathing check."

Again, the signal passed from front to back. Again, no one stepped out of line with a problem.

The JM turned to the intercom. "We're ready back here."

"Okay," the pilot replied. "Hang on. I'm dropping the ramp now."

"Secure for ramp opening."

The Pathfinders grabbed straps dangling from the upper bulkhead while the ship's aft bulkhead opened downwards and turned into a narrow ramp reaching out over the abyss. The jump bay's air pressure dropped, tugging at the standing Marines.

Wind howled through the small craft, making speech, even thought, impossible. The Pathfinders stared at the black opening as if hypnotized. Those who weren't absorbed by the daunting task of keeping their instinctual fears away thanked the gods of war for a cloudy sky. They would be less visible to ground watchers, and therefore less vulnerable to ground fire.

The JM made a broad chopping gesture with his right arm.

"Stand by!"

The four files shuffled forward until the lead troopers were level with the edge of the opening. Above the red jump lights, a glowing chronometer counted down the remaining seconds. When the digital readout reached zero, the lights changed to green, a screeching siren filled the bay, and the JM made a sweeping motion with his arm, releasing the Pathfinders into the night sky.

Almost like a single mass, the thirty-three troopers and one retired noncom jogged to the edge of the ramp and flung themselves into the void, arms and legs outstretched. Within seconds, the bay was empty. A final glance back and the jumpmaster let go of his strap, joining the black swans swooping down in Pacifica's tropical sky.

*

Decker and the one-hundred and twenty-five Pathfinders flew through the night air for a long time, guided only by their helmets' targeting computers, using their bodies as wings and rudders. The sky around them and the ocean below were both of the same unrelieved black. Deep space had more orientation markers. If it weren't for the tug of gravity, and the rush of wind, they could have been floating in a dark limbo where there was no up or down.

Zack reveled in the exhilaration of flight. Only crazy people would jump out of a perfectly good shuttle, trusting their lives to a square of material strapped to their backs, but Decker was one of those, and he knew it. You had to love parachuting to be a Pathfinder. And he loved being a Pathfinder.

At a thousand meters, the kite-parachutes popped open, and the Marines' descent slowed to a shallow glide. By now, they could make out the richer black of the island as it grew in their visors. Lights too had begun to separate land from sea as Amali's compound came into view.

Tugging on the wires above his shoulders, Zack controlled his 'chute's course, his computer projecting a target grid on the inside of his visor. This was the most dangerous moment. They were close enough for a sharp-eyed watcher with night vision gear to spot them and then kill them. But Amali's mercenaries didn't expect a Marine assault on a Commonwealth planet, let alone a tricky and dangerous airborne attack. Surprise, as always, would be the Pathfinders' best ally.

And if all else failed, they could always call on the Warthogs, whose shallow glide had brought them to a nearby, deserted island.

*

"Everything quiet?" The mercenary noncom hitched up his trousers as he walked into the compound's operations room.

"So far, sarge," the duty tech replied. "Our Lord and Master can have another night of undisturbed sleep."

"More like undisturbed perversion, if you ask me."

"Dangerous talk, sarge, especially since that fucking Marine got away. The boss has been acting vicious."

"Scared is the word you want to use." The sergeant sat on the corner of a console and burped. "He's fucking scared that Marines will come down here and wipe the island off the face of the planet."

"Would they do something like that?"

"Naw. It'd be against the fucking law. Only the buggering Senate can authorize military action on a member planet, and there's damn little chance they'd to do it for this place. The boss' family and friends own half the cocksucker politicians. This is just bullshit we're doing, acting as if we're a fucking Marine base on the edge of the fucking Shrehari Empire. Still," the noncom burped again, grimacing this time as acid rose in his throat, "gotta keep up appearances, so pay attention to your screen and make sure the logs are complete."

"Yeah, yeah, sarge. Cover my ass. I know the drill." The tech turned back towards his screen and yawned. "Nothing out there but a flock of stupid birds coming in."

He pointed at the indistinct blips a few hundred meters away from the shoreline and the same distance up.

"Hah," the mercenary sergeant cackled, "with any luck they'll be geese, and we'll get some hunting tomorrow morning."

"Doubt they're geese, sarge. Too big. Must be another kind of bird. Maybe they'll make good hunting anyways."

"Yeah. What's weather say for tomorrow?"

"Another storm coming up, as big as the one the other day, when this Decker guy vanished."

"Fucking hurricane season's started early."

"Yeah."

"Take it easy. I'm going to go have a crap and then take a walk outside."

The tech yawned again and gave his sergeant an ironic wave. The noncom grinned and replied with the rigid digit salute before leaving the ops room.

*

The ground came up fast under Zack's feet, and he could no longer judge the distance. Facing in the direction of his drift, he bent his knees slightly and waited for the impact.

It came as a surprise as it did every time.

His feet hit the ground with a jarring thump, and he took several quick steps forward to absorb his momentum. Then, when he was sure he had his balance, he knelt to reduce his silhouette while his canopy collapsed to the ground with a sigh. Around him, muffled thuds and the rustling of parachutes were the only signs of Third Troop's landing. To Zack's ears, they were incredibly loud, but he knew the jungle's nightly concert of bird chants and predatory yowls would cover the noise.

With practiced ease, he freed his carbine and swung it out while his other hand twisted the 'chute harness buckle, releasing him from its anchor-like drag. His helmet visor, set to light intensification, showed the estate in detail. He marked the building he'd been taken to after his arrival and quickly spotted the door.

Two red blips suddenly appeared in his visor's targeting grid. A loud shout of alarm rang across the tarmac, and a bright plasma shot split the night.

Instinctively, Decker raised his carbine to his shoulder and lased the merc who'd shot. When his weapon's sight found the target, an exercise that took less than a second, he pulled the trigger twice, in double-tap fashion. His shots were true, and the merc died without another sound. A trooper beside him dispatched the other sentry with the same efficiency and speed.

But neither had been fast enough. The night gave birth to the eerie wail of an alarm siren.

The troop leader slapped Zack on the shoulder.

"C'mon, Decker, let's shag. Let the CO take care of the opposition."

They reached the relative safety of the blind walls after a short sprint. Zack was pleased to see he wasn't even breathing hard though the weight of the armor dragged at his body.

From somewhere on the other side of the estate, a mercenary machine gun opened up, but it was silenced quickly when a Marine rocket launcher whomped in reply.

Ignoring the developing fight, as Major Ryent had instructed them to do, Zack slipped around the corner of the building, carbine at the ready. He immediately came face-to-face with a five-man merc patrol emerging from the barracks. His reflexes still ran true, and he mowed them down in a sustained burst from the hip, nearly cutting two of them in half at the waist, while the others died when his shots flash-boiled their innards.

With the sounds of a growing battle around him, Zack sprinted from cover and headed straight for the dark rectangle that led to the labs, and ultimately the hive.

*

Walker Amali moaned with pleasure as his latest lover, the daughter of a Senator with more ambition than ability, rode him with consummate skill. She had arrived on the island earlier in the day, sent as an offering by her father, who wanted to join the select circle of politicians who held the real power, and he knew Amali was the financing behind that power. He also knew the head of ComCorp had a weakness for well-rounded and pliable women. His daughter Yelena was both.

Amali's climax was building when the alarm siren started wailing and mounting panic replaced the pleasant warmth of lovemaking. It turned to a sick feeling of nausea when he heard gunshots outside.

He pushed the girl away and rolled off the bed, stabbing his vidcom terminal. She protested at the treatment but fell silent when she saw the look in his eyes. Gunfire lit up the night, and he thought he saw black shapes move with deadly swiftness among the shrubs and trees of his gardens.

"Amali here. What the hell is happening?"

"Technician Hillier, sir," a frightened voice replied. "We're under attack by Marines."

"What?" Amali demanded, wide-eyed. A tic tugged at the left corner of his mouth.

A sweaty, panicked face replaced the tech's. "Sir, they're Pathfinders. We're under airborne attack. I figure there's more'n a hundred of 'em, a full squadron. The captain is down, and we're getting slaughtered."

Amali was stunned, speechless. Not only had Decker escaped, but the bastard had also come back with a commando force.

He abruptly cut the link and headed for his walk-in closet. All that mattered now was to flee and save himself. The girl looked at him, frightened by what she heard, but even more frightened of the tortured expression on his face. She remained silent.

The magnate quickly dressed in a black one-piece outfit and strapped on a pistol belt. The Marines had murdered his cousin and wouldn't stop at killing him either. As for the experiment, he mentally shrugged. It was over. There would always be more experiments. One day, the Navy would pay for all the outrages. He swallowed the bile that had risen in his throat.

Walker looked at the girl, still naked, still beautiful and still a whore, sent here by a pimping father who lusted for power. She whimpered softly, flinching every time a burst of plasma came too close to the windows. Amali couldn't take her with him, she'd be a liability, and he couldn't afford to leave her behind to tell the Marines about his bolthole. Her father wasn't important enough to matter. The daughter mattered even less.

Slowly, he pulled out his pistol and aimed it at her head. She stared at him, wide-eyed. With deliberate care, as if he were on a shooting range, he breathed in and out, tightening his finger on the trigger.

The shot punched a small hole in the girl's perfect forehead, leaving a smoking hole in its wake. But its exit wasn't so neat. The plasma flash boiled her brain on the way out, and when it blew away the back of her skull, pinkish-white matter bubbled out, splashing all over the bed. She voided herself as she died and a strong odor of urine and feces mixed with the smell of charred flesh.

Without warning, Amali vomited on the plush carpet, sickened by the stench. He had never killed anyone with his own hands before. Someone else had always done his dirty work for him. Trembling, he heaved until nothing but bile joined the growing stain at his feet. Sounds from the mansion's front hall snapped him out of his misery: the Marines were inside.

He ran to an ornate wooden panel in one corner of the room and placed his palm on an elaborate design in its middle, opening the door to a hidden lift. No one but his father knew about it, the builder having long since died in an accident.

Walker slumped against the lift's curved walls as the doors closed, his entire body trembling. He was swept down into the island's underground warren, where a submarine waited to whisk him away. But when he stepped out of the lift and into the tunnel, the sound of exploding charges from the submarine pen pushed his panic to a peak.

He ran to the pen's door and poked his head around the corner. A squad of Marines in black armor had found a way in and were busy sabotaging everything in sight. One of the troopers spotted him and pointed in his direction.

Amali vaguely heard a voice call his name and order him to stop, but his instincts drove him back into the tunnel, towards the other door that opened into the jungle. His father had used that one for solitary walks and quiet assassinations.

The thick steel door opened with a creak at his command, and the humid night air hit him like a fist. Pounding feet echoed behind him, and he ran out of the tunnel into the dark forest. With a loud clang, the door slammed shut again, cutting off his pursuers.

When he stopped running, deep in the jungle, Walker Amali realized he had nothing but a small handgun with a half-empty magazine. All the Marines had to do was come pick him up.

Hidden and alone, the most powerful man on Pacifica trembled, fighting his fear and rage, unable to think of a way out of his predicament, except hope the Marines didn't come after him.

Things like this weren't supposed to happen. The Amali family thought itself above the law.

*

A single shot fried the door's locking mechanism, and Zack pried it open. Major Ryent and his troops had turned the raid into a full-scale battle, distracting every mercenary in Amali's employ. Most of the arc lights had died, shot by snipers, plunging the compound into a darkness punctuated by the flash of plasma ammunition, rocket exhaust streams, exploding grenades and satchel charges.

One of the Pathfinder troops had already taken out the ops center, cutting the island off from the rest of the universe. Another had captured the fusion reactor, selectively cutting power to enemy-held areas, while a third was rounding up everyone in the private part of the estate, looking for Walker Amali himself.

Helmet visor switched to infrared, Decker stepped into the darkened corridor and put his back against the wall, to reduce his silhouette. There was no one in sight, no unusual heat signatures, and no booby traps. He signaled for the troop's scouts to join him.

Two armored figures slipped past, one holding a sensor, the other covering him. They moved carefully but quickly, searching for signs of life, human or alien. At the first door, they stopped and signaled. Zack didn't need to look inside to know what it was.

"Interrogation room," he said over the radio.

"Clear it," the troop leader ordered.

"Roger. T'chin, Douala, number one team. Sisulu, Rajmurti, security positions. Move."

The two scouts crouched on either side of the corridor, weapons pointed into the darkness. Number one team stepped up to the door, one on each side, concussion grenades in hand. Corporal T'chin slapped the lock pad, and the door slid open with a sigh. In unison, the two Pathfinders armed and tossed their grenades into the room.

Before the explosions died down, the team burst into the room, weapons at the ready, eyes scanning for survivors. Decker followed them in. Other than the slight damage from the grenades, it was unchanged. Seeing the mind probe, he remembered every painful second of the interrogation. A crimson curtain of hate closed before his eyes, and a murderous rage gripped him.

"Someone in the back," the scout warned, "single human, no sign of weapons."

"Cover me, Dal." T'chin cautiously neared the door, keeping to one side and out of the line of fire. He palmed the lock, and it opened. "Whoever's in there, surrender or die."

"Don't shoot, don't shoot," a quavering voice replied. "I'm coming out."

Zack knew that voice intimately. When Doctor Cantos crossed the threshold, the former sergeant stepped forward and grabbed him by the throat.

"Remember me, you fucking mind rapist? Or did you see so many customers in the last week you forgot Zachary T. Decker?"

"N-n-no," the doctor croaked weakly. "P-please let me go."

Zack laughed. It was an ugly, hate-filled sound.

"Not a fucking chance, Cantos. You raped my soul, now it's time to pay the piper for your fun."

Decker lifted the man and threw him into the reclining chair he'd occupied so recently. Snapping the restraints into place, he lowered the probe over Cantos's head.

"What are you doing, Zack?" A low voice asked from the doorway. "We've still have a mission to complete."

"Your major said I could get my revenge, Reggie," he snarled back. "It'll just take a moment."

Sergeant Reginald Warwick, the troop leader, shrugged and ordered his men to continue their advance down the main passageway. Decker, true to his word, spent little time fine-tuning the probe. He switched it on and set the automatic programming to the most acute setting. Cantos screamed in terror as he felt the awful tendrils of the machine bore through his skull and sink into his brain, infiltrating his mind and tearing at his soul.

In a few minutes, his personality would start to break down, and he would slowly, irreversibly, turn into a human vegetable, alive only because the probe could not destroy the brain's autonomous functions. Without a backward glance, Decker left the room and shut the door behind him.

A rape for a rape, and a soul for a soul: frontier justice had come to Pacifica.

The red haze lifted enough for him to remember his duties, and he rejoined the scouts. The mercs had abandoned the laboratory complex where the gunner had been held prisoner, ordered outside to fight off the Marines. They met a few technicians who gladly surrendered. A loaded plasma gun was a convincing argument. Quickly, they cleared out sophisticated labs, taking precise recordings of the extraordinary array of powerful scientific equipment.

"This is it." Zack pointed at an unremarkable door on the right side of the corridor, just before the passage ended at a set of heavily armored portals. "That's the room where they showed me the bugs."

"So it probably figures the hive is behind those starship hatches there," Warwick replied. "It'll take more than we have to blow them."

"No problem. The window in there'll give under a rocket."

"Your call, Zack."

The viewing room was as dark as the rest of the compound, and the scouts slowly scanned it before anyone else went in.

"Human, hiding behind the sofa," one of the scouts warned. "No weapons."

"Another of your friends?"

The gunner stepped past the scouts and stopped at the sofa.

"You can get up now, Professor Rocheford. I promise that you will come to no harm."

He still remembered her silent tears when Amali had displayed the depth of his depravity in this very room. The woman rose unsteadily, unable to see him in the dark.

"W-who are you?"

"We met a few days ago, Professor. I was strapped into the chair over there while Amali showed me his home video of Diego Strachan getting eaten by a bug."

"The Marine."

"Retired Marine, Professor. Zack Decker, in case you forgot. But the people with me are still serving. We're here to destroy the hive."

Rocheford sighed and reached out to steady herself.

"Then the nightmare is finally over."

"Yeah."

"I didn't know what he intended to do with the Quas, Mister Decker, I swear."

"Later, Professor, later."

But the floodgates had opened. She had to justify her part in this experiment, rationalize her participation in cold-blooded murder.

"He hired me from the University as a private researcher, promised me the best labs and facilities. And money, lots of money. By the time I realized what he wanted, it was too late. He would not let me go." She sobbed. "He's sick, Mister Decker. I had to do as he ordered."

"I know, Professor." Zack laid a gentle hand on her trembling shoulder. "You're as much of a victim as I was. Sergeant Warwick, can you escort Professor Rocheford out of here and keep her safe?"

"Sure, Decker. C'mon, Prof."

"No, wait. What will happen to all this?"

"We're going to kill every bug, pupa, and egg, and then wipe the hive from the face of the universe, along with the labs and all."

"Good." She shuddered. "The hive is behind the window. On the other side of the hatchery is a tunnel. The left side leads to the nursery, the right side to the queen. Amali has placed his two remaining soldiers in a special holding pen in another part of the facility. I can show you where."

"Thanks, Prof, we'll get to it right after this."

"And Amali?"

The anger and loathing in her voice rung a chord with Zack's own feelings. Their eyes met for a few seconds.

"Dunno. Wait." Decker switched to the squadron net. "Niner, this is Gunner One. Can you give me a sitrep on Amali, over?"

"Two Niner here, Gunner One," the leader of the second troop replied. "He escaped into the jungle through an underground tunnel. If we have time, Niner says we can go look for him, over."

"Gunner One, thanks, out."

When he told Rocheford what he had just learned, the woman's face hardened into a mask of hate.

"I can find him for you, Mister Decker, by using the two soldiers in the pen."

Her eyes met his and held him in their powerful grip.

"I guess that makes two of us who want to see Amali receive what he deserves," Zack growled. "We'll do it. Right after we clean out the hive."

He turned towards Warwick. "Unless you have objections, let's do this."

"Right. Everyone, clear out of the room. Berenguez, take the Professor back to the last bend in the corridor. Grabowski, arm your LAW and prepare to fire on order."

Moments later, the only people left were Decker and Trooper Grabowski. The latter lifted the LAW's disposable launch tube to his shoulder and aimed.

"Ready, sarge."

"Fire."

Spouting a tongue of flame, the short, stubby missile erupted from the tube and slammed into the window. It exploded, shattering the reinforced plas alloy and lighting up the room bright as day. The back blast knocked Grabowski and Decker off their feet.

Zack rose and breathed in deeply. But instead of smelling the familiar scent of burnt explosives, a dry, acrid stench assaulted his throat.

"God Almighty," Grabowski swore. "I haven't smelled something like that since we destroyed a vytyrek nest on New-Tasman."

"It's the stench of bugs, Trooper." Zack walked to the window, shattered plas crunching under his booted feet. "Prepare another rocket."

The hatchery was bathed in orange light, but the eggs glowed with their own internal luminescence. Decker felt the rest of Third Troop gather behind him as he looked at the obscene, glistening spheres. He was oblivious to the curses, comments, and half-jokes circulating among the Pathfinders.

With slow, deliberate care, he raised his carbine to his shoulder and aimed at the first egg. He pulled the trigger twice and watched it burst in a spray of gelatinous, off-white matter. The sound was sickeningly wet and gooey, like throwing a rock into a hot mud pit.

Chitin rubbed against chitin as three drones burst into the hatchery, bent on protecting the precious eggs. Even without a soldier's stinger, Quas drones were formidable killing machines.

"Grabowski, target the bug on the right. You," Decker grabbed another trooper with a LAW by the arm, "take the one in the middle. Someone else with a LAW, front, and center and take the left one. Move! Fire when you're ready."

The words were barely out of his mouth when Grabowski fired. The rocket hit the bug squarely in the upper segment and exploded. A bare second later, the center bug also vanished in a flash of light. When the explosions subsided, nothing remained of the two drones except a few jagged pieces of chitin. A bright smear of ichor decorated the wall behind the bugs. Oblivious, the last bug kept on heading for the invading Marines, but a trooper with a medium machine gun fired his weapon on full automatic and disintegrated the Quas.

Zack methodically started shooting at the eggs again, one round per egg, one egg after the other. By the time he'd done ten, several more Pathfinders had joined him by the broken window, and each took their own row. Gradually, the acrid stench of Quas succumbed to the even more sickening odor from the burst eggs.

The Marines worked in silence, dispassionately; they stopped merely to concentrate their fire on the eyes of a fourth drone that belatedly came to check on its charges. It survived only marginally longer than its three comrades did. When the last egg disintegrated with a splash, Zack jumped over the window ledge and into the unhealthy miasma of the slime-covered hatchery. After a moment's hesitation, the others followed.

The nursery was exactly as Decker had seen on the vidscreen: a honeycomb-like structure with dozens of niches occupied by white, moving blobs: Quas pupas, rapidly maturing into fully-grown adult bugs.

The gunner stepped back and slammed a fresh magazine into his carbine. He sent a burst into the first niche, puncturing the pupal bag. An eerie, nerve-rending screech erupted from the hurt creature as it thrashed about in pain, ichor flowing from half-dozen shot holes. Taken aback, Decker lowered his carbine and stared, but only for a moment. Other Marines joined him, and the wholesale slaughter of immature Quas began, to the horrific concert of alien death screams.

More shots resonated from the corridor as the Marines massacred the remaining drones rushing to defend their charges. When the last pupa died, the Marines suddenly realized that another, desperate voice had been answering the dying bugs. Chills ran down Decker's spine at the horrible sound.

"The queen," he whispered, and jogged off deeper into the hive, towards the chamber.

As he entered the warm, stifling room, he saw the immense female Quas writhe, as if fighting something. Then, with a nauseating sound, she tore free of her egg sack and stood up, raising her wet, glistening, and stinger-equipped tail in challenge. She bellowed something in her chittering, incomprehensible tongue and charged at Decker.

Sudden terror gripped the gunner, and his finger closed around the carbine's trigger, spewing round after round of plasma at the huge bug. The plasma splashed off her chitin like drops of water as she kept coming. Her tail swooped around her lower legs, and the stinger scraped across Zack's chest armor with a scream of tortured metal.

The sound somehow snapped Decker's ancient, racial fear of killer insects and he aimed his stream of plasma where it would do the most damage, in the eyes. Before he could punch through to the creature's brain, her tail swept at Zack again, knocking him down. The female bellowed, but her triumph was cut short by a rocket from the entrance to her chamber. She exploded in an apotheosis of light and sound, her body transformed into chitinous shrapnel that rattled against the Marines' armor like hail. Decker was drenched in sticky fluid and nearly vomited in his suit. When he finally hauled himself up, he turned his blank visor towards Warwick.

"What the hell took you so long, Reggie?"

"Don't you know it's impolite to enter a queen's palace without an appointment?"

"And I suppose the royal chamberlain wasn't available to make one."

"Yeah. C'mon, let's find you somewhere to wash off."

While the troop leader and his Marines placed explosive charges in the hive and the adjoining labs, Zack returned to the shower room where he'd punched out a merc on his last visit and washed the queen's bodily fluids off his armor. As he did so, he remembered Rocheford and the two penned-up soldiers.

He found the researcher waiting in a lab nearby, eyes bright with hate. She explained her idea in a few sentences and Zack, after calling Ryent, took her to the ops center.

"I can't say I approve of this, Decker," Ryent told Zack, after introductions, "but we have a bit of time. You have one hour to find Amali. After that, we leave, whether he's dead or not."

"Aye, aye, sir. I need just one thing to help, and that's an airborne sensor to pinpoint his location so the Prof can vector the bugs."

"The Warthogs are inbound. I'll have them overfly this side of the island in a standard search pattern. In the meantime, the Prof can start by directing your bugs towards this area." He pointed to the spot on the tactical display that corresponded to the secret exit.

The search took very little time.

"Got him." Zack's tone held no particular pleasure. The sensor feed from the hovering Warthog was impersonal as if the quarry wasn't a human being.

"Roger," Rocheford replied, "vectoring the soldiers to the spot. Shall I release them from control to take Amali?"

"No. Keep them from attacking until I tell you. I still need to talk to the bastard."

"You can use the Warthog as a relay, sergeant."

"Thanks, sir."

*

Walker Amali heard the rustling of chitin and the chittering of hunting Quas in the darkness. A fear he'd never believed possible burned through him. Somehow, the soldiers had escaped from the pen and were hunting for food.

They were near, very near, yet the richest man on Pacifica was unable to move from the spot, paralyzed by his terror. His nose twitched as he caught a hint of the Quas' acrid scent. A sudden chatter on his right drew his attention, and he saw the outline of a soldier, close enough to touch.

Wetness ran down his legs as he voided his bladder in fear while tears ran down his cheeks as he sobbed, mind teetering on the edge of madness. A brilliant beam of light stabbed through the canopy of leaves and illuminated his hiding place. The two Quas appeared in all their terrifying bulk, stingers sweeping the bushes as they waited for their controller's next command.

"Amali," a loud voice called him from above, from the source of the light. "It's your old friend Zack Decker. Remember me, your second test subject? I promised you I'd come back and see you die for your crimes. We'll I'm back, but I've had a better idea. I'll let your little monsters take care of you as you wanted them to take care of me. Fitting isn't it: a punishment that measures up to the crime."

The richest man on Pacifica fell to his knees and weakly raised his hands towards the voice.

"Please, no." The desperation in his whine made Decker want to puke. "I'll make you a wealthy man. You know I can. Just call these things off. I haven't done anything. I demand justice. I have the right to a fair trial before a jury of my peers."

"You lost that right when you used me like a fucking guinea pig." Decker trembled with rage as he shouted into the comms unit. Major Ryent laid a calming hand on the gunner's shoulder and spoke.

"Mister Amali, we found the body of a young woman in your bedroom. Your work, I believe."

"Yes, yes, I admit it. Just get me out of here."

"Then you admit to committing murder, Mister Amali?"

"Yes." The twitching Quas were pushing him into the arms of full-blown panic. "I'll tell you anything, admit to everything. Just call them off."

"Too late, Mister Amali," Zack Decker whispered. He nodded at Rocheford to release the soldiers.

He and the Professor forced themselves to watch the video feed as the Quas, responding to their primitive instincts, tore a screaming Amali apart and ate him. The Marines turned away, unable to face the horror exposed by the Warthog's uncompromising illumination.

When it was over, Ryent, in a quiet voice, ordered the pilot to destroy the last two Quas with the Gatling gun slung under the Warthog's nose.

Decker and Rocheford stared at the screen for a long time after the picture had faded, trying to come to terms with what they had done. Revenge was rarely, if ever, satisfying. This time had been no exception.

In the end, Walker Amali hadn't been a rich, perverted monster whose ambitions could have led to another civil war. He had been a wretched, terrified human being who, for all his crimes, did not deserve such a horrible end.

Zack knew the final image would remain with him for the rest of his life. He had appointed himself judge, jury, and executioner. That a real court would probably have acquitted a man like him, with his political friends and money enough to subvert any judge, didn't make it any more justifiable.

"You know, sir," he said, throat tight with long suppressed emotions suddenly boiling to the surface, "revenge is a dish that is better not eaten at all. There is no honor in something like this."

"I know, sergeant, I know." Ryent gripped his shoulder in sympathy. "I've been there myself. You never get it out of your memories, but if you remember the next time, you won't do it again, and that's something we can claim over those of Amali's bent. They never learn the price of honor. If it makes you feel any better, we couldn't let Amali live after this. That he died at the hands of his illegal pets was justice of a kind."

"The kind that had best not happen too often," Vanlith chimed in softly, "even if it sometimes must."

"Time to go, people. Professor, we'll have to take you with us. What will happen to you depends on the Fleet."

Rocheford shrugged.

"I've deserved any punishment they want to give me."

"Your help tonight will be noted, and will mitigate whatever the authorities decide." Ryent turned towards his executive officer. "Mo, order the load-up. Sunrise is in less than an hour, and a nasty storm is brewing to the north. We won't have a better time to slip away unnoticed. Release all the prisoners and tell them to head for the hills. This place is about to become a massive bombing range. If they're lucky, someone will come and save them before they die of hunger or disease."

Ryent invited Decker to sit in the lead Warthog's empty co-pilot seat, to give him a front row view of the compound's devastation.

With a precision born of long practice, the four gunboat pilots methodically destroyed the estate's aboveground buildings, swooping down like birds of prey. The charges set by the Pathfinders added to the havoc.

Zack's final view of the island where he'd nearly lost his life was of eight fuel-air bombs exploding in a huge ball of flame that flattened and charred everything on the shores of the lagoon. Amali's estate vanished, along with everything he and his people had done there.

The few survivors in the jungle would spread the word *pour encourager les autres*. Even if they didn't survive, the thoroughness of the attack was a strong enough message to the Coalition.

— NINETEEN —

"It's been a hoot having you on the mission, Zack." Vanlith beamed at Decker. "Here's a little souvenir for your collection." He pressed one of the 251st's squadron crests into Zack's hand. "If ever you feel lonely, call us. We'll keep a scout suit your size handy."

"Will do, Gus," Decker grinned, but his smile didn't quite reach his haunted eyes.

"Sergeant, you're always welcome in the 251st," Ryent offered his hand. "The Corps didn't do itself a favor by retiring you at the end of your hitch. If you ever re-enlist, give us a yell."

"Thanks, sir. But it wasn't much. A baby could've walked into Amali's shit hole, what with all the ordnance you guys brought down." Decker shrugged.

"Whatever you say, sergeant," Ryent smiled at the man's off-hand embarrassment. "But you can be sure your name will come up in my report. I wish you and Captain Ducote could stay for the post-jump blast."

"Sorry, sir, but we better be on our way. The less time *Demetria* spends attached to *Charles Martel*, the less trouble we'll encounter later. She's back to normal now and has a living to earn."

Ryent locked eyes with Decker. His excuses were plausible, but the major knew it wasn't that. The retired sergeant had suffered too much and had let his desire for revenge go beyond his own moral limits, and he needed to distance himself from direct reminders of the events. It probably wasn't the healthiest way to deal with the problem, but he couldn't force the man. He could only hope

Decker wouldn't self-destruct. Though God only knew what the probe had done to his mind.

"We all do things we regret later, Mister Decker." Ryent's voice was soft. "The important thing is not to let the regrets destroy us. In the end, what's the difference between killing a man with a shot between the eyes, and letting his own horrible machinations destroy him? I'll tell you what the difference is: none. Dead is dead, and that's what Amali deserved. Only you can decide whether what you did was dishonorable. I have no right to judge, nor does anyone else, because none of us went through what you did. For what it's worth, I think you're a hell of a Marine, Decker, an honorable Marine and I'd be proud to see you in my unit. Take care."

Zack snapped to attention. "Sir."

With a final nod, Ryent and Vanlith left the airlock. Decker and Talyn were alone. She was wearing a commander's dark blue uniform, with an impressive row of ribbons on the tunic.

"I'd like to talk to you in private before you leave, Mister Decker."

"Sure," Zack shrugged, the mask of the carefree warrior slipping now that Ryent and Vanlith were gone. He looked exhausted, driven by ghosts and haunted by his memories. "Down in *Demetria.*"

"I'd prefer it if we were alone."

"And I'd prefer it if Avril was there. Whatever you want to say to me, you can say in front of her."

"Very well," she acquiesced, knowing that Avril's presence would tilt the balance against her offer. "After you."

*

Ducote broke off her pre-flight check and came to stand beside Zack, placing a possessive hand on his shoulder.

"I spoke with my superiors earlier today. They're impressed by your performance and agree that you should never have been retired. They authorized me to offer you reinstatement in the Marine Corps, with a promotion to warrant officer and detail to Intelligence, where your natural talents will be put to good use. Your records will show you never left the Corps but came to my department the day of your original retirement. And you'll receive all the back pay too. It's only fair, since you worked for us all along, even though you didn't know it. And as a warrant in Intelligence, you'll have a good shot at a direct commission to captain in two or three years."

Zack Decker was speechless. He felt Avril tighten beside him. Talyn had just offered him the one thing he had dreamed about for so long. To be back in uniform, back in the Corps. A genuine Marine warrant officer no less. Then why where there so many butterflies in his stomach?

He turned his head to look at Avril, see what she had to say and found his answer. Her eyes pleaded silently, and that touched him deep down. She didn't want him to leave, yet didn't want to stand in his way either.

"Does your offer of employment still stand, Captain Ducote?" He asked in a strangled voice.

"Yes, Zack, it does," she whispered. "But if you want to go back to the Corps, take what Hera is offering. It's what you deserve." Tears formed in the corners of her eyes. She seemed convinced he would leave her to return to his world.

A band of steel tightened around his heart, and he felt torn in half, between the Marine Corps and Avril Ducote. He no longer doubted that she loved him. She had comforted him two nights earlier when he finally broke under the strain of the last few months. Holding his head tightly against her breast, she had stroked his head and gently talked him through the worst of it. Avril Ducote had shown him understanding, acceptance, and tenderness. He couldn't leave her, even though she had set him free, even though he didn't love her as she loved him. Yet.

At that moment, Zachary T. Decker realized that he had finally left the Commonwealth Marine Corps for good. He wanted to face the future with Avril Ducote, and live the life of a free trader, far from the intrigues and the violence Hera Talyn's offer carried. His healing would take a long time, but with Avril, that time would be bearable. He smiled sadly at Talyn.

"Sorry, Commander. I've already accepted a better offer. Avril and I are going to make a go of it." Zack sensed rather than heard Avril sob and pulled her against him tightly.

Talyn smiled back.

"Somehow, that's what I figured, and I told my superiors you'd turn it down. I guess there's nothing left but to wish you good luck. You're both extraordinary people who deserve happiness. Your service record will still be amended to read that you voluntarily retired today, at your old rank, after a detail with Intelligence. You'll be getting your back pay, eventually."

"Thank you, Commander."

"If ever you change your mind, or want to contact me," she tossed a small data wafer at him. Zack caught it with his right hand, "the procedure's on there. Remember, the Fleet needs all the friends it can get to stop scum like Amali."

"Friends like Kinnear?"

"And you, I hope."

"I'll try commander, but no more manipulation."

"Promised. Good luck, Pathfinder, Avril. Oh, yes, one last thing. If you go to Trevan's Shipyards at Wyvern, they'll give you a new rear ramp for *Demetria*. Trevan's already have a credit note in your name to cover the cost. It's the least we can do."

"Thank you," Avril nodded. "Goodbye."

Without glancing back, Talyn climbed up the ladder and vanished into the frigate's airlock.

Less than an hour later, the two ships separated. Zack and Avril watched from the cockpit as *Charles Martel* gracefully sailed away, magnificent against the backdrop of stars. With a flash of light, she vanished into hyperspace, off on a new mission.

"Any regrets, darling," Avril looked at him anxiously, stroking his cheek with the back of her hand.

"No." Zack sighed. "Sure I wanted to go back, but I don't know if I could have handled it." He shrugged. "After all this shit, I don't really know who I am anymore, but I do know you're more important than anything else in my life right now. And if I need to find my balance again, I'd rather do it here, with you."

"I love you too, Zack," Avril smiled and softly kissed him on the cheek.

"Where are we off to?" He asked.

"Any Outworld will do. We must find a cargo and get the ship working again."

"Then how about Aramis?"

"Zack!" She eyed him suspiciously. "You're not thinking of taking your friend Tren to task for his little deception, are you?"

"Nah," he gave her his patented aw-shucks grin, "not at all."

"I don't believe you, Zack Decker." She frowned.

"Okay, okay." He raised his hands in surrender. "So I still think the bastard deserves one on the kisser but don't worry. We'll knock each other around a bit, but after we each put a few good ones in, he'll pull out a bottle of whiskey and we'll get stinking drunk telling each other lies about fights we were both in."

"You're bloody impossible, Zack." She laughed at his disingenuous manner. It proved he was on the mend, and that made her happy. "Course two-one-five mark seven-zero, Mister Decker."

"Two-one-five mark seven-zero it is, Captain. And if those little green squiggles are more than just decoration, the sublight drives are ready, with the hyperdrives standing by."

"By God, I do believe we'll make a true spacer out of you."

"Only if you know how to teach an old monkey new tricks. What's our heading anyways?"

"Aramis. It sounds as good a place as any to start. I would like to hear more about your past from your friend Tren Kinnear."

"Just make sure you don't believe everything he tells you. And never take him up on a job offer. I know how dangerous that can be."

"Yes, but it has some nice side-effects."

"Aye, Avril, that it does. Perhaps I'll just buy Tren a big drink to thank him. After all, if it weren't for him, we wouldn't have met."

"Maybe, maybe not. But somehow, I'm sure we were fated to meet, eventually."

Before Zack could reply, Avril engaged the hyperdrives and set the autopilot. She rose and held out her hand.

"The ship can sail herself now, Zack. What do you say we celebrate your signing on as first officer and shareholder of *Demetria*?"

About the Author

Eric Thomson is the pen name of a retired Canadian soldier with thirty-one years of service, both in the Regular Army and the Army Reserve. He spent his Regular Army career in the Infantry and his Reserve service in the Armoured Corps. He worked as an information technology specialist for a number of years before retiring to become a full-time author.

Eric has been a voracious reader of science fiction, military fiction, and history all his life. Several years ago, he put fingers to keyboard and started writing his own military sci-fi, with a definite space opera slant, using many of his own experiences as a soldier for inspiration.

When he's not writing fiction, Eric indulges in his other passions: photography, hiking, and scuba diving, all of which he shares with his wife.

Join Eric Thomson at:

http://www.thomsonfiction.ca/

Where you'll find news about upcoming books and more information about the universe in which his heroes fight for humanity's survival.

Read his blog at:

https://ericthomsonblog.wordpress.com

If you enjoyed this book, please consider leaving a review on Goodreads or with your favorite online retailer to help others discover it.

Also by Eric Thomson

Siobhan Dunmoore

No Honor in Death (Siobhan Dunmoore Book 1)
The Path of Duty (Siobhan Dunmoore Book 2)
Like Stars in Heaven (Siobhan Dunmoore Book 3)
Victory's Bright Dawn (Siobhan Dunmoore Book 4)
Without Mercy (Siobhan Dunmoore Book 5)
When the Guns Roar (Siobhan Dunmoore Book 6)

Decker's War

Death Comes But Once (Decker's War Book 1)
Cold Comfort (Decker's War Book 2)
Fatal Blade (Decker's War Book 3)
Howling Stars (Decker's War Book 4)
Black Sword (Decker's War Book 5)
No Remorse (Decker's War Book 6)
Hard Strike (Decker's War Book 7)

Quis Custodiet

The Warrior's Knife (Quis Custodiet No 1)

Ashes of Empire

Imperial Sunset (Ashes of Empire #1)
Imperial Twilight (Ashes of Empire #2)

Ghost Squadron
We Dare (Ghost Squadron No.1)